HER SHOW
OF FORCE

MAHONEY AND SQUIRE, Book 1

MIKE KRENTZ

- Mike Krentz -

FREE BOOKS and OTHER PRIZES

Sign up to receive Mike's regular newsletter that offers insights into military and emergency medicine, news about Mike's books, and a monthly contest for gift cards, novellas, and signed paperback books. No spam.

Join Mike's newsletter mailing list here:

https://mikejkrentz.com/newsletter

NOTE TO READERS

This story was originally published in 2012 as RIVEN DAWN, by Mike J. Krentz. The current revised second edition has been substantially rewritten and upgraded, but the core story remains the same.

To the women and men of the United States Seventh Fleet,
warriors and heroes all.

Phase Zero: Shape

Chapter One

March 21, 2003, Persian Gulf

Weapons spent, the F/A-18 Hornet streaked over the coast of Iraq into total blackness over the Persian Gulf.

At the controls, Lieutenant Commander Kate "Scarlett" Mahoney announced "feet wet" into her helmet microphone, climbed the jet to three-thousand feet, and let herself relax for the first time since the mission began three hours ago.

Flashes of warning lights from the instrument panel interrupted her in mid-breath.

Left engine fire.

Kate pushed the fire extinguisher button and shut down the engine. The jet rolled left, as expected when flying with an unopposed right engine. She made the proper control corrections, confirmed the fire was out, and continued a gradual single-engine flight toward USS *Constellation* (CV 64), the aircraft carrier from which she had launched three hours earlier.

The photo of Patrick smiled at her from where she'd pasted it to the instrument panel. "Almost home, kid."

The Hornet lurched into a violent left roll. Kate pushed the control stick to the right.

No response.

Kate reached between her legs as she announced her dilemma. "Lost controls. I'm, uh, ejecting."

She yanked the yellow/black-striped handle. The jet's canopy blew away a second before the ejection seat holding Kate shot into the overcast night. The crippled jet fighter plunged away toward the Persian Gulf.

Hang on tight, Patrick.

The acceleration force caused her to black out. In seconds, the seat separated, the parachute deployed, and Kate's limp body transitioned from projectile to falling leaf. The sudden deceleration and the groin straps yanking on her distended bladder jerked her into consciousness. So did the intense pain in her dislocated left shoulder.

Patrick had disappeared from her mind.

She peered up to confirm the dim outline of a full parachute. Her wingman circling overhead would report "good chute" to *Connie*.

Overcoming the pain in her shoulder, Kate inflated her flotation vest and snapped the waist lobes together. A glimpse of the carrier's distant light appeared against the black horizon, no doubt launching the rescue helo in her direction. She steadied her breathing.

Less than a thousand feet before water entry.

When her boots hit the water, Kate released the parachute straps just before her body submerged. In seconds, she popped through the surface and used her uninjured arm and two muscular legs to swim away from the parachute.

She floated on her back. Euphoria rolled over her in harmony with the sea swells.

"Woo-hoo!"

Besides her first combat sortie, delivering "shock and awe" to Saddam Hussein's Baghdad on this night, Scarlett Mahoney had survived an engine fire and shut-down, single-engine flight, catastrophic hydraulics failure, loss of flight controls, and low-altitude ejection. A water rescue would complete the scenario.

The docs would fix her shoulder. Scarlett would fly again. She would reunite with Patrick.

What more could a girl want?

Chapter Two

March 22, 2003, San Bruno, CA

"Happy birthday, dear Patrick. Happy birthday to you."

Aunt Colleen set the cake in front of Patrick as his friends and their mothers gathered around the table. He took a big breath and blew with all his might. Four candles went out right away, but he needed a quick second puff to put out the fifth one. Everyone clapped and cheered. Patrick stared past the chocolate-frosted cake to the presents on a side table in the mall's party room. He couldn't wait to open them, especially the one in blue wrapping tied with a white ribbon. Aunt Colleen had said Mommy sent it all the way from Eye Rack. That must be far away. Mommy had been gone forever. Why didn't any of his friends' mommies ever go to Eye Rack?

His aunt dished out the cake and ice cream. Patrick gobbled it down. Once they all ate, he could open presents. He got mad when some kids wanted seconds.

Time came to open the gifts: a dump truck, an ambulance with flashing lights and a real siren, Power Rangers action figures, a Transformer, and a tablet he could draw on then erase. Aunt Colleen had saved the present from Mommy for last. She made him listen to

9

her read the card first.

"Dear Patrick. Happy birthday. I miss you very much. They don't have malls or toy stores where I am, but I found something I hope you enjoy. I love you. Mom."

He tore open the wrappings. His fingers touched something hard and leathery. A strange animal with a long neck and a lump on its back. Patrick wrinkled his face as he turned it over in his hands.

"It's a leather camel," Aunt Colleen said. "Camels are animals that live near where Mommy's ship is. She got it on liberty in Bah Rain."

Patrick searched all over the animal, but he could not find a switch. Maybe it needed batteries. He didn't see a battery hole. He tried to move the legs, but they were stiff as pencils. The neck too. He handed it to Aunt Colleen.

"How does it work?"

The mommies giggled.

"It's a model, a beautiful leather model. It doesn't move or have batteries. Put in on the shelf in your room so when you look at it, you can think of Mommy."

Patrick stuck out his lip and turned back to his new Transformer.

Later, Patrick and his best friend, Mei Li, helped her mother and Aunt Colleen pack up the presents. He held onto the leather camel. Outside the party room, he saw a man watching them.

At the mall exit, Aunt Colleen turned to Mei Li's mother. "I'll get the car and pick you up here. No point in carrying all this stuff through the garage."

As soon as Patrick's aunt left, Mei Li had to go to the bathroom, "real bad." Her mother sat Patrick on a bench. "Wait right here while I take her to the ladies' room. Don't move. Your aunt will be right back." She took Mei Li's hand and rushed into the bathroom.

Patrick sat and examined his camel.

"Hi, son." The same man who had watched them leave the party room. His smile made Patrick shrink against the bench.

The man pointed to the box of presents and the camel in Patrick's hand. "Someone had a birthday party."

Patrick nodded.

"How old are you?"

Patrick held up five fingers.

"Five years old. You are a big boy, aren't you?"

Patrick looked away. He felt like crying.

The man dropped to one knee. "What's your name?"

Patrick stared at the floor. "Patrick Walker."

A car pulled up outside, and Aunt Colleen got out.

When Patrick looked back, the man had left.

Chapter Three

March 23, 2003, An Nasiriyah, Iraq

Senses poised against surprise attack, the warriors of Amphibious
Assault Vehicle Platoon, Charlie Company, First Battalion, Second
Marine Regiment, inched across the dusty flat terrain. They
approached the Northern Saddam Canal Bridge on the periphery of
An Nasiriyah, Iraq, 350 kilometers southeast of Baghdad. The
company formed one element of Task Force Tarawa, charged to
clear a path through the southern Iraq city for the First Marine
Regiment rolling up from behind. With enemy fire in An Nasiriyah
suppressed, that fast-moving assault regiment could rush through
unimpeded toward Baghdad.

　　　　Three bridges over the Euphrates River opposed Task Force
Tarawa. The first, on the city's outskirts, had already fallen. The
other two, further into An Nasiriyah itself, presented more
formidable threats. Charlie Company was assigned to seize and
control the Saddam Canal Bridge inside the city. The path to success
lay through an environment where the enemy could entrap and
ambush the US force.

　　　　Riding an AAV-7A1 assault vehicle near the rear of the Task

Force advance, Major Preston Davis, USMC, poster-fit and poised even in dusty desert-hued battle dress, scrutinized the hostile surroundings. Sporadic radio traffic had reported a nearby ambush of a US Army maintenance convoy. The convoy had suffered casualties and given up prisoners, including two female soldiers. Preston squinted against the bright sunlight.

Here, the Iraqis will stand and fight.

From the beginning, Operation Iraqi Freedom had faced only token opposition. But now the conflict promised to turn grim. Preston sensed the nearby phantom enemy measuring his force. He sweated from the desert heat. Or was it the impending conflict? He turned to Doc Esperanza, the Navy hospital corpsman riding next to him.

"Doc, keep everyone hydrated."

"You got it, Major."

Preston placed a hand on the young man's shoulder. "No matter what happens, Doc, do not charge into enemy fire without cover. Once they realize you're the corpsman, you become a prime target."

"I know, sir." The medic shrugged at being told the obvious.

Moments later, the sky rained brimstone and chaos.

Rocket-propelled grenades and mortar rounds exploded all around. Automatic rifle fire sizzled from too many directions. Radios crackled with strident voices. Thunderclap explosions, whistling projectiles and rattling cacophony filled the air. Vehicles exploded into plumes of black smoke. Those still mobile scrambled into defensive positions. Frantic voices shouted uncoordinated orders.

Doc Esperanza jumped out of the vehicle and ran crouching toward the closest smoking vehicle. Preston forced his own legs and arms into action. His boots hit the sandy road just as the corpsman dove to the ground under a burst of automatic gunfire. Preston crouched low and hurried toward his doc. As the medic got up, another volley of gunfire kicked up sand around them. Preston tackled the corpsman and covered him with his own body. He kept the doc pinned beneath him until the enemy gunfire gave way to return fire from the US Marines.

Preston rolled aside. The corpsman sprang up and ran toward the smoking vehicles. Not thinking, Preston followed.

A cloud of acrid smoke choked him. Through the fog, he saw dozens of Marines wounded or killed. He caught up to the corpsman, who pulled wounded Marines from a burning vehicle. Preston rushed forward to assist.

Heat from the conflagration seared Preston's skin and clouded his vision. He grabbed a fallen Marine under the armpits and dragged him from the vehicle. Beneath one armpit, the man had only a bloody stump and a missing arm; two stumps where legs used to be.

Dead.

Rifle and machine gun fire rattled the scene again. Preston dropped the dead man and hustled back to the shattered vehicle. Doc Esperanza bent over another fallen Marine. He stood and waved Preston away.

"You don't belong here, Major. Get the hell out. Take cover, sir!"

A whistle and a thud. The corpsman's throat burst open in a spray of blood and tissue. He grasped at his neck, eyes wide and white. Frothy blood spurted around his hands. The corpsman stumbled toward Preston and fell forward in front of him. His face thumped into the sand. Blood spurted from his neck for a few

14

seconds, slowed to a trickle, then stopped. The doc didn't move.

Preston turned his corpsman over. The gaping hole in the man's neck, no longer spewing blood or air, told the major what the lifeless eyes affirmed.

I killed my doc.

 .

Phase One: Deter

Chapter Four

April 8, 2012, South China Sea: USS *Shenandoah* (LCC 21)

Captain Kate Mahoney awoke to the familiar ache in her left shoulder. Disoriented, she scanned the darkness. As the sleepy mist around her senses lifted, she recognized the rocking ocean motion, humming machinery noise, faint aroma of oil and metal, and windowless confines of her stateroom in USS *Shenandoah*, the converted amphibious assault ship that served as flagship of the United States Seventh Fleet. Kate rolled onto her back in the narrow bed—"rack" in Navy parlance—and reached above her head to flip on the bulkhead-mounted fluorescent lamp. Eyes squinting against the harsh glow, she found her glasses and looked at her watch. 0430. Sunday morning.

Kate had expected to sleep late while *Shenandoah* plowed the placid South China Sea toward Singapore. She needed a relaxed holiday routine now that the flagship neared the halfway point of its ninety-day deployment from home base in Japan to Asian ports vital to US interests.

She swung her legs over the side of the rack and stretched, still wearing the olive green Nomex flight suit from the previous day. A paperback romance novel lay opened on the deck where she'd dropped it. She undid her US Navy-regulation chignon and shook out long auburn hair that tumbled over her shoulders.

Gotta get it cut in Singapore.

Kate returned the book to the shelf over the light fixture. Three steps from her rack, she sat at her desk, switched on the lamp, and booted up one of two computers connected to a single monitor. As the screen came to life, she calculated the time and date in California, on the other side of the International Date Line.

Just after 1:30 pm, Saturday, a day behind here. Patrick might be online.

Had less than a month passed since Kate left Patrick in Colleen's care and started the trans-Pacific journey to her next Navy challenge and adventure? It seemed longer.

Logged onto the internet, Kate opened her Facebook page and scanned for messages and new posts. Nothing from Patrick, but the green dot next to his icon showed him logged on. Kate clicked the cursor over that icon and typed into the text box.

Chapter Five

April 8, 2012, Yellow (West) Sea: ROKS *Bucheon*

Republic of Korea Navy (ROKN) Commander Kwon Nam-Yung had just stepped out of his tiny shipboard shower when an urgent call shattered his morning routine. "Captain, we have an unidentified contact advancing on the NLL. Could be KPN with hostile intent. Please come to the bridge."

"On my way." Kwon pulled on his drab blue working uniform with the brand-new rank insignia and hurried out the door. In the passageway, he cursed the apparent threat to his first patrol as skipper of the Republic of Korea Navy (ROKN) corvette, ROKS *Bucheon*. If the so-called Korean Peoples' Navy (KPN) to the north approached the Northern Limit Line (NLL) with hostile intent, this day could be cataclysmic—for him and the free nation he'd sworn to defend.

When he reached the bridge, sweat beads dotted his forehead, despite the chill of harsh winter's reluctant withdrawal from the Korean peninsula.

The officer of the deck reported. "Contact now bearing three-two-zero, range two-five miles, moving southeast."

Kwon gazed at the radarscope. An ominous blip approached the Northern Limit Line that divided Korean territorial waters between north and south. The blip appeared to be closing on *Bucheon*.

"KPN," he said. "Hail it on bridge-to-bridge."

The junior officer keyed the transmitter. "Vessel approaching Northern Limit Line, this is Republic of Korea Warship Seven-Seven-Three. Please identify yourself and say intentions."

Silence.

"I say again, vessel approaching NLL, this is ROK Warship Seven-Seven-Three. You approach Republic of Korea territorial waters. Acknowledge and say intentions."

No reply.

North Korea People's Navy patrol ships often feinted at the NLL. The approaching vessel could break off at any minute, but as the ROKN patrol commander, Kwon must regard it as a legitimate threat. The Armistice Rules of Engagement (AROE) limited his options against the potential invader. He could not legally fire on the other vessel unless challenged.

Should he prepare a warning shot? Was this the initial sortie in an all-out assault on his homeland, or an isolated provocation from the new young leader's regime in the Democratic People's Republic of Korea (DPRK)? Why choose this morning to harass a routine ROKN patrol? Did they mean to test his resolve?

Kwon stood tall. They would find him a formidable adversary.

He took the transmitter from the junior officer. "Vessel approaching NLL, this is the captain of ROK Warship Seven-Seven-

Three. You encroach on ROK sovereign waters and place yourself in jeopardy. Acknowledge and say intentions."

* * *

Twenty-five miles to the northwest, the Korean People's Navy *Sariwon*-class corvette continued southeast. Commander Kim Lee Jung, the veteran skipper, smirked at his ROKN opponent's bravado broadcast. "Nervous fool." Kim did not lift his own transmitter. "We will make him squirm more. Increase speed to twelve knots."

As the *Sariwon sped up*, the ROKN skipper's higher-pitched voice came back over the receiver. "Vessel approaching NLL, this is ROK Warship Seven-Seven-Three. Final warning. Reverse course or face dire consequences."

Commander Kim chortled. "This simpering mouse dares to provoke the tiger? Northern Limit Line indeed." He spat on the deck. "Proceed on course. All ahead full. Sound general quarters." He turned on his heel and left the bridge to his watch team. He would view the intensifying battle picture on the video display in the combat information center below decks.

* * *

On *Bucheon*, Commander Kwon's heart raced as the threatening radar blip closed to fifteen miles from his ship.

They did intend to test him!

Rivulets of sweat streaked his face as he shouted commands. "Sound general quarters. Prepare to fire cannon. Arm Exocet missiles. Get Second Fleet on a secure line."

Should this confrontation go awry, Kwon refused to become a sacrificial offering for his ROKN superiors' political face-saving. He must co-opt the chain of command now to affirm his intentions. He had to expect the North Korean ship to cross the NLL. When it

21

got within range—twelve miles, but Kwon could wait for ten—he planned a warning blast from *Bucheon*'s 76mm cannon across the invader's bow. His KPN adversary would get the next move, but not for long.

AROE be damned.

At close range, Kwon dared not allow the North Korean to fire on him first. The warning shot should prove his resolve and stop this childish game. If the marauder kept his course, Kwon resolved to cram an Exocet missile into the detested communist's belly.

Chapter Six

April 7, 2012, San Bruno, CA

Perched on the back of Shen-zin Su, the giant turtle, Fanpanzhe scanned the alien terrain. The unexplored realm of Pandaria bore no resemblance to Azeroth, not even before the Cataclysm. Fanpan must hasten to find Horde allies for the first quest to win the global war against the Alliance and restore order to a world broken by the Cataclysm.

With the mind-hand skill of a nascent drone pilot, Patrick Walker manipulated the keyboard and mouse to maneuver his avatar across *World of Warfare* on the computer screen. Just past his fourteenth birthday, Patrick's experience-honed gaming skills surpassed those of many older gamers.

Fanpan ventured into the lush green Jade Forest, seeking a monk. He needed chi energy to enhance his warrior strength for melee attacks against the verming and mantoids. The Horde must overcome these new Panderan races to move on to the next phase. To his delight, on the screen, a monk approached from the forest.

The text box popped open.

> **Fuchou:** *I am Fuchouzhe, the Avenger. Come with me to the Temple of the Jade Serpent.*

Patrick's fingers rippled over the keyboard.

> **Fanpan:** I am Fanpanzhe, the Rebel. With our martial arts and joint force, we will win.

> **Fuchou:** *Greetings, Fanpan. Let us lead the Horde to vengeance against the Alliance. The world will be ours!*

Together, the new friends charged into the Jade Forest. They gathered other players as they went, building a powerful army. The Horde would destroy the despots of the Alliance and reunite Azeroth under Panderan influence. When the Horde achieved ultimate victory, Fanpanzhe and Fuchouzhe would become the reigning masters.

They came under a fierce assault from a gang of Alliance warriors and magi. Fanpan executed his spinning crane kick that took down all enemies within eight yards. Fuchou rallied orcs and dwarfs to protect Fanpan's flank. Other Horde allies rushed to join the melee. Fanpan and Fuchou deployed their most skillful martial arts. The Alliance attack faltered.

A high-pitched *beep* invaded Patrick's headset. His mother on Facebook. He ignored the interruption and kept his mind on the game.

Beep, beep.

No use. She knew he was online, and she would persist until he responded, or she would give up in anger—for which he would later pay. He typed into the game's text box.

> **Fanpan:** AFK. Back soon.

Patrick opened his web browser and clicked the Facebook

tab. His mom's message appeared.

Scarlett: *Hey, Patrick.*

He used his Facebook screen name.

PatWalk: Hi, Mom.

From where had she last e-mailed him? Somewhere in the Pacific Ocean.

Scarlett: *How are you?*

PatWalk: Okay.

Scarlett: *Just okay?*

Like she even cared.

PatWalk: Fine, Mom.

Scarlett: *I'm sorry I didn't email or text you sooner. It's been crazy here.*

PatWalk: Yeah.

Her life was always "crazy."

Scarlett: *How's school?*

PatWalk: Okay.

Scarlett: *Studying hard?*

PatWalk: Hard enough.

Scarlett: *How are your grades?*

PatWalk: Okay.

Could we get this over?

Scarlett: *What's your favorite subject?*

PatWalk: History, I guess.

Scarlett: *What do you like about history?*

Patrick pounded his forehead. *Geez!*

PatWalk: It's easy.

Scarlett: *You like it because it's easy?*

PatWalk: Yeah.

25

Scarlett: What do you take that's hard?

PatWalk: Nothing. They're all easy.

Scarlett: What's your least favorite?

PatWalk: Math.

Scarlett: Why math?

PatWalk: Teacher's a jerk.

Scarlett: How come?

PatWalk: She's stupid.

Scarlett: How so?

PatWalk: Dumb homework.

Scarlett: You do your homework, right?

PatWalk: Of course.

This was beyond pain. Patrick split the screen and rejoined his team. He would play and text with his mom at the same time.

Scarlett: How's your social life?

PatWalk: Huh?

Scarlett: Friends, girlfriend, whatever?

PatWalk: Geez, Ma.

In the game, he tried a spinning crane kick, but the texting distraction foiled his timing and the attack failed. The enemy force had doubled, and the errant kick had diminished Fanpan's energy. Patrick recharged his avatar for another counterattack. Meanwhile, Fuchou and the others held the attackers at bay. His mother continued her texting attack.

Scarlett: I'm interested in your life, Patrick. I want to know how you're doing. I miss you.

Patrick rolled his eyes. Yeah, right.

PatWalk: I'm fine, Ma. Anything else?

He rejoined the game. Fuchou had gained power while orc

reinforcements arrived. They could still win the battle.

His mother continued to fill the Facebook text box.

> **Scarlett:** *I'm fine too, in case you wondered. Some days are better than others. I wish I could be with you.*

Patrick ignored her text and led his charges into the fray. Outnumbered and outmaneuvered, they died within minutes. Fuchou retreated. Patrick left the game. Frustrated, he resumed the Facebook chat.

> **PatWalk:** I miss you too, Mom.
>
> **Scarlett:** *Thanks for saying that.*
>
> **PatWalk:** When will I see you?
>
> **Scarlett:** *When I get home from this current underway period, in about a month. I'll take leave and visit you there.*

Patrick sighed.

> **PatWalk:** I'd rather visit you in Japan.
>
> **Scarlett:** *But your studies.*
>
> **PatWalk:** No big deal. I always get good grades. You're more important.
>
> **Scarlett:** *Make you a deal. Keep up the grades for another month and you can come to Japan.*
>
> **PatWalk**: Deal!
>
> **Scarlett:** *Hope the new kid in North Korea doesn't mess it up for us.*

Patrick scowled. He should know better than to get up his hopes on one of her promises. She'd broken so many. He didn't dare believe this one. Eager to return to his game, he typed with angry fingers.

> **PatWalk:** Gotta go.

Scarlett: _Okay. Be good. Have fun. I love you._

Yeah, right, Patrick thought.

PatWalk: You too.

He closed Facebook and reopened the game. Fuchou waited for him. Their forces had restored to maximum health. Together, they rejoined the battle.

Chapter Seven

April 8, 2012, South China Sea: USS *Shenandoah*

Kate tried to work after her Facebook chat with Patrick. She fell asleep at her desk. The phone's shrill blare jolted her awake. She picked it up before the second ring.

"Ma'am?" She recognized the voice of recently promoted Captain Eric Mikleson, Seventh Fleet Assistant Chief of Staff for Intelligence (N2).

"Eric, we are now the same rank. Please don't call me 'ma'am.' I'm not your mother."

"Aye, ma'am." Mikleson caught his breath. "Sorry. Distressing intel from the Pen. ROK Fleet reports a showdown between ROKN and KPN ships in the West Sea near the NLL."

"Crap. How long before they might engage?"

"Maybe an hour, maybe eight hours, maybe never. Depends on who blinks when."

"Roger. You notify the chief of staff. I'll round up the others. Meet in COS's office in ten minutes. I need caffeine first."

"On it, ma'am." Eric hung up.

"Another routine Sunday morning at sea," she said to the framed portrait, taken a year earlier, of herself in civilian clothes with her arm around Patrick.

He looks too much like his father.

Kate padded into her cramped but private head, a treasured perk of her rank and position. She had long since wearied of shared bathrooms and shit-and-shower familiarity with other women—officers and ladies notwithstanding. The shower had to wait. She washed her face, put her hair up into a tight bun, and donned her glasses. Her reflection in the mirror looked more like a forty-something school marm than Seventh Fleet Deputy Chief of Staff and Director of Operations (N3).

Without changing her flight suit or undergarments, Kate tugged on and laced her boots, left her stateroom, and bustled down the passageway toward the flag mess.

Even on Sunday, officers and sailors of the Seventh Fleet staff and *Shenandoah* crew roamed the ship performing the thousand daily tasks needed to keep a US Navy fleet afloat and the commander's staff battle-ready 24/7. Men and women in digital blue working uniforms, sarcastically called "aquaflage," made way as Kate hurried toward the flag mess. Her mind distracted, she ignored or half-nodded to their polite greetings.

She entered the private dining room known as the flag mess. The size of a small café, the mess contained several rows of tables and a buffet-like serving area. Behind that, enlisted mess specialists prepared four meals per day: breakfast, lunch, dinner, and "mid-rats," for "midnight rations" available to officers working night shifts. A large screen TV mounted on a bulkhead showed news clips from the Armed Forces Network, a compromise between those officers who preferred CNN and those who relied on Fox News.

Staff officers sat together in small groups at the various tables. Several of Kate's friends ate breakfast together. The fleet surgeon, Captain Matt "Doc" Cushing, was a kind yet tired man in his late fifties, drinking black coffee from a large Starbucks mug with *Kuala Lumpur* and a relevant graphic printed on it. He ate fried eggs, bacon, and grits. Across from Doc sat Commander Russell "Rusty" Simmons, the public affairs officer (PAO), a stout middle-aged man who resembled a stereotypical used-car salesman. His breakfast included fried eggs, bacon, sausage, and pancakes.

The third member of the group was Commander Alexis Sideris, the judge advocate general (JAG) representative with specific expertise in international law. A slim woman, Alex sipped a glass of orange juice and nibbled on a bowl of granola-sprinkled fruit.

"Over here, Kate." Doc Cushing pulled out a chair. "We're making plans for Singapore and the dining out."

"Sorry, Doc." She sidestepped the chair and made straight for the coffee service. "No time to chat." She carried a Starbucks mug similar in size to Doc's, decorated with the words *Hong Kong*. She filled it three-quarters full of coffee and topped it off with creamer. Then she chose a miniature muffin, stuffed it in her mouth, and headed to the door.

She paused at the table of friends. Rusty turned to her. "Kate, is it true that tiaras are authorized for wear with female mess dress?"

Kate ignored the question. "JAG, PAO, come with me to the COS, now."

The two officers glanced at each other with puzzled expressions as they rose to follow her. Kate preceded them out the door, scurrying toward the chief of staff's office.

Chapter Eight

April 7, 2012, San Bruno, CA

After eight hours of gameplay interrupted only for bathroom and snack breaks, Fanpan and Fuchou had achieved powerful synergy. Their Panderan army gained footholds deep inside the Jade Forest. A knock on his door broke Patrick's concentration. His aunt leaned into the room.

"Patrick, you should be in bed."

"In a minute, Aunt Colleen. I'm almost done."

"You are a slave to those games. Does your mother know how much time you spend on them?"

"Mom doesn't care. She's on the other side of the world."

"Your mother cares. She'll care more if you don't do well at school. Did you finish your homework?"

"Don't have any." He stared at the screen so his aunt would not catch the lie in his eyes.

"Get to bed. We're going to early Mass in the morning. Did you forget tomorrow is Easter Sunday?"

This woman could be a worse bitch than his mother.

Patrick shrugged. "Whatever."

"Do not expect to spend the entire day tomorrow in front of that monitor. You need to get out more. Do something with friends. Have a life besides computer games."

"Might go to the mall."

Aunt Colleen stood her ground in the doorway. She would nag him to the point of losing the battle—unlike his mom, who would eventually give up and let him play. Mom had her own distractions.

"Okay. I'll go to bed now."

As soon as she left, Patrick signed off the online game, locked his door, and turned off the overhead light. With the room illuminated solely by his computer screen, Aunt Colleen would think he'd gone to bed. He opened his Facebook page, surprised by a new message.

> ***Fuchou:*** *Fanpan?*

Excited, Patrick typed.

> **PatWalk:** How'd you find me?
>
> ***Fuchou:*** *Wasn't easy.*
>
> **PatWalk:** I'm not allowed to use my name online.
>
> ***Fuchou:*** *Me neither. Parents can be so paranoid.*
>
> **PatWalk:** No shit.
>
> ***Fuchou:*** *Dude, check this out.*

A hyperlink appeared in the text box. Patrick clicked on it. The screen displayed a photo of a young woman, naked above the waist. She leaned toward the camera. Seductive eyes looked right at him.

Patrick had explored internet porn sites on his own, but how did this friend—?

> **Fuchou:** *Like it?*
>
> **PatWalk**: Yeah. How did you know?
>
> **Fuchou**: *From playing with you all day. Your WOW name is Chinese for rebel. We are alike.*
>
> **PatWalk**: Yeah.

He scrolled through similar photos on the link.

> **Fuchou:** *Enjoy.*

He signed off.

Patrick closed Facebook and left the photos on the screen. He stripped to his underwear and stuffed a bathrobe along the doorjamb.

Chapter Nine

April 8, 2012, South China Sea: USS *Shenandoah*

"Wacko sons of bitches!"

Captain Leo LeBlanc, USN, Seventh Fleet Chief of Staff (COS), ranted into a portable telephone handset as he paced around his stateroom like a choleric gorilla. He had just donned cycling shorts and a singlet for his stationary bike workout when Eric Mikleson's phone call interrupted his morning routine.

"Yeah, yeah. My office. Right. Ten minutes, okay." He threw the phone onto his unmade bed. "Son of a bitch!"

Leo pulled on blue coveralls over his cycling togs. Before he opened his adjoining office, he cast an indignant glance at the Trek bicycle and Kinetic stationary trainer in his bedroom. His cherished workout had just given way to another potential crisis on the Korean Peninsula.

"Why can't these people behave? Churlish bastards pick Sunday to squabble and ruin my ride."

At his desk, he logged onto his secret-classified network

computer and clicked through a dozen messages heralding the West Sea confrontation. They had arrived in the ten-minute interval between his morning coffee, email scan, and change into cycling clothes.

The chief of staff's cabin in *Shenandoah* featured two rooms. The bedroom provided a full-size bed, ample storage, and enough deck space for Leo's bike and trainer. A larger adjoining office doubled as a small conference room. An L-shaped desk in one corner hosted three computers and two monitors cabled to two different networks with different origins and classification levels. A fifty-inch LCD screen hung from the opposite bulkhead. In front of it, a sofa and chairs formed a U-shape, emulating a family room. On the other side of the room, a six-seat conference table, ornate Japanese credenza, and étagère completed the furnishings.

Memorabilia displayed around the office highlighted Leo's twenty-three-year Navy career. Polished wood plaques, dark blue ball caps with gold trim, and elaborate foreign mementos and knick-knacks adorned most of the room's surfaces. By strategic positioning, those items rendered homage to two prized trophies perched on the antique credenza: the bruised gold helmet that Leo had worn as a wide receiver for the US Naval Academy, and a handcrafted model of a US Navy destroyer. The side number *97* identified the ship as the USS *Halsey*, which he had commanded five years earlier.

Kate Mahoney and her usual entourage entered. Eric Mikleson followed in close trail. Leo scrutinized the senior officers gathered around his desk. Each belonged to the elite leadership team designated as "ACOS and SA," for "Assistant Chief of Staff" and "Special Assistant." By standard nomenclature, each assistant chief of staff headed a directorate described by a number following the letter "N," hence Kate's designation as the "N3" and Eric's as the "N2."

Leo frowned. "Where's the seven?" He meant the N7, ACOS for Theater Security.

"Couldn't find him," said Eric. "Didn't answer his phone. We'll fill him in later."

Leo leaned forward like a quarterback taking command of a gridiron huddle. "Okay, boys and girls, what do we know?"

Eric answered. "Sir, ROK Fleet reports that a probable North Korea *Sariwon* encroaching on the Northern Limit Line threatens *Bucheon*, their patrol corvette in the West Sea. The KPN ship does not broadcast AIS identification signal and does not answer radio queries. At last report, the ships were twenty miles apart and closing, with the NLL between them. The ROKs say they will engage if the *Sariwon* threatens their ship. They won't risk another *Cheonan* embarrassment."

Leo raised a hand, directed his gaze at Kate Mahoney. "For benefit of the new kid on the team, the N2 refers to the surprise sinking of a ROK corvette, *Cheonan*, in early 2010, allegedly by a torpedo launched from a North Korea *Yono* submarine—although the DPRK denied it."

Mahoney scowled. "I know about that one, sir."

She leaned into the group. "The ROK captain threatened consequences if the *Sariwon* doesn't reverse course."

Leo threw his head back like a roaring lion. "Big farking deal, Kate. Those people play chicken along that line all the time. They taunt each other like street brats with rocks and sticks. Do we go to general quarters on a Sunday morning over a minor squabble?"

Kate's voice trembled. "Sir, this is an escalating tactical situation and—" Leo's steel-eyed glare caused a brief pause, but she continued. "We don't know what the new leader up north might do. The *Sariwon* may have hostile intent."

Leo returned fire. "I have hostile intent because these jokers upset my Sunday." He shot a derogatory look at the PAO. "Less prime-time limelight might discourage them." He eyed each officer in the room. "Does anyone here believe they will shoot each other?"

Alexis Sideris, the JAG, stepped forward. "Sir, North Korea doesn't acknowledge the NLL. This could be a 'FON,' freedom of navigation sortie to flaunt their disrespect for it. They've challenged it before with fishing vessels. Crossing the line with a warship would be a flagrant provocation, but the AROE still apply. The ROKs can only engage against a direct threat."

Leo grinned at Kate. "AROE refers to the Armistice Rules of Engagement that limit military action by the ROKs, and us. But you knew that, right?"

Mahoney stared at him without speaking.

Leo shrugged. He scowled at the JAG. "The ROKs can't give a shot unless they take one first, right?" He rolled his eyes. "That sounds fair. You willing to bet on it, Commander?"

Alexis' face flushed. She did not reply.

Kate spoke. "Can we afford to take that chance?"

Leo's eyes narrowed. "You have something in mind, Captain?"

"We can't play spectator. We need to prepare a response for the admiral in case they act out and go kinetic."

Leo laughed and clapped his hands. "Let's hear it for the rookie. She scarcely knows where to piss in this bucket, and she's already itching to start a war. That is ballsy, Kate, if you'll pardon the expression." He chuckled. No one else seemed amused.

Mahoney's cheeks turned crimson, but she did not respond.

He pressed. "The name of the game in this region, Captain Mahoney, is DIME, with a capital 'D' for diplomacy. We parlay before we draw weapons. I realize you have a twitch in your trigger finger because you Hornet jockeys get off by shooting stuff. I love to blow things up too, girl. In different circumstances, I might join you in taking a whack at the bastards." He shook his head. "It doesn't work that way."

Mahoney's voice quivered with anger. "I understand the DIME paradigm. I maintain that we support diplomacy, information, and economics with military power. President Theodore Roosevelt articulated that concept succinctly. Sir."

He waved her off with a dismissive hand. "If you want to waste your Sunday playing military board games, be my guest. Just ask before you shoot. Okay, sweetheart?"

Leo enjoyed Mahoney's struggle to control her anger. He put on his most withering air as he waited for her to continue. When she spoke, her voice squeaked. "Yes, sir. Also, we should launch P-3 reconnaissance. We need our own source of information, beyond what the ROKs give us."

"You got one right, Captain." He struck his most imperious pose. "Why haven't you already done that? As fleet N3, you have that authority. The P-3 should be over the scene by now. Please don't tell me you waited to play 'COS may I' first."

She glared at him, eyes narrowed, face florid. "Consider it done, sir."

Leo rolled his eyes, then turned to the rest of the group. "Okay, team." His voice was no longer confrontational. "Despite my yanking the N3's chain, we must conduct increased surveillance and plan a response. The admiral flies aboard tomorrow as we close on Singapore. We have him for less than a day before he heads to the

ASEAN summit in Kuala Lumpur. We owe him a complete brief on courses of action, including military escalation. If we recommend escalation, he needs enough time to direct movement of ships and aircraft into position. You all know what to do." He scowled at his N3. "Get that damned recon bird in the air and then work up tactical options for the admiral to consider."

She replied in a steady voice. "Aye, sir."

"Consult the N7 before you finalize any plan. He holds the expertise on Korea."

Kate flinched. "Aye, sir."

"Get to it, folks," Leo said. Like first graders responding to a recess bell, his minions rushed from the room.

* * *

In the passageway outside Leo's office, Kate turned to Alexis. "What a dick."

Alex placed her hand on Kate's arm. "That conversation alone gives you grounds to—"

"Forget that." Kate hurried away, leaving the nonplussed JAG staring after her.

Kate bristled at the thought of talking to Colonel Preston Davis, the Fleet Marine Officer who also served as the N7 (ACOS for Theater Security). She knew his storied reputation as a military planner and warfighter, and his expertise in East Asia matters. But she had felt uncomfortable in their few interactions since she joined the staff. She must follow the chief of staff's order, but she would make her own decisions. With any luck, the colonel would stay out of touch. From what she'd heard, he sometimes disappeared for lengths of time—unusual behavior for a senior officer in a warship at sea.

- Mike Krentz -

Chapter Ten

April 8, 2012, South China Sea: USS *Shenandoah*

In a spartan stateroom on the *Shenandoah* VIP flag level, Colonel Preston Davis, USMC, thrashed on his rack. The thin top sheet lay in a heap on the deck, tossed off during his fitful sleep.

In a dream as real as life, Preston pulled wounded marines from a burned-out armored personnel carrier. No matter how many men he extracted, more bodies remained. A Navy corpsman shouted for him to take cover. He backed away, leaving his men screaming in agony as the APC burst into flames. From the blaze, a blood-soaked Marine emerged like a specter out of black fog, one arm missing below a jagged stump of a shoulder, his face burned black, red froth bubbling from a hole in his neck. He lurched toward Preston, then fell forward. His face struck the sand with a wet thud. Preston kneeled by the fallen Marine, rolled him over, and gasped. Staring at him through the charred eschar, the same eyes he saw every day in his own mirror.

Except these dead eyes had no light.

43

Preston sat up. Sweat dripped from his forehead. The soaked
bottom sheet reeked of stale perspiration. His hands quivered. He
slowed his breathing, trying to relax.

He had thought himself rid of the dreams. Not so. He let out
an exasperated sigh, then switched on the light over his rack and
sucked in the cool air of the ship. The oil and metal odor assuaged
his memory of the charred-flesh stench from a past battlefield.

Preston tumbled out of bed, pulled the wet skivvies off his
rump, and dropped them onto the deck. Naked in the adjoining head,
he splashed cold tap water on his face. He glanced away from the
mirror as he opened the medicine cabinet. From behind a canister of
shaving cream, he retrieved a bottle labeled "Listerine." He drew an
eager swig, savoring the burn as golden whiskey flowed down his
gullet. Grateful for the warm tingle coursing through his body, he
leaned over the sink. A furtive glance into the mirror projected that
deathlike face. Raw terror set his skin and sinew afire. Yet he
shivered.

He took another liberal quaff, turned on the shower to mid-
hot, and stepped in. The water soothed him while the whiskey did
the same from within. Then he shut off the flow and lathered himself
with urgent vigor.

The jarring ring of the phone in his adjoining room
interrupted.

"Damn."

He let the phone ring.

Ten minutes later, close-shaven and wearing clean skivvies,
he stepped from the head into his unembellished habitat. As he did
every morning, he looked at the two photos taped to the bulkhead
over his workspace. One, a four-by-five-inch grainy black and white
print, depicted a young army officer in Vietnam-era battle dress,

brandishing a rifle. The second, a larger color photograph, showed a beaming Major Preston Davis posing with a prior commandant of the Marine Corps. Both marines wore dress uniforms highlighted by rows of campaign and personal commendation medals. Inscribed across the bottom in gold ink were the words, "To Pres Davis. Semper Fi! George Jones, USMC."

Preston spread the blouse of a fresh digital olive-green camouflage uniform on his now tightly made rack. He used a ruler to roll up the sleeves to precise Marine Corps specifications. Once dressed, with no crease or fold out of place, he inspected himself in the full-length mirror on the bulkhead. A squared-away US Marine Corps bird colonel gazed back at him.

"Oorah, Marine."

Chapter Eleven

April 8, 2012, Yellow (West) Sea: ROKS *Bucheon*

Even in the chill of *Bucheon's* bridge, Commander Kwon sweated inside his Kevlar vest and helmet. He watched his crew focus on battle tasks. Some men cast furtive glances in his direction, silently pleading for decisive leadership. Below decks, the lives of a hundred ROK sailors hung on his next decision.

Kwon swore not to let them down. He would not subject their families to grief and shame. He would not give up his ship to the evil force from the north. Resolute, he scrutinized the radarscope.

Without a nanosecond pause, the threatening blip crossed the Northern Limit Line and continued straight toward *Bucheon*. As the invader closed to ten miles, Kwon maneuvered his vessel to a position ahead of the enemy's bow.

He admonished himself. *No hesitation.*

He hesitated.

Kwon clenched his damp fists. Seconds more delay would remove his options and put his crew in immediate danger. He licked his lips and turned to the first officer.

"Fire!"

The confused younger officer stared at his captain in disbelief, not moving.

"Fire NOW!"

The ship shuddered as volleys erupted from the fore-mounted cannon.

"Evasive maneuver!" shouted Kwon. On his mind's edge he sensed something out of place, unexpected: a deadly force in the water, an amidships disturbance. Did his men launch an Exocet?

The last conscious thought of his life.

* * *

Aboard the *Sariwon,* the officers on the bridge reported *Bucheon*'s cannon shot to their captain in the combat information center.

"The fool fired?"

Commander Kim ordered a retaliatory cannon fusillade and then rushed to the bridge. As he climbed the ladder, he felt a rumbling crescendo from beneath the ship.

Did that dipshit shoot an Exocet? He shouted up the ladder well. "Evasive maneuvers!"

He was between decks when pandemonium erupted.

A detonation from deep below shot a meter-wide jet of water upward into the belly of the *Sariwon.* The erupting geyser splintered the aging hull like a dry stick broken over a knee. Secondary explosions, escaping steam, bursts of flame from igniting fuel, flying shrapnel fragments, and gushing plumes of seawater caromed through the ship.

Many sailors of the Korean People's Navy died in an instant. Others fell or jumped overboard into the churning sea. Caught on the ladder between the CIC and the bridge just above the plume's impact point, Commander Kim Lee Jung was one of the first casualties, crushed and drowned at once.

* * *

Ten miles away and seconds later, a similar eruption tore into *Bucheon*. An up-rushing bubble imploded on the ship's hull and thrust the vessel out of the water. It splashed down in two useless hunks of fractured steel.

The sudden impact threw Commander Kwon and his bridge team forward. Kwon's body shot like a missile through the thin Plexiglas, bounced like a rubber doll on the crumpling deck below, and plunged into the sea. None of the panicked ROKN sailors, struggling to keep their own footing, noticed their skipper's corpse sink without ceremony.

Almost in sight of each other, the broken North and South Korean ships foundered as the few surviving sailors struggled to save themselves and their shipmates. Those still alive dove into the chilly water, swimming away from the pandemonium, searching for flotsam on which to alight. Others, buoyed by inflated float coats or life preservers, treaded water, numbed by the magnitude of death and destruction around them. A few lucky souls climbed into the few lifeboats that had withstood the explosions.

* * *

Sometime later, a US Navy P-3 Orion maritime patrol plane arrived over the scene. The four-engine aircraft descended to five hundred feet above the surface and circled the chaos. From her left-front pilot's seat, Lieutenant Commander Jessica "Cricket" Squire, USN, radioed position coordinates to a US Navy destroyer, USS *Stethem;* the closest US Navy ship. The destroyer sailed at maximum speed northward, diverted into the West Sea while underway to a scheduled port visit in the southern ROK port of Mokpo.

Cricket flew the P-3 in sequential figure-eight tracks over the water around both doomed warships. The aircrew transmitted photos and videos back to their base in Okinawa, Japan, from where they would be relayed to USS *Shenandoah*. Nothing else to do. The P-3 had no rescue capability, and Cricket knew that *Stethem* would arrive too late to save the perishing humans below them.

"What the hell happened down there?"

* * *

As the broken vessels sank out of sight, the few survivors, leaderless and alone, clung to their flotsam or lifeboats and prayed for deliverance. They grieved for their doomed shipmates, whose bodies descended to their last resting places on the bottom of the West Sea.

Below the surface, the denizens of the deep swam around the sinking cadavers and scrutinized the new arrivals to their maritime domain, not at all concerned about which came from north or south of an imaginary line on the surface above.

Phase Two: Seize

Chapter Twelve

April 8, 2012, South China Sea: USS *Shenandoah*

"Once Catholic, always Catholic," Margaret Mary Mahoney had often declared that in her clipped Irish brogue. "You can quit comin' to Mass. Go to them Protestant churches. You never stop bein' Catholic." Kate pictured her mother's ruddy complexion and intense green eyes, now five years after their light extinguished.

Movement in the small ship's chapel brought her back to the Easter Sunday Mass in progress. She rose with the rest of the congregation, a dozen sailors of diverse ranks, as Father Felix Armando, the sixty-year-old benevolent fleet chaplain, intoned the Lord's Prayer.

After leaving the chief of staff's office, Kate had ordered the P-3 to launch, directed her crisis action team to work the Korea response plan, and then stole thirty minutes for her cherished Sunday morning respite from the chronic chaos of a forward-deployed warship.

Like many cradle Catholics, she had fallen away from the

church of her youth several times. True to Margaret Mary's dictum, she had returned. Not that Kate was religious. She did not remember the last time she'd said an actual prayer. Over her life's stormy waves, she had realized personal comfort in the practice her mother had taught. She gravitated to Sunday Mass underway because Father Felix encouraged his flock to sit instead of kneel, to relax and enjoy refuge from the duty demands on their energy. Plus, he gave pithy homilies.

"The peace of the Lord be with you," the priest said.

"And also with you," the group responded.

"Offer each other a sign of peace."

Kate smiled and shook hands with Father Felix and the surrounding sailors. Then she sat to prepare for communion. Her thoughts wandered to her first combat sortie, the "shock and awe" phase of Operation Desert Storm when she had ejected over the Persian Gulf. Her career had soared after that mission. She wished Dodger had survived to congratulate her, but he had been the sole fatality of that fateful night.

As her first squadron commander, Leroy "Dodger" Jackson had become the surrogate father who taught her not only how to lead, but how to attack when under fire. Years after the shock of his death over Iraq, Kate still refused to admit she'd never see him again.

Kate Mahoney had not always been tough.

"You're a great stick, Kate, but too tentative in a skirmish." Dodger had plunked a finger into the nugget pilot's chest. "Somewhere in there you have a killer instinct. I've seen it in your eyes, the way you stare down men who harass you. They back off from that look. In the cockpit, you won't see the face of the guy coming after you, but give him the same what-for. Never retreat.

Attack."

In her sortie into Iraq a few years later, leading her flight through heavy fire to destroy a strategic building in downtown Baghdad, she had discovered her courage. The faces of Tom Mahoney and Luke Walker, late father and ex-husband, became the faces of the enemies she needed to stare down.

"A lady never fights back," Mary Margaret had often said. "You stay strong and silent. You take it." Her mother had lived what she preached, even when Tom Mahoney had taken to beating her in the late stages of florid alcoholism. Kate shivered at the memories.

This lady fights back.

After that night's ejection and rescue, she had earned a reputation for on-the-edge courage, keen to fly through hostile fire and bring the fight to the enemy when men might hesitate. No Navy pilot flew into combat as fearlessly as Scarlett Mahoney.

For eighteen years in naval aviation, she had endured the likes of Leo LeBlanc and his old-school chauvinism. The air medal with the combat *V* and the distinguished flying cross she wore on her dress uniform deserved respect from her male colleagues. But men gazed at her chest to ogle her breasts, not to admire her military decorations. Throughout her career, she relished verbal sparring with her male counterparts, no matter how heinous their affronts. Earlier in life, she had developed thick skin and honed a razor tongue as a defense against three aggressive brothers.

In battles of wits, most men come unarmed.

Why, at the peak of success, should she have to face off with a jerk like Leo LeBlanc? Why did each new rung on the career ladder force her to prove herself anew to sexist tyrants? This latest fool was no match, but Kate no longer savored the battle.

I am tired of it.

Communion had begun. Kate rose and approached Father Felix, who raised the consecrated host in front of her. "The Body of Christ."

"Amen."

He placed the bread into her hand. Transferring it to her mouth, she started toward her seat when a petty officer beckoned from the rear of the chapel.

"COS wants you in the MOC right away, ma'am."

Holy Christ. Not even divine worship can spare me from that man.

She thanked the messenger and hurried from the chapel.

* * *

The *Shenandoah* Maritime Operations Center (MOC), normally dormant on Sunday mornings, was abuzz when Kate arrived. She stopped when she entered the room, surprised by the frenzy. Phones rang non-stop. The central video screen displayed a graphic of the Korean peninsula and surrounding waters, with lines superimposed to show the demilitarized zone (DMZ) over land and the NLL over the West Sea. Colored icons depicted the locations of ships: blue for US, green for ROK, red for DPRK and PRC (People's Republic of China), white for others. Just below the NLL, one green and one red icon blinked at each other.

Another screen carried live news feed from CNN. A banner ran across the top, with white letters against a red background. "Breaking News: Crisis in Korea." The video cycled through stock images and B-roll of North and South Korean naval vessels, interspersed with replays of young Kim Jong Un, the untested new leader of North Korea.

A smaller banner appeared at the bottom of the screen. "Korean warships attack each other in Yellow Sea."

She approached Commander Paul Sadler, her deputy N3, typing on his computer.

"What happened?"

Stadler glanced at her, then turned back to his screen. "Korean ships shot each other, ma'am. COS came looking for you. He said to go straight to his office."

"Thanks, Paul. Keep me informed." She scurried from the MOC.

Chapter Thirteen

April 8, 2012, South China Sea: USS *Shenandoah*

Kate entered the chief of staff's office to find Eric, Alexis, Rusty, and several others present. The tall Marine leaning against the bulkhead in the back of the room drew her attention. His high-and-tight haircut and physique-hugging green camouflage uniform set him apart from the Navy officers attired in baggy blue coveralls or digital-patterned blue-and-gray "aquaflage." Colonel Preston Davis, USMC, the Seventh Fleet N7, rendered Kate a superficial nod.

Although annoyed at his condescension, Kate's deferential return nod piqued her more.

A "grumph" from Leo got her attention. "Thanks for joining us, Captain." He gazed at her with open disdain. "Looks like you got that war you wanted."

"Sir, I didn't—"

He raised his palm. "Yeah, yeah. Lighten up."

Kate frowned.

Leo turned to Eric. "What do we know?"

"Sir, it appears the Koreans sank each other's ships. First reports assess that the ROKs fired first. The KPN retaliated."

Hearing that, Kate shook off her unease and shifted her brain into operational mode. "Not likely. The ROKs wouldn't fire without a clear and present danger. They understand the AROE."

"Nevertheless, they did," Eric said. "We're still collecting satellite imagery, and ROK Fleet won't share any substance with us until they complete their own analysis. The P-3 is on scene. We'll have photos and videos soon."

"Survivors?" Kate asked.

"The P-3 reports some in the water. Rescue operations are just getting organized."

Leo addressed Kate. "Can *Stethem* arrive in time to help?"

"I don't know her present position. I doubt it. We can support salvage operations, but not rescue ops."

Leo sneered. "Am I the only one bothered that the N3 doesn't know where in the Pacific her friggin' ships are?"

Kate flushed. "Sir, I came straight from church. I can get her exact position, but based on her last known location, she's too far away to rescue anyone, even steaming at top speed."

Leo did not respond.

Kate shifted the subject. "We should get *Denver* underway from Sasebo; embark CTF-76 as the flag officer to command and control Navy support of the salvage and personnel recovery."

"Do it."

Kate continued. "We need to plan our military response. We have to show support for the ROKs, and we need to prepare to defend them if the North attacks."

Leo half-rose from his chair. "Whoa, Nellie. Did you not hear the N2? The ROKs fired first. If we rush to their side, we become co-aggressors."

"Aggressors?" Kate's voice rose with a slight quiver. "Regardless of how it looks in the early fog, we know the ROKs won't start a war with the North."

"Of course not," said Leo. "But a ROK ship fired on a KPN ship. Maybe a rogue ROKN captain got an itchy trigger finger and violated AROE. Doesn't matter. Either way, it's provocation. The DPRK will denounce the ROKs, the US, and the rest of the free world. The international press will have a field day. We can't fan those flames by charging in with sabers drawn."

He took his gaze off Kate to sweep across the entire group. "Boys and girls, the admiral arrives tomorrow. He will want answers and solutions. Prepare to advise him."

"Nothing."

All eyes turned toward the authoritative voice. No longer leaning on the bulkhead, Colonel Preston Davis stood tall. "We tell him to do nothing."

Kate raised her eyebrows. "Nothing? We're the United States Seventh Fleet. One of our closest allies is threatened. We can't do nothing."

"We can, and we must." The colonel regarded Kate with patronizing eyes.

"We have a responsibility here."

"To. Do. Nothing." The colonel articulated each syllable as if Kate were a slow learner. "A simple skirmish got out of hand. They play this game from time to time. Both sides will posture and brandish their manhood at each other, but nothing serious will happen. The last thing we do is escalate it into a substantial conflict."

Kate faced him, hands on hips. "A contingency plan is not escalating."

Preston moved closer to her. "Look, Captain. You're new here, so let me give you some advice. Stop thinking like an American. Consider where we are. In this region, we're not the cops. This incident is not a ghetto street fight. People here skirmish. They do it for sport, and the Koreans have done it for decades. Stifle your compulsion to rush in with guns blazing at the first sign of trouble. Think about the rest of the region. Do you want to pull the PRC into this little feud?"

Kate took a few seconds to control her exasperation. "No matter what we do, China will side with North Korea. The Russians might, too. They may make disparaging speeches and challenge our intentions, but they won't risk war with the world's most powerful Navy."

"Can you be certain of that?" Preston rolled in for the kill. "Do you want to take that chance? You understand the PRC's military build-up and North Korea's asymmetric capabilities, their weapons of mass destruction, do you not?"

Before Kate could respond, Leo broke in. "This debate is taking us nowhere. Can we get back to business, please?"

Colonel Davis ignored him. "We do nothing. PacFleet will say we do nothing. PACOM will say we do nothing. So will SecDef and SecState. POTUS won't stick his neck out for this, not when he's running for re-election. Our leaders will seek a diplomatic solution to this crisis." He addressed Kate. "We. Do. Nothing."

Kate flushed. She turned to the COS, trying to control the tremolo in her voice. "Sir, we can't sit on the sidelines. We don't know what happened. If this is a deliberate North Korea provocation, we must support the ROKs. I can't make a show of force on a moment's notice. We need to plan it now so we can execute on short notice, move ships into position, get carriers and aircraft ready to launch."

Leo scoffed. "Welcome to the real world, Kate. This is not a War College assignment. Nor is it Strike U, where you lead a Hornet squadron with dummy bombs into mock attack against cardboard tanks in the Nevada desert. And certainly not 'shock and awe' over Iraq. We play hardball Asian politics here. You lay off the heaters." He looked at her like a parent to a child. "Baseball analogy."

Kate flushed. "I had the best heater in the league when I pitched high-school softball. I get it. Again—"

Leo waved her silent. "Everything we do gets scrutiny, from Pyongyang to Beijing to Honolulu to Washington. On this staff, we don't get extra credit for bravado."

Kate struggled to control her rising frustration. She labored to keep her tone calm and resolute. "COS, let me do my job. I oversee fleet operations, and I need to plan an executable operation in response to this crisis. We can't afford to cower in political fear. Lack of action puts our allies and our own forces in danger. Higher authority can decide whether to execute, but we should not preempt their decision."

Colonel Davis scoffed. "Higher authority will keep our sword sheathed."

Kate turned on him. "Even in its sheath, a sword must stay sharp, Colonel." She surprised herself at the vehemence in her voice, which had not trembled. She felt a sudden confidence, like when she had flown bombing missions in Iraq. The colonel had given her the face she needed.

Leo waved his arms. "Fine, Kate. Make your plan and prepare to present it to the admiral. Pres, you work the diplomatic option. We'll let the boss decide what to recommend up the chain of command. The rest of you know what to do in your own areas. Now get to it."

"Aye, aye, sir," they responded in unison and filed out in silence. No one spoke to Kate.

Chapter Fourteen

April 8, 2012, South China Sea: USS *Shenandoah*

In her office, Kate telephoned her subordinate N3 in Task Force 76, CTF-76, the command responsible for amphibious ship operations in the Seventh Fleet. Based in Okinawa and Sasebo, Japan, CTF-76 was commanded by a one-star admiral who reported to the Seventh Fleet commander.

A brief knock at the open door heralded the uninvited arrival of Colonel Preston Davis, who ushered himself in and took a seat on the small couch facing Kate's desk. With the phone in hand, she nodded to him, and then faced away to continue the conversation.

"I understand that Rear Admiral Sanchez prefers to embark in *Denver* when it sails north to join the salvage ops, but I won't delay the ship's movement for his return from Phuket to Sasebo. Sorry to cut short his vacation, but your admiral needs to fly aboard *Denver* from somewhere enroute, probably Seoul."

She frowned as the voice on the other end objected.

"I'm telling not asking, Commander. Get that ship underway

soonest. Your boss can meet her in transit. He'll have to miss the Sasebo media hype. This operation is to support the ROKs, not his ambition for a second star." Another pause as she listened, scowling. "Do it, Commander."

Kate slammed down the phone, then remembered the presence in the chair behind her. She whirled around to face Preston.

"I have no idea why some Navy people consider you a bitch, Captain." His ingratiating smile did nothing to soften the sting of his words. "You'd make one hell of a Marine."

"I'll take that as a compliment, Colonel."

He did not reply.

Uncomfortable, she broke the silence. "To what do I owe the honor of a visit from the Seventh Fleet's senior Marine?"

He sat back with hands behind his head, flexing his biceps. "To convince you not to push a military response to the Korean crisis."

Kate folded her arms over her chest. "You're welcome to try, Colonel, but my recommendation supports our commander's overarching strategy and priorities. The civilian and military politicians can play defense and worry about 'the message,' but as the operational command for the world's most powerful Navy and the ROK's closest ally, we must prepare to respond with force. We would be remiss in our duty to our commander if we let him get caught unprepared if the North Koreans escalate."

Preston regarded Kate like a kindly father to a feisty daughter. "You've never served in this area of operations, have you? You came from the east coast, I understand?"

Kate's distraction by the colonel's sculpted arms annoyed her more than his patronizing air. "I came here from command of VFA-213 in Virginia, from where I made my second CentCom deployment. But I have been in this AOR as CAG OPS for CVW-5 in Atsugi. We deployed in *Kitty Hawk*."

Colonel Davis responded with a thin smirk. "I caught the clever reference to your command and combat experience, Captain. I have noticed your distinguished flying medal. Consider your warfighting credentials established." He leaned toward her as if to share a secret. "I will tell you something about this region you don't appreciate. For all their vaunted capabilities, the North Koreans are second stringers. It's about the Chinese and their military growth. We make no decisions without considering the impact on the PRC, and their probable response. To be blunt, if you want to protect the Seventh Fleet commander and our mission, you don't let Admiral Lewis stick his, uh, nose where he'll get it cut off."

Kate feigned puzzlement. "You said as much in COS's office. Do I require a personal tutorial?" He remained silent, so she continued. "I get your point, Colonel. But the Korean People's Army is the world's third-largest military. A firm response to North Korea's provocation is the right message to the DPRK and the PRC. My proposed response targets both."

Davis shook his head. "That decision is above our pay grade, Captain."

Kate flushed. "Oh, c'mon, Colonel. I don't know what you think your job is around here, but mine is to give solid tactical and operational advice to the fleet commander so he can recommend an informed course of action to higher command. The Navy and Marine Corps didn't put us here just to make plans on paper and create pretty PowerPoint slides."

Preston raised a conciliatory hand. "I get it. May I suggest we examine all the facts and available courses of action before we advise the admiral to ready, fire, aim? We owe him an honest assessment of all the nuances."

Kate glowered. "Such as?"

"The world will believe the ROKs started this fracas."

"You can't buy that story. You know they didn't."

"What I know or believe doesn't count. We don't have all the facts at this point. If we charge in without proof, our adversaries will paint us as aggressors. The DPRK and PRC could perceive or portray your 'preparation' as 'provocation.' That puts not only our commander, but the entire chain of command up to and including the Commander-in-Chief, on the defensive. Do you really want to hand our adversaries another justification for offensive action?"

"You've said as much three times now. I got the first two, and I hate redundancy. You're wasting our time repeating yourself. Unless you have something new, I have work to do."

She turned toward her desk, then turned back to face him. "Another factor that I assumed you would understand. Our job in this area of operations is to manage risk, not run away from it."

Davis raised his hands as if to surrender. "Oo-rah, Captain."

He rose from the chair, towering over her. "One other item. As senior leaders, you and I should not disagree in front of the admiral."

Kate whirled her chair around and stood to face him. "Is that why you came here? You want to avoid a confrontation in front of the boss?"

Preston said nothing. His height forced her to look up at him. Kate hated that her short stature often put her at a disadvantage against men. She hated that her voice trembled when she became angry or upset.

She blinked and imagined herself in the cockpit over Iraq. Her voice became steady. "I won't play that game. As you said, the admiral deserves honest, data-driven options, not groupthink. I won't let you drive his decision any more than you want me to do. That's not my job and not my style."

The colonel shrugged. "We agree to disagree. We'll see how the boss plays it."

"Yes, sir, we will."

He paused at the door. "We're the same rank, Kate. You need not call me 'sir' or even 'Colonel.' I'm 'Preston,' or just 'Pres.'" He smiled, less condescending.

"Sorry, sir, I won't do that. As professionals, we should address each other with proper respect."

"Suit yourself, Kate." He smirked and left her office.

Don't call me "Kate."

The words never reached her lips. She stayed at the doorway for a moment, watching Colonel Preston Davis stride down the passageway as if he owned it.

Chapter Fifteen

April 8, 2012, San Bruno, CA

Patrick locked his bicycle into the racks on the north side of the mall. He found his friend Gavin inside the entrance.

"About time," Gavin said. "We've been waiting a half-hour."

"Had to finish something first."

"Sure thing, gamer ace. Nice of you to come spend some time with your human friends. Hurry up. The others are at the food court."

Patrick, Gavin, Omar, Marcie, Olivia, and Mei Li sipped sodas and munched on cheeseburgers and fries at a table in the food court. Omar shared Patrick's enthusiasm for video and computer gaming. Gavin was a sports fanatic who had made the varsity football team as a freshman. Marcie and Olivia were into clothes and boys.

Patrick had known Mei Li since preschool, during the times he'd stayed with his aunt when his mother deployed. Now he and

Mei Li were "going together" as high school freshmen. Mei Li was less developed than the other girls, but she got straight A report cards at school. Since Fuchou had linked Patrick to the pornographic website, he had wondered when Mei Li would grow tits like the women in the photos.

As the fries disappeared, Patrick held court. "The Panderans are like super-trendy martial arts warriors. Their world is like China, even has a Great Wall. They look like pandas, except with long chin beards; they wear those cone hats like people in Asia. They fight with bare hands and use weapons only to finish off their foes. The Monks have healing powers. My friend, Fuchou, is a Monk. He's one of the greatest teachers in the world."

"Dude, give it a break," Gavin said. "It's fantasy."

"I think it's interesting," Marcie said. "It's highly analytical. Teaches problem-solving and stuff."

"Who is this Sue Chow?" Mei Li said.

"Fuchou," Patrick said. "A guy I met online in the game world. His screen name is Chinese for 'Avenger.'"

"Where does he live?"

"No idea. Doesn't matter. Could be anywhere in the world. That's the advantage of online gaming. You're not limited by geography. You can have friends anywhere."

Mei Li pursed her lips. "I'd rather have friends I can see." She sounded jealous, which confused Patrick.

Gavin asked, "Do you just play games together, or do you have, like, online chats too?"

Patrick rolled his eyes. Gavin had never touched a video or computer game, or he would not have asked such a naïve question. "Usually the games, but many of my friends chat or text as well. It's called 'multi-tasking,' dude."

Marcie batted her eyelids at Patrick. "I love Facebook chats. I play some online games too. It's cool that you make friends around the world, Patrick."

Mei Li moved closer to Patrick. "Maybe someday I'll be good enough for Patrick to let me play games with him."

He ignored her and spoke to Marcie. "You just gotta play a lot." Looking at Marcie, he felt something different than he did with Mei Li.

Chapter Sixteen

April 8, 2012, San Bruno, CA

Back home, Patrick closed the door and logged onto his computer. A
Facebook message icon blinked. Marcie.

> **MarcieD:** *Whassup? You gonna WOW all night? Or be
> human for a change?*

He considered how Marcie shared his interest in gaming. Mei
Li had tried to play with him, but the games bored her and she didn't
care to watch him play. Marcie had flirted with him at the mall. He
would like to spend time with her.

> **PatWalk:** I might.
> **MarcieD:** *Might what?*
> **PatWalk:** Go out. Got anything in mind?
> **MarcieD:** *Olivia is here. Let's all hang. Don't need to do
> anything special. Get to know each other better.*

Olivia had a mature figure and a reputation to go with it. By
rumor, she'd already "done it," more than once, but with older guys,
not freshmen. Hanging with those two might be fun.

70

PatWalk: Can you get away?

MarcieD: Sure. You?

PatWalk: Have to wait till my aunt's asleep. She won't let me out late, not with girls.

From out of nowhere, an idea hit him.

PatWalk: You girls wanna go for a ride?

MarcieD: On your bike? LOL.

He typed in haste as the plan unfolded in his head.

PatWalk: I can use my aunt's car.

MarcieD: You drive? You're not old enough.

PatWalk: How hard can it be?

MarcieD: You're weird, dude.

PatWalk: How else we going to get together? Too far to walk. A car gives us privacy.

MarcieD: You wish. LMFAO.

PatWalk: You game or not?

Marcie did not answer right away. Patrick reasoned she was huddling with Olivia. Excited, he waited.

MarcieD: You're on. Where and when?

PatWalk: Two hours. Your corner.

MarcieD: Okay, wild man. Don't stand us up or you are dead.

PatWalk: I'll be there.

He grinned and clicked off the messenger and started the online game. He opened a chat with Fuchou.

Fanpan: Guess what I'm doing later.

Fuchou: Beating off?

Fanpan: Better. Picking up chicks for a joy ride.

Fuchou: On a bike?

Fanpan: No, doofus. My aunt's car.

Fuchou: Radical. Since when do you drive? You old enough?

Fanpan: Got my license.

Fuchou: What's the big deal? I drive girls around all the time.

Patrick searched for a quick answer.

Fanpan: My aunt's strict. I don't get the car much.

Fuchou: Whatever. Wait. Did you say, girls? Plural? Bold, man. Wish I could join you.

Fanpan: Me too.

Fuchou could be an ally in this adventure. He seemed more experienced, like he knew things that Patrick only imagined.

Fuchou: Wouldn't it be weird if we live in the same town?

Fanpan: Yeah.

Fuchou: Where's home, Dude?

Patrick hesitated. He'd heard stories, but then he doubted Fuchou was a stalker. He was too cool, and he enjoyed gaming. No harm in a vague response.

Fanpan: San Francisco Bay Area.

Fuchou: Bummer. I'm in Florida. Couldn't be farther apart. But we might meet up one day.

Fanpan: Maybe.

Fuchou: Maybe you'll get lucky with those chicks. You got rubbers?

Patrick hadn't thought beyond taking the car. He hadn't planned on what Fuchou implied. The notion frightened him.

Fanpan: Sure. Now let's kill aliens.
Fuchou: Right on, Bro.

Chapter Seventeen

April 9, 2012, South China Sea: USS *Shenandoah*

"Flight quarters, flight quarters. The ship is at flight quarters. All designated personnel man your flight quarters stations. Wear no covers topside; throw no items over the side. All hands not involved in flight quarters remain forward of the superstructure. The smoking lamp is out. Now flight quarters."

The 1MC overhead announcement, accompanied by a test blare of the ship's collision and fire alarms, roused Kate from a heavy sleep on her rack. She and her staff had worked most of the night on the Korean response plan, and she had endured long, contentious phone conversations with her PacFleet and PACOM counterparts. Those higher commands to which Seventh Fleet reported were based in Hawaii. The eighteen-hour time difference made it their Sunday morning, in contrast to deep night in the South China Sea. Her higher-echelon counterparts' relaxed aloha wear on the video teleconference annoyed Kate almost as much as their steadfast refusal to support her aggressive military strategy.

By 0400, she had put the finishing flourish on a complicated PowerPoint presentation that included animated icons to depict ships' and airplanes' movements in various schemes of maneuver. Aggravated and drained, Kate had settled down for a brief rest and slept through both reveille and her own alarm clock. It took the ship's call to flight quarters to rouse her.

Kate's commander would arrive on *Shenandoah* within the hour. She undressed and dashed into her shower.

* * *

A polished olive-green HH-60 Seahawk helicopter swooped in majesty through the haze aft of the ship. Thumping rotors beat the air as the helo flew a steady descent to the flight deck. The words, *Commander US Seventh Fleet,* stood out in bold white letters against the glossy painted fuselage, as did the three white stars on the door—heralds of the rank and status of the aircraft's occupant.

In the chief of staff's office, Leo and Preston lounged in soft chairs watching their commander's arrival in fuzzy black-and-white on the bulkhead-mounted LCD screen. When the helicopter touched down, eight bells sounded over the 1MC loudspeaker, followed by the announcement to all hands.

"Seventh Fleet, arriving."

Leo turned to Preston. "Showtime. Game face." Both men rose and left the cabin. In the passageway, the COS proceeded aft toward the superstructure ladder, while the N7 walked forward to his office.

On the flight deck, as the helicopter rotors slowed to a safe speed, sailors wearing float coats, safety helmets called "cranials," and goggles darted beneath the blades to chock the wheels and chain the aircraft to tie-downs. Another sailor opened the passenger door and saluted the stocky figure who alighted wearing a green Nomex

flight suit, white float coat, cranial, and goggles. Three silver stars
on the cranial's brow identified the wearer as Darnell C. Lewis, Vice
Admiral, United States Navy, Commander US Seventh Fleet.

One sailor escorted the admiral past the rotor arc, around the
tower, and forward to a door leading into the superstructure's
ceremonial passageway. Eight sailors serving as side boys in rows of
four saluted as the admiral walked between them. At the entrance,
the chief of staff rendered a snappy salute to welcome his direct
superior aboard. Admiral Lewis preceded Leo into the passageway
as the helicopter's rotors wound to a stop.

Chapter Eighteen

April 9, 2012, South China Sea: USS *Shenandoah*

At 0930, Vice Admiral Lewis, designated by the code N00, met with his senior staff to discuss the Korean crisis. He commanded from the head of a conference table in his plush office/stateroom, similar in design but more spacious than his chief of staff's quarters. COS and the ACOS group sat along both sides.

In her seat next to Leo, Kate fumed as he and Colonel Davis stole the conversation. Hard copies of her PowerPoint presentation sat on the table, unread. She pictured herself as an orphan child at a family supper table, seated but not allowed to talk.

Break in, soon.

Lewis listened, giving complete attention to his advisers' viewpoints. Stout but fit, he wore typical aviator working garb: the Nomex green flight suit with three silver stars on each shoulder yet sported the symbol of a submariner on his royal blue name tag.

Kate considered that incongruous. In the competitive spirit among Navy warfare communities, no self-respecting "bubblehead" would dress like an "airedale," and vice versa. Fleet commanders could wear any organizational uniform—but only the warfare device earned.

Everyone respected the imposing presence before them. A legend as an all-American fullback at the Naval Academy, Darnell Lewis' career had soared from plebe to the commander of the most extensive fleet in the Navy. His ascendancy was neither by accident nor in deference to diversity. Esteemed as both a shrewd strategist and intrepid warrior, he also had a well-earned reputation for political astuteness. Few doubted that higher command and a fourth star awaited him beyond his current assignment.

Kate tuned back into the discussion as Colonel Preston Davis continued his monologue. She wondered if N00 shared her impatience with the Marine's obvious posing. She had heard that Lewis and Davis were friends from previous joint service. Perhaps the colonel enjoyed credibility with the boss that she had yet to earn for herself.

"With the upcoming two-plus-two talks with the PRC, the White House won't risk giving them an excuse to sabotage those negotiations," Preston said. "The Koreans get into these cockfights." He glanced at Kate, but she stared past him. "They may brandish swords, but neither side is serious enough to cause an all-out war."

The admiral raised his hand with the palm outward, his well-known stop signal. "Sinking each other's ships and killing several hundred second or third cousins might be considered serious in some quarters."

Kate seized that moment to jump into the fray. "Indeed, sir. We should consider it serious. We can't sit this one out. Failure to respond says we don't honor our commitments in the region." Her voice quavered, so she stopped speaking.

Colonel Davis regarded her as if she were a pesky fly. "Admiral, if we side with the ROKs, we push the PRC into overt support of the DPRK, perhaps with force. We cannot afford to confront China, for both diplomatic and military reasons. We must treat this as a local conflict between two factions that have hated each other for decades."

"You recommend a prevent defense," Lewis said.

Kate spoke, but Leo talked over her. "Admiral, Colonel Davis is right. We shouldn't risk provoking the PRC. Higher authority will agree."

Livid, Kate erupted, her voice firm. "Why are we here at all, sir, if we refuse to accept risk in supporting our allies? What does that say about our commitment? Why not pack up our ships and our planes and our sailors and marines and leave? Let higher authority run the show from six thousand miles away with no up-close visibility."

Kate shifted her sharp gaze at Colonel Davis. "Do we let our allies believe we don't have the balls to face up to bullies? No one in this region wants a timid sister."

She paused in realization that everyone, including the admiral, was staring at her. She turned to him and continued in a measured voice. "Sir, you command the forward deployed naval *force*. Why let the world perceive you as reluctant to wield that power against aggression? If the United States Navy stays on the sidelines and won't support our closest allies, you can bet the wavering nations in this region will flock to the PRC. If force is really not a choice, send our expensive military toys somewhere else and let us all go home to our families."

Embarrassed silence descended as she remembered to append the word, "sir," to her rant. All eyes bounced between Kate and the admiral.

He leaned toward her and spoke in a soft voice, "What did you have in mind, Captain?"

"Sir, I refer to the PowerPoint brief in front of you. I recommend a visible show of force in the West Sea. Deploy the Carrier Battle Group straight to the NLL and park it on KJU's ass. Fly jets off the carrier day and night. Bring P-3s from Okinawa to conduct constant surveillance. Cycle our cruisers and destroyers through Pyeongtaek on the west coast and Donghae on the east. Show the ROKs and the DPRK we're in the neighborhood, fully operational and ready to fight—any time."

She glared at Preston. "We show North Korea and the PRC that we will not hesitate to launch our overwhelming military force against any provocation."

Admiral Lewis sat back, immersed in thought. When he spoke to Kate, a hint of a smile showed in the corners of his mouth. "What do PacFleet and PACOM think of your idea?"

Kate deflated. "No support from the operations shops. I spoke to both. They believe the plan carries too much political risk."

The admiral snorted. "What a surprise."

Colonel Davis began, "Sir, with respect, again I say—"

Lewis raised a hand to cut him off. "I got it, Colonel. You advise that we defer the decision to higher authority without an aggressive recommendation from us. Well, PacFleet will fret and wring hands and waffle till the sun sets, but they sure as hell won't act. They will defer to PACOM. PACOM will spend all their energy churning over the message and the optics, not the action. At the end of another day, they won't act either. They'll run it up to the Joint Chiefs and the Interagency Committee, where it will get staffed and studied and diluted—to control the message, not the outcome.

Finally, they will present it to the national command authorities, where—you guessed it—they will take a pass. By then, with no influence from us, this crisis will be over, and our adversaries emboldened. We'll be staring down a larger threat." He shrugged. "We can defer that one higher too and start the cycle all over.

"One day, not tomorrow, but sooner than later, the North Koreans will storm over the DMZ and the NLL to 'unite' Korea. The ROK will turn to us for help while we just sit and suck our thumbs because we're not in a ready position. How much blame do you think higher authority will take for that debacle?"

Davis and Leo spoke at once, but the admiral turned to Kate. "How quickly can you execute?"

"I've already put the carrier battle group on a ninety-six hour prepare-to-deploy order. We'll achieve full mission capability within a week."

"Do it now, Captain, while it's the weekend in Hawaii and Washington, before the uniformed bureaucrats recover from their mai-tai and martini hangovers."

Admiral Lewis swept his eyes over the entire group and spoke in a firm, authoritative voice. "Gentlemen and ladies, the United States Navy Seventh Fleet does not sit on the sidelines. Not on my watch. I hope the PRC sticks its beak into this because I would love to bust it off. We have a duty to defend freedom and US interests in this region." He slammed a fist on the table. "By God, we will execute our obligation."

He smiled at Kate. "At least someone here has the ovaries to stand up for what's right."

Kate and the Colonel stared ahead, stone-faced, neither daring to look at the other. The other officers inspected the deck at their feet.

81

"Now get to it," the admiral said.

Before anyone could move, the admiral's aide entered without knocking. "Sorry to interrupt, sir. The battle watch asked me to pass an urgent message to Captain Mahoney."

As everyone else fled the room, the aide handed Kate a folded note. She waited to open it until she was in the passageway. Her face paled when she read it.

"Call your sister as soon as possible."

Patrick?

Chapter Nineteen

April 9, 2012, South China Sea: USS *Shenandoah*

Kate hurried to her stateroom to make the call. Her older sister answered the phone on the second ring.

"Colleen, what's going on? Is it Patrick?"

"He's okay, but there's been an incident."

"Incident?"

"He took my car. He got arrested."

"Your car?" She looked at the photo of Patrick on the desk. "He's okay?"

"He didn't get hurt. No crash."

"What happened?"

"A police officer called at one in the morning. Asked if I knew where my car was. Obviously not in the driveway where I left it. They caught Patrick three miles from here, driving my car without headlights."

Kate gasped. "He could have been killed."

"There's more. He had two girls in the car. The cop told me

83

to come get him or they would take him to jail. Thank God my neighbor was home to drive me. When I got there, they had him handcuffed. The girls' parents had picked them up and left the scene."

"Handcuffed? He's fourteen."

"Policy, they said. At first, he told them he was sixteen. He told the truth only when they asked for a driver's license."

Kate's head spun. In her windowless gray confines on the rocking ship, the conversation felt spectral. She squeezed her eyes to quell onrushing tears, struggled to find her voice. "What's next?"

"He has to appear in court. They charged him with reckless driving and endangerment, plus driving without a license. They wanted to make it auto theft, but I refused. I pointed out that you are in the Navy, deployed overseas. One cop said Patrick might get off with probation and community service because he doesn't have a record. They will hold off the exact court date for a while until you can go with him." Her voice took a tone of authority. "Come home, Kate. Your son needs you."

She rubbed her forehead where a monster ache had begun.

"Where is Patrick now?"

"In his room."

"Please get him."

When he came on the line, Patrick sounded far away. "Mom?"

"Patrick, Patrick. What did you do? Why?"

"Just did."

"You could've died. Those girls might have been killed, or maimed."

"Sorry." Monotone.

"Don't say you're sorry unless you mean it."

"I mean it."

Was this Patrick on the line? He sounded like his father, Luke Walker. She couldn't think straight.

"You still there, Mom?"

Kate didn't know what to say. "I'm happy you're okay, but I have to think about what to do. I'm angry and sad." She choked on the words. "I can't talk to you right now."

"I am sorry, Mom. Don't hate me for this." Was he crying, or acting?

"I will never hate you. I want to believe you're sorry, but I need to figure out how to handle this. Please, stay out of trouble until I get there."

"I will."

She had nothing else to say.

"Do you need to speak to Aunt Colleen again?"

"Please."

"I love you, Mom."

"I love you too, son."

Drained, Kate explained to Colleen that she could not come until the ship made port in Singapore in two days. Then it might be problematic because of a pending international crisis. In the big-sister stern voice Kate had always dreaded, Colleen insisted Kate needed to be with Patrick. Kate promised to call back within a day.

She hung up and sobbed. Thank God she had Colleen, divorced and childless, to look after Patrick. Her sister was right. Patrick needed his mother now, not an aunt. But how?. . .

After a few minutes, she washed her face and sat at her desk, staring at nothing.

What the hell do I do now?

A gentle knock interrupted her misery. Still seated, she

85

reached over to open the door. Preston Davis stood in the doorway.

"Not now, please." She tried to close the door, but the colonel blocked it.

"Are you okay? We're all worried about you."

Phase Three:

Dominate

Chapter Twenty

April 9, 2012, Yellow (West) Sea: USS *Denver* (LPD 9)

"Task Force Seventy-Six, arriving."

The dull gray MH-60 Seahawk helicopter touched down on the flight deck of the *Austin*-class amphibious ship, USS *Denver (LPD 9)* idling in the West Sea. It would serve as temporary command ship for Expeditionary Strike Group Seven/Task Force-Seventy-Six (CTF-76) as it assisted the ROK Navy in the salvage of ROKS *Bucheon*.

Once the aircraft was safely chocked and chained, Rear Admiral (Lower Half) Rafael "Rafe" Sanchez, USN, Commander Task Force Seventy-Six, disembarked and followed his escort to the ship's superstructure. He offered a perfunctory salute to his chief of staff and entered the ship, shedding his float coat and cranial as he proceeded down the passageway. The ceremonial protocol for embarking this one-star admiral emulated that observed for his immediate superior, the three-star Seventh Fleet commander, on USS *Shenandoah*. But since *Denver*'s current mission was grisly business, Rear Admiral Sanchez had no use for niceties.

A few miles away, the remains of *Bucheon* and her crew had surfaced. From the *Denver* bridge, Sanchez gazed upon the larger ROKS *Dokdo*, the ROK Navy's new amphibious ship. As soon as his own staff briefed him, Sanchez would fly to *Dokdo* to join the ROKN Second Fleet commander who controlled a small flotilla of US and ROK ships conducting the salvage operations. With the North Korea People's Navy engaged in similar operations on its own destroyed ship ten miles away, the atmosphere on board *Denver* was thick with tension and depression. Few sailors, US or ROK, had ever been close to, or imagined, such a tragedy.

A career surface warfare officer, Sanchez refused to wear a flight suit, even when authorized. Clad in his Navy working uniform, he descended the ladder to the conference room below the main deck. Inclement weather had impeded diving and flight operations during the early course of the salvage mission. Today had seen the first unencumbered efforts.

Foul weather had also delayed the admiral's circuitous route to his rendezvous with *Denver*, an added burden for which the disgruntled Sanchez blamed the Seventh Fleet N3, one Captain Katherine Mahoney. She had ordered *Denver*'s immediate departure from Sasebo in southern Japan before the CTF commander could return from leave in Thailand.

As if a half-day delay would matter in the face of this tragedy.

Now Rafe must play serious catch up before joining the ROKN admiral in less than an hour.

"What do we know?" Sanchez asked the officers gathered around the conference table.

The chief of staff spoke. "Sir, so far, the ROKs have

recovered twenty-six bodies, including the *Bucheon* captain, positively identified. They have also recovered debris from the ship, but nothing specific, and no indications of cause. The hull, I mean the pieces of the hull, are still submerged. She seems to have broken in two, just like *Cheonan* in 2010."

"What about the weapons systems?" asked the admiral.

The N3 operations officer responded. "Sir, we've begun dive operations today, and have no report on that. The ROK divers care less about the weather. They dove yesterday, and we think they inspected at least part of the weapons systems. No word on what they found."

"Get it," said Sanchez. "I need that information before I brief Seventh Fleet. What's the weather outlook for the next few days?"

"Clear today and tomorrow, sir. Another storm system is developing to the west, so conditions will deteriorate after tomorrow."

"Then make the most of it while we can," Sanchez said.

As the group departed, Sanchez freshened up in his stateroom before embarking on the helo for the short flight to *Dokdo*. He did not relish the stiff formality and diffidence that stifled direct dialog between the two nations' military leaders. This was not a time for politeness and ceremony, much less inscrutability or veiled mistrust. The next two days would be critical, not only for the salvage operations, but for the careers of his ROKN counterparts and, more important, his own.

Two hours later, Sanchez sat in the office of Rear Admiral Yee-Dongsun, Commander, ROK Navy Second Fleet. After the initial exchange of pleasantries over tea, Admiral Yee asked all others to clear the room. Sanchez noted the wan, harried expression of a man who had not slept in days, and whose professional career teetered on extinction.

When they were alone, the Korean pursed his lips and looked at the deck before speaking. "I have serious information that I may share only with you." He shot Sanchez a wary eye before he continued. "Yesterday our divers inspected the hull of *Bucheon*, including the weapons systems. Both missile launchers contained Exocets." He paused for his words to take effect.

Sanchez whistled through his teeth. "That suggests—"

"*Bucheon* did not fire missiles before she was hit."

Sanchez blew out a deep breath. The two men looked at each other with mutual appreciation that *Bucheon* did not fire on the North Korea ship with the intent to kill. The unanswered question caused both men deep dread.

After a long pause, Sanchez gave it a voice. "If *Bucheon* did not sink the *Sariwon*, who did?"

Chapter Twenty-One

April 9, 2012, South China Sea: USS *Shenandoah*

Before entering his own office after the conference with the admiral, Leo LeBlanc poked his head into the small office across the passageway. The door plaque read *Flag Secretary*, but the incumbent, Lieutenant Commander Elijah Kramb, USN, was no secretary. The FlagSec served as the chief of staff's right hand in all matters administrative. Kramb controlled the calendar, the priorities, and management of the COS and the senior staff. Lieutenant Commander Kramb had the toughest job on the ship: high demand, low reward.

Leo found the FlagSec in his usual harried pose, bent over his computer, hammering the keyboard. Elijah looked up, but his fingers kept moving.

"I need exercise," Leo said. "Bar the door till I tell you I'm ready to rejoin the rat race."

Elijah smiled. "Aye, sir."

As Leo turned to leave, Kramb said, "Sir, I put the draft *5050* for Singapore on your desk. We need to get it out to the staff before the port-visit brief this evening." A gentle yet firm reminder to Leo that a fleet chief of staff should never expect uninterrupted personal time, least of all for exercise. Elijah's portly frame suggested that the same applied to the FlagSec. Despite the warning, Leo guarded his exercise time because, teetering on the edge of sanity, he needed therapeutic endorphins as much as a junkie craving a fix.

"I'll review the *5050* right after I finish my workout," Leo said. Elijah had already turned back to his computer.

Entering his office, Leo shunned the paper pile that Elijah had left in his inbox. The draft *5050* instruction—a standard Navy document that promulgates details, rules of conduct, and behavior for specific events such as port visits—mocked Leo from the top of the pile. The entire stack stood more than a foot tall. The folders in the bottom four inches had not moved in three months.

Leo fought off his habitual urge to open the email on either his classified or unclassified computers. Those inboxes would overflow with electrons the same as the physical inbox on his desk choked on paper. He would steal the time to work out right now, even though he would pay it back twofold later. The constant demands on the chief of staff would extract their due from Leo's chronic sleep deprivation.

A few minutes later, clad in cycling shorts and a singlet, Leo spun his legs on the stationary bicycle. The chronograph on the handlebars showed only a ten minutes' workout so far.

Damn, this is boring.

Endorphins slowly wore the edge from Leo's tension. Usually he plugged an iPod into his ears and listened to loud rock music as he spun, but the battery had drained the last time he worked out—what was it, a week ago?—and he'd forgotten to recharge it.

Using the remote, he flipped on the large screen TV in his stateroom to watch the Armed Forces Network's tape-delayed NBA playoff game. The ship's overworked satellite reception scrambled the video into bursts of multicolored pixels interspersed with only random frozen vignettes of actual play. Even with perfect video feed, the inane AFN promotions instead of commercials would annoy anyone, let alone a hard driving chief of staff. Frustrated, he turned off the TV. He was alone with his endorphins and his thoughts.

Captain Mahoney Baloney. My job isn't hard enough. Now I gotta deal with her? Bitch causes trouble wherever she's stationed. Wraps suckers like Lewis around her damned finger.

Sweat dripped off Leo's brow as he intensified the workout pace. He had never worked with Kate Mahoney before, but he knew men who had. Few said anything flattering about her. Most former subordinates and colleagues used the words "ambitious, overbearing, short-tempered, cunning," or worse, to describe Scarlett Mahoney. Yet she prospered in the elite aviation community dominated by hard-hitting, ballsy, spirited men who had accepted women on their team only when given no choice. Not only had Mahoney moved up the ranks, she wore that distinguished flying medal from operations over Iraq.

"Someone manned her cockpit before she got that award," he'd heard one aviator say.

There must be some truth in it.

Other women succeeded in the Navy—even in naval air—without acquiring bitch reputations. Mahoney must deserve at least some of the tarnish. But how much?

Mahoney leaves a boatload of angry men in her wake wherever she sails. Now she's my problem. I cannot let this woman take me down.

Leo harbored no illusions about his own ambitions. A successful stint as Seventh Fleet chief of staff would position him for selection to admiral. His carefully managed career had reached the brink of the ultimate affirmation that he deserved. A successful track record here, plus a glowing fitness report from Admiral Lewis, would put him over the top. If he continued to play his cards right, for his next job he would wear a silver star on each of his collars.

Kate Mahoney blocked his pathway to greatness. She had persuaded Lewis to buy her reckless, jingoistic response plan to the Korea crisis. That spelled trouble, especially for Leo.

If things go sour on the Pen, no one will blame untouchable Darnell Lewis.

De facto pre-selected for his next star, the admiral's supporters in Congress and the White House would not allow any offal to stick on him.

My face will catch it.

Leo dared not risk that outcome. How to deal with Mahoney, especially now that she'd won the admiral's support?

I've clipped pilots' wings before. I can do it again.

Leo completed his workout with a vigorous animosity-fueled spin. Panting, he dismounted the stationary bike and paced his stateroom, gulping water until the sweat stopped flowing. He considered what he'd heard about Mahoney's last squadron tour, first as executive officer and then commanding officer. Rumor had it that promising careers disintegrated because of her. In certain quarters, Kate Mahoney was openly called "a ruthless bitch."

Need more information.

He took a quick shower, donned a clean working uniform, and fired up his office computers. The Outlook inbox on his unclassified machine filled up with bold-formatted subject lines of unread e-mails. Leo ignored them and pulled up his contacts list, searching for a name that he could not remember. No help.

"Drat." Then he slapped his hand against his head. "Will I ever figure out the easy way to use this technology?"

He brought up the unclassified US Navy internet site and navigated through the index for the home page of VFA-213, the east coast aviation squadron that Mahoney commanded before coming to Seventh Fleet. Clicking on *Command Leadership,* he found what he needed. The current commanding officer, Commander Ira "Less" Leskowitz, would have been Kate's executive officer when she commanded that squadron. The website provided the CO's email address. Leo cut and pasted it into the address line of a new message:

Less:

We met in the past. How goes command? Greatest job in the Navy, right?

To the point, I'm asking for your help with something, and I'd appreciate keeping it in absolute confidence between you and me. Can we set up a telcon? I need information about your predecessor. Next couple of days would be good. We'll be in Singapore, but don't worry about the time difference. I'll make myself available at your convenience. Look forward to talking to you.

VR/ Leo LeBlanc

After hitting *Send,* he lifted the draft *5050* from the top of his paperwork inbox. Chuckling, he turned to the last page, signed it, and tossed it into the outbox.

Chapter Twenty-Two

April 8, 2012, San Bruno, CA

Ignoring the game play on his screen, Patrick texted Fuchou.

Fanpan: I got caught.

Fuchou: By your aunt?

Fanpan: Worse, the cops.

Fuchou: No way, Dude? You got captured? How?

Fanpan: Headlights off.

Fuchou: Dude, that's basic. Chicks in the car?

Fanpan: Yeah. Cops called their moms. Not good.

Fuchou: Bummer.

Fanpan: They cuffed me.

Fuchou: No way, man. Police brutality.

Fanpan: Whatever.

Fuchou: Jail?

Fanpan: Nah. Aunt came and got me. I gotta go to court.

Worse, she called my mom on a ship somewhere near China. Seriously pissed.

Fuchou: *What can she do from a friggin' Navy ship?*

Fanpan: You don't know my mom.

Fuchou: *Brutal, huh?*

Fanpan: Strict as they come.

Fuchou: *You did nothing awful. Not like you screwed those girls or gave them booze or drugs.*

Fanpan: Stole a car. Drove it on the street without a license, no headlights. Stupid.

Fuchou: *Chill, Fanpan the Rebel. Don't go soft now.*

Fanpan: Easy for you to say.

Fuchou: *Hey. I've done stuff. Still here.*

Fanpan: You been in trouble with the law?

Fuchou: *No kidding. Got through it. Not so tough.*

Fanpan: What did you do?

Fuchou: *Can't say. Worse than taking my aunt's car on a joy ride.*

Fanpan: She at the door. Gotta go.

Fuchou: *Later, Rebel. Hang in there. Proud of you.*

Fanpan: Sure.

Aunt Colleen opened the bedroom door. "Go to bed, Patrick. Tomorrow's another day."

"Okay." She left the room. Patrick shut down his computer, changed into pajamas, and went to bed. Hours passed before he could sleep.

Chapter Twenty-Three

April 9, 2012, South China Sea: USS Shenandoah

Preston Davis stayed in Kate's doorway with arms folded and no apparent intent to move. Like he didn't believe she was okay.

"Migraine coming on," she said. "I get them sometimes."

"Everything all right at home?"

She shrugged. "Teenage son."

"Been there. It gets better."

"Speaking as a father?" Kate didn't know whether he was married or had children. She noted the absence of a wedding ring.

"As a former teenager. Also, as a father, in a past life. Long story. Not relevant now."

Kate's curiosity piqued, but she hesitated to drift into a personal conversation with the man she considered a nemesis. The throbbing in her head would make conversation painful, anyway. "I really have a headache. I'm going to lie down for a while." She shut her eyes and rubbed her forehead.

"Roger," he said. "Hope you feel better soon."

"Thanks." Kate looked up, but the colonel had left. She
stared out the door for an instant before closing it. She switched off
her desk lamp and lay down on her rack. The glow of the computer
monitor lit the room in eerie blue. Kate closed her eyes and thought
about the conversations with Colleen and Patrick.

*What kind of mother am I? Why am I here and not there?
Why do I want to stay away from there, even now, when my son
needs me?*

She thought about her aspirations when she agreed to take the
Seventh Fleet job. After her squadron CO tour, she wanted to
command a carrier air wing. Her competitors for the few available
air wing slots had all been men, some with lesser records than hers.
Yet she failed to select. She couldn't blame gender. Other women
had served in that role. Was it because of her reputation as a "bitch"?
Undeserved as it was?

After that disappointment, Kate failed to select for command
of an aircraft carrier, which would have been a welcome consolation
prize. Reputation again? Thinking that her career had hit a dead end,
Kate had considered bailing out. After nineteen years of naval
service, she had the option to retire before the end of her next
assignment.

Then Vice Admiral Lewis handed her the Seventh Fleet job,
a chance to excel and prove her capacity for greater responsibility.
Success at Seventh Fleet would put her back on the upward track,
maybe to land that air wing job after all. Failure here, or only
satisfactory performance, would consign her future to humble staff
positions with no hopes of advancement. If that happened, she would
give up and retire.

Leo LeBlanc would enjoy that.

She chuckled at the chief of staff's transparency. He

100

considered Kate a threat to his own ambitions; hence, his unrelenting passion to discredit her.

The computer monitor blinked off, leaving the windowless room pitch black.

I say again, why am I here?

Kate smiled at the sardonic pathway of her thoughts, running in a circle, not toward a conclusion.

What the hell do I want? Why do I care about advancing? What difference would it make for Patrick? CAG or carrier CO, either is sea duty. More separation. Would he act out again, do something even more dangerous? I could lose him. If I haven't already.

Her older sister's divorce had enabled Kate's move to Japan and Seventh Fleet. She and Colleen had been close when growing up, comrades in a dysfunctional, abusive family. The arrangement for Patrick had seemed perfect. Colleen cherished her nephew. She had practically insisted that he live with her, and it spared Kate the tough decision of moving him to Japan then finding care for him when she was underway on the ship. It had seemed the perfect arrangement.

She had failed to consider how Patrick's relationship with Colleen might change when he entered adolescence, or how Colleen would handle a rebellious teenager. Neither their alcoholic, abusive father or passive, dependent mother could serve as stellar parental role models for Kate and Colleen. Whatever the circumstances, they both had had to wing it with children. Neither was prepared for the roiling emotional turbulence of teenagers.

Kate squeezed her eyes tight against the mounting head pain and nascent tears. She could hardly blame Colleen for her own life choices. She, not Colleen, was Patrick's mother.

101

Am I any better than Tom Mahoney as a parent? True, I'm not an alcoholic. Am I drunk on ambition instead?

Kate's eyes sprang open. She flipped on the light, leaped from her rack, and admonished herself in the mirror. "Get your head right, woman. You have only one option."

Logging onto her unclassified computer, she intended to pull up the internet site for the Defense Travel System to book a flight from Singapore to San Francisco and Patrick. True to form, the website ground away, taking five minutes to load.

The phone rang.

When she picked it up, Eric's excited voice spilled into her ear. "Kate, it's Eric. You were right. The ROKs didn't start it."

"What?" It took a few seconds to shift her mind back to the Korea situation.

"I can't say over the phone," he said. "Come to the MIC."

"On my way." She closed the internet page, locked her computer screen, and bolted out the door.

Chapter Twenty-Four

April 9, 2012, South China Sea: USS Shenandoah

An hour later, Kate and Eric sat on the leather couch in the admiral's office, flanked by Vice Admiral Lewis and the chief of staff in plush side chairs. Eric had just finished describing the salvage team's discovery that *Bucheon* had not fired an Exocet.

The admiral leaned forward in his chair. "Any thoughts on what really happened?"

"I'd rather not speculate," Eric said. "We don't have enough facts."

Leo shot Eric a derogatory look. "How do you propose to fill in the blanks?"

Eric did not flinch under Leo's glare, but turned to address the admiral. "Salvage operations have just begun, sir. I expect other clues will surface."

Kate addressed the admiral. "In the interim, we should reconstruct a chronology from what data we have; an instant replay."

She smiled at the chief of staff. "Sports analogy, COS."

Admiral Lewis chuckled, then turned to Eric. "Can you do that? Do you have enough data?"

"We do," Eric said. "I agree with Captain Mahoney. If we scrutinize the data from all angles, we may see something we missed in the heat of the moment."

"Nothing to lose except your own time," the admiral said. "Do it."

The three captains closed their briefing books and rose to leave.

Lewis said, "Kate, could you stay for just a minute?"

Leo shot Kate a withering stare. He hesitated. "Should I stay too, boss?"

The admiral waved him away. "No."

Puzzled, Kate stood at her place until Eric and Leo had left. The admiral motioned her to sit. He tented his fingers under his chin. "You got an urgent message at the end of this morning's meeting. Is everything all right? Anything I need to know?"

Kate found it hard to respond. She wondered whether Preston Davis had mentioned anything to the admiral. She wanted to dodge the question but noted the kindness in the admiral's eyes. They reminded her so much of Dodger that she held her breath for a second. She let out the breath, willing her shoulders and back to relax. "My son, sir. He's gotten into some trouble back in the US."

Lewis said nothing, his eyes and open posture prodding her to continue.

She told him the entire story. By the time she finished, a film of tears blurred her vision.

The admiral smiled. "Teenagers." He shook his head. "They can hurt us in so many ways. At least that phase of life is time limited. It will pass."

"That keeps me sane, sir. Except sometimes I wonder if either of us will survive till it passes."

"You will." His eyes turned serious. "I assume you'll go home."

"I don't know, sir."

"Let me rephrase. You will go home to support your son."

"But Korea—"

"Will still exist when you return." Reaching out, he touched her sleeve. Unusual contact from a flag officer to a subordinate. Paternal in this case. "Someday, you will finish this Navy gig, Kate. We all do. You want Patrick in your life when you put away the uniform for good. That means you go home now, for however long it takes."

Kate needed all her effort to keep from crying. When she answered, her voice broke. "Thank you, sir.

"

Chapter Twenty-Five

April 9, 2012, South China Sea: USS *Shenandoah*

"Colleen, hi."

Back in her room, Kate held the phone away from her ear, anticipating her sister's angry retort.

"Kate? Christ, I thought the North Koreans had gotten you. Otherwise, you would have called before now."

"We had a crisis."

Two heavy breaths blew through the receiver before Colleen responded. "So did Patrick."

Kate seethed. "I'm doing the best I can, Sis. World conflicts don't pause for one family. I'm on a combat ship at sea. Can't just jump off and swim to California. I'll get there as soon as I can."

"When might that be?"

"We pull into Singapore in a day. I'll try to get emergency leave and fly home from there."

"Try? Try, Kate? What could be more important than your own son?"

"Needs of the United States Navy, the ultimate trump card. I can't talk about what's going on here. We may have a battle on our hands. My chief of staff is not a sensitive man. He gets to approve or disapprove my leave request. He's not my fan, Colleen. Even if the crisis settles down, he could deny my request out of spite."

"Jeez, Kate. How can you work for an organization that puts its own needs or someone's spite between a mother and her son?"

The question struck Kate in the chest like a sledgehammer, leaving her breathless.

"Kate? You still there?"

She found her voice, her falsetto voice. "I'm here. Just thinking."

Colleen was right, of course. "I'll make it happen, Colleen. I'll figure out a way." Admiral Lewis had all but ordered her to go. If COS disapproved her leave request, she would go straight to the admiral.

Her sister's voice became less peevish. "I understand your situation, Kate. I appreciate what you do. Patrick's okay for now, but he needs you. He needs the one parent still in his life."

"Is he there? Can I talk to him?"

"Not home from school yet."

"Tell him I'll call this evening, your time."

"No. I won't tell him that. We're never sure that you'll call, even when you promise. Patrick thought you'd be in touch before now. He'll be home if you call, but I'm not going to set him up for more disappointment. He might do something more reckless to get your attention." She paused. "You understand that his grand-theft-auto adventure was to get your attention, don't you?"

Kate seethed again, but not at Colleen. "I will call."

"Hope so. Get here soon, Kate." She hung up without a

goodbye.

Chapter Twenty-Six

April 9, 2012, South China Sea: USS *Shenandoah*

Later that afternoon, Kate stood at parade rest—shoulders square, feet apart, hands clasped behind her back, eyes straight ahead—in front of Leo LeBlanc's desk as he studied her emergency leave request. She had asked to depart when *Shenandoah* reached Singapore, and to return before the ship went back to sea a week later.

COS lingered over the document, as if scrutinizing every word, parsing every sentence. The sneer on his face confirmed he was making her wait on purpose for his answer.

"You don't say why." He did not look up from the paper. "Strange time to request leave, what with Korea and all."

"My son got into some trouble. He needs me. That's all you need to know . . . sir."

Leo's return glare made Kate think he might storm over the desk. "That's not for you to say, Captain. What trouble?"

Kate blinked. "Arrested for stealing my sister's car. I need to go to court with him."

Leo snorted. "You got coverage?"

"Commander Sadler, my deputy. I'll have my Blackberry if anyone needs to reach me."

COS stared at her, his eyes aflame. Then he smiled. "Very well, Mahoney. Sometimes a parent needs to be present for a child. The Seventh Fleet will survive without you. We did quite well before you got here. Be sure you and the N2 finish that instant replay crap before you go." With a flourish, he signed the request and handed it to her. "Come back before we depart Singapore."

"Thank you, COS." Despite herself, she rendered a non-required salute.

When she reached for the door, Leo spoke again. "Brief Colonel Davis on your thoughts about the Korean crisis. If anyone can figure it out, he can."

"Aye, sir."

He smiled as she turned to go. "Teenagers do grow up."

You didn't.

"Thanks, sir." She left without looking back.

Kate charged down the passageway toward her stateroom. She pulled up short when she noticed the fleet surgeon's door ajar. A handwritten sign taped just below the Seventh Fleet logo stated, *The doctor is in.* Besides his operational duties, the avuncular physician maintained an active counseling service for the oft-stressed senior staff.

Kate glanced through the gap in the doorway. Doc stared at his computer monitor. "Doc, sorry to interrupt. You got a moment?"

The man's face showed immediate concern when he noted her expression. He pointed to his computer screen. "Just my daily Facebook fix. Come in and sit down." He motioned to the couch opposite his desk. "You look upset."

Kate sat on the couch, then bounced up and paced the small room. "I need to vent, Doc."

"Venting allowed. Confidentiality guaranteed." He pushed the door almost shut for a modicum of privacy, but with a small slit in the doorway to assure passersby that he and the woman in his stateroom were doing nothing more than talking. "What's up?"

"The COS. I've had it with that man." Her hands tightened into fists.

"How so?"

"He gives me shit, just for his own pleasure."

"Leo is hard on everyone," Doc said. "He makes it his mission to be tough. It's a generic COS thing. Do you feel singled out?"

Chaotic emotions distressed Kate. She tried to organize her thoughts, opening and closing her fists.

Doc remained silent.

Unwanted moisture fogged Kate's eyes. He handed her a small box of tissue from his desk. She took one and then chided herself for needing it. Her voice turned to steel. "He has it in for me, Doc."

"How?"

"He doesn't like girls in his clubhouse. I threaten his old school chauvinist world. He baits me, pushes my buttons."

"Buttons?"

"Anger. He says things to piss me off. He pushes me to the edge. I can't retaliate. I have to take it."

"Why?"

"He has all the power. If I strike back, I go down."

"Strike back. Interesting metaphor."

111

A vision flashed across her mind, a man hitting a woman with his open hand. In a single breath, the specter vanished. She dabbed at her eyes with the tissue.

Doc leaned back in his chair. "You've been in naval aviation your entire career, right?"

Kate nodded.

"Surely COS is not the first aggressive male you've encountered, even in a superior-to-subordinate role."

She nodded again.

"Yet he frightens you? Have others affected you that way?"

She thought back over her career and nodded. "I put them in their place. I don't recall ever feeling this intimidated."

"So, why now? Why Leo LeBlanc?"

A curtain closed over her thoughts and emotions. Her mind went dark.

"Drawing a blank here, Doc." The surroundings now seemed banal. Why was she standing in a small metal cubicle inside a floating hunk of metal and machinery, with tears in her eyes, sharing confused intimate feelings with a male colleague with whom she sometimes socialized in a group?

"I have to go, Doc." She headed toward the door.

"Sure," he said. "Come by any time you want to talk, or vent, or escape the madness; even to chat about nothing important."

She was already in the passageway. She turned to look back through the open door. "I'll do that, Doc. Thanks again." She had no intention of returning.

Kate sensed the doctor watching her retreat down the passageway.

Chapter Twenty-One

April 10, 2012, Singapore Strait: USS *Shenandoah*

Colonel Preston Davis slept in fits, disturbed not by the ugly dream of the prior night but from worry over the lost debate earlier that day. He had underestimated the lady jet jockey. Never did he suspect that Kate Mahoney would prevail with his old friend, Darnell Lewis. The admiral had invited Preston to Seventh Fleet, insisting that he needed Preston's experienced wisdom, and promising to make the move career-enhancing. Preston assumed Darnell would appreciate his practical advice to lie low while diplomats sorted out the Korea situation. He did not expect Mahoney's appeal to Darnell's warfighter spirit. Albeit chagrined, the hardened Marine admired the Navy woman's boldness.

She's earned her blue-ribbon attack pilot reputation. Fearless against opposition.

Aside from the blow to his competitive spirit, Preston worried that Kate's aggressive plan would backfire politically. His argument had not been mere rhetoric. The PRC's economic ties to

Pyongyang would demand support for their bombastic ally's untried new leader—especially in the face of US military power.

Mahoney hadn't thought enough moves ahead. She'd fallen into the American habit of instant gratification. "Slam, bang, thank you for playing. Next contestant." Did she not understand the history of this region? Bullies did not survive. You could defeat the closest adversary, but you never saw the nimbler guy hiding around the corner, waiting to pounce on you from behind. Around the corner from North Korea, the nation that spawned Sun Tzu waited patiently for an arrogant adversary to weaken itself.

Kate will play right into their hand.

Why lose sleep over it? Her plan would never see the light of day. Cooler heads at PACFleet and PACOM would see to that. Darnell must know the score. Had he just thrown a bone to his new N3, a "Welcome to Seventh Fleet" present? Perhaps. Later on, when the plan never reached fulfillment, he could blame the military bureaucrats up the chain of command for spoiling the fun.

Darnell could be that nimble. Mahoney's inflated ego would not see the ruse. On the other hand, Preston knew Darnell well enough to recognize that his friend was impressed—if not with the plan, certainly with the style in which it was presented.

The woman is persuasive. I'll give her that much.

Preston turned over in his rack. Why worry that a sole female aviator could embarrass the United States on the international stage? He gave her far more influence than she deserved. Weightier issues did not rob his sleep as much as this.

He had to admit that his angst involved more than the contentious debate over the operations plan. His mind pictured flight-suit clad Kate Mahoney rolling in for the attack. Creeping warmth stole into his groin.

Stop that.

Long ago, after a bitter divorce, Preston had sworn off serious relationships with women, satisfied instead with shallow dalliances and one-night stands. He seduced vulnerable younger women, enticing them to gratify their inner daddy yearnings by mounting the illustrious colonel—no strings, no paybacks. When they moved on to more mature relationships, others like them waited in the wings for their turn on Preston's stage.

Kate Mahoney was a unique challenge. As much as she might appeal to his virile imagination, Preston could ill afford any familiarity beyond professional repartee. His career destiny precluded a relationship with a naval officer, or any military woman. Success in this Seventh Fleet tour as the master of theater security would culminate in his selection for brigadier general. Then he would command sizeable forces and ultimately rise to positions of broad influence and political power. Internecine relationships, even if not forbidden by policy, could derail his progression. He must never allow that.

As he closed his eyes and struggled for sleep, he resolved to maintain a safe, professional distance from one Katherine Mahoney. Then the vision of Kate in that damned flight suit arose again in his consciousness.

Suck it up, Marine.

He turned to his side and concentrated on other thoughts.

Chapter Twenty-Eight

November 16, 1965, Fort Benning, GA

Two-year-old Preston Davis played with his wooden building blocks on a thin rug spread over the bare concrete floor of the sparsely furnished apartment in junior officer housing at Ft. Benning. Mommy sat on the couch with the nasty bundle pressed to her bare breast. Mommy called the bundle "Baby Sister."

Preston hated Baby Sister. Baby Sister took his Mommy. Baby Sister stole *his* place. Baby Sister sucked the nipple that Preston wanted. His nipple, not hers! After Baby Sister came, when Preston was hungry, Mommy poured yucky, slimy stuff into his mouth where she used to put the nipple.

Bad Baby Sister!

Preston wanted to hit Baby Sister on her soft head with one of his blocks. *Kapow!* Then he would get the nipple back for himself.

"Brrring."

Preston always startled at the sound the door made when a

stranger came. He usually felt scared of a stranger, but this time he was glad. Mommy would pull her nipple out of Baby Sister's mouth. That would make Baby Sister cry.

Yay!

Preston smacked his lips when Mommy lifted the brown nipple out of Baby Sister's mouth. Baby Sister cried.

Good.

Mommy didn't try to calm her. She looked out the window. Preston looked, too. A dark green car sat on the street. Mommy liked strangers, but now she seemed scared. If Mommy was scared, Preston felt scared. His throat dried up. Mommy put the tit back into its pouch, closed her blouse, and went to the door. Baby Sister screamed in her arms. Preston followed Mommy to the door. When she opened the door, he hid behind Mommy's skirt.

"Mrs. Davis?" The voice sounded strange. Peeking around Mommy's skirt, Preston saw two big men wearing familiar dark green suits with shiny gold buttons. He sensed Mommy's fear, and he became so afraid he didn't utter a sound.

Baby Sister stopped crying. Maybe she felt afraid, too.

"Mrs. Davis, I'm Major Harris, and this is Chaplain Chumley. May we come in?"

Mommy shrieked. "NOOOOOO!" She almost dropped Baby Sister. Baby Sister screamed. Preston hid behind Mommy's skirt and clutched her leg.

"NOOOOO!" Mommy wailed. She tried to close the door, but the two men didn't let her. "Get out! Get out! Get out! You can't come in. Please don't come in. I don't want to hear it." Mommy was crying hard now. Baby Sister was crying. Preston cried, too. He didn't know why he was crying, but he had never seen Mommy cry like that. Something was very, very bad.

The men came in.
Preston felt sooo sad.

Chapter Twenty-Nine

April 10, 2012, South China Sea: USS *Shenandoah*

Hunger awakened Preston a few hours after he'd fallen asleep. A half-hour remained before reveille. He rose and flipped on the light over his desk, illuminating the faded black-and-white photograph of his father, the only likeness that survived Preston's turbulent post-childhood life. The young soldier dressed in vintage drab BDUs and toting an M16 rifle stared from the photo with eyes that haunted Preston's nightmares.

Unlocking the secure file drawer that held his valuable personal documents, he found an aging manila envelope and emptied the contents onto his desk: a tarnished bronze medal mounted on a faded red ribbon with a single blue and white vertical stripe, and a plastic folder containing a yellowed sheet of paper, the typed print now a faint shade of gray.

DEPARTMENT OF THE ARMY

THE PRESIDENT OF THE UNITED STATES
TAKES PLEASURE IN PRESENTING

THE BRONZE STAR (POSTHUMOUSLY)

TO

FIRST LIEUTENANT PRESTON J. DAVIS, JR.,
UNITED STATES ARMY

FOR SERVICES SET FORTH IN THE FOLLOWING

CITATION

FOR GALLANTRY IN ACTION AGAINST AN ARMED
ENEMY, WHILE SERVING AS RANGER RIFLE
PLATOON LEADER, 7TH CAVALRY REGIMENT,
UNITED STATES ARMY, DURING THE BATTLE OF
IA DRANG, VIETNAM, ON 15 NOVEMBER 1965.
CAUGHT BETWEEN HOSTILE CROSSFIRE OF AN
ENEMY AMBUSH, FIRST LIEUTENANT DAVIS PUT
HIMSELF IN THE LINE OF DEVASTATING FIRE
AS HE MANEUVERED HIS TEAM TO A COVERED
POSITION FROM WHICH TO RETURN FIRE ON
ENEMY POSITIONS. THOUGH MORTALLY WOUNDED,
HE CONTINUED TO DIRECT FIRE UNTIL HE
SUCCUMBED TO HIS FATAL WOUNDS. HIS
LEADERSHIP UNDER FIRE INSPIRED HIS MEN TO
CONTINUE THE FIGHT AT GREAT RISK TO THEIR

```
OWN SAFETY, RESULTING IN THE ENEMY'S
RETREAT. FIRST LIEUTENANT DAVIS' PERSONAL
COURAGE, TACTICAL EXPERTISE, AND
PROFESSIONAL COMPETENCE WERE DIRECTLY
RESPONSIBLE FOR HIS PLATOON'S SURVIVAL.
HIS LEADERSHIP AND BRAVERY UNDER FIRE
REFLECTED GREAT CREDIT UPON HIMSELF AND
THE UNITED STATES ARMY.

FOR THE PRESIDENT,
(Sig)
STEPHEN AILES
SECRETARY OF THE ARMY
17 MARCH 1966
```

Even in the blurred photograph, Preston recognized his own eyes in the proud gaze of the young soldier, unaware that he would soon die. What other traits did he share with the father he'd never met?

His mother never talked about him.

Preston shook himself back to the present, took a quick Marine shower, and dressed in his BDUs. Though morning routine had not yet begun for the ship, he knew the culinary specialists would have fresh coffee brewing in the flag mess.

When Preston entered the flag mess, his eyes fixated on the feminine figure in the green Nomex flight suit standing at the coffee service. With her back to the door, Kate did not notice his presence. He indulged in a second of covert admiration before he approached her. She turned around when she heard his footsteps. Her face went flat.

"Good morning, Kate."

"Morning, Colonel." She did not look at him.

"You have trouble sleeping, too?"

She nodded. He stood by as she poured cream into her coffee. The awkwardness of the moment forced her to interact. "I had to call PACFleet and PACOM. On their hours, of course."

"How did that go?"

"Not well."

"No surprise, right?"

"No. They said many of the same things that you did yesterday, especially the J3." She referred to her counterpart at Pacific Command. The director of operations there was a one-star Navy admiral.

Preston scoffed. "Aloha land, a different world. They have to take the broader view."

"Broader view?" Kate's voice quivered and her face flushed. "They stick to the middle of the path. Wouldn't dream of risking their precious necks on the edges. They don't care a whit about strategic imperatives, winning the peace, or even fighting for it. They only care about image, perception, political fallout, and—ultimately—how the Seventh Fleet's reaction to the crisis might affect their own career ambitions."

Her eyes flashed.

She has green eyes.

"Perhaps they intend to avoid a fight that we can't win."

Kate waved him off. "When did the world's most powerful Navy become so terrified of risk?"

"Long view, Kate. Whatever we do here affects the nation's interests across the world. Can't ignore those effects."

Kate's eyes flashed again. "'Never negotiate out of fear.' A

123

famous Commander-in-Chief said that."

"JFK also said, 'Never fear to negotiate.'"

"From a position of strength," Kate said. She turned to leave. "We'll see how it turns out, Colonel. Have a good day."

Preston watched her stride to the door. The Nomex draped her as if tailored to fit the curves.

Damned flight suit.

Chapter Thirty

April 14, 2012, Singapore: USS *Shenandoah*

Nestled in the confluence of the Strait of Malacca and the South China Sea, the island city-state of Singapore was a robust hub of economic and strategic significance. A steady flow of maritime traffic between the Indian and Pacific Oceans traversed the Malacca Strait, and most transiting ships pulled into Singapore for provisions, refueling, crew rest and recreation. The steady influx of international visitors augmented the Lion City's ancient Asian heritage, making Singapore not only one of the world's busiest commercial seaports and cultural melting pots, but also a popular tourist destination.

Engines rumbling, a team of tugboats nudged *Shenandoah* alongside the pier at the expansive Changi Naval Base on the eastern outskirts of Singapore. Sailors of the Republic of Singapore Navy (RSN) retrieved mooring lines rifle-shot from the *Shenandoah* main deck by US sailors wearing orange float coats and light blue hard hats. Once the flagship was secured to the pier, the boatswain's whistle and 1MC announcement informed the crew.

"Moored. Shift colors."

The US flag, known as the national ensign, was hauled down from the ship's mast. On the stern, sailors in dress white uniforms hoisted another ensign on the jackstaff protruding aft from the flight deck, thus shifting the colors from at-sea status to in-port status.

Cranes lifted into place two gangplanks, known as brows, one forward to serve the main quarterdeck for official arrivals and departures, the other aft as a secondary point of embarkation/debarkation and to unload supplies and offload trash. On the pier, the RSN band played martial music. Once the brows were in place, an official Singapore welcome party was piped aboard for a brief visit with Vice Admiral Lewis.

Because of its strategic location on the Strait of Malacca, coupled with technological prowess equal to that of the United States, Singapore played a crucial role in US relationships in South Asia and throughout the western Pacific. This visit by the Seventh Fleet commander and his flagship played a key role in the theater security strategy of the US Navy. Besides formal talks between the leaders of the two navies, the men and women of the Seventh Fleet staff and *Shenandoah* crew would act as informal US ambassadors, roving throughout the city to spread goodwill and American dollars to win the hearts and minds of a people ethnically related to China.

Once the arrival process and ceremonial niceties were completed to her satisfaction, the ship's executive officer ordered the officer of the deck to make the 1MC announcement that all sailors, regardless of rank or location, relish in any foreign port.

"Liberty call. Liberty call. Liberty call for all hands authorized liberty."

Dressed in a wide variety of civilian clothes corresponding to their age and maturity, sailors and officers streamed over the respective brows and walked seventy-five yards down the pier to buses that would take them to Changi's front gate, a half-mile away. There they would disembark, process through a controlled security building, and embark other buses outside the front gate. Those buses would ferry them for several miles to the nearest public transportation stops, and from there the temporary US ambassadors would disperse throughout Singapore. Many sailors carried duffel bags or small suitcases, eager to spend a few nights in hotels away from shipboard life, to feel and behave like normal human beings after several weeks in the artificial environment of a ship at sea.

With laptop and carry-on bags slung over her shoulder, Kate lugged her suitcase down the brow to a waiting van that would drive her to Singapore's international airport. Bone weary and emotionally spent, she dreaded the seventeen hours of air travel to San Francisco via Tokyo.

Kate felt torn between two priorities. She had so learned to compartmentalize her professional and personal lives that she found it jarring to leave *Shenandoah* with the unfinished business of the Korean situation; never mind that she was not solely responsible for the crisis or its resolution. Would she return in time for the dining out event scheduled on the next-to-last night in port?

More important, what would happen when she reunited with Patrick? How would they work through his latest crisis? At least she would have the better part of a day to make a gradual transition. Kate had scored some Ambien from Doc, so she hoped to spend the first leg of the flight asleep to recharge her batteries and give her frayed nerves the chance to recover. During the flight from Tokyo to San Francisco, she would figure out what to do about Patrick.

And the rest of my life?

Chapter Thirty-One

April 14, 2012, Tokyo, Japan: Narita International Airport

Kate realized on descent to Tokyo that she had been more exhausted than she'd thought: she had slept for most of the seven-hour flight from Singapore. During the two-hour layover before her next flight, she found a small lounge where she drank two glasses of wine and munched on Japanese rice crackers.

Maybe not a good idea, the wine. Need to work out the Patrick situation during the next flight.

Nine-and-half hours would be enough time to come up with a plan, even if she slept for part of the journey.

Fat chance of that.

Her boarding pass for the flight to San Francisco put her in the middle of a five-seat center row at the back of the aircraft, one of the Defense Travel Service's favorite low-fare selections.

Hell with it.

At the departure gate, Kate sacrificed some of her abundant frequent flier miles—a benefit of multiple trans-Pacific flights, courtesy of US taxpayers—for an economy plus upgrade. She rationalized that the economy upgrade, rather than a seat in coveted business class, would leave enough miles in the bank for a future trip to somewhere exotic with Patrick.

Kate boarded the flight and settled into the cherished aisle seat. She left the romance novel in the carry-on bag stuffed into the overhead. No distractions from the task at hand.

Should be easier than planning a military operation in the Yellow Sea. Should be.

When the jumbo jet reached cruise altitude, Kate reclined her seat, stretched out, and pondered how to plan the various options and choices ahead of her and Patrick.

Let's start at the very beginning.

Chapter Thirty-Two

November 1991 to May 1992, Milton, FL: Naval Air Station Whiting Field

Fresh from Officer Indoctrination School at nearby Pensacola Naval Air Station, Ensign Katherine Mahoney straightened the solitary National Defense ribbon above the right pocket of her brand-new khaki uniform. She checked to be sure the edges of her buttoned shirt, polished brass belt buckle, and pants fly formed a perfect "gig line." Satisfied that her attire conformed with US Navy regulations, Kate used tissues to buff her already gleaming brown shoes, then left the ladies' head in search of the classroom for Training Squadron TWO (VT-2), where she would begin earnest pursuit of her dream of becoming a naval aviator.

She would have collided with a young man coming out of the men's head had she not made an agile pivot at the last second. Embarrassed, she apologized but couldn't find her voice.

Trim and fit in a tailored uniform with the olive-green trousers and form-hugging khaki top with second-lieutenant bars on the collars, the man looked as if he were born with a perfect gig line

131

already in place. He might have come straight from a Marine Corps recruiting poster.

He extended a hand. "Sorry, ma'am. Too eager to get to my first day in naval air."

Kate didn't know whether she could take the proffered hand, so her arm stopped in the space between them. Chagrined, she tucked it to her side. "No. No problem." She forced a smile. "Me, too."

"VT-2?"

"Yep. The 'Doerbirds.'"

He held out a hand again. "Luke Walker. Folks call me 'Sky.'" He chuckled. "I know. Lame."

This time, she shook his hand. "Kate Mahoney. People call me, uh, Kate." She thought she would fall through the deck from mortification.

Luke tilted his head, scrutinized her. "Okay, 'Kate,' but you'll need a proper call sign before we graduate."

"I'll think about it."

"Nope. You don't get to pick your call sign. No one does." He looked into her eyes. "Hmmm. I'm thinking 'Scarlett.' Green eyes and all."

Kate huffed. "I don't think so."

Luke chortled. "Frankly, my dear . . ." He put a hand on her back and guided her down the passageway. "Let's find those Doerbirds. Sooner we get started, sooner we climb into those jets."

As she walked beside Luke "Sky" Walker, Kate felt a sensation new and exciting inside her. She couldn't put a name to it. Later in life, she would know it as lust.

Early in their primary flight training, Kate and Luke became shipmates and eventual lovers. Both excelled in aviation science and demonstrated natural aptitudes for flying. When it came to skill in the cockpit, Kate surpassed everyone in her class, including Luke.

When the time arrived for follow-on aircraft-specific training selection, her squadron commander lauded Kate in front of her classmates.

"Best stick we've seen in a long time."

Kate scored the only available slot in the tactical jet pipeline.

Luke got helicopters, an important role for any Marine Corps aviator, but not his dream of flying jets.

As the squadron celebrated their pipeline selections with liberal libations at the officers' club, Kate allowed herself to believe what Luke told her.

"I'm proud of you, babe. You won the prize fair and square."

"You're not angry that I finished ahead of you? You don't regret that I got jets instead of you?"

"You are the ace, babe. I love you all the more for being so friggin' good."

Smitten by his words, Kate failed to see the first crack in their storybook romance. She ignored the truth, that "Sky" Walker never settled for second place in anything.

Just before graduation from flight school, Kate and Luke hurried away from Whiting Field Naval Air Station on Friday afternoon, drove directly to Panama City, checked into a hotel, and made torrid love before the sun set. As they lay together, spent and satiated, Kate turned to him.

"We could get married."

"What?"

"Think about it. The Navy will co-locate us if we're married. Otherwise, we'll be apart after we graduate."

Luke sat up, moved away from her; his face hardened to

stone. "You willing to give up jets for that, Kate? You'll transition to helos and stay here with me? Because I sure as hell can't move up to jets and go to Meridian with you."

"I would—" She stumbled on the words, couldn't finish.

"I didn't think so."

They did not discuss the subject again.

Later, as she unpacked her toiletries, Kate remembered that she'd intended to refill her birth-control pills before they left.

How could I be so careless?

She tried calculating her risk of conception, but she'd never been regular. She had no idea when she ovulated.

I have to tell him.

Luke had already changed into his swimming shorts and opened a beer from the minibar when she came out of the bathroom. "Luke, I screwed up."

He chortled. "No, baby. You were on top. I screwed up." His laugh faded when he saw the panic in her face.

"What?"

"I forgot to refill my pills. We're at risk."

He stared at her, his eyes aflame. "How . . .?"

She shrugged. "Too hot to trot." She sighed. "I lost my head. I meant to refill them on the way out of town. Sorry."

Luke gazed out the window, his lips taut. Then his face softened, and he blew out a breath. "No big deal."

He stepped away from the window and sucked down the rest of his beer. "What happens, happens. We were going to get married anyway, right?" His smile might have seemed genuine, if not for the angry chug on the beer. He put down the bottle and hugged her. Within minutes, they were naked on the bed, where they remained the rest of the evening and night.

Neither of them broached the birth control topic again as the weekend unfolded. Their frequent lovemaking became a frantic crescendo, as if each time was the last. Sated and exhausted by late Monday, they drove back to Whiting Field in complete silence.

* * *

Kate missed her next period. The home pregnancy test was a formality.

When she told Luke, his face turned red and then pale. "You can get rid of it."

Kate responded with a fury that surprised her. "Never. I'm Irish Catholic. I could never forgive myself, or you." She advanced on him, stuck a finger in his chest. "You can walk away. I will have this baby, with or without its father."

A month later, Kate Mahoney and Luke Walker exchanged vows in a low-key ceremony in the base chapel at Pensacola Naval Air Station. Kate would be stashed in a desk job there until after the baby was born. Then she would transition to primary jet training at Meridian Naval Air Station in Mississippi.

Luke stayed at Whiting Field for helicopter training. Aside from the priest, Kate's brother and sister were the only witnesses at their wedding. Her parents refused to come. Luke did not invite his family.

Three months after they married, stabbing pains in her pelvis awakened Kate in the early morning darkness. Luke had gone on an overnight cross-country training flight. Kate sat up and reached for the beside light, but a new pain spasm doubled her over.

She gasped at the realization that she sat in a puddle of blood. She stumbled out of bed, nearly fainting at the effort. Unable to stand, she propped herself against the bedside stand, turned on the light, and called 911.

Kate slumped onto the floor, where she lay half-conscious on the carpet until the paramedics arrived.

Kate was admitted to Naval Hospital Pensacola, where she underwent D & C for an incomplete miscarriage.

Luke came to see her as soon as he returned from his training flight.

"Well, that sure changes things."

"We can try again. On purpose this time."

He scrunched his mouth. "Yup."

The next day, Luke went on another cross-country overnight flight. Kate got a ride home from the hospital. In the bedroom, a maroon trail led to a blotch of dried blood embedded in the light gray carpet next to the phone.

Luke had been home but had not bothered to clean up the mess.

Not his mess, after all.

* * *

Kate and Luke spent the next eight years more often apart than together. Despite the Navy's policy to collocate married couples, the "needs of the Navy" gave them separate assignments.

After a successful first operational tour flying Hornets off the deck of USS *Theodore Roosevelt*, Kate got an assignment to Meridian Naval Air Station as a jet instructor. Scarlett Mahoney had become a darling of naval air. Now she would pass along her knowledge and skills to a new crop of men and women assigned to tactical jet aviation.

Luke flew CH-53 helicopters in Haiti and transferred to Meridian for shore duty as a Marine Corps recruiter.

For the first time since the miscarriage, they would live together as husband and wife.

Luke never outright accused Kate of manipulating him into marriage, but his behavior said it. He turned surly and selfish and drank to excess. From their first year together in Meridian, Luke belittled Kate and her accomplishments. Tenderness disappeared from their bed, giving way to abuse and humiliation. Without understanding why, Kate endured it; even when it brought tears to her eyes and left welts on her buttocks.

Maybe I deserve it.

Luke frightened her. She found excuses not to be in bed with him, especially when he was drunk. She would stay up late or feign sleep to avoid making love with him. His relentless, twisted passion usually overcame her resistance.

Kate no longer wanted to conceive a child with Luke Walker.

A year later, she gave birth to Patrick.

Chapter Thirty-Three

April 14, 2012, San Bruno, CA

Fanpan and Fuchou advanced through Pandaria, leading the Horde to higher levels as the Alliance forces withered under the partners' furious chi-enhanced assaults. If they could win a few more battles, they would qualify for the next gaming level.

"You are on top of your game today," Fuchou's voice said through Patrick's new headset.

Patrick grinned. The total dominance and control filled him with energy. He felt invincible. "Onward, friend. Let's carry this through to victory."

A knock on the door interrupted. Without waiting for a response, Aunt Colleen opened the door and leaned into the room. She spoke in a stern voice. "Patrick, we leave for the airport in twenty minutes. You're not even dressed. Your mom's plane is on time. Please get in the shower and get dressed."

Patrick did not look up from the game. "Just a minute."

"No just a minute. Now, young man. We can't be late to pick

her up."

Patrick kept his attention on the computer screen. "Do I have to go to the airport?"

Colleen threw up her hands in exasperation. "Your mother is flying all the way across the Pacific Ocean to be here for you. The least you can do is meet her plane."

"I can meet her here just as well."

Colleen raised her voice. "How would you like it if you were in her position?"

"I would never be in her position."

Her voice trembled with anger. "Shut down the game and get dressed, Patrick. Now."

On the screen, he executed a perfect crane kick, taking down several enemies at once.

"I'm almost done."

Chapter Thirty-Four

April 14, 2012, San Francisco International Airport

Who names a kid "Preston"?

"Raise your seat for landing, ma'am." Startled from half-sleep, Kate opened her eyes to see a flight attendant speaking to her from the aisle by her seat.

"We're on final approach to San Francisco."

"But I'm not done. I don't have a plan."

The flight attendant gave her a condescending smile. "Please raise your seat, ma'am."

Kate blinked herself back to reality and complied.

She had fallen asleep reviewing her history with Luke Walker and woke up thinking about Preston Davis.

WTF, Scarlett?

Kate felt no more rested than when she left *Shenandoah*. Yesterday was it? She looked at her watch. The date had not changed. She had crossed the International Date Line, making "today" last forty hours. Now she would struggle with jet lag when she should focus on Patrick. So much for figuring it out en route.

She sat through the approach and landing with a blank mind. When the aircraft reached its gate and the seat-belt sign extinguished, the crush of passengers rushing to gather their belongings and get off the plane annoyed her. She remained in her seat until most had deplaned. Finally off the plane, she made an immediate sortie into the first restroom she could find before proceeding to immigration and customs.

When she reached the immigration lobby, Kate groaned at the long lines ahead of her. It would take at least an hour to get through. Like others in the line, she ignored the sign prohibiting cell phone use, powered on her Blackberry, and waited till it picked up a signal from a local provider. The instrument went into buzzing paroxysms as incoming Seventh Fleet e-mails flocked into the inbox queue. She ignored them and texted Colleen.

Here. Customs. Long wait.

An immediate reply lit up the screen.

No problem. I'm here.

Eighty minutes later, Kate emerged into the arrival lobby, pulling her rolling suitcase. She scanned the crowd of waiting people, but she did not see Patrick.

"Kate." Her sister's voice came from behind her. Colleen approached just as Kate turned around. When they hugged, Kate looked past her for Patrick. Maybe he was in the restroom.

"So glad you're here," Colleen said.

"Me too." Kate looked around again, understanding what she had sensed all along. "Where's Patrick?"

Colleen glanced away. "He decided to wait for you at home." Kate's sister looked sad and ashamed. Maybe it was Kate's own disappointment. She sighed.

Off to a terrific start here.

Chapter Thirty-Five

April 14, 2012, San Bruno, CA

Fanpan and Fuchou rode over the horizon together, moving on to the next game level. Deep into Pandaria, they chased after the Alliance, whose forces had retreated in disarray. A vast Horde army followed the two Panderans across the lush landscape.

"We will chase the miserable Alliance army and demolish it in the next level," Fuchou announced. "We ride to total victory."

Patrick glanced at his clock. "Dude, my mom will be here any minute."

"Yeah, well, I gotta go, too." Fuchou's voice sounded angry through the earphones. "My mom will take the belt to me if she realizes I never went to bed." The two online friends had played their game throughout the night.

"Don't kid about stuff like belts," Patrick said.

"Okay, no belt, but she'll be pissed, anyway. We got these guys on the run, so—"

Sudden flames and arrows came across the computer screen

143

from everywhere at once, cutting down the Horde's advance. The Alliance was executing a massive ambush and counterattack.

"Can't leave now," Fuchou said. "Our asses will be grass if we don't hang in against this assault."

Patrick's fingers flailed furiously over the keyboard as he and Fuchou fought off the Alliance attack. At the height of the battle, his iPhone ring tone sounded. He looked at the tiny screen. Aunt Colleen.

Shoot.

"Fanpan, your flank," Fuchou's voice yelled into his headset.

Patrick looked back at the computer monitor to see his avatar wilt under a surprise fire attack. He ignored the ringing iPhone and fought furiously to save himself. He would not have enough energy to withstand the attack from multiple Alliance players. Fearing failure, loathe to let down his fellow warriors, he redoubled his effort. His fingers pounded the keyboard as he struck multiple rapid blows and spinning kicks, trying to stay alive, to prolong the battle until Fuchou could arrive to help. He could see Fuchou's avatar holding off a multi-player attack, coming to his rescue. Fanpan was down to his last bit of energy when Fuchou finally broke through, mounting a vicious counterattack that forced the assault away, enabling Patrick's avatar to recharge.

Fuchou had rescued him. His friend had the enemy on the run, his own energy level ebbing as he chased after them. Other Horde players arrived to defend their two Panderan mentors. With the Alliance in retreat, the battle had turned in the Horde's favor. But Fanpan and Fuchou were too low on energy to pursue. They would need a brief rest before moving on—

"Hello, Patrick."

Patrick turned toward the familiar voice. His mother stood in the doorway.

Chapter Thirty-Six

April 14, 2012, San Bruno, CA

"Gotta go," Patrick said into his microphone. He took off his headset, stood, and embraced his mother. "Hi, Mom. Sorry about the airport."

"It's okay," Kate said, feeling not okay. She hugged him and then held him at arm's length, looking him over. "You've grown in the four months since Christmas. Maybe it's the hair. You have three extra inches on top there."

Patrick squirmed. "Nice to see you too, Mom."

After an uncomfortable pause, Kate gestured toward the computer screen. Some sort of game action. "What's that on your computer?"

"It's my online game, the newest version of WOW. My friend Fuchou and I are kicking Alliance butt."

Kate furrowed her weary brow. "Butt? Fuchou? Is that one of your school friends?"

"Someone I met online. We play together as a team because

we're at the same ability level. He's a little better than me, actually."

"Does Fuchou have a real name?"

"Probably, but I don't know it. He's an online friend, Mom."

"Meaning you don't know anything about him except his screen name and gaming ability?"

Patrick shuffled. "Don't need to know anything else."

"Where does he live?"

"Florida."

"So, you know something about him. Does he know where you live?"

Patrick looked down. "Just California is all."

Kate chewed on her lower lip. She had always worried about Patrick succumbing to online predators, but she didn't want to have that conversation now. They had other issues to discuss. She wondered, though, how much his online "friends" may have contributed to his recent behavior. She'd always thought him impressionable, too eager to please his peers. Maybe the only difference from her peer group as a teenager was that she knew her friends' real names and saw them as real people. They influenced her anyway. How could Patrick know whether this Fuchou was his same age? Could he be a predator adult pretending to be a kid, waiting to strike? She forced the thought out of her mind. That was not why she'd flown halfway around the world.

Focus.

"Okay." She moved further into his room. "We need to talk. Can you shut off the computer and come downstairs, please?"

"Aren't you tired from your trip?" Patrick glanced at his computer monitor.

"I'm exhausted," she said. "But I don't want to put this off any longer. I've been so worried about you. I'm going to the bathroom to freshen up. Meet you in the living room." She walked out without giving him the chance to object.

Chapter Thirty-Seven

April 14, 2012, San Francisco, CA

Fuchou watched both his and Fanpan's avatars return to full strength. "Let's roll, dude."

"I have to sign off," Fanpan said. "My mom's here."

Of course she was. "Parents always spoil things. No problem, Fan. I gotta deal with an old lady, too. Be strong, Panderan."

"I will," said Fanpan. He exited the game.

Fuchou logged off the internet and removed his headset. He lit a cigarette, took a deep drag, and blew the smoke at the computer screen. "Have a great time with your bitch mother, boy. In the end, you will come to me."

When he'd finished his smoke, he stood, stretched, and walked from the darkened living room into the adjoining kitchen to pour himself a cup of coffee from the percolator next to the empty can of Folgers. Hungry, he removed two slices of bread from the pantry and opened the refrigerator. Nothing remained from his supply of lunch meat.

149

"Damn. Used it up last night." He closed the refrigerator, chewed on the bread, and sipped the coffee.

Back in the living room, he emptied the full ashtray into the trash, then collected last night's empty beer bottles and put them into the recycling container. He raised the window shade. The early morning fog had cleared. On the street below his apartment, people were about to start their days. He would have to go out. Low on coffee, low on beer, almost out of cigs, and no lunch meat.

A quick stroll to the Haight Street Market would clear his head. Then he could plot the next moves in his real-life game with Patrick Walker.

Chapter Thirty-Eight

April 14, 2012, Changi Naval Base, Singapore: USS *Shenandoah*

With the admiral off the ship making official calls in Singapore, and most of the staff on liberty ashore, Leo LeBlanc took advantage of the solitude to catch up on his email and clear his paper inbox. A knock on the door interrupted his concentration.

"Enter," he called.

The door opened to admit Captain Nick Juel, the Fleet Logistics Officer (N4), a wiry figure dressed in biking shorts and a fluorescent yellow cycling jersey. He carried a matching helmet and Oakley sunglasses with yellow frames. A small rear-view mirror extended from the frame's left temple.

"Up for a ride, COS?"

A hard-core cyclist, Nick claimed to log five thousand miles a year. He and Leo often rode together when the ship was in port. Leo knew Juel held back his pace to let Leo keep up with him.

"Give me twenty minutes?"

"Sure. Meet you on the pier in twenty."

Leo finished his immediate task and changed into black cycling shorts and a faded red jersey. Just as he removed his bike from the Kinetic trainer, a yeoman second-class from the Flag Administration office knocked and entered his office. "Sir, you have a call from a Commander Leskowitz. He said you tried to reach him?"

"Thanks, YN2." Leo beamed. "I'll take the call." He leaned the bicycle against his desk and picked up the phone.

"Less? Leo LeBlanc here. Thanks for returning my call. Working late on the east coast? Or is it early? I can never figure the time differences in my head."

A weary voice on the other end of the phone replied. "Back from a night carrier qual, sir. Trying to keep my NATOPS current while running a squadron." He paused. "Sir, I got your email and thought I should call you right back."

"Thanks. I appreciate that." Leo sensed his caller's eagerness to get to the point. "I'd appreciate your full candor. This conversation is strictly off the record."

"Solid copy, sir."

"You were Kate Mahoney's XO and then followed her in command, right?"

"Aye, sir."

"How would you rate her as a leader?" Leo almost salivated as he sat at his desk.

A pause. "Candid and off the record, sir?"

"As I said, Commander."

"Total bitch. When I took command, the squadron morale wasn't just in the toilet, it had flushed into the holding tank."

"Specifics?"

"No one was ever good enough for her. No one performed to her satisfaction. Perfect didn't even work. She won't take suggestions. It's her way or no way."

"That could describe many senior naval leaders," Leo said. "High expectations and strong opinions don't make one a bitch, especially in today's Navy."

"This one has a temper, sir, and she's unpredictable. You never know when she will pop off, or what will make her blow."

"I've known flag officers like that. What makes Mahoney different?"

"Shit don't stick to her. She's careful. Clever at managing upward. Minds her manners in front of superiors, works the issues, and keeps it professional. But, if a subordinate crosses her, she busts his balls—in private, of course."

Leo leaned forward, as if he could close the distance to his caller and get more dirt. "You know that for a fact?"

"My nuts are still sore. She kicked me hard several times."

"You were the XO. Your balls were fair game for any CO. It comes with the job."

"Different game with Mahoney. She makes it personal and permanent. Holds a grudge till she takes you down for good."

Leo leaned back, shook his head. "Anyone file charges on her?"

Leskowitz chortled. "You know the US Navy won't do that, sir. She's a poster child for women in naval air. She gets all the slack she wants. We just sucked it up through the eighteen months she had command. Now that she's gone, no one will step forward with any dirt. They are glad to be rid of her."

"Did she mistreat everyone in the squadron, or just some?"

"Not everyone. She had favorites, her inner circle of trustees.

They got away with all kinds of crap. Others never got a break. You couldn't keep a hair on your ass if you got on her bad side."

Leo looked at his bike and then at his watch. Nick would be waiting for him, and Nick was not a patient man. "Listen, Less. I have to get to a meeting. I'd appreciate specifics if you can get them, anything credible. Need documentation, not hearsay or sour grapes. Again, off the record and non-attributable."

"Roger, sir. I'll make some subtle inquiries around the squadron."

"Appreciate it, Less. Enjoy command. Your life goes downhill from there. Believe me."

"Aye, sir." Leskowitz hung up.

Leo replaced the receiver. "Damn." He grabbed his bicycle and hurried out the door.

* * *

Two hours later, Leo and Nick rode side-by-side to Changi Naval Base on the cool-down leg of their ride. The breather gave Nick the chance to discuss his favorite topic, himself.

"Logistics is all about marketing. Most of life boils down to marketing. I have a degree in marketing. I have one in accounting too, but in marketing I have an advanced degree. Effective marketing is the key to success in leadership and logistics. All warfare is logistics, as you know, and all logistics is marketing."

Leo smirked. "You should have that discussion with our N3."

"No shit. Not my favorite ACOS."

"She could use help on her marketing skills."

"That's her rep."

Leo slowed his pedaling cadence. Nick followed suit. "What rep?"

"She was a tyrant as an XO, worse as a CO. Guys left the

Navy on account of her."

Leo turned so quickly toward Nick that he almost toppled his bike. "You know that for sure?"

Nick cast a sideways glance at Leo. "The supply guy at ComLogWestPac here in Singapore came from the air wing where Mahoney was CO of one squadron. When he heard I was on Seventh Fleet staff, he told me to watch out for her. He didn't work with her, but he said the other squadron COs hated her. She had the CAG snowed. Made the rest of them look incompetent."

Leo smiled. Fitness was not the only benefit of a bike ride with Nick Juel. "Can you get me in touch with that supply guy while we're here?"

"No problem." Nick picked up the pace.

Leo struggled to keep up with him.

Chapter Thirty-Nine

April 15, 2012, San Bruno, CA

The night had not gone well. The day started worse. Caught in the throes of jet lag, Kate had awakened early. By chance, Patrick's school was on spring break for the week. As Patrick and Colleen slept and the sun rose, Kate sat alone in the kitchen. She poured her third cup of coffee and brooded over her future and Patrick's.

Had the fantasy world of video and computer games traded places with real life in her son's soul? Did he live in a virtual reality, only sometimes stepping out to plug into his actual persona? When not sitting in front of his computer, his mind seemed never free from the latest game scenario. Was this an escape? Was his life with a single mom and absent father so intolerable that he had to retreat into a make-believe digital reality?

Thinking that she must commit herself to him above all else, she shuddered at the thought that she may have already lost him. How to break that spell?

By mid-morning, Colleen awoke and joined Kate in the

kitchen. Kate learned that Colleen shared the same concerns about Patrick.

"It's impossible to get him off that computer," Colleen said. "He won't budge, no matter how I threaten or cajole him. What am I going to do? I can't drag him off it. He's bigger than I am. Sometimes I threaten to unplug it, but I can't watch him all the time. He'll just plug it back in. One time I tried hiding his mouse and keyboard. He made my life so miserable I finally gave them back. He promised to limit his playing time. Never happened."

"It's not your fault, Sis. Not your responsibility, either. He uses those games to fill the void in his life. Where are his parents? His mom is off at sea, halfway around the world fighting God-knows-what, and he—" She shook her head. "He never knew his father."

Colleen touched Kate's arm. "Luke was such an evildoer. I can't imagine Patrick being better with that jerk in his life. You did what you had to do. Luke would have destroyed both you and Patrick."

"Oh, I never doubt the wisdom of the clean break," Kate said. "But Patrick is a boy without a father—at an age when boys need a dad." She thought of her conversation with Patrick when she arrived. "I worry about his online friends filling that void. Cyber-predators exist. Even if not a predator, what influence does this 'Fuchou' have over him?"

"For what it's worth, I haven't seen any telltale signs."

Kate sighed. "Would you recognize the signs? I wouldn't."

Colleen looked at her with widening eyes. "Maybe taking my car was a sign. That's not like Patrick."

Kate grimaced. "What I've been thinking."

* * *

157

Kate and Colleen tag-teamed Patrick out of bed in time to shower
and get dressed for the last Mass of the morning. Fifteen minutes
later, alarmed at not hearing the water running, Kate went back to his
room and found him sitting at his computer playing a game. Angered
beyond control, she hauled him out of the chair and pushed him into
the bathroom. He raged at her through the closed door, but she held
the door shut and refused to let him out. He quieted down. After a
few minutes, she heard the shower water run.

Returning to Patrick's room, Kate noted a text box open on
his computer monitor. She gasped as she read the text.

Fanpan: My mom's trying to make me go to church.

Fuchou: Dude, that's harsh. You should choose whether
you go.

Fanpan: Not going.

Fuchou: Right. Show her she can't bully you.

Fanpan: She's at the

Fuchou: Hello?

Fuchou: Dude?

Fuchou: Still there, Fan?

Kate stared at the blinking cursor. She turned her head
toward the door. Down the hall, the shower water was still on. She
sat down at Patrick's desk and typed.

Fanpan: This is his mother. Who are you?

The cursor blinked. No response. She typed again.

Fanpan: I don't like what you told my son.

Still the blinking cursor, no response. She typed.

Fanpan: Stay away from him.

Blink, blink, blink. She typed more.

Fanpan: I will forbid him to communicate with you.

Blink, blink, then words appeared.

Fuchou: *Fuck off, bitch.*

Kate reached under the desk and yanked the plug out of the wall. The screen went black.

Chapter Forty

April 14, 2012, San Bruno, CA

After Mass, Kate and Patrick waited for their order at a local pancake house. Colleen had walked home to give them time alone. Every few minutes, Patrick pulled out his iPhone, stared at it, and sometimes tapped out a text. Too exhausted from the jet lag and the emotion of the morning to chastise him, Kate waited until their meals arrived, knowing that Patrick's hands would be engaged in devouring the massive breakfast he'd ordered.

Ignoring her own omelet, she started as soon as Patrick started pouring syrup on his waffle. "Patrick, I'm worried about you."

He looked up. The annoyance on his face reminded her of Luke. "Please, Mom. Not now. I went to Mass, okay?"

"I'm worried about how much time you spend on video games."

"What do you do for a living, Mom? I've seen where you play games on that ship. You've got four giant monitors in that big room." He stuffed a large wad of waffle into his mouth. "You play video games, too."

"That's real world, Patrick. Those are actual operations. Those screens display real ships. My job is to prevent war, not play at it."

"Sure," he said around the half-chewed wad. He washed it down with a swig of orange juice. "My world is real, too. To me."

Kate raised her voice, louder than she meant to do. "That's why I'm worried. If you believe that world is real, you are deluded."

He crammed an entire sausage patty into his mouth and talked around it. "I know the difference between games and the real world. When I play, that's a real world. That's why they call them RPGs, for role-playing games. I can choose to be whoever I want."

"You can do that in life, too. You have choices. Good choices."

"Right." He gulped another swig of orange juice. "In my life right now, I choose to be role-player in computer games."

Kate stared at him.

He gazed at her over a fork-full of scrambled eggs. "Geez, Mom. At least it's not drugs."

What's the difference? Kate had first-hand knowledge of addiction. Denial, defensiveness, evasion, rationalizing, lying, blaming others; her son showed the signs of a hard-core user.

Kate ordered another cup of coffee for herself and another orange juice for Patrick, to keep them at the table a while longer.

"Tell me again why you took Aunt Colleen's car."

Patrick scrunched up his face. "I told you, because I could."

"Did anyone put you up to it?"

He put down his fork, squinted his eyes, made an ugly face. Luke again. "What's that mean, Mom?"

161

She swallowed hard. No time like the present. "I can't imagine you thinking it up and taking Colleen's car on your own. You had help."

He looked down, stirring the remains of the eggs around the plate with his fork.

"Whose idea was it, Patrick?"

"Mine."

"I don't believe you."

He shrugged. "That's your problem."

"No, it's *our* problem. I will not let you lie your way out of it. You may not know this, but I was always the best at those stare-and-blink games. I never blinked first. I'm not about to start with you."

"Can't make me blink, Mom."

"There. You admit you lied. Otherwise, you wouldn't worry about blinking."

He looked at her, dumbfounded.

"Gotcha," she said.

He sat back, arms folded, lip protruding. "Still not saying."

"I'll keep your computer disconnected until you tell me the truth."

He laughed. "You unplugged the monitor, Mom. The computer is still on. If you unplug that, I'll hook it up again after you leave."

Kate narrowed her eyes. "Maybe I won't leave."

"You have to leave."

"What if I don't? What if I quit the Navy and stay home with you?"

"You'd be AWOL, or whatever. They'd send the MPs after you."

"I have enough years to retire."

White lie. Almost enough years.

"I send a letter and it's done. My admiral will support me."

"You'd never do that, Mom."

"For you, I would. I love you that much."

He drank his juice in silence. He wasn't going to tell her what she wanted to know, so she asked for the check.

When they got up to leave, Patrick blurted out, "It was the girls. They dared me to do it."

* * *

They drove home in silence. Kate wanted to believe Patrick's story that the two girls had goaded him into stealing the car. She might have done something similar when she was that age, rebellious and yearning to dominate young males. She figured he had not told her the whole truth, but she decided not to push him.

After they pulled into Colleen's driveway and Kate shut off the engine, Patrick turned to her. "Are you going to disconnect my computer?"

She let out a deep breath, unhooked her seat belt, and faced him. "No, I'm not. I will not stoop to that level. I don't believe you're telling me the whole truth. Someone else influenced you, someone you know online. Except you don't really know him. He is taking control of your judgment and urging you to do things you wouldn't do on your own." She shook her head. "I can't stop that. All I can do is to be your mom and continue to teach you right from wrong and hope that you make the right choices in your life. I can't make those choices for you. Until you're an adult, I have the responsibility and the right to protect you from harm."

Kate sighed and gazed through the windshield into a middle distance. "I did that when you were a baby, and I swear I will do it

163

now—whatever it takes to keep you safe."

Patrick did a double take, looked at Kate with wide eyes. "What did you do when I was a baby?"

Whether it was exhaustion, the tension, the jet lag, or her frazzled nerves that broke down her wall, Kate never knew. Her son deserved to hear the truth from which she had sheltered him over the years.

"I went after your father with a knife to keep him from beating you."

Patrick's mouth gaped open, his face turned white. His unblinking eyes pierced hers.

Kate touched his arm. "Come inside. I'll tell you the complete story."

His face turned red. "Not inside, Mom. Right here, right now."

She took a deep breath, leaned over the center console, and put her arm around him. "I was naïve and in love . . ."

Chapter Forty-One

1999, Meridian, MS: US Naval Air Station

Kate heard one-year-old Patrick's scream the instant she got out of her vehicle in the driveway of their junior-officer military housing on board Meridian Naval Air Station. She had concluded night landing approaches with her jet aviator students at 2100. Without changing from her flight suit, she drove straight home. Luke should have put one-year-old Patrick to bed and fixed dinner.

Frightened for Patrick, she rushed through the front door. Her baby's screams intensified to a panic level Kate had never heard. Between the shrieks, Luke shouted obscenities. Dropping her flight bag, she charged upstairs.

"Luke, what's wrong with Patrick—?"

The scene inside the toddler-cute bedroom scorched her with rage, as if she'd charged full bore into a furnace. Luke bent over their baby son's crib, his hand raised, poised to strike.

"Luke!"

Kate jumped across the room and seized his wrist. Startled,

he broke her grasp, dropped his arm, and turned to her, his face crimson, breath boozy. He spread his hands in a conciliatory gesture and spoke with slurred speech.

"Me and the kid comin' to an understandin' about he's s'posed to be quiet at night."

Kate pushed past her husband, lifted Patrick from the crib, and cradled him in her arms. The baby kept crying. She carried him past Luke into their own bedroom and pushed the door closed with her foot. She hugged and coddled Patrick for several minutes until he calmed down. His pajama bottom was soaked. His diaper reeked of urine.

Changing him would mean going back into the nursery. Kate did not want to confront Luke, not in his current state. She laid Patrick on the bed, removed the diaper, and let Patrick recline naked on the bed. As he quieted, she inspected his body for bruises or scratches. Finding none, Kate heaved a sigh of relief.

Got home just in time.

Once Patrick seemed comfortable, Kate swaddled him in a bath towel and rocked him in her arms. Cracking open the bedroom door to peer into the hallway, she heard the television blaring on the ground floor. Luke had gone downstairs. Kate tiptoed to the nursery, diapered Patrick, and gently placed him back in his crib. She hummed to him until he fell asleep.

Kate watched Patrick sleep for ten minutes before she left the room. Back in the master bedroom, she washed her face and steeled herself for what must happen next. She started to shed her flight suit to take a shower, but changed her mind. Dared not be out of earshot from Patrick. She had to confront Luke now, before more booze rendered him incapable of understanding her. She took a deep breath, left the bedroom, and went downstairs.

In the living room, Luke sucked on a beer as he watched a football game on TV.

Football and beer. Always.

In the kitchen, Kate opened a beer for herself. She took a generous chug, strode back into the living room, and switched off the TV. She turned to face Luke.

"What the hell? I'm watching the game."

"What were you doing to Patrick?" She forced a stern tone to overcome her quivering voice.

Luke let out a disgusted snort. "Just some old-fashioned Marine Corps discipline. Kid needs to learn when to be quiet."

Kate's eyes narrowed. "Did you strike him, Luke? Tell me the truth. Did you hit our son?"

Luke scoffed. "You see any bruises on him? I didn't hit my son. What do you think I am?"

"You were about to hit him when I came in, weren't you?"

He waved at her as if she were a fly. "Back off, bitch." He took an angry swig of his beer.

Kate sipped her beer, trying to calm her rage. "Treat me with respect, Luke. I am your wife and Patrick's mother. You don't talk to me like that."

"Well, excuse me." His nostrils flared. "I was gettin' his attention. Kid needs discipline."

Kate pointed her finger at him. "Zip it, Luke. You can't discipline a one-year-old. He doesn't understand your words."

Luke shrugged. "Needs discipline."

"No. If you had checked him, you would have found the filthy wet diaper. If you had changed him, he would have gone right back to sleep." She tossed her head toward the stairs. "You hear any crying now? All I did was change his diaper."

167

Luke shook his head. "Good for you. Now turn the game back on—please, ma'am." His voice reeked of sarcasm.

"Not yet." She crossed her arms. "We need to talk this out."

Luke rolled his eyes and groaned. "Christ, Kate, we got nothing else to say about it. I didn't hit the kid." He put his arms out in a pleading gesture. "I would never hit my son."

The beer had mellowed her. Kate reckoned him sincere. "Don't ever touch him in anger. You do, I will kill you. I mean it, Luke."

He half-rose from the chair, tight-faced, florid. Cords stood out on his neck. Small drops of spit sprayed from clenched teeth. "Sure you will, shit-hot lady fighter jockey." He pointed a finger at her. "You better have a strong wingman with you before you try to take down this Marine."

The ugliness left his face as quickly as it had come. He shook his head and grinned. "Hey, wouldn't happen, anyway. Like I said, I would never hit my son."

Kate glowered at him for a second, then backed off. "Okay."

"Good. Now please turn the game back on."

Kate flipped on the TV. "I'm going to bed now. I've got an early flight tomorrow."

When she left the room, Luke called after her. "Grab me another beer on your way past the kitchen, babe."

Back in the bedroom, Kate drank a second beer, then lay on the bed, limp from emotional exhaustion. She did not change out of her flight suit nor remove her boots. If Patrick woke up, she would rush to his crib before Luke could get there. Kate could not let him be alone with Patrick, not tonight as drunk as he was.

Tomorrow. I'll figure it out tomorrow.

The nursery remained quiet. Exhaustion and the beers

dropped Kate into a deep slumber.

* * *

At first, Kate thought she dreamed of the screaming baby. She startled awake to the reality of terrified screeching from the nursery, and Luke shouting over Patrick's wails.

Kate bounded out of the bed and raced to the nursery. Luke held Patrick in both hands, squeezing him so hard that his little face turned crimson.

"Get your hands off him!" She charged at Luke and struck him hard on his back.

Luke tossed Patrick into the crib like a football. He turned and swatted Kate across the face with the back of his hand. The force of his blow knocked her to her knees. He grabbed a fistful of her hair, yanked her across the floor, and shoved her through the door.

"Get the fuck out of here, bitch!"

Even in her rage, Kate was no match for the powerful Marine. She raced down the steps two at a time. In the kitchen, she flung drawers open, searching for a weapon. She grabbed the largest kitchen knife she could find.

Kate charged back up the stairs. "Mommy's coming, Patrick!"

She found Luke holding his hand over Patrick's mouth.

Gripping the knife, she advanced on Luke to show what she had in her hand, but not close enough for him to disarm her. "Put him down. Put him down gently, or I swear to God I will kill you."

A look of disbelief crossed Luke's face. He backed away and did as she'd demanded. She glanced at Patrick, but also kept her gaze on Luke. His eyes never left the knife as he inched away from the crib toward the nursery door. Moving to the crib, Kate kept the knife pointed at Luke's midsection. Patrick's cries sounded coarse

169

and gasping. He had cried so hard he no longer had saliva in his throat.

Kate looked at him for a second too long.

Lithe and quick, Luke charged at her, ducked, grabbed her knife-holding hand by the wrist and twisted it hard. Searing pain shot up her arm. She struggled to hold on to the knife. Planting her left foot on the carpet, she pivoted and struck Luke in the groin with her right knee. He went down with a heavy grunt, just as her hand lost grip on the knife.

Luke writhed on the floor, both hands grabbing his crotch. Kate soccer-kicked him hard in the solar plexus and again in the chest. His ribs cracked under the force of her steel-toed flight boot. She tried to pick up the knife, but intense pain swelled in her right wrist. The fingers went numb. She reached for the knife with her left hand.

Luke pivoted beneath her, also reaching for the knife. Their hands collided, the impact causing the knife to skitter underneath the crib. Luke struggled to his knees to reach it. Kate soccer-kicked his groin, forcing him back down. She added another direct kick to his temple. As he writhed on the floor, she pinned him down with her knee on his chest.

"Crawl out of this room like the viper you are, or I will drag you out dead. Now!"

Luke groveled out the doorway. As soon as his feet left the room, Kate slammed the door shut and locked it. Then she sat on the floor, using her back to barricade the door. Her whole body convulsed. Patrick cried, but she dared not leave the door unprotected until she was sure Luke would not try to break back into the room.

She cooed across the room. "You're okay, baby boy.

Mommy will protect you."

Footsteps clambered down the stairs. Kate prayed for Luke to leave the house. The refrigerator door opened and closed. The footsteps came back up the stairs toward the bedroom.

"Have another beer, Sky," Kate whispered. "Have a whole case."

Finally, silence. Patrick had stopped crying. Kate remained still for a full hour and a half until just past 0300 by her watch. Patrick slept. The house was quiet.

Kate still trembled.

Cautious with every silent movement, she cracked the door. She peered into the hallway. Luke's motionless body sprawled across the floor between the nursery and the bedroom. A glob of vomit circled his head. Kate thought for a second that he might be dead until she heard a raspy snore. Not even an earthquake would wake her husband from this drunken stupor.

Kate wrapped Patrick in the crib sheets, sidled around Luke, and ran down the stairs. Grabbing her purse off the entryway floor, she fled out the front door. The cool fall air filled her lungs as she buckled Patrick into his car seat, jumped in, started the car, and raced away.

She drove to the base hospital, where she asked for military police to be called while the doctor on duty examined first her baby, then her.

In her haste to get away, she'd forgotten about the knife under the crib.

Chapter Forty-Two

1999, Meridian, MS: US Naval Air Station

Sprawled across the threadbare carpet runner on the hallway floor, Luke regained consciousness to the stench of vomit and the ache in his groin. A painful lump blossomed on his left temple. When he raised his head from the stinking goo, thunderous pressure pounded inside his head. He rolled over and tried to stand, but a quick catch in his chest seized his breath and dropped him back to the floor.

After a few minutes, the pains eased. Luke struggled into a sitting position. Cradling his throbbing head between his hands, he looked around through the foggy blur in his vision.

The door to Patrick's bedroom stood ajar. Luke considered his counterattack.

Fighting the agony, he forced himself to stand. He braced his back against the wall and made three faltering steps to the door. Breathing became easier when he pressed his left arm against his chest, but the blurred vision and the pressure cooker inside his head worsened by the second.

Luke wanted to charge through the door to surprise Kate before she could react. His weakened legs didn't respond. He swatted the door, only to realize his right hand had gone numb. As a last resort, he leaned against the frame and kicked his foot back at the door.

"Come out of there, bitch."

Silence.

He kicked again. "You got no right." He panted for breath between each word. "You got no fucking right."

No sound from within.

Luke summoned all his energy and lurched into the room.

No Patrick. No Kate.

Pressing both hands to his head against the ballooning pressure, he slumped to the floor and rolled into a fetal position. He spotted the kitchen knife under the crib. When he reached for it, a sharp crack in his chest stopped him short. His vision narrowed, as if seeing a fading light through a long tunnel.

He moaned. "You got no right."

All went gray.

* * *

Luke awakened to heavy pounding on the downstairs front door, but he could not force himself up. The door burst open, followed by rapid footsteps climbing the stairs and entering the room.

"Major Walker," a disembodied voice said.

Through his fogged vision, Luke made out two sets of legs in olive green camouflage battle dress uniforms.

Someone shook his shoulder. "Major Walker. Naval station police. We'll help you up."

Two sets of hands lifted Luke to a sitting position. A young sergeant-at-arms looked into his face. "What happened here, Major?"

The brief glimmer of an idea flared through the clouds inside Luke's head. He almost smiled as he focused his blurry vision on the man closest to him. "My wife. She shook the baby. I stopped her." He tilted his head toward the crib and the knife beneath it. "She attacked me with a knife and took my son."

The pain inside Luke's head exploded a nanosecond before everything went black.

Chapter Forty-Three

1999, Meridian, MS: US Naval Hospital

Uncomfortable on the gurney in the naval hospital's meager emergency room, Kate shivered, more from fright than cold. Like a penned sheep, she occupied one of four curtained cubicles in the tiny treatment area. She held a dripping ice bag to her swollen cheek and eye while a hospital corpsman taped an elastic wrap to her right wrist. Her open eye squinted against the harsh fluorescent lighting. The pervasive antiseptic smell nauseated her.

From somewhere outside the space, she heard the muffled sounds of Patrick crying.

"Keep that arm elevated, ma'am," the corpsman said in a southern drawl. "Won't swell so much."

"My baby?"

"Your son will be out of X-Ray soon, ma'am." The young man closed the dingy curtain around the gurney and departed. Ignoring stains of old blood and mucus on the curtain, Kate stared through the slender opening, desperate for someone to bring Patrick to her.

She fretted that Luke would storm into the cubicle instead.

Kate startled when a shadowy figure loomed on the other side of the curtain. A man's hand pulled the drape back, and she sprang to defend herself.

Not Luke.

She relaxed and smiled at the young Navy doctor whom she had first seen when she rushed into the ER with Patrick in her arms. As he talked, he avoided eye contact.

"Your son has fresh contusions on his chest and back, consistent with squeezing. At his age, the ribs are pliable, so none broken. We need to get a CT scan to rule out intracranial hemorrhage from shaking."

Kate dropped the ice bag. "When can I—?"

A nurse bustled through the curtain and grabbed the physician by the arm. "Doctor, we have an ambo."

They left Kate with the curtain wide open. A siren approached, then stopped outside. Within seconds, paramedics careened through the ER doors, pushing a wheeled litter with a motionless body on top. She couldn't see his face, but Kate recognized Luke's worn cowboy boots.

The frenzied ER team moved him into the first cubicle and closed ranks around him.

Fifteen minutes later, the chaos from across the room had stopped. The ER staff had rushed Luke to another part of the hospital. Kate heard someone say "O-R" as the doors shut behind them.

In the stillness, Kate listened for Patrick's cries. Nothing. She did not know where he, or anyone else, had gone. She got off the gurney, pulled the curtain fully open, and found herself alone in the room. Across from her cubicle, debris and discarded instruments attested to the frantic effort to save Luke's life.

Kate could wait no longer. She had to find Patrick and get out of that place. She zipped up her flight suit and laced up her aviator boots, a clumsy task with her sore ACE-wrapped wrist. As she started to bolt, a young man dressed in khaki Dockers and a dark Navy golf shirt entered the cubicle. A woman followed, also wearing casual civilian clothes. Two enlisted sailors came in behind her, both in camouflage battle dress uniforms with pistols strapped to their hips. Kate recognized them as naval station police. They stood on either side of her.

The man in Dockers addressed Kate. "Mrs. Walker—"

Kate raised her hand. "Please. I'm Lieutenant Commander Mahoney."

The man made a show of scanning the area where Kate was the only patient. He looked back at her. "You are married to Major Luke Walker?"

Kate frowned. "Yes, but I prefer you to address me as Lieutenant Commander Mahoney. As you can see from my flight uniform, I am an active-duty naval aviator, assigned to the VT-7 training squadron as a jet flight instructor."

The man lifted a palm in a "who cares?" gesture. "Very well. I'm Special Agent Hargrow from Navy Criminal Investigative Service, NCIS. This is Ms. Gonzales from Navy Family Services."

Kate relaxed. At last, the cavalry had arrived. "Where is my son?"

"He's safe," said Ms. Gonzales.

The woman's tone alarmed Kate. She stiffened, looked from one civilian to the other. "I need to see him."

"We are going to keep him for a while," Ms. Gonzales said.

"Until we figure out what happened," the NCIS agent said.

Kate's face burned. A sharp pang struck her chest. "You what? No. You can't. I—I just—I rescued him." She squared her stance, hands clenched into fists.

"We don't know what happened, ma'am," the NCIS agent said. "We have a battered child, a knife found at the scene, and a Marine Corps major, your husband, with a fractured skull—"

Kate interrupted him, pointing to her swollen face. "You have a battered wife here!"

The agent did not react. "Major Walker is undergoing surgery right now to remove a blood clot on his brain. He may not survive."

Kate gasped. "But I—"

"Before he lost consciousness, the major said that you shook the baby, and you attacked him when he tried to stop you."

Kate exploded. "That's a damned lie." Rage and fear boiled inside her. Her ears pounded, nostrils flared.

The agent stepped back. The two military policemen moved to either side of Kate.

Kate had to get Patrick. Escape this nightmare. She barreled toward the accusers. One police grabbed her arm. She tried to pull away, but he tightened his grip. Desperate, she swung around and kicked his shin with the steel toe of her flight boot.

In the next heartbeat, the policemen had Kate face down on the floor, her arms pinned behind her, one man's knee planted solidly in the middle of her back. The other man shoved her head to the deck. They clamped handcuffs on her, the right one so tight around the bandage that it caused stabbing pain in her wrist.

They hauled Kate to her feet. "Sorry, ma'am," the younger man said. "We have to take you into custody."

Kate stopped struggling. Her knees weakened, and her shoulders sagged. Tears filled her eyes. Her lips trembled.

"I want to call my commanding officer."

Chapter Forty-Four

April 16, 2012, Singapore: ComLogWestPac

The United States Navy maintained in Singapore a strategic logistics function—ComLogWestPac (CLWP), for "Commander, Logistics Group, Western Pacific." The one-star rear admiral and staff commanding CLWP worked from a modest US facility at the Sembawang commercial sea terminal on the northern edge of the island. That admiral also reported to the Seventh Fleet as Commander, Combined Task Force Seventy-Three (CTF-73). With Military Sealift Command, CTF-73 directed a fleet of over forty supply and special-mission vessels to support and replenish US Navy warships throughout the Seventh Fleet area of operations. In a mission related to its strategic location in the AOR, CTF-73 also planned and supported bilateral military exercises with partner nations throughout the Western Pacific.

Representing his boss, Leo arrived via driver to Sembawang for a courtesy call with Rear Admiral Susan Hancock, the incumbent LogWestPac commander. First, he sought the senior supply officer to whom Nick Juel had attributed not-so favorable opinions about one Captain Katherine Mahoney.

Leo found Captain Andy Hale in his office. This logistician's appearance was the antithesis to his cycling fanatic colleague, Nick Juel. Leo wondered how the corpulent officer could pass the semiannual Navy physical fitness assessment. Leo had never met a non-eccentric officer of the US Navy Supply Corps; he wondered what Andy's shtick would be.

Making short shrift of the opening pleasantries, Leo asked about Kate Mahoney.

"I didn't know her well," Andy said. His eyes darted to the right as he spoke.

Leo countered. "You were the CAG supply officer, right? When she was a squadron CO?"

"Right." Eyes darted left.

"You must have interacted with her."

"Not much. Mostly I dealt with her supply guy." Eyes darted upward.

Leo paused, willing the Navy captain to catch his cues to take the conversation in the intended direction. The other man stared at his shoes—brown shoes in concert with the gold aviation supply warfare device pinned over the left chest pocket of his khaki uniform.

Leo pitched a hanging curve ball, nearly begging Hale to take a swing. "I heard she's rough on her people."

"Wouldn't know about that."

"I heard some guys quit on account of her."

"None that I know."

Leo came back with the high hard one. "Nick Juel said that you warned him about coming to the Seventh Fleet Staff and working with her. He said you told him to watch his back."

Hale did not answer. He studied his fingernails. Finally, he raised his head and—for the first time in the conversation—looked Leo in the eye.

"Said nothing like that. Nick must be mistaken."

Leo's body slumped. "You're sure?"

"Yep." Hale looked at his shoes again.

"Okay," Leo said. "Here's my business card. If you think of anything I should know, please get in touch."

"Sure." The supply officer took the card and stared at it, not moving from his seat.

Leo showed himself to the door.

Ten minutes later, accepting coffee from Rear Admiral Susan Hancock, Leo admired the patrician features of the woman sitting across from him. In her mid-fifties, Hancock maintained a trim, athletic figure. She wore service khakis that appeared tailored for her, with an impressive row of ribbons parked exactly one-quarter inch below her naval aviator's wings of gold. Her brown shoes sported fresh polish, buffed to a high gloss.

An early female pioneer in tactical naval aviation, Hancock had carved a path for younger women aviators like Kate Mahoney. Susan was one of the first women to qualify in jets, and the first to command an F-14 Tomcat squadron in combat. From that success, she'd risen quickly through the ranks, served the mandatory Pentagon penalty tour, and then commanded a carrier air wing. An accomplished leader and strategist, as well as superior tactical aviator, she earned her star and the plum assignment as ComLogWestPac.

"Good to see you again, Leo." She offered a sincere smile as she lifted a small cookie to her mouth. They had served together at the Pentagon and shared similar culinary tastes, as well as perspectives on the Navy.

"You too, ma'am," Leo said. "Congratulations on your promotion and assignment."

"Forget the 'ma'am.' I'm still 'Sue' to you." She winked. "I hope to congratulate you in the not-distant future."

"Thank you, ma'am." Leo could not bring himself to address any admiral by first name, even when invited to do so.

Admiral Hancock chuckled. "Still the same stodgy SWO you are."

"Too old to change, ma'am."

A brief silence ensued as both sipped their coffee and chewed the last of the cookies.

Hancock put down her coffee cup and faced Leo. "How's your new N3 doing?"

How is it that flag officers always know what you want to discuss?

"Do you know her, ma'am?" The question did not sound as innocent as Leo intended.

Her eyes flashed. "Cut the crap, Leo. We've known each other long enough, so drop the phony formality. You know I know her. Naval air is a tight community, and we don't feed on our young like you surface warfare guys. Women in naval air are even closer because we are so few. Women in tactical air? I know them all like sisters."

She scowled and pierced Leo with laser-like eyes. "I know you well enough to understand that you didn't put on a uniform and come all the way up here from Changi for a courtesy visit. You have some compelling reason to be here instead of riding a bike, tearing up a golf course, or sitting on a barstool. Get to it."

Leo put down his coffee cup and faced the admiral. "What can you tell me about Kate Mahoney?"

Hancock wrinkled her brow and smiled. "Thanks for being straight." She put down her cup and leaned forward. "Kate is a hell of a stick, one of the most gifted pilots I've ever seen. But she can be a real hothead. She's ambitious, aggressive, arrogant, self-absorbed, stubborn and fearless. The perfect jet jockey—if she were a man. Give her the slightest opening in a fight and the next thing you know, she's on your six and you've got a missile up your ass. She'll do it without hesitation and without flinching. In combat, you want her in front, leading the formation." She tilted her head, lowering her voice in a confidential tone. "But you may not want her running your operations."

Leo nodded. "I'm beginning to see that."

The admiral continued. "She'll do a good job strategically. Kate is smart and creative. She knows her tactics and won't hesitate to push the envelope. But she has difficulty playing nice with others, especially men. Some say that she bears all the charm and diplomacy of a wildcat."

"Seen that." Leo paused for the admiral to continue, but she sat back and sipped her coffee. He pressed. "I've heard she can be abusive, especially to subordinates."

Hancock did not take the bait. "Couldn't tell you about that. I've never worked for her." She took another sip of coffee, seeming to deliberate on her next words. "I've been in this environment long enough to appreciate that a woman can be called a bitch—or worse—for character traits and behaviors praised in a man. I won't go there, Leo. I suppose you've heard the same buzz that I have, but I have no personal knowledge of any abusive behavior."

"Understood, ma'am." For the second time in an hour, Leo's

body slumped.

"You have a leadership challenge with her, Leo, but gender has nothing to do with it. I've seen the same challenge aplenty with male aviators. You need to channel her aggressiveness to your benefit."

"I'm the Seventh Fleet Chief of Staff, not a damned counselor."

The admiral chuckled and shook her head. "Leo, Leo, Leo. Kate Mahoney can either help or hurt you. If she doesn't learn to handle the pressures of a major staff job in a positive way, she will one day go down in flames. Don't let her drag you down with her." She reached out to him. "I'm telling you that as a friend."

Leo shuddered. He dropped the formal tone. "Thanks, Sue. I appreciate your advice and your candor. I will watch my six, as you aviators say."

After the two had engaged in a less serious discussion, Leo thanked the admiral for her time and rose to leave. Then he remembered his strange conversation with Andy Hale. "I spoke with your senior logistician earlier. I had heard that he knew Mahoney, but he denied it. Strange guy. A credible source told me that Hale harbors resentment toward Kate."

"No kidding." Hancock motioned Leo back to his seat. She addressed him with an air of confidentiality. "Hale lied to you. With reason." She paused. "Andy Hale is a notorious womanizer. He considers any woman in the workplace as a potential target, married or otherwise. He deployed with the CAG staff to the Med when Kate was a squadron XO." Another pause. "One night, a group of officers held court at a bar in some liberty port. Andy came on to Kate. I heard he groped her. She turned on him, grabbed his crotch, and said if he didn't get away from her, and stay away, she would rip out his balls and feed them to the goats."

"Ouch." Leo gulped. "Kate didn't file a harassment complaint?"

"Not her style. She's an attack pilot. Prefers to take the fight straight to the adversary." Susan Hancock chuckled. "Hale damned sure left her alone after that night."

Andy Hale was a dead end. Leo again thanked the admiral and rose to leave. She led him to the door, stopped, and turned to him. She chewed her lip, weighing her words, then relaxed.

"One other thing. After her nugget operational tour, Kate did a stint as an instructor in Meridian. Something happened there that caused her command to take her off flight status. Soon after, she was reinstated and given orders to an operational department-head tour in Japan. We heard rumblings that someone had pulled strings for her. Some years later, when I was the aviation detailer, I got a look at her record. Pristine. No mention of any down time from flight status— ever."

Leo stroked his chin. "Were the rumors about her losing flight status untrue?"

Hancock shrugged. "I've said all I can. I believe that something happened there." She twisted her mouth. "Kate's wouldn't be the first record to get buffed up before a selection board."

Leo tilted his head. "So . . .?"

"Kate was married to a Marine aviator when she went to Meridian. She went to Japan as a divorcee with a child. No one knows what happened to her ex-husband. He's no longer in the Marine Corps."

Susan Hancock opened the door and ushered him out. "Good day, Leo. Enjoy the rest of your visit to Singapore."

Chapter Forty-Five

April 16, 2012, San Bruno, CA

With the mother in the house and liable to overhear their conversations, the gamers had reverted to texting instead of using their headsets.

       Fuchou: *Dude, we missed you yesterday. Couldn't advance without you.*

       Fanpan: My mom made me go to church. We stayed out afterward.

       Fuchou: *You went to church? Pussy.*

       Fanpan: Hey!

       Fuchou: *Pussy, pussy, pussy. Mama's boy.*

       Fanpan: Screw you. Let's play. I have to go to juvie court later.

       Fuchou: *Sure, Dude. Let's hit these guys.*

    Fuchou pursed his lips as the game launched. His fingers banged the keys with new intensity.

The bitch is getting to him. Time to ramp it up a notch or two.

* * *

Forty minutes later, Patrick's mother knocked on his door. "Time to get up, Patrick. We leave in an hour."

How pathetic was that? She didn't know he'd been up for hours.

Fanpan: Gotta go. Need to get ready.

Fuchou: Sure. Hey, don't sweat that court crap.

Fanpan: I am worried about it.

Fuchou: Act all meek and sorry and you'll be OK. I'll send you some good stuff when you get back.

Fanpan: I don't know. If my mom sees that, I'm toast.

Fuchou: Lock your screen, dipshit. Lock your door too. Damn, you turning weenie?

Fanpan: I'm not. Send them. I'll be extra careful.

Fuchou: Cool. I got some raw stuff last night.

Fanpan: Okay. I'm gone now.

Patrick logged off the game and chat screen. He had not stopped thinking about what his mother had told him the day before, about his father. She had always refused to talk about the man, even when Patrick asked. He had fantasized that his absent father had been a war hero, or maybe a CIA agent, or international spy, maybe a POW. Probably dead. Why else would a man never contact his son—if he knew he had a son? Patrick had fantasized his father riding into his life like a video-game mega-hero.

His mother had told him that his father was no hero, but an evil man, a drunk who hurt Patrick's mother and tried to hurt him. She had to use force to take Patrick from him. They ran away, like some video-game minions fleeing an evil villain's rage and power.

Can I believe all she said? Not like she always tells me the truth.

She told him she had lost track of the man's whereabouts after that long-ago night. She never wanted to see him again. Patrick was better off not knowing him. That she had thought about pretending that Luke Walker was killed in a war, that he was a hero. Why couldn't she just tell him the truth?

Yesterday had been the day. In tears, his mother apologized for her lie, and said that keeping the truth from Patrick had been just as wrong as letting him believe his father was something else.

Maybe what happened was not all his father's fault. Maybe his mother was as much to blame. She could be a mean bitch. Maybe she had terrorized Patrick's dad and driven him to drink.

Maybe . . .

Patrick didn't know enough. He had only his mother's version. His dad's story could be way different. Patrick couldn't make all the pieces fit. How does a man just disappear? Wouldn't he still want to know his son? Maybe he didn't know where his mom and he had gone. Or maybe he really was dead.

A thought hit him. His mother had said that Luke Walker had been a Marine. Patrick logged onto the internet. In the Google search box, he entered the name *Luke Walker*. As he clicked the search icon, his mother opened the door to his room. Like lightning, he minimized the web browser.

"Patrick," she said. "You need to turn off the computer and get in the shower. We cannot risk being late." She left the room, but the door remained open.

Thankful that she had not seen his Google search, Patrick refreshed the screen. Very few entries matched his search, and none seemed to mention the Marine Corps. He saved the Google search, shut down the computer, and headed to the shower.

Chapter Forty-Six

April 17, 2012, Singapore

Awakened by the morning glare through the full-length window, Eric Mikleson slipped into the hotel room's bathroom. He dressed in silence, then tiptoed from the room as his wife Melody, ten-year-old son John, and eight-year-old daughter Melissa slumbered. Like other Seventh Fleet family members, they had flown from Japan to Singapore to be with Eric while *Shenandoah* remained in port. The fleet's business never stopped, least of all in the face of a looming international crisis. Eric planned to return to the ship to put in a full day's work. His family would wake up late, share a leisurely breakfast, and enjoy sightseeing and high-end shopping in Singapore. By evening, Eric would return to the hotel in time to meet them for dinner.

When he arrived at the pier where *Shenandoah* was tied up, an assortment of eager sightseers and shoppers descended the brow and hurried down the pier to the liberty buses. Some of them had been on shipboard duty and missed the first night's revelry. Their eager faces and cacophonous banter suggested they would make up the deficit well before sunset.

Eric stopped in the nearly deserted flag mess for orange juice, coffee, scrambled eggs and ham, then descended to the MIC to boot up his computers. New items in his classified email elaborated on the ROKs' discovery of *Bucheon's* Exocets intact in their launch tubes. An inveterate puzzle-solver, Eric worked through the lunch hour, intent on unlocking the poser of what happened that fatal dawn in the West Sea.

Under his direction, a skillful, dedicated team of officer and enlisted professionals leaned into the challenge. Eric drove them nearly to the point of mutiny, but their work ethic and sense of pride thrived under the workload. Many were die-hard introverts, self-styled geeks who preferred their reclusive cryptologic environment over extreme shopping or elegant dining anywhere in the world. They sifted through a wealth of classified and unclassified material: memos, e-mails, satellite images, news clips, videos, aerial photos, radio intercepts, reports from other agencies and friendly nations, and top-secret sources—including embedded human intelligence agents (HUMINT)—many of those sources unknown to most of their shipmates. The intel staff's expertise and honed professional judgment wove these diverse data points into an intricate tapestry that Eric hoped would reveal the truth about the fates of *Bucheon* and its North Korean adversary.

Alone in his office, Eric scanned three different computer screens, synthesizing raw data and rolled-up summaries prepared through the night and early morning by his staff. He scrutinized the materials for new information from the ongoing salvage operation in the West Sea. Collating the data, he began a detailed reconstruction of the sequence of events, reviewing the minute-by-minute movements of the two Korean ships on the morning of the hostilities. He created a detailed timeline directed at the basic question, "Who shot at whom when, with what, and who hit whom with what? And why?"

By four PM, his blurred vision begged for a reprieve from consecutive hours fixated on computer screens, assuaged only by several cups of coffee and small bags of Cheetos from the vending machines on the mess decks. With a sigh, Eric shut down the computer and prepared to head back to the hotel. Two hours in heavy afternoon traffic on bus and subway would get him to his room with enough time to shower and change for dinner.

His secure phone rang.

"Captain Mikleson, this is Admiral Sanchez calling from *Denver*." The encrypted voice sounded like the admiral was submerged in an underwater cave instead of riding atop the ocean. "I couldn't get your COS, so I'm calling you. Someone needs to act on this. Our divers found the remains of a torpedo on the ocean floor in the area where *Bucheon* went down. Two large pieces bore Chinese markings."

Eric frowned. He would be late for dinner. No, he would miss dinner and be late for breakfast—assuming he got off the ship at all for the rest of the port visit.

Chapter Forty-Seven

April 16, 2012, San Mateo, CA

Kate and Patrick walked in silence through the parking garage of the San Mateo County Courthouse, both immersed in private thoughts after Patrick's hearing. Not until they buckled their seat belts in the car—the same one that Patrick had stolen—did Kate speak.

"Could have been worse."

Patrick folded his arms, stared at the floor. "Not much. That judge treated me like a criminal."

"You committed a crime, Patrick." She did not mean to sound so harsh.

"Geez, Mom. I feel crappy enough. Now you gotta rub it in."

Kate touched his shoulder. "I'm sorry. I felt awful for you." She shot him a stern look. "Maybe you'll learn from it."

He scowled. "The judge thought you were my aunt, not my mother. I could rub that in, but I won't."

Kate forced a smile. "Thanks."

They drove from the garage in silence. Kate mentally

flagellated herself.

I'm a failure as a mother.

If she had done a better job, neither of them would have suffered the humiliation they'd just endured. Was Colleen right? Did Patrick intend to send Kate a message when he took the car? She glanced sideways at her son as she maneuvered the car through traffic. "I still don't understand why you did it."

"You think I do? It just happened, Mom."

"Fair enough." She shrugged. "We don't always understand why we do things. I sure don't."

More silence. Kate had just merged into the traffic flow on the Bayshore Freeway when her Blackberry buzzed on her belt. It could only be Colleen or someone at Seventh Fleet—neither trivial. She pulled off at the next exit, maneuvered into a convenience store parking lot, and stopped the car.

Patrick frowned. "What are we doing?"

"Sorry. I just got a message."

"So?"

"It might be serious."

Patrick turned away, stared out the window. "Yeah, sure."

Kate pulled the Blackberry off her belt. A text message from Eric Mikleson.

> *About that sporting event we've been following. Looks like another team is in play. The big dogs. Coach wants you back in the game.*

"The friggin' PRC?"

"Huh?" Patrick said.

Kate did not answer him. Her thumbs flew over the small keyboard.

> *Very interesting. Wrapping up here in the next day or so.*

196

Expect me back before the next period.

She replaced her Blackberry and turned to Patrick. "They need me back on the flagship."

Patrick turned back to the window, silent.

* * *

Colleen was not home when Kate and Patrick returned.

"We should talk," Kate said.

"I don't want to talk right now. Can't it wait?"

"We need to figure out what we're going to do."

"Sounds like you already decided."

"Patrick—"

He clenched his fists, glared at her. "Let me think about it, Mom. Please. Give me some space."

"So you can go upstairs to your computer game and avoid thinking about it?"

"Can I just take a break?" He sounded desperate.

Kate needed a break, too. "One hour. Then I want you back downstairs. I'll fix some lunch. We have to talk, Patrick."

"Whatever, Mom." He ran up the stairs.

To contact his online friend? Kate shook her head.

I can't watch him all the time.

* * *

An hour later, Kate and Patrick sat at the kitchen table. She'd stormed upstairs to get him off the computer after the allotted one-hour "break."

"Did you chat with your friend?" Kate took a bite of her fruit salad to keep from snarling at him.

Patrick chewed on his grilled ham and cheese sandwich before answering. "What friend?"

"Your online gaming friend."

He tossed his head. "Yeah. So?"

"Does he know you're in trouble?"

He looked away. "Yeah."

"How does he know? I thought you had friends online for playing games."

"We talk and text, too. Everyone does."

Kate swallowed her anger. She did not want to spoil what little rapport she had with Patrick. She took a breath. "Okay. Let's talk about where you can do your community service."

"I did a Google search. There's a place called Homer House. It's like a day care for abandoned kids."

A little too eager? Rehearsed? Or was she too suspicious?

No choice but to play. "Where is it? How far from here?"

Patrick took a generous bite of his sandwich to chew on as he mumbled. "The City."

Kate shook her head. "No way. Not The City. We'll find some place closer."

"Like there's anything worth doing here in suburbia with all the rich and privileged kids."

"Community service doesn't have to involve anything more than picking up litter. You can do that over at the park, without commuting to The City."

Patrick looked at her, defiance written on his face. "Sure. Just put in the time, go through the motions? Is that what you taught me to do, Mom?"

Kate bit her lip. "That's not what I meant."

"You said you want me to learn from this. How better than to spend time with younger kids whose parents abandoned them?"

"Not in The City, Patrick. That's a hard 'no.'"

"I know my way around there, Mom. Lived here half my life

while you've been everywhere else in the world. I can do it."

"No, you can't, and no, you won't. It's not safe."

"Fine!" Patrick jumped up; his chair clattered to the floor. "I won't do anything. They can put me in jail. How safe do you think that will be?" He stormed out of the room and ran up the stairs. Kate heard his bedroom door slam.

Kate buried her head in her hands, not knowing what to think; or what she felt.

A few minutes later, she Googled *Homer House* on her laptop. Located on Haight Street in San Francisco, it appeared to be a legitimate establishment that sought to combine day care and counseling services for children of broken homes. Students from the nearby University of San Francisco volunteered there as counselors, often in conjunction with their psychology or sociology courses. Kate picked up the phone and dialed the number on the website.

Later, Kate rested her chin in her hands as she looked across the table at Patrick—his mood much improved since she'd relented on the Homer House idea. "I really am considering leaving the Navy," she said. "I'm eligible to retire in another year. Could get an airline job. You and I could find our own place. I could be a real mom for once."

"When you're not flying, you mean?"

"I wouldn't be at sea for months at a time." She reached across the table and held his hand. "You deserve a full-time mom, especially now that you're a teenager. This thing that happened—with the car—was a wake-up call for me. You're the most important thing in my life. I need to be here for you."

A scornful look crossed his face. "Thing?"

Kate let go of his hand. "You know what I mean. Give me a break. Don't dissect my every word."

"You've made promises before, Mom. Lots of them."

She reached her hand out again. "Some things you won't understand until you're an adult, until you have children of your own. You grow up thinking your parents are perfect, and it hurts when you find out they are not. No parents are perfect. Least of all me. I've made mistakes, big ones. I've put myself and my career ahead of you. That was wrong, Patrick, and I'm sorry. I want to make it up to you now. I want to be your full-time mom."

"Yeah, sure."

"It will take time for you to trust this idea, I know. Can you promise you'll work on trusting me?"

He shrugged. "Okay. We done now?"

Across the table, Kate saw a young man whom she barely knew, slipping away from her like a receding tide.

She raised her hands in a surrendering motion. "Fine. Go upstairs. Try to enjoy the rest of your spring break." She bit her lip. "Meanwhile, I'm still in the Navy and I have to get back to the ship. I leave tomorrow afternoon."

Patrick looked across the table at her, his face expressionless. Then he squeezed her hand, stood, and bounded up the stairs toward his room.

She called after him. "Homework before gaming. You must have some."

He turned in mid-stairs, smirked. "Hello, Mom. Spring break. Guess you forgot."

For several minutes, Kate stared up the empty stairs. A single tear rolled down her cheek.

Chapter Forty-Eight

April 17, 2012, San Francisco International Airport

Kate stuffed herself into the middle seat of the center row at the back of the 777 jetliner for the first leg of her return journey from San Francisco to Tokyo to Singapore. This time, she hadn't tried for an upgrade.

What would be the point? I'm a zero at personal planning.

A hefty young man wearing ear buds entered the row, stuffed a backpack beneath the seat in front of him, avoided eye contact, and plunked into the seat next to Kate. She fought and lost the battle for the armrest. The guy was a pro.

Kate leaned to her right to get some space. A Japanese woman occupied that seat.

"*Sumimasen*," Kate said in apology for invading the woman's personal space.

The woman smiled. "*Daijoubu.*"

Of course, the woman would say it was all right. Over her time in Japan, Kate appreciated the Japanese people's politeness and concern for others—qualities that apparently had fled from her own culture.

By the time the jet started its takeoff roll, Kate and her Japanese neighbor had figured out how to share the armrest. As soon as the seat belt lights went off, Kate retrieved the romance novel from her purse and read. A welcome escape from the challenges of single parenthood and sexist superiors.

Ten minutes later, she closed the book and rubbed her eyes. The printed words had failed to block images of Patrick, Luke, Leo LeBlanc, and Preston Davis from invading her mind. She thought about her revelation to Patrick about her skirmish with Luke. She hadn't told him about the aftermath. Aside from those involved, no one, not even Patrick, needed to know those details.

Chapter Forty-Nine

1999, Meridian, MS: US Naval Air Station

A week after her arrest for the alleged abuse of Patrick and assault on Luke Walker, Kate glowered across the table at Lieutenant Alexis Sideris. The young Navy JAG would serve as the defense lawyer in Kate's military trial.

"You dare to accuse me? I'm the victim, Lieutenant."

"I'm not accusing you, ma'am. I'm on your side. Kept you out of the brig, remember?"

Kate bit her lip. "Sorry."

When Kate's commanding officer, Commander Tyler Fox, learned of her plight the night of the fracas, he called the local naval legal services office where Lieutenant Sideris stood duty. The skipper and the lawyer convinced the naval station police to release Kate to their cognizance instead of incarcerating her in the Navy brig. Kate was restricted to the naval air station and prohibited from returning to her home in officer housing. The duplex unit assigned to her and Luke constituted a crime scene.

Kate had no desire to return there, least of all without Patrick. She got a single room in the Meridian Naval Air Station bachelor officers' quarters (BOQ). The squadron flight surgeon had removed Kate from flying status, so her jet students rescheduled with other instructors. Embarrassed by her squadron mates' wariness the one time she showed up in the squadron spaces, Kate did not return. Other than taking meals in the naval station galley, she spent her time holed up in the BOQ, reading and watching mindless TV shows.

Why do I feel like a criminal?

Patrick was in capable hands. Commander Fox had persuaded Child Protective Services to allow his wife, who often babysat Patrick, to care for him in their home. He argued that they could provide an environment less stressful than a custodial facility. Overwhelmed with cases, CPS officials jumped at the opportunity to get the temporary custody matter out of their hands; so long as Kate would not have access to Patrick.

Kate was relieved to keep the haughty Ms. Gonzales from Navy Family Services away from her baby.

"We have to consider your plea, ma'am," the JAG's voice brought Kate back to the present. "The case pits your word against Major Walker's. The only hard evidence from the scene is a knife with your fingerprints—*only* your fingerprints—and the vomit and blood in the hallway. You and the major both had blood alcohol levels in the intoxicated range."

Kate recalled giving a blood sample in the ER, without knowing the purpose.

"I told you what happened," Kate said. "I rescued my baby. I thought Luke would kill him." She frowned at the JAG. "I had two beers after I got home from my night flight and argued with Luke."

204

She wrinkled her forehead. "Maybe I had three, or part of a third. I was upset."

Lieutenant Sideris shrugged. "Major Walker claimed he caught you harming Patrick and that he wrestled the child away. You returned with the knife and attacked your husband. He disarmed you, but then you took him down with a groin kick. You kicked him in the chest, and then you fractured his skull with another kick to the head. Steel-toed flight boots, right?"

Kate didn't answer.

"The resulting brain bleed, technically epidural hematoma, didn't kill him, thanks to medical intervention. He will suffer permanent disability. He will never fly again. Probably he will be unfit for continued duty in the Marine Corps. He will lose his livelihood." The JAG made a tent with her hands. "He can make a convincing case against you. Ma'am."

Kate hated the woman in front of her. The lady JAG's bobbed brown hair, meticulous khaki uniform, and solitary national defense ribbon irked Kate. Her defense counsel wore no deployment ribbons, no personal medals, no warfighting qualifications, and no wedding ring. What could this fresh-out-of-law-school ingenue know about military marriage, much less about child abuse?

"I rescued my child," Kate said. "Any worthy mother would do the same."

The JAG folded her arms. "So would a worthy father."

"Luke Walker is not a worthy father. He is a vile, drunken, abusive man." Kate's voice quivered as she pointed to her discolored face. "How the hell did I get this smashed face, Lieutenant? What about *my* evidence? The police photos, and the ER staff who saw me rush in with my baby. I was in a panic. Why is it all about the damned knife?"

"You attacked your husband with a lethal weapon. Your face may look swollen from that non-mortal bruise, and your wrist may be sprained, but the major almost died from your assault."

"What about Patrick's wounds?" Kate was crying now. "I didn't cause those. Who wouldn't understand a mother's rage against the man who did?"

The JAG remained silent while Kate composed herself. After a minute, Lieutenant Sideris leaned forward, looked at Kate with empathy. "I believe you. But the court, all of whom are male officers, might buy your husband's version and find you guilty of assault and child abuse."

Kate quelled her tears and steeled her eyes as she looked up at the JAG. "He never wanted Patrick."

The lieutenant sighed. "The major will show up in court sober, dressed in his best Marine Corps uniform, with a high-and-tight haircut to show the surgical scar on the side of his head. He will limp and slur his speech to emphasize his permanent disability.

"On the other hand, unless you change your aggressive attitude, Mrs. Walker—"

Kate protested, but the JAG stopped her with a raised hand.

"They will call you 'Mrs. Walker,' regardless of what you want."

Kate sagged back into the chair.

The JAG continued. "You, Mrs. Walker, will come across as a domineering, pushy shrew capable of inflicting lethal force. You could lose your child and your career; serve time in Leavenworth too." She watched Kate absorb the impact of her words.

"You can plead guilty to a lesser charge. Claim that you were out of your mind with stress. You had both been drinking, so your judgment was impaired. A domestic squabble got out of hand. You didn't want to hurt your husband or your baby. You just flipped out.

"You're okay now, court have mercy. Take your lumps, reconcile with your husband, and get your child back. Move on with your life."

"Stop!" Kate leaned over the desk on clenched fists, her face inches away from the younger woman. "For the last time, I did not attack my baby. I attacked a drunken, wicked man who abused my son and assaulted me. Did what any mother would do. I rescued my baby." Her eyes flared. "Reconcile? I'll see him burn in hell first."

The lawyer leaned away from Kate's wrath. "I respect your feelings, ma'am, but I can't guarantee what the court will do with the evidence. My first concern is that you not lose your child."

"Then change your tune and get ready to fight, Lieutenant, because I have my evidence. I will tear that court apart before I let them take Patrick away from me."

Lieutenant Sideris blew out a deep breath. "You realize that by fighting, you choose all or nothing?"

"It won't be nothing."

"To win, you must destroy him before he destroys you."

"Damn right."

The JAG threw up her hands. "So we fight to the death." She looked Kate in the eye. "I need all the dirt on him you can give me. Start with what you meant when you said he didn't want Patrick."

Kate sat back in her chair and bit her lip, grasping the price she must pay for victory.

So be it.

She squinted against tears as she glared back at the JAG. "Luke raped me. That's how we made Patrick."

Chapter Fifty

1999, Meridian, MS: US Naval Air Station

After three months barred from seeing her son, Kate's finger hesitated over the doorbell to the Fox home. She sensed Patrick inside. Even in the warm Mississippi dusk, a chill washed over her.

Kate had sworn a statement about Luke's prior abuse and agreed to testify in gut-wrenching detail. But she dared not count on a favorable verdict. With little to lose, Luke would stoop to any depth to exact his revenge by removing Patrick from her life. He would not try to prove himself a fit parent, because he had no intention of keeping Patrick. Forcing Kate to lose custody would be victory enough for him. No matter how hard Kate fought for justice, Luke would never lay down his weapons and retreat.

He is a Marine, after all.

Lydia Fox's early afternoon phone call had surprised Kate. "Would you like to see Patrick?" Kate had thought that she had misheard.

Now here she was, pressing the doorbell.

209

Footsteps approached from inside. The door opened. Lydia held Patrick by the hand. "Here's mommy."

Patrick shied away from Kate.

She swept him into her arms and hugged and kissed him. "I've missed you so much, baby boy."

Patrick jerked his head back, pushed away from her, and cried.

Lydia led them to a cozy family room. "You two get reacquainted while I serve up some drinks."

Patrick had stopped crying but became agitated when Lydia left the room. Kate bounced him on her knee as she used to do in happier times. The familiar action soothed him.

From behind her, a man spoke. "Hello, Kate." She turned to see Commander Fox approach with two soft drinks in his hand. He handed one to her, then took a seat across from the sofa. "Looks like you and Patrick are getting to know each other again."

"Thank you, sir." Kate decided to be upfront with her superior. "Why am I allowed to see him now, with the trial weeks away?"

The commander smiled as if he'd just won the Super Bowl. "No trial. You can take Patrick home with you today if you're ready to have him back."

Kate stared at her boss. "No trial?"

"Luke Walker made a sworn statement. He admitted you told the truth."

Kate's eyes widened. Her mouth opened and closed before she could speak. "I don't believe that. Luke never backs away from a fight."

"Believe it," the Commander said. "Your hotshot JAG will tell you the same thing tomorrow after the judge signs the papers."

"But how?"

"You don't need to know."

She stared at him until he had to say something. "Luke learned what would happen to him if he lost at trial."

"What?"

"He chose an honorable medical retirement from the Marine Corps, with full disability, over a prison term and dishonorable discharge."

Kate shook her head. "He bought that? Without a fight in court?"

The commander winked. "You represent the future of naval aviation, Kate. People in high places look out for you. They can be quite persuasive."

Kate remained skeptical. "Does Luke get to see Patrick?"

"He's renounced all paternal claims to your son. You will never see Luke Walker again."

Kate scoffed. "I don't believe that. Not for one second."

Commander Fox raised his hand. "Believe it, Kate. Re-settle in your home. Reunite with your son. When you're ready, and you arrange childcare, I need you back on the flight schedule. We have students eager for you to teach them to fly jets. They want to learn from the best."

Kate stared at her mentor, desperate to trust what he said. Seven years of hellacious marriage warned her otherwise.

Luke Walker never accepts defeat.

- Mike Krentz -

Chapter Fifty-One

April 18, 2012, Singapore: Changi Naval Base

Following a vigorous bike ride into the heart of Singapore and back, Nick Juel cleaned up and donned his mess dress white uniform in time to board the last bus transporting officers from *Shenandoah* to Raffle's Hotel for the formal dining out, a longstanding Navy tradition. He sat himself in the middle of the vehicle, from where he regaled junior officers making their first visit to the popular Asian capital.

"Think of Singapore as a manicured society. Look at those boulevards: not a blade of grass out of place, no weeds, no dogshit on the sidewalks, no garbage on the street. You won't step on old chewing gum because chewing gum is illegal here. Spitting, too. This place is so ordered that it may seem sterile. But you can get fabulous cuisine of any ethnic variety you want, rich night life, plenty to do." He winked at two female ensigns sharing the seat in front of him.

"The cycling weather is ideal. Singapore is one degree off the

212

equator, so not much variation in temperature or humidity. Hot and moist year-round. You acclimatize to the heat. I ride my bike in the middle of the day here. Just gotta keep hydrated. 'Get busy living or get busy dying,' you know." He looked around at the blank faces. "*Shawshank Redemption*. I'm a movie nut, too."

Nick shifted in his seat to entertain another group of young officers. "Raffles Hotel, where we're going, is a genuine nineteenth-century historical landmark. Raffles founded Singapore. Presidents and heads of state have stayed there. Gents and ladies, you won't find a more inspiring setting for a dining out anywhere else in your naval career. You gotta visit the Long Bar for a drink. You can get an original Singapore Sling, because that's where it was invented." He paused for emphasis. "I'm a single malt scotch guy myself."

Nick leaned back in his seat, basking in the attention of the junior officers hanging on his every word. "Shipmates, if you have any salt in you at all, tonight you will make unforgettable Navy memories."

Chapter Fifty-Two

April 18, 2012, Singapore: Raffles Hotel

The imposing white colonial facade of Raffles Hotel lived up to Nick's description. Promenading through the ornate lobby and ascending an oaken staircase, he led several natty officers and gentlemen across an interior terrace to an elegant foyer outside the main ballroom. The transformation from the dingy gray steel confines of *Shenandoah*, with its narrow passageways, constant noise, machinery smell and temperamental climate control, to this international landmark intoxicated the retinue and fueled the officers' expectations of a fine evening, like young men on respite from a tired old mother finding themselves in warm consort with a wealthy and attractive international socialite.

When Leo and the ship's captain arrived, the celebration was well on its way. The two senior officers ordered drinks and joined the pre-dinner fellowship and camaraderie. Other officers, many of whom had checked into hotels in the area, continued to arrive as the cocktail hour progressed. Some brought spouses, their elegant evening gowns and handsome tuxedos adding splashes of color to the white and black livery of the naval officers. Eric and Melody Mikleson arrived as one such couple. Eric sported new four-striped captain's shoulder boards, but even with its polychromatic rows of medals, his dress white dinner jacket made drab contrast to Melody's model-like features, flowing brunette tresses, and a chic lavender gown.

In another corner of the foyer, Colonel Preston Davis held court. He wore the traditional Marine Corps mess dress uniform, a full-length dark blue jacket with two rows of thirteen small gold buttons. The jacket opened diagonally outward from a choker collar to reveal a red vest over a pleated white shirt and royal blue trousers. His martial appearance contrasted with the starched *maître di*-like all-white attire of his Navy counterparts. Preston's five rows of anodized medals—including a bronze star for valor in combat—hung from multicolored ribbons over the left breast. The tailored uniform draped perfectly over his rugged physique, enhancing his battle-toughened facial features. Like groupies adoring a rock star, an audience of junior naval officers hung on his every word. The two female Navy ensigns whom Nick Juel had entertained on the bus stood enraptured at the front of Preston's admirers as he launched his battle tale.

"They called it 'Ambush Alley.' We secured the bridges into Nasiriyah so the fast-moving invasion element could speed through to Baghdad. My unit got pinned down by RPG and sniper fire." He took a sip of his drink, then continued in a somber voice. "We lost good marines that day."

A hush fell over his listeners. Some gripped their drinks; others swigged. Preston waited for the effect of his last words to set up the audience before he continued. "But the mother battle was

Fallujah. Much bigger challenge. I was—"

A stir near the room's entrance interrupted his soliloquy and broke his spell on the devotees. Looking toward the commotion, Preston saw that Kate Mahoney and Alexis Sideris had entered. Besides the prescribed mess dress uniform, each woman wore a Navy-blue cloth tiara with embroidered naval officer's crest in the center and gold embroidered scrambled eggs emanating along each wing.

When did Kate return from the US? Today?

A flock of white-jacketed officers and gentlemen quickly surrounded the newcomers, diminishing Preston's audience to the two ensigns and a few lusty male junior officers.

* * *

Doc and Rusty approached the newly arrived senior female officers with drinks from the bar.

"Glenmorangie neat, as ordered, Captain." Doc smiled and handed Kate her drink.

She thought the doc overzealous, but rewarded him with a grateful smile. "Thanks, Doc."

As she savored the liquid's welcome warmth in her throat, over Doc's shoulder Kate noticed Preston staring at her. The intensity in his eyes caused a curious bloom throughout her body. She returned his gaze, but then averted her eyes. Did her face flush?

Just the scotch on top of jet lag.

Chapter Fifty-Three

April 18, 2012, Singapore: Raffles Hotel

Suitably pre-lubricated, the combined officers of *Shenandoah* and Seventh Fleet staff paraded into the main ballroom, where they sat by order of rank at long rows of lavishly set tables. The chief of staff and the *Shenandoah* commanding officer, Captain Henry Longman, occupied a head table, along with the guest speaker, the commodore of a Royal Australian Navy ship that was in port at the same time as *Shenandoah*. In front of the head table, a large crystal punch bowl brimmed with traditional Navy grog, a potent concoction of various rums and orange liqueurs. Officers who broke the rules of the mess would be sentenced to quaff from this mixture. Most would not consider it punishment.

At the opposite end of the room from the head table, Lieutenant Commander Elijah Kramb dined alone at a table set for one. For this occasion, the FlagSec served the traditional role of "Mr. Vice," the event's official master of ceremonies and enforcer of the rules of the mess.

Delighted to escape the bland cuisine served on the ship, the merry revelers feasted on a traditional roast beef dinner with paired wines.

"So this is what pink meat looks like," joked one junior officer.

After the meal, the guest speech, and the prescribed formal toasts, the group launched into the most enjoyable business of the evening: ludicrous informal toasts and jocular jabs at fellow celebrants. If Mr. Vice ruled an officer in violation of the rules, he could order said officer to pay a monetary fine to the mess fund and make a trip to the grog bowl.

An uncomfortable Lieutenant Junior Grade rose at his place. "Mr. Vice."

Elijah recognized him with a deep intonation. "Lieutenant JG Hazelton."

Red-faced, the junior officer addressed the head table. "Mr. President, respectfully request permission to ease the springs."

Captain Longman chuckled. "Very well, Lieutenant. However, your profound lack of mission planning and your inefficient fuel management require retribution to the mess. Mr. Vice?"

Mr. Vice cackled. "Indeed, sir. For improper fuel management, I fine Lieutenant Junior Grade Hazelton ten dollars, plus a trip to the bowl—*before* departing the area."

The officers—many with legs pressed together against the rising pressures in their own bladders—applauded the young officer's predicament. He took quick steps to the grog bowl, his body hunched forward at the waist. He chugged a draft of the swill, then dashed from the hall toward the restrooms.

As the laughter died down, Colonel Preston Davis rose at his seat. His sonorous voice commanded rather than requested recognition. "Mr. Vice!"

Mr. Vice responded as the room hushed. "Colonel Davis, sir."

The colonel scanned the entire gathering and then addressed the head table. "Mr. President, a point of order." He made sure that he had everyone's attention before he proceeded. "I note with grave concern that two of our senior officers exhibit deplorable leadership by entering the mess improperly attired."

"Go on, Colonel," said Captain Longman.

Davis eyed Kate as he continued. "Mr. President, Captain Mahoney and Commander Sideris entered the mess not only with heads covered but wearing audacious headgear that derogates the solemn nature of this auspicious occasion."

Kate and Alexis rose to stand at their places as required whenever accused of malfeasance toward the mess.

Captain Longman addressed them. "Captain Mahoney, Commander Sideris, how do you respond to this grave allegation from the senior Marine officer?"

Kate cleared her throat as she pulled herself fully erect. "Mr. President, I am shocked and awed by Colonel Davis' ignorance. Navy uniform regulations authorize formal tiaras for female officers attending events of this nature. My colleague, a respected judge advocate general, will so attest."

Alexis took the cue. "Indeed, Mr. President. Captain Mahoney is correct. In fact, . . ." She extracted a sheaf of paper from beneath her cummerbund. "I have a copy of the US Navy uniform regulations, should you or the Colonel wish to peruse them." The other officers in the room tittered.

Kate continued. "Mr. President, the Staff Judge Advocate

and I proudly wear this authorized Navy headgear as a respectful compliment to our fellow officers of the mess. Perhaps Colonel Davis regrets he cannot emulate, but—sadly for him—he is not an officer of the United States Navy, nor is he a woman."

The room erupted in laughter.

Struggling to contain his own laughter, Captain Longman pounded the gavel to regain order before pronouncing sentence. The room stilled.

"Captain Mahoney, Commander Sideris, you are indeed in authorized uniforms, including the tiaras. Therefore, I must impose an amercement on Colonel Davis for improperly accusing senior officers of the naval service. Mr. Vice?"

"Aye, aye, sir," said Mr. Vice. "For improper accusations against senior officers of the United States Navy, I fine Colonel Davis twenty dollars and a trip to the bowl for two quaffs, one for each officer offended."

Preston Davis marched to the grog bowl, stood at attention, and with exaggerated formality drank two full cups of grog. Passing Kate's chair on returning to his own seat, he muttered, "Well played, Captain."

Kate pretended she didn't hear him.

When the colonel sat down, Ensign Clarissa Zipp, a recent US Naval Academy graduate serving her first operational tour, stood and leaned on the back of her chair. In the foyer earlier, she had fixated on Colonel Davis' monologue. A red wine stain next to her solitary national defense ribbon soiled her dress-white jacket.

"Misser Vice!" Her voice shrilled.

Mr. Vice shrugged. "Ensign Zipp."

The disheveled ensign faced the head table. "Misser Prezzent, I strenosly object to your lasht ruling." She waved her arms in frustration as she quit trying to emulate the stilted rhetoric of her seniors. "Okay, so maybe they can get away with wearin' those terras cuz they're all senior and stuff, but they're showin' up the rest of us women here."

Across the table, the other young female who had admired Preston's cocktail monologue rose from her seat. Ensign Tamika Robinson's dress white jacket featured an enlisted surface warfare badge and an enlisted good conduct medal. As a former deck sailor who had transitioned to officer ranks, she was older than Ensign Zipp. She turned to the head table with unabashed confidence, bypassing Mr. Vice.

"Mr. President! I join in my colleague's objection. Do you know what those things cost? Junior officers can't afford crap like that. They—"

Mr. Vice interrupted, "Ensign Robinson, you are out of order. You may not address the President of the Mess unless first recognized by Mr. Vice."

"So, recognize me, *sir*. I'm standing right in front of you."

Captain Longman pounded his gavel to draw everyone's attention back to the head table. Uncomfortable silence filled the room.

"Ensigns Zipp and Robinson, you are both out of order. The matter of the tiaras has been settled and is not subject to further discussion. Now be quiet and take your seats. Proceed, Mr. Vice."

The two women sat down as Mr. Vice said, "For improperly addressing the mess, I fine Ensigns Zipp and Robinson five dollars each." He did not order a trip to the grog bowl. Neither lady appeared to need any more spirits.

Ensign Zipp spoke across the table to her colleague, loudly enough to be heard throughout the room, "What bullshit is that?"

221

An embarrassed silence gripped the assemblage. Kate threw down her napkin and stood up. "Mr. Vice!"

Mr. Vice seemed grateful. "Captain Mahoney."

"Mr. President." Kate's voice quivered with anger. "Respectfully request permission to ease the springs. In the interest of efficiency and continuing the business of the mess, I respectfully request for Ensigns Zipp and Robinson to join me."

Captain Longman smiled. "Thank you, Captain."

Kate proceeded toward the door, stopping at the table where the two ensigns sat. "Ladies," she said, "Come with me. Now."

Scowling, the two young women rose and followed her out of the room. Behind them, a young male officer stood and diverted the gathering to a more jovial topic.

Chapter Fifty-Four

April 18, 2012, Singapore: Raffles Hotel

Kate didn't take the young officers to the restroom. She pulled them into a quiet alcove where they could talk in relative privacy.

"What the hell is with you two?"

"Just trying to have some fun, ma'am," said Ensign Robinson. "No big deal."

"No big deal? Could you be that naïve?" Kate moved in closer to the younger women. She spoke in a measured, distinct voice. "Listen, ladies. We live and work in a male-dominated environment. Female officers—all of us—must maintain a higher standard."

Ensign Zipp rolled her eyes. Kate looked the younger woman in the eye. "Don't you roll your eyes at me, Ensign." She glared at the insolent face looking back at her. "Hear this, young lady. These guys may act like friends, and they may treat you nice, like you're one of the guys. But you're *not* guys, and they very well know the difference. The minute you lose control of your dignity, you become

223

a fair target."

Ensign Robinson chortled. "You speaking from experience on that, ma'am?"

Furious at the woman's impudence, Kate fought to maintain her composure. She pointed her finger at the ensign's face. Her voice trembled when she addressed the young woman. "You don't talk, girl. You listen. Got that?"

"Yes, ma'am," the woman muttered.

Kate calmed her voice. "I know from experience, painful experience. Many women suffered a boatload of mistreatment and abuse and shed buckets of sweat and tears to earn a place of respect in this Navy, to make opportunities for you. I will not watch you throw that away with stupid behavior. Start behaving like officers and ladies instead of sluts in a cheap saloon." She put her face so close to Ensign Robinson's that she almost gagged on the odor of half-digested wine on the woman's breath. "Do you hear me now, Ensign?"

Ensign Robinson stared Kate in the eye, unblinking. "Loud and clear, ma'am."

Kate stepped back. "Believe me, ladies. These guys are not your friends. Many of them do not respect you as officers." She took a breath. "Targets. You are targets. If nothing else, remember that." She stood over them, hands on hips. "You two clean up your acts right now, or I will personally escort you back to the ship. Is that clear?"

"Aye, aye, ma'am," the two women responded in unison.

"Now carry on." Kate spun on her heel and left the alcove.

As soon as Kate was out of earshot, Ensign Robinson turned to her companion. "Bitch needs to get laid."

"Aye, aye, ma'am." Ensign Zipp mocked with a sloppy

salute.

"Let's go find dick," said Ensign Robinson.

"Roger that, shipmate!" Ensign Zipp smoothed her mess dress and ran her fingers through her hair to loosen it a bit. The two women headed toward the bar where the officers of the mess now gathered. The formal dinner had ended.

* * *

Shaken by the confrontation, Kate composed herself in the ladies' room before entering the bar area, now occupied mostly by junior officers. Seeking to avoid conversation, she nodded in reply to their polite greetings but did not break stride.

Lieutenant Commander Elijah Kramb's imposing frame stood between her and the bartender. "Good evening, ma'am. May I have the honor of buying the captain a drink?"

"I would prefer the honor of buying a round for you, Mr. Vice."

She led the way to the bar, where she ordered a Glenmorangie neat for herself and a draft beer for the FlagSec. She made small talk as the scotch slowly assuaged the smoldering fire in her head. After what she considered a proper polite interlude, she excused herself and went out to the balcony for much needed fresh air.

Chapter Fifty-Five

April 18, 2012, Singapore: Raffles Hotel

On the ornate balcony overlooking Singapore, senior officers gathered in small groups, jabbering while they sipped after-dinner drinks. Some smoked cigars. Kate stood apart, leaning over the sculpted white railing to stare at the multicolored city lights stretching to the Malacca Strait. On top of her jet lag, the scotch combined with the dinner wine seemed to disengage her brain—a welcome fugue sensation before her return to the accelerated operations tempo of a fleet command.

A familiar voice from behind disrupted her mellow state. "Plotting a strategic assault on Singapore, Captain? Winning the battle of Korea not enough for you?"

Kate stared straight ahead for an instant to steel herself, and then turned to face Colonel Preston Davis. "Just getting fresh air, sir." Her head felt hot even as she hoped to sound cool.

Preston leaned against the railing next to her. "Welcome back to the squirrel cage. I didn't see you on the ship. When did you

226

arrive?"

"Earlier today. I haven't been to the ship. Commander Sideris was kind enough to bring out my mess dress and let me crash in her room here in the hotel. I spent the afternoon sleeping off the jet lag." She shrugged, wondering why she felt the need to explain her time management to him.

"Rough week?"

Kate scoffed. "Pretty much." She didn't want to get into details, not with Preston Davis. She backed away from the railing. He matched her step.

"I wanted to compliment you," he said. "You've bested me twice in a week."

She furrowed her brow. "Bested?"

"Just now, with the toasts." He gestured toward the dining room. "And when you sold your show-of-force plan to the admiral. That was an impressive first sortie."

"I wasn't selling anything." Was it the dim light or the scotch—or both—that cast Colonel Davis less threatening here on the hotel balcony than on the ship? "The admiral assessed the situation the same as I did. I wasn't competing with you, or anyone."

"Modesty duly noted, Captain." He sounded sincere. "I meant it as a compliment."

Kate softened. "Compliment accepted, sir. That means a lot from someone of your stature."

He held out his glass in a toast. Kate hesitated, then clicked her glass on his, but averted her eyes.

After a brief pause, Preston went on. "Last overnight in port. You didn't get a hotel room here?"

"I'm going back to the ship." She turned away to look out at the city. "Got a lot of catch-up work."

Preston moved beside her, saying nothing as he also gazed outward. Then he spoke in a lowered tone. "I have a room at the Fullerton on Clark Quay. Close to here. The night is still young. Work can always keep."

Flushed, Kate stared straight ahead. She slugged down the rest of her drink and moved away from him. "I'm going inside." She hurried off to the bar area.

Kate spotted Eric at the bar and hurried to join him.

"Glenmorangie, neat," she said to the bartender.

"I'll pay for that one, too," Eric said. He handed Singapore dollars to the bartender and received his change. Then he and Kate moved away from the bar.

Eric regarded her with concern. "Are you all right? You look upset."

"I'm fine. Just had an unpleasant conversation."

Eric looked toward the balcony and then back at her. "Good to have you back. Not much traction with the game plan while you were gone."

"I'm not surprised, with the boss off the ship and COS in charge."

Eric rubbed his brow. "I can't tie all the pieces together. That frustrates me."

A wave of fatigue washed over Kate. Was it just yesterday that she'd been with Patrick? "If anyone can figure it out, you can."

"Thanks," Eric said, "but enough work for now. We are supposed to be enjoying an evening of elegance." He raised his glass as a toast, gestured toward the dining room. "Nice job handling the colonel in there."

Kate forced a smile. She looked him in the eye and clicked her glass with his.

"Whatever you two are celebrating will have to wait." Kate and Eric both cringed at the interrupting voice. Leo LeBlanc had come up behind them like a stealth fighter.

"Kate," Leo said, "I've been looking for you. Eric, you need to hear this, too." He moved them into the same alcove where Kate had confronted the ensigns. He turned his back to the larger room and spoke in a low voice, using metaphors to disguise his disclosure of strategic information in a non-secure setting. "I just got a call from the boss. PACOM called a timeout. The game is on hold."

"On hold?" Kate said. "Why?"

Leo spoke just above a whisper, forcing the other two to lean toward him. "The ROKs won't play, and we've seen no offensive moves from the other team. PACOM wants to wait for the head coach to call the next move."

Kate rolled her eyes and glanced at Eric. He looked stunned.

A twinge of a smile crossed Leo's face. "No ship movements are authorized for now."

Eric rubbed his forehead. "If we delay, we lose strategic surprise." He looked around for anyone listening, then spoke in code anyway. "We still don't believe our team committed the foul."

Leo gloated. "Who hit first doesn't matter now. You two go back to the ship now and work on a new plan. That other one is dead in the water." He smirked at Kate. "This time, Captain, consult the N7 and me *before* you bring anything to the admiral."

Kate glared back at him. "Aye, aye, sir. I had planned to leave the party now, anyway."

"You do that, Captain." He stared at her for a moment, then did an abrupt about-face to rejoin the crowd of revelers at the bar, seamlessly shifting his persona to that of hale fellow, host of the mess.

Eric turned to Kate. "Sorry, ma'am."

She turned on him. "What did I say about that 'ma'am' shit?"

Eric raised his hands. "Guilty. And sorry."

Kate relaxed. "No, I'm sorry for snapping at you."

"I share your frustration, ma—Kate."

She shrugged. "Why should we be surprised? We were never really in the game."

The two moved out of the alcove, but Kate stopped and touched Eric's arm. "Don't go back to the ship. Stay here with your family. No one's at work in Hawaii right now, anyway."

Eric smiled with obvious relief. "Thanks, Kate. You may have just saved my marriage. I'll come aboard first thing tomorrow to resume connecting dots."

"Don't rush to get there," Kate said. "Plenty of time once we are underway. Not like anyone up the chain is salivating to get our product."

Eric shook his head. "We don't know the whole truth about what happened in the West Sea. We have to find it. I will be there in the morning."

"Fine," she said. "Now get back to your wife before she wonders if we've got something going here besides work."

Eric walked toward the bar area where Melody waited for him, but then he turned back. He hesitated before speaking. "Don't let the COS push you around. You've earned your stripes. Besides, the admiral's got your back."

"Only so long as I'm right." Kate smiled, genuine. "Thanks. I appreciate the support. Now please go enjoy your evening."

Eric didn't move. "Will you discuss a plan with the colonel?"

She shook her head. "I've talked to him enough for now, thanks. You can speak to him."

"Roger." Eric turned and walked toward his wife.

Kate looked at her watch. 2200.

Patrick!

She rushed to the elevator bank, avoiding the officers engaged in full-out attack on the remains of the evening.

Chapter Fifty-Six

April 18, 2012, Singapore: Raffles Hotel

Kate scurried into Alexis's hotel room. She calculated that 2200
Singapore time would be seven AM in San Bruno. She could still
Skype Patrick before he left for school. Fumbling (*I didn't drink that
much*), she removed her laptop from its case and turned it on,
drumming her fingers as the machine took its time booting up and
connecting to the hotel's wireless network. She opened the Skype
program, ready to click on Patrick's number.

My headset.

She looked through her case for the USB headset but
couldn't find it. She turned the case upside down and dumped all the
contents on the bed. No headset.

Damn! Did I leave it at Colleen's?

She searched the room to see if Alexis had a headset, but she
found none. She looked at her watch. 2215. Patrick usually left the
house at 0720.

I have only five minutes.

Retrieving her Blackberry from her purse, she found it out of power. She'd forgotten to charge it after the long flights. In desperation, she tried dialing Patrick's iPhone from the hotel room phone, but she got only a high-pitched beeping sound.

Kate returned to her laptop and Skype-texted Patrick in haste, not paying attention to accuracy.

Scarlett: Patrick. You ther?

She stared at a blank screen, and then words popped up.

PatWalk: Hey, Mom.

Scarlett: In Singpore. I forgt my heeadset so I can't talk to u. U okay?

PatWalk: Yeah. Gotta go to school now.

Her fingers flew over the keyboard with minimal accuracy.

Scarlett: Got her ok. One mor day til we sale. Try to call u tomorro. Want to kno about Homer Hous. Love u.

PatWalk: Sure, Mom. You too. Bye.

PatWalk is offline.

Kate typed back anyway.

Scarlett: K-bye.

She considered checking her personal email or her Facebook page, but then she sighed, logged off, shut down the laptop, and replaced it into its case. She had to start back to the ship, but first she wanted to change out of her mess dress into civilian clothes. When she opened the closet door, the woman reflected in the full-length mirror took her by surprise. Kate had forgotten about the tiara perched in her hair. Now it seemed silly. It belonged on someone younger. She jerked it out of her hair and tossed it onto the bed.

"So much for female officer dignity," she said aloud.

Kate sat on the edge of the bed with her head in her hands.

"What the hell am I doing here?"

The empty room did not answer.

After a few minutes, Kate washed her face and tidied her hair. Deciding not to change out of the mess dress, she slung the computer bag over her shoulder, picked up her suitcase and garment bag, and started toward the door. She tucked the tiara into a side pocket of her garment bag, where she found the USB headset exactly as she had packed it before she left San Bruno.

* * *

Kate zigzagged through the lobby to avoid small groups of naval officers planning assaults on Singapore's eternal night life. Many still wore their mess dress, while others had changed into more casual party attire. Those with more lucrative means would head out to popular night spots in Clark Quay and Orchard Row, while the more frugal members would seek less costly dance venues in the local area. They reminded her of a different time in her Navy career.

Like forever ago.

Clear of the revelers, she proceeded through the main lobby door and approached the doorman. "A cab to Changi Naval Base, please."

The doorman directed her to a queue thirty yards to her right.

When she reached the line, she saw Preston Davis approach the lead cab. With him, talking and laughing loudly, were Ensigns Zipp and Robinson. All three still wore mess dress uniforms.

Colonel Davis held the rear door for the two young women. Kate tried to hide behind the person in front of her, a short woman. As he got into the cab, Preston looked straight at Kate and then announced loudly to the driver, "Clark Quay, please." He pressed into the back seat next to Ensign Robinson. As the cab pulled away, he looked over his shoulder at Kate.

A minute later, Kate reached the front of the queue and slunk into a cab as the doorman loaded her bags in the trunk. She slammed the car door behind her before the doorman had the chance to close it.

"Changi Naval Base," she said to the driver. As the cab left the historic hotel and drove into the night, Kate Mahoney felt a hot tear run down her cheek. She wiped it away with her sleeve, refusing to let another one follow.

Way to go, Scarlett.

The cab maneuvered through traffic and headed westbound. Kate watched the city lights speed by the window. Then her gaze searched the darkness beyond the passing lights. She did not know what her eyes sought.

Kate's thoughts drifted to the night of her first combat sortie into Iraq, before her ejection and rescue. Dodger, her beloved mentor, had led the flight of Hornets to their targets. Just as Scarlett rolled into her first bombing run, Dodger's voice blared in her headset.

"Give the bastards bloody hell, woman!"

Dodger never made it back from that mission.

What would he say to me now?

Chapter Fifty-Seven

April 18, 2012, San Bruno, CA

"My aunt took me to Homer House today. I met a counselor and signed up for my volunteer service."

With his mother gone and Aunt Colleen at work, Patrick chatted with Fuchou on his headset without fear of being overheard.

"Cool, Dude. Did you meet Homer?"

"He wasn't there, but his assistant seemed nice."

"I don't know Homer," Fuchou said. "I hear good things."

"In Florida?"

Fuchou took a few seconds to answer. "His reputation extends from coast to coast. Tell me more about what you'll do there."

Patrick spoke in an excited cadence. "I'll work every Saturday for six hours. That's when my aunt can take me. I could ride the BART into The City, but my mom insisted my aunt take me and pick me up each time. I can't game on Saturday mornings until this is done."

236

"Dude, you got caught, tried, convicted, and sentenced. You gotta serve your time. Get over it."

"Yeah."

"Next time you cruise, turn on the lights."

"No next time. My aunt hid the keys." He frowned. "My mom would kill me."

"Someday you'll figure out that your aunt and your mom don't run your life."

"Someday."

"Sooner than later, I hope. C'mon, let's play."

Fanpan and Fuchou entered the fantasy world of Pandaria and continued their quest. Victory became more difficult as the Alliance threw stronger warriors and more sophisticated tactics against them. After four hours of intense game play, they ascended to another level. As the trailer for the next level played, both gamers relaxed.

"How'd you like the last pictures?"

"Awesome." Patrick had never seen photos of real people engaged in sexual intercourse. He had stared at them long enough to masturbate twice. He did not want Fuchou to know his naiveté. "I mean, they were pretty good. Nothing I didn't see before."

"Got something better for you. Videos. I'll send you the link."

"Videos? You mean live?"

"Live when they were filmed."

"People do that? Let someone film them doing it?"

"You'd be surprised what some people will do, dude. Some real sickos out there. Be careful."

* * *

"Sickos, indeed." Fuchou gloated after he signed off the game and swilled down the rest of his beer. "I am proud to be one of them, darling Fanpan. You have no idea how sick a man can be, but you will learn soon enough. So will your witch mother."

He lit a cigarette, hobbled to his refrigerator, and extracted another beer. The limp seemed worse tonight. Must be fatigue. He'd had a long day, busy as an industrious spider spinning his intricate web. He vowed to remain patient.

Soon we will catch a fly—or two.

Chapter Fifty-Eight

April 19, 2012, Singapore: Changi Naval Base

The last busload of raucous, drunken Americans passed the Changi Naval Base main gate just before 0200, the Seventh Fleet-imposed liberty curfew. A few speeding taxicabs returned late revelers within minutes after the last liberty bus disembarked its passengers.

The RSN sentries relaxed. With the US sailors tucked into their ship, the rest of the night should be uneventful. In a few more hours, they could turn the watch over to the day shift.

Forty minutes later, approaching headlights alerted the guards. A taxicab raced up to the checkpoint and screeched to a stop. Alarmed, the forward sentry's right hand perched on his holstered pistol as he scrutinized the vehicle. The rear window on the driver's side rolled down, and an American woman poked her head out. The guard noted the female officer's disheveled white US Navy uniform and took his hand off his holster. Just a very tardy and very drunk returnee from the night's festivity. No matter which US ship was in port, there was always at least one late return past their curfew.

The woman flashed an ID card at the sentry. Her head swayed in the window space as she spoke. "I am Ensign Robinson. We are all officers of the US Seventh Fleet. Let us go through to the USS *Shenandoah*."

The sentry did not budge. "Regrettably, ma'am, public vehicles are not allowed on the base at this hour without prior authorization. We've received no authorizations tonight."

The woman poked her head further out the window. "As an officer on the Seventh Fleet Staff, I authorize you to let this vehicle through the gate."

The sentry remained polite. "With apologies, ma'am, that authorization must come from the Republic of Singapore Navy."

Another woman in a similar uniform emerged from the opposite rear door of the cab. Realizing that she also was drunk, the sentry signaled his colleagues in the guardhouse. Observing the developing situation, the other guards approached the vehicle.

The new woman walked around the car and stood in front of the sentry. "Whaddaya wannus to do, Mishter? We godda gedda our ship."

The other female officer got out of the vehicle. Both women advanced on the sentry, now flanked by two other guards. The American and Singaporean sailors confronted each other only three feet apart.

The senior guard politely addressed the American officers. "We cannot allow this unauthorized vehicle through the gate. The last bus to the US ship ran at 0200. You must proceed on foot through this checkpoint, then walk to your ship. We regret there is no other way."

"Walk!" The first woman put her hands on her hips, legs spread. She gestured to the inside of the vehicle, "Colonel Davis

240

there is a very important senior officer, and he don't walk. He gets an escort."

Inside the vehicle, a colonel in rumpled US Marine Corps dress uniform lay sprawled across the back seat. He snored loudly, oblivious to the verbal skirmish taking place on his behalf.

The implacable sentry maintained his composure. "You may escort your colonel to your ship on foot."

The first woman moved closer to the guard, her face inches from his. The sour alcohol blast of her breath nearly took him down. "Listen, Bozo. I am ordering you, on behalf of the colonel here, who is the senior officer present, and a decorated combat Marine, that you must let this car through the gate to take us back to our ship." She raised her finger at him. "I mean now, mister!"

Whether intentional or because her alcohol-impaired brain misjudged the distance, her finger plunked the RSN sentry squarely in the chest. In an instant, the three guards took down and pinned the two drunk females to the asphalt. Weapons drawn, they hauled the somnolent colonel out of the vehicle and pinned him to the ground as well.

The taxi took off with the rear door flapping in the slipstream of its accelerated departure.

The RSN sentries handcuffed all three American officers before allowing them to sit up. The second woman vomited on herself and the Marine colonel.

Inside the guardhouse, the RSN officer-in-charge picked up a phone.

Chapter Fifty-Nine

April 19, 2012, Singapore: Changi Naval Base: USS *Shenandoah*

Kate tossed in her rack. Her restless body felt every chink in the thin mattress.

After returning to the ship from the dining out, she had tried to spend time at her computer catching up on email and rethinking the Korea response plan. Thoughts of the evening's events, interrupted by painful memories of Dodger, impaired her concentration. Soon after midnight, she gave up and went to bed.

I didn't need that last drink. Or two.

With the ship in port, Kate missed the machinery noise and gentle sway of the waves that often lulled her to sleep like a baby in a cradle. She continued to fret, unable to find the "off" switch for her churning mind. The harder she sought sleep, the more elusive it became. She snatched only short bursts of fitful napping.

Waking abruptly from one abbreviated respite, Kate punched the light button on her digital wristwatch. 0222. She turned on her side and took steady, even breaths, then lapsed into a fugue, half dreaming, half remembering.

A rough hand touched her shoulder and caressed the back of her neck. Soft lips kissed her hair and spoke tenderly into her ear. "I didn't mean to hurt you, baby."

Luke's hated voice, yet it warmed her.

"I didn't mean to—"

Not Luke's voice. Dodger? Preston? She turned toward the seductive whisper. Ice daggers pierced her heart as she stared into the penetrating eyes of Thomas Patrick Mahoney.

Kate jolted awake. She hyperventilated. Sweat drenched her skin. Kate's heart hammered against her chest. Where was she? Who was with her? She sat up and wiped the glaze from her eyes. The familiar surroundings of her stateroom emerged into gray focus against the darkness.

Another nightmare.

Kate's bounding pulse slowed.

What dream?

She could not remember. The nightmare had retreated to some deep psychic cavern, there to wait for a future night when it would rise like a silent demon to attack her unshielded slumber.

Kate flipped on her reading light, drank from the water bottle next to her rack, and looked at her watch. 0235.

She steadied herself. "Just a dream," she said aloud. She got out of the rack, went into the head, teased the sweat-soaked locks off her forehead, and washed her face. Back in her rack, she rolled onto her side and tried to go back to sleep.

* * *

The shrill ring of her phone brought Kate bolt upright in bed. The crown of her head struck the metal frame of the reading light over

her rack. Sharp pain stabbed her scalp. Shaken by the rude
awakening, she probed the painful spot with her fingers. Sticky wet.
She flipped on the light. Blood.

The phone continued to ring. Kate pressed her scalp with one
hand, got up, shuffled to her desk, and answered it with the other
hand.

"Captain Mahoney?"

An enlisted watch officer spoke into her ear with an excited
voice.

Kate interrupted him as he continued to ramble. "What the
hell time is it? 0250? Did you call COS? He stayed in town? I'm the
senior officer on board?"

Her pulse sped up, quickening the flow from her scalp
wound. She was now wide awake.

"Got it," Kate said into the phone. "Have the duty driver
meet me on the quarterdeck." She gathered her thoughts. "I'll need a
master-at-arms." Another thought. "And the duty corpsman.
Thanks."

She slammed down the receiver.

Kate padded quickly into the head, turned on the light, and
sat on the commode. She dabbed toilet paper onto the cut in her
scalp. The tissue came back stained with fresh blood. She stuffed a
wad of toilet paper back into the wound and held tight pressure as
she finished urinating. Gingerly, she lifted the tissue. Just flecks of
blood. She had stanched the bleeding. She stood at the sink and
looked in the mirror.

"God, you're a mess," Kate said to her reflection of swollen
red eyes and tangled hair glistening with sweat and blood. She took a
cold wet washcloth to her face and then leaned forward to view the
cut. It lay too far back from her forehead to see. At least it was

behind her hairline. She dabbed the wound with the washcloth, which returned a few drops of bright red blood. Again, she applied pressure.

"No time for stitches." Kate stood in front of the mirror and held constant pressure on the wound for a full three minutes by her watch. Lifting the washcloth, she saw no sign of fresh blood. She dabbed again with a tissue.

Bleeding stopped.

She yearned for a quick shower to wash her hair but feared restarting the bleeding. A glance at her watch reminded her she should be on the quarterdeck. Kate cleaned herself up as best she could, then donned fresh underwear and a royal blue tee-shirt before climbing into her flight suit.

* * *

Fifteen minutes later, Kate emerged from the ship's duty van at the Changi Main Gate. A burly master-at-arms and a female hospital corpsman alighted behind her. Before departing her stateroom, Kate had stuffed more toilet tissue into the scalp wound, combed her hair over the white paper, and tied it into a tight bun. She then pulled on her blue Navy ball cap and tipped the brim forward to hide the injury.

She had pressed cold compresses on her eyes and applied just enough makeup to dull the redness. Hopefully, that had transformed her into a proper senior officer in the United States Navy, about to conduct difficult official business with a host nation.

The two ensigns and Colonel Davis sat handcuffed under a spotlight outside the guard shack, guarded by two RSN sentries. The women wept. Davis slept with his head on Ensign Zipp's shoulder. Kate wondered whether the vomit stain on the front of the ensign's white jacket had come from Zipp or the colonel, or both.

245

Pulling her ball cap tighter onto her head to assure it hid her injury from view, Kate approached the scowling RSN officer who appeared to be in charge of the scene. She returned the officer's crisp salute. "Good morning," she said. "I'm Captain Katherine Mahoney, the senior US Navy officer present. I am here to take custody of these officers."

The officer spoke in terse, accented English. "They assaulted an RSN sentry."

"I understand, sir." Clueless about the rank of the RSN officer, Kate did not know how to address him. "The United States Navy takes full responsibility. I suggest that because of the hour, you allow us to take custody of these suspects. We will confine them in USS *Shenandoah*. We can sort out the details later, in the light of day." She tried to sound friendly yet authoritative, wondering under the surface if gender mattered in this host nation's military. "We will, of course, make them fully available to RSN authority when required."

The man in charge remained silent, seeming to weigh the value of turning his prisoners over to the US Navy now against the complex procedure of incarcerating them in the RSN brig, a process that would keep him and his watch team on the base well past their usual quitting time.

"Very well, ma'am," he said. "We will file a full report via the chain of command."

"Please do. I assure you that the US Navy will treat this incident with all due seriousness. I most sincerely apologize on behalf of my commander."

"Thank you, ma'am." The sentry moved aside to allow Kate to approach his captives. She slid a finger under her cap to touch her wound and felt the sticky wetness of fresh blood.

Make this quick.

Kate kneeled on one knee in front of Colonel Davis and lifted his chin off Ensign Zipp's chest. "Good morning, Colonel." She put on her most sarcastic tone. "I trust you enjoyed your hotel room tonight."

Davis stirred. "Whad de fugh?"

He was barely conscious. Alarmed, Kate motioned to the corpsman. "Get him to Medical asap."

The corpsman and master-at-arms lifted the colonel to his feet and dragged him to the duty van. Kate turned to the two ensigns, both of whom managed to stand on their own power. She glared at them. "You ladies are so screwed."

Ensign Robinson offered her a sloppy salute. "You got that right, ma'am, and it was mighty fine." Defiant, she stared into Kate's face. "How'd you do? You get any tonight?"

Fuming, Kate turned to the duty driver. "Get them out of here. To medical. They need to sleep it off where someone can watch them. Don't wait for me. I'll walk back to the ship."

The driver and master-at-arms escorted the women into the van next to Preston. The vehicle sped off. Kate turned back to the RSN officer, offering her business card before signing the turnover documents. "I apologize again on behalf of the United States Navy." She scowled and shook her head. "The United States Marine Corps, too."

The RSN officer saluted her. She returned the salute, did an abrupt about-face, and strode down the pier toward the ship. Fresh blood trickled through her hair under the ball cap. She reached into her flight suit pocket and found some tissue to wipe the ooze.

Kate held pressure on the wound as she relished the long, solitary walk back to *Shenandoah.*

247

- Mike Krentz -

248

Chapter Sixty

April 19, 2012, Koampo, People's Democratic Republic of Korea: Korean People's Army Base

Tucked within an inlet along the southwest coast of North Korea, the Korean People's Army (KPA) military base in Koampo, South Hwanghae Province, became the scene of heightened yet clandestine activity. Each night under cover of darkness, a new platoon of combat-ready marines arrived, increasing the base population to invasion strength. The KPA troops joked that they could smell their southern enemy's stench on Baengnyeong Do, the closest of the ROK-controlled Northwest Islands, sixty kilometers away.

As troops arrived by land and air, the Korean People's Navy (KPN) moved to Koampo seventy *Kongbang*-class hovercraft landing vessels that the Americans called LCPAs, for landing craft, personnel, air-cushioned. Each air-cushioned gun vehicle could accommodate a platoon of fifty-five soldiers in full battle dress. At fifty kilometers per hour over shallow water or even tidal mudflats, the hovercraft could reach Baengnyeong Do in less than sixty minutes. As a flotilla, the seventy vessels would support an island invasion force of some two thousand North Korean marines.

The invasion plan counted on tactical surprise. First, heavy artillery fire would incapacitate the northwest island defenders. Then the agile assault force would launch from Koampo to overrun Baengnyeong Do before the ROKs knew what hit them. With a forward operating base at Baengnyeong Do, the KPA could then launch successive invasions of the other Northwest Islands, seizing strategic initiatives and forward operating presence from which to launch further provocations or attacks on the South Korean mainland.

* * *

In late 2010, following an unprovoked North Korean attack on Yeonpyeong Island ("Y-P Do"), the Republic of Korea military had established a Northwest Island Defense Command to bolster security on the five Northwest Islands. Concerned that the recent *Bucheon* incident might presage more aggressive KPA provocations, the ROK prepared to defend the strategic islands—with support from its US ally. In response, elite US Marine Corps weapons companies and special forces units joined the twelve thousand ROK marines ready to defend the islands.

Koampo and Baengnyeong Do thus became a microcosm of the infamous demilitarized zone that meandered through the midsection of the Korean Peninsula. Two bands of brothers, whose ancestors once fought together to defeat a more powerful enemy, now girded loins to spill each other's blood over a dividing line born not from geography, but from the political consequences of history.

Each side claimed righteousness and assumed confidence of ultimate victory.

Chapter Sixty-One

April 19, 2012, Singapore: Changi Naval Base: USS *Shenandoah*

Kate stood bleary-eyed along with Rusty and Alexis in front of Leo LeBlanc's desk. After the *Shenandoah* corpsman had sutured her laceration, Kate managed an hour's nap before she had to shower and dress for the day. The local anesthetic injection had worn off, giving way to a burning sensation in her scalp.

Leo glowered at Kate while he spoke into the telephone. "Yes, sir. Fully understood, sir. We will deal with all three officers. Admiral Lewis deeply regrets this unfortunate incident. As you know, sir, he had to depart Singapore yesterday or he would apologize in person. He will call Admiral Chow himself later in the day. Yes, sir, we will keep you informed, sir. Thank you, sir."

He slammed the phone receiver into its cradle. "Damn it, Kate! Why didn't you control those little brats? You knew they were trouble. You should have brought them back to the ship with you."

Kate stood her ground. "Sir, when I last saw them at Raffles, they were in the company of a respected senior officer of the United States Marine Corps. I trusted they were in capable hands."

Leo's eyes narrowed. "Don't wise off with me. As the senior female officer on staff, this travesty is on you, not on Colonel Davis. Certainly not on me. You should have exerted stronger leadership."

Kate flushed, but kept her voice under control. "Should I have exerted leadership on Colonel Davis as well?"

COS glared back at her. "You are on very thin ice here, missy. Mind your tongue."

Kate stared at the wall over his head and replied in an exaggerated monotone. "Aye, aye, sir."

"You get to help with damage control. Put on dress whites and meet me on the quarterdeck in twenty minutes. We have to kowtow in person to Admiral Chow."

"Aye, aye, sir." She turned to leave, but his voice stopped her.

"I haven't dismissed you yet, Captain Mahoney." He glowered at her over tented fingers. "You still owe me a revised plan for the Korea situation, on my desk today. I trust you've had enough of a fling in Singapore that you won't need to leave the ship today."

Kate turned back to face him. "The plan is almost done. I'll have it for you shortly after we return from RSN headquarters." Kate moved closer to Leo's desk. "I consulted the N7 early this morning. His only comment was 'Whad de fugh?'."

Leo jumped out of his chair and leaned forward on knotted fists, his livid face less than a foot from Kate's. "We will deal with your smart mouth and insubordination later, Mahoney. First, we have to untangle the mess you made with the Sings. Now get out of here and get ready."

Kate snapped to attention. "Aye, aye, sir."

She followed Alexis and Rusty as they hurried from the room. In the passageway, Alexis turned to Kate. "Why did you provoke him? Do you want to make things more difficult?"

Kate glared at her. "I'll take no more crap from that man. I've had it with his disrespect."

Alexis scowled. "Please be careful. I can help only so much legally if you dig yourself into a hole."

Kate stared her down. "I can take care of myself, Judge. You, of all people, should know that."

Chapter Sixty-Two

April 19, 2012, Singapore: Changi Naval Base: USS *Shenandoah*

A polished official black sedan pulled up to the *Shenandoah* brow. COS and Kate alighted, their dress white uniforms damp and crumpled from the heat and humidity. By protocol, Kate hung back and stood at attention as the Seventh Fleet Chief of Staff ascended the brow to the quarterdeck. Six bells sounded, and the 1MC blared.

"Staff, Seventh Fleet, returning."

Once Leo was officially bonged aboard, Kate ascended the brow. When she entered the ship, he was waiting for her in the ceremonial passageway. "My office. Fifteen minutes." It was the first time he'd spoken to her since they departed the ship an hour earlier.

"Aye, sir."

Walking back to her stateroom, Kate noted the fleet surgeon's open door. She paused for a moment, then leaned in. Doc sat at his computer as usual. He looked up and smiled when he saw her.

"Doc, I have to change clothes and get back to COS's office, but could I ask you something?"

"Sure."

"My alarm startled me this morning, and I hit my head on the reading light. I got a cut just here." She leaned over to show him. "The corpsman in medical sewed it up, but I still feel oozing. Would you look at it?"

Doc took a flashlight from his desk drawer. "Sit here in my chair where I can get a good view."

As they transferred positions, he said, "Why didn't you call me when it happened?"

"It was the middle of the night. I didn't want to bother you."

He raised his eyebrows.

She shrugged. "I had to rush to the main gate to take care of an incident."

"So I heard."

"I guess everyone has by now."

Holding the flashlight in his teeth, Doc used both hands to spread her hair and expose the sutured laceration. "It looks fine. The corpsman did a neat job. The ooze is normal. It's not bleeding. You can wash your hair today."

"Good to know, Doc, since I already did."

"To be honest," he said, "you could spit into a scalp wound and it would heal. The blood supply is that robust."

"Yuk." Kate grimaced as she stood up. "Thanks, Doc."

She hesitated at the door.

Doc responded to the clue. "Anything else?" When she didn't answer, he continued. "I hear you and COS had to apologize to the RSN admiral. How'd that go?"

"Rough. COS holds me responsible for what happened last night. No matter what I do, things get worse. Like you can't recover an airplane caught in a death spiral."

"You know how to recover that airplane."

"Let go of the controls. Pulling harder on the stick tightens the spiral. Most airplanes will correct themselves if allowed."

"Maybe you should just let go. Control what you can and let the rest do whatever. You know what happens if you try to over control an airplane. Life is no different." He sat back in his chair and regarded her with kind, patient eyes.

"I have responsibilities."

"You do, but at the end of the day, it's a job. An important job, national security and all, but it's not your whole life. Never let your job define who you are."

She thought of Patrick and then remembered a flash from the prior night's dream. "Sure, Doc." She backed toward the door. "I have to go. COS is waiting for me."

Doc gave her a knowing look. "You can always come back. Door's usually open."

"Thanks, Doc." She rushed off to her stateroom, feeling all at once choked by the dress white uniform.

* * *

Back in her comfortable flight suit, Kate stood in front of Leo LeBlanc's desk while he held an encrypted phone to his ear. He still wore dress whites. Kate's gaze wandered to the large video monitor on the bulkhead. CNN showed a continuous loop of Kim Jong Un ranting. The streaming banner below the images caught Kate's attention.

PRC: "No one listening to us."

Kate furrowed her brow, pressed her lips together. *What are the Chinese saying now?*

COS spoke into the mouthpiece. "Aye, aye, sir. Solid copy. We will. Thank you, sir."

He hung up the phone and smirked at Kate. "Well, Captain, we'll have to put our misbehaving ensigns on hold for a bit. That was the boss. On direction from the White House via SecDef, PACOM directs a complete stand down of any operations in the West Sea."

Kate was stunned. "But—"

COS raised his hand to interrupt. "National command authorities, Captain. We don't argue. We execute. We knew from the git-go that Hawaii and DC would not let us drive our big guns into the middle of a minor skirmish."

"If we back down now, we concede future advantage to the North Koreans."

Leo dismissed her protest with a wave of his hand, as if shooing an annoying fly. "So far as the US is concerned, this was an isolated event between two errant vessels not acting on the authorities of their respective governments. Absent any credible signs of North Korean build-up, which we have not seen, the United States will not escalate it into an international crisis." Leo leaned back in his chair, hands behind his head. "That's the end, Kate. Now be a good girl and order those ships to stand down. Then treat yourself to a good time on our last day in Singapore." He smirked again. "Just be sure you return to the ship before curfew."

Kate's ears felt on fire. She struggled to keep her voice under control. "Sir, you know about the Exocets still being in the launchers on the *Bucheon*, don't you?"

"So?"

"Then you also know that *Bucheon* could not have sunk the

258

North Korean ship."

Leo blew out a breath and crossed his arms. "I don't know what happened in the West Sea. I do know that by direction from higher authority, it's not our affair."

Kate threw up her arms in exasperation. "How can you say that? If we don't know what happened, then we owe it to higher authority to figure it out so they can make informed decisions."

He shrugged. "So figure it out if that's what you want to do. Fine by me if you and the N2 choose to spend your liberty time chasing imaginary dragons." He grinned. "*After* you carry out the lawful orders given to you."

Kate calmed herself. Whether intended, Leo had just given her and Eric permission to continue investigating. "Aye, sir."

"Thank you for your cooperation, Captain. After you execute that order, you can write up those two ensigns for admiral's mast."

Kate frowned. "Aye, sir." She started to leave the room, but then turned back. "Did you want me to write up Colonel Davis too, sir?"

Leo fumed. "I'll take care of the colonel, Captain. You just concern yourself with those two little sluts."

Kate didn't move. "Sir, Colonel Davis, as the senior officer in that small group, had the prime responsibility and culpability. If we hold the ensigns accountable but not him, we condone a double standard. Respectfully, sir, I can't support that."

Leo's mouth dropped open. "What are you saying to me?"

"You and I both have a responsibility to the admiral in this matter. We must hold all three officers accountable. We risk the appearance that the colonel gets different treatment because he's a senior officer." She paused for emphasis. "And male."

"Different indeed, and justifiably so. Colonel Davis has a

259

stellar record. He is highly respected not only in the US Navy and Marine Corps, but among our allies. He's earned the right not to suffer public humiliation, not to have his career scuttled for one misjudgment."

Kate stood still. She opened her mouth to speak. Leo raised his hand. "That will be all, Captain."

She could not make her feet move. She should retreat, but a deep internal force pushed her. "COS, I know the colonel's record and I understand the esteem in which he's held. I realize the investment the US Navy and Marine Corps have in his career. But last night was not an isolated misjudgment. If we really respect him, we must confront his behavior."

Leo came out of his chair again. She raised her hand to stop him. "Hear me out. I've been down that road. I know what happens if we don't intervene."

He sat back and frowned. "What?"

"My father was an alcoholic. It ruined his career and broke his family. He had a bright future, but he died a tragic, disgraceful death. If only someone had intervened—" She caught her breath. "Colonel Davis deserves the chance for a better outcome."

Leo looked at her without emotion. "Why women shouldn't be senior officers. Bleeding hearts can't lead in this Navy."

"Call me whatever you want. But if you really care about Colonel Davis, make him get help—before it's too late."

COS cocked his head to the side and blinked. After a silent moment, he nodded. "Okay, Kate. I'll make him see the doc. But we'll still do the legal stuff separately. He's earned that much."

Kate felt limp, drained. "Thank you, sir." She turned and left the room.

Walking down the passageway, she passed the fleet

surgeon's office and saw Doc through the open door. She paused for a second and then entered his field of view. "Doc, can I talk to you again, please?"

He beckoned her into the room.

Chapter Sixty-Three

April 19, 2012, Singapore: Changi Naval Base: USS *Shenandoah*

Later that afternoon, Preston and Leo sat on the couch in Leo's office. Neither smiled.

Leo sighed. "You really dicked the dog on this one, Pres. What the hell were you thinking?"

Preston shrugged. "I needed to let off steam. One thing led to another, and it got out of hand."

Leo forced a laugh. "You and I go back a few years. We earned our stripes in combat, and we've had some terrific times on liberty. But the Navy and Marine Corps team we knew has changed. Touchy-feely now. We can't do crap. We damned sure can't expect top cover if we screw up. You're lucky the media didn't get hold of it, or we'd all be toast."

Preston frowned. "What will the boss do?"

"You know Darnell Lewis. He will come down on you hard, first out of principle—you know how he feels about officers and dignity. Second, because you've left him no choice. He almost had to come back here to kowtow to Admiral Chow. I did it for him, which was damned unpleasant, thank you."

Leo leaned in, speaking in a confidential tone. "This is Singapore, Pres. They take little things seriously here. Can't chew gum or spit on the sidewalk without risking a fine. You don't touch a woman in public here. Then you do the drunken gyrene act. I told Chow that we'd give you the Navy equivalent of caning. Otherwise, you and those two harlots would be up against a different wall."

"I owe you for that, Leo."

"No shit, shipmate. But frankly—and I mean this—the United States Navy owes you, too. You've pulled our butts out of the deep fry enough times. It's our turn to save your hide." He lowered his voice. "You have to trust me and do exactly what I tell you."

"Not seeing another choice here, Leo. What do I have to do?"

"Talk to the doc."

Preston's eyes narrowed. "The doc? About what?"

"You know, Pres."

Preston's fists knotted. "Say it, Leo."

"Alcohol. Alcohol and you."

Like a cornered tiger, Preston turned on Leo. "Alcohol? That's why you called me in here? You want me to see the doc about alcohol?" He crossed his arms and legs. "You can't be serious."

"Serious as a funeral. Yours, if you don't do what I say."

"You call yourself my friend, Leo? You go drinking with me on liberty, how many times? Now you tell *me* to see the doc about alcohol?" He pointed at Leo. "Why don't you go see the doc?"

"I didn't break curfew. I didn't have two drunk young women with me, and I sure as hell didn't cause a ruckus with the Sings."

Preston looked Leo in the eye. "You're doing this to save face, aren't you?" He glared. "What's this really about?" He unlocked his arms and leaned forward, his voice sinister. "Did Mahoney get to you?"

Leo grimaced and shook his head. "Not about Mahoney and not about saving face. Pres, you may have a problem. We need to find out so you can do something about it."

"I don't have a problem."

"Then you have nothing to lose by seeing the doc."

"And if I don't?"

"I'm giving you a direct order, Colonel. Fail to obey it and there will be consequences. Make this easy for all of us. Just go talk to the doctor." He leaned closer to Preston, spoke in a near-whisper. "I still have your back, Pres."

Preston rose and strode toward the door. "Fine, COS. I'll talk to the doc." He opened the door, stopped, and then turned to confront Leo. "We'll find out if you can still call yourself my friend." He stormed out.

Leo leaned back on the couch, sighed, and closed his eyes. He napped for ten minutes, then got up and went to his desk, picked up the phone, and dialed the Fleet Surgeon.

"Doc, I need to talk to you about Colonel Davis."

Chapter Sixty-Four

April 19, 2012, San Francisco, CA

Since Patrick was still on spring break after his mother left to rejoin her ship, he convinced Aunt Colleen to let him start his community service sooner than planned. The Thursday morning drive up the peninsula from San Bruno took less time than expected. They arrived fifteen minutes early at Homer House, near the corner of Haight Street and Masonic Avenue in San Francisco. Aunt Colleen waited in the car while Patrick approached the two-story building. Tentative, he stopped at the door and waved her away.

Once her car turned the corner, Patrick entered through the front door into a tiny reception area. Homer House occupied the ground floor of a townhouse. A side staircase led to what looked like a second-story apartment. A cheerful college-aged youth greeted Patrick, asked him to wait, and disappeared into the back. Minutes later, the youth returned, followed by a middle-aged woman.

The woman shook Patrick's hand. "Welcome to Homer House, Patrick. I'm Mrs. Fleming, the lead counselor." She handed him a clipboard and a pen. "A few forms to fill out. The most important is the time sheet. That's the one we will send back to the court to validate your hours. If you don't fill that in each time you're here, you won't get credit. Then you'll have to put in more hours than you need."

Patrick sat in the single chair in the reception area and went to work on the first form. "When you're finished with those," Mrs. Fleming said, "I'll show you around and introduce you to some of the junior counselors."

Fifteen minutes later, Patrick followed Mrs. Fleming into a narrow hall. In rooms on either side, he spotted children, appearing to be between the ages of eight to twelve, playing games or working on crafts. Youths ranging in age from fourteen to eighteen helped them. A couple of young adults, who appeared to be college age, circulated among the rooms.

Mrs. Fleming led him into the last room off the hallway. "We'll start you out here with the younger children." A half-dozen children in the six- to seven-year-old range sat at two tables. At one table, they worked simple jigsaw puzzles. At the other, they played with Lego blocks. Mrs. Fleming got the attention of a young adult hovering over the Lego table. "Mr. Owen, this is Patrick Walker. He's come to help us out on weekends for a few months."

Mr. Owen was a large, bespectacled young man with shaggy hair and an unkempt beard, but his face seemed gentle. He held a beefy hand out to Patrick. "Hi, Patrick. Owen Carver. Welcome."

"I'll let you finish Patrick's orientation," Mrs. Fleming said to Owen. She left the room.

With a smile, Owen sized up Patrick. "I'm guessing court-ordered public service. What'd you do, steal a car?"

Patrick's jaw dropped. He stuttered his response. "Yes. How

266

did you know?"

"More than a good guess. Happens a lot." He clapped Patrick on the back. "You may find this duty more rewarding than you think. Let me introduce you to the kids. This is Joel. That's Mark. Jolene. Pete. Casey and Jen. Hey, guys. Say hello to Patrick. He's going to help us out for a while."

The children barely looked up as they grunted hellos.

Several hours passed. Patrick played with three boys building a Lego airplane. He had not done Lego himself for many years, and it surprised him to enjoy it. The boys warmed to his suggestions. For the first time in his life, someone looked up to him.

I might like this counseling bit.

"Patrick." Mrs. Fleming stood in the doorway and beckoned to him. "Mr. Homer wants to meet you now."

She led Patrick to an office at the back of the hallway. A thin, long-haired, bearded man in his mid-forties stood at his desk and reached out a hand. "Hi, Patrick. I'm Homer. Welcome to Homer House."

As he shook the proffered hand, Patrick sensed that the man's touch lingered longer than a typical handshake. Homer's face seemed a little tense, yet he flashed a winning smile. His shoulder-length sandy brown hair and trimmed beard reminded Patrick of the painting of Jesus Christ on display in Aunt Colleen's hallway. Passionate blue eyes peeked out from beneath Mr. Homer's hairline. The eyes intrigued Patrick. He didn't know why.

"Thank you, sir," Patrick said in his best Catholic-schooled military child voice.

Homer sat behind the desk, gesturing Patrick to a casual chair just opposite. He picked up the forms that Patrick had filled out, held them in front of his face, and studied them. Then he showed just his eyes and forehead over the top of the papers. "Auto theft?"

"Yes, sir. I took my aunt's car."

"Why?"

Under the gaze of those piercing eyes, Patrick felt like he was on trial again. He looked at his feet. "Girls."

"Of course." Homer chuckled. "Behind any man in trouble, you will find a woman who drove him to it."

Patrick didn't know what to say.

Mr. Homer became serious. "Joy ride?"

"Yes, sir."

"You said girls, plural?"

Patrick nodded. "Yes, sir."

"What's with the 'sir' thing? You got a dad in the army or something?"

"My mom's in the Navy."

"Well, save the formality for her. We go by first names here." Another chuckle. "Again, girls, plural. How many?"

"Just two."

"*Just* two? Most men have trouble handling one."

"I wouldn't know about that, s—" Patrick stopped himself from saying "sir."

Homer leaned forward over the desk. "Starting a long and illustrious career of skirt-chasing, Patrick?"

The question made Patrick uncomfortable, and he didn't know how to answer. He shrugged. Homer sat back in a more casual pose. "The important thing is that you got caught before you hurt yourself or those girls. Do you realize how lucky you were?"

"Yes, sir." Patrick looked down. "I mean Homer."

"Good," Homer said. "For you to help these kids here, you have to be strong enough to admit when you've messed up.

Otherwise, they mark you as a phony. Then you have no credibility, and you're no use to us. I know you're not here permanently, but I'll tell you the same thing I tell my full-time counselors. Here you can make a difference in the life of a kid who might otherwise grow up to a miserable existence. If you alter that course—even a little—for one of these youngsters, you've done something exceptional. Understand?"

"Yes, si—"

"Good. We'll talk more during your time with us." Homer rose and reached across the desk, again offering his hand. Patrick stood and shook the man's hand. Homer gave him a look that Patrick did not comprehend, but it made him feel warm inside. Embarrassed, he darted from the room.

Later, as he helped young Josh put the roof on the Lego palace they had built, Mrs. Fleming tapped him on the shoulder. "Time to wrap it up, Patrick. Your aunt is here for you." Patrick had not expected the six hours to pass so quickly. He bid a reluctant goodbye to the boys and left the room. On his way out, he looked around for Mr. Homer, but he was nowhere to be seen.

As Aunt Colleen maneuvered the car into traffic, she asked, "How did it go?"

"Good."

"Did you meet Mr. Homer?"

"Yeah."

She glanced sideways at him. "Tell me about him."

"He seems nice."

"Did you learn anything about the home?"

"I can change a kid's life."

Chapter Sixty-Five

April 19, 2012, Singapore: Changi Naval Base: USS *Shenandoah*

His eyes glued to the computer screen, Eric Mikleson's fingers groped in vain for another French fry. The styrofoam plate was empty. Eric understood the importance of a decent meal break, but he often found his work too demanding. A to-go container brought from the flag mess to the MIC allowed him to eat and work at the same time. Tonight, unanswered questions in his pursuit to reconstruct the Korean conflagration vexed him. Not only did he save time by eating at his desk, but he could not stomach inane mess chatter about sports and movies until he figured out the puzzle that might hold the key to resolving the tensions in Korea.

He reviewed the PowerPoint slide showing the timeline and confluence of events during that fatal morning in the West Sea.

- The ships approach each other near the NLL.
- The KPN ship accelerates and crosses the line, heading

directly at *Bucheon*.

- *Bucheon* fires cannon.

- The KPN ship returns a cannon shot just before taking a hit amidships.

- *Bucheon* suffers a similar hit.

- Both ships break in two and sink.

What am I missing?

Eric recalculated the reported speeds of the two vessels against their tracks gathered from electronic intelligence and their presumed locations when they fired on each other. The root cause still eluded him.

"Fire, fire, boom, boom. Fire, fire, boom, boom. Wait a minute . . ."

He squinted at the screen, then minimized the PowerPoint and brought up the Seventh Fleet staff contact directory. He found the number for "Fires" buried in the convoluted N3 directorate listing and dialed it as fast as his fingers could move.

"Lieutenant Commander Nathan, it's Captain Mikleson, the N2. I need your expertise on Korean weapons systems. It's urgent. No, I'll come to you."

Eric locked down his computer and hurried out of the MIC.

* * *

Returning to the MIC twenty minutes later, Eric ran through the images and timeline once more to confirm the conclusion that the weapons expert had validated. Based on the reconnaissance photos and open-source videos of the damage to both ships, neither Korean vessel could deliver the fatal blow to the other within the time and range on the timeline, much less to cause each vessel to break apart amidships. The weapons expert opined that "bubble-jet effect" explained the damage scenarios. A mine or torpedo detonating in the water beneath a ship would create a rising bubble. At the surface, a column of water would strike the ship's hull like a high-energy jet, causing severe damage.

Both ships broke in two from underwater explosions.

Two ships encountering mines almost simultaneously ten miles apart? No way. Someone else was there! Who are you? Where were you? Did you fire Chinese torpedoes? Why?

Eric reviewed the P-3's videos showing the initial damage to the ROK ship. Then he opened another video window and replayed file footage of the *Cheonan* salvage from the spring of 2010. The extent and nature of the damage to the two ships appeared nearly identical. The ROK investigation of that incident had concluded— with the concurrence of everyone but the DPRK and its PRC and Russian allies—that the *Cheonan* damage resulted from bubble-jet effect from a North Korean torpedo, most likely fired from a *Yono-c*lass "midget" submarine.

He tapped his forehead and then dialed another number. "I need to review all the imagery of North Korean and PRC sub bases around the West Sea for the several days before and after the *Bucheon* incident. Right away, please."

Somebody else has bloody hands.

Chapter Sixty-Six

April 19, 2012, Singapore: Changi Naval Base: USS *Shenandoah*

In the *Shenandoah* operations office, Kate huddled with her staff members not ashore on liberty. She had chosen not to recall anyone to the ship. No sense spoiling everyone's day. With dismay, she realized that most of her minions had still been on the ship when she called the meeting. They were a dedicated, hard-working lot, mostly mid-level officers of the O-4 (lieutenant commander) and O-5 (commander) ranks. Many aspired to career progression similar to Kate's. For them, hard work and personal sacrifice paved the avenue to future success.

"You guys should get out more," Kate often told them. "Quality of life matters as much as professional growth."

Like I'm a role model.

Kate told her officers about the direction from higher authority to cancel the show of force. She looked around the room, making eye contact with each of them. "We're not going to do that, not exactly.

"Whoever started this sequence of events in the West Sea may not be done. Those who don't live in this AOR may be content to stand down, or they may honestly believe the whole affair was an isolated event. We live here and know better. We can't afford to wait and hope that nothing else happens. We anticipate, and we seize the initiative."

Kate knew the fleet could not mobilize fast enough from home or distant ports to thwart another event in the West Sea. In high school, she excelled in soccer, and she later sparked the intramural team at the College of William and Mary. She preferred scoring goals over playing defense.

In this game, she needed to play both ends of the field.

"Don't look at where the ball is now," she said. "Run to where the ball will be next. Get there first and kick the ball into the enemy's face. That's what we need to do."

As they worked through the various operational scenarios and possible responses, a daring plan emerged. Kate expected that higher authority would not take the risk that the plan required.

"We'll have to sell this plan to the admiral. Like everything else in life, operational planning is all about marketing, right?" Her smile faded as the blank stares from her audience suggested they did not know Nick Juel, the N4.

Kate hoped that Vice Admiral Lewis would support her, but even if not, she would take whatever risk the plan required. Even if her career went down in flames, she could hold her head high. She would rather Patrick know his mother as a courageous warrior than a weak woman.

Patrick!

"What time is it in California?"

She looked to the bulkhead, where an LED clock showed multiple time zones. It was 1830 in Singapore, 0330 in the morning on the US west coast—on a school night. She had missed the time window to call or text him.

She had also missed dinner in the flag mess.

Kate left her team to work out the last details and to prepare PowerPoint slides for the response plan. Returning to her stateroom computer, she opened her email and scanned an inbox full of new messages. None from Patrick. Then she logged onto the internet and pulled up her Facebook page. No message from Patrick. He had made several posts to his page, obscure references to video games and pop culture that she did not understand. He had addressed nothing to her.

She sent him a private message.

> **Scarlett:** Sorry, Dude. Natives got restless last night, and I had to subdue them. Bummer. I didn't get to call you. Never left the ship today. I will try again before we leave this port. Hope you're doing okay. I'm eager to hear about Homer House.

Kate paused, wondering what else to write. Her mind could not make the leap from hectic war-planning to the suburban milieu of San Bruno. Patrick seemed more than a world away. Drained, she logged off the internet. Running her fingers through her hair, she felt the early scab around the site of the scalp laceration. Had it been just last night—or, more accurately, this morning—that it happened? She was about to go to the flag mess in search of some fruit or leftover bread when her phone rang.

Alexis' voice. "Last call for alcohol. COS is off the ship for the evening, and we get underway tomorrow. Liberty call till midnight for officers. I'm rounding up the usual suspects and

276

heading to Clark Quay for dinner and drinks. You come."

Exhausted and jet-lagged, Kate started to beg off. Then she decided she could use a drink or two, and a decent dinner. She had to stay up late anyway, to contact Patrick when it was morning in San Bruno.

"Okay."

"Brow in thirty. Be there."

"I said okay, Alex."

When Kate hung up the phone, her spirits lifted. What had the doc said? Your job is not your life?

Here's lookin' at you, Doc.

Chapter Sixty-Seven

April 19, 2012, Singapore: Changi Naval Base: USS *Shenandoah*

Preston Davis had not been in hack since an inebriated sortie with a colonel's daughter when he was a footloose second lieutenant back at Quantico. He didn't remember many details of the event that led to his involuntary grounding.

Flagrante delicto?

No, that had been a different escapade. He chuckled at the memory.

Alcohol had played a major role. He remembered the sober aftermath with crystal clarity. Turned out the young lady had a history of targeting Marine junior officers, so Preston's chain of command had given him a break. He had spent the rest of that tour in hack but suffered no permanent blot on his record.

Stretched out on the rack in his stateroom, he tried to reconstruct what had happened the previous night. He had gloated at Kate Mahoney's transparent discomfort when she saw him board the cab with the two ensigns. He somewhat recalled drinking and dancing with the women at various hot spots in Clarke Quay. He remembered talking about a Fullerton Hotel room he had never booked.

Preston rubbed his forehead, willing his memory to return. No, he did not mention a hotel to the ensigns. He wasn't that loaded. Earlier in the evening, he had lied about it to Kate Mahoney—a deliberate pass at her, retaliation for her besting him in the dining out repartee. He knew she'd take umbrage at the suggestion of naughtiness—at least with him.

Why did I do that?

In the cold confines of his stateroom, Preston recognized the prank for what it had been: a deliberate, mean attempt to discomfort her. A warning perhaps? He was attracted to Kate. Did he drive her away on purpose? For her own good?

If his tactless balcony remark didn't repulse her, the degrading scene at the Changi gate must have. How did he and the ensigns find a taxi and return to Changi? He remembered spewing some gibberish about using his rank and position to excuse them all from being out after curfew. He had passed out as soon as the car moved. His next memory was Kate's stunning green eyes piercing him with such contempt and anger, and him being too smashed to say the word, "Sorry." Although he felt it. He felt it more now.

I'm an idiot.

Preston looked at his watch. 1820. He was hungry, but he wanted to avoid the flag mess. Earlier, at 1100, before the mess opened, he had sneaked in to grab a quick peanut butter and jelly sandwich and return to his room without crossing paths with others. Now evening, most staff officers would dine in town on their last night in port. Preston would wait until after dinner hours before stealing back to scrounge another sandwich for his evening meal. He did not want to run into anyone who remained on the ship for duty or for an urgent workload, least of all the N3.

Need a drink.

From the head, Preston recovered the hidden Listerine bottle. Sitting on his rack, he unscrewed the bottle's lid. The whiskey aroma wafted immediate comfort. The bottle was down to a third full. He had drunk more than planned by this stage of the deployment. He could smuggle more whiskey on board in Thailand—if he was out of hack by then. Otherwise, he would have to ration what he had until the ship returned to Japan.

Preston stared at the bottle. How might last night have been different if—? He would never know, because he never had a sober encounter with an appealing woman. Why should he give a damn about Kate Mahoney, anyway? Especially after last night? Why should he care about any woman? Women caused problems.

He took a long quaff from the bottle and sat on his rack until the warmth spread through his body. Then he went back into the head and carefully replaced the bottle in its hiding spot.

He brushed his teeth, gargled with real Listerine, and took a hot shower. Emerging from the bathroom dry, mellow, and fortified by the whiskey, he put on clean BDUs. Then he stole into the flag mess. He scanned the room, thinking that he might see Kate. He saw no one. Heaving a disappointed sigh, he helped himself to bread and peanut butter and hurried back to his stateroom.

Chapter Sixty-Eight

April 19, 2012, Singapore: Clark Quay

Singapore night life came alive as darkness descended to cool the city. Kate, Alexis, Rusty, Doc, and Nick enjoyed Mongolian barbecue at an outdoor table in Clarke Quay. Nick waxed on about the merits of the Navy's Thrift Savings Plan, as if he had invented it. Dispirited, Kate's thoughts wandered to her own issues. Looking at her watch, she reminded herself to call Patrick at 2200, when it would be 0700 in San Bruno. She could catch him before he left for school.

She had not seen Preston Davis since that early morning encounter at the Changi gate. He must be staying in town or maintaining a low profile somewhere on the ship.

Why would I think about him?

After dinner, the group found a nearby Irish pub with Wi-Fi. Kate sat off by herself, opened her laptop, and Skyped Patrick. She caught him as he got ready for school. The pub noise invading her headset made conversation difficult.

"Hey, Patrick, it's Mom."

"Yeah, Mom. I know."

"How are you?"

"Okay."

"Just okay?"

"I'm fine."

"Sorry I didn't get to you call you sooner. It's been crazy since I got back."

"Sure, Mom."

Kate waited for him to talk, but heard only silence. She would have to take the lead in this conversation.

"Did you start at Homer House?"

"Yep."

"How is it?"

"Okay."

"Details, Patrick."

"What do you want to know?"

"Tell me about Mr. Homer?"

"He's okay."

Kate decided she could wait in silence for as long as it took him to talk. It didn't take long.

"He seems kind of cool."

"How so?"

"He likes kids. And he likes video games."

"Really? How old would you think he is?"

"I don't know. Middle-aged, I guess. Like you."

Ouch! "You think it will work out?"

"Why wouldn't it?"

Kate raised her voice, loud enough to elicit looks from patrons at a nearby table. "I ask because I care, Patrick. I'm sorry I had to come back here so soon. I'd rather be with you. I'd rather see this through with you." Just then, a group of Australians at an adjoining booth erupted in laughter. Kate wondered if Patrick had heard them.

"No big deal, Mom." He had heard. She pulled the microphone closer to her mouth and tried to shield it with her hand.

"It is a big deal. I've never had a son who stole a car and had to do community service."

Silence filled her earphones. Then a monotone. "I said I'm sorry. Don't beat me up about it."

Kate bit her lip. "That's not what I meant. You don't need to apologize again."

Neither spoke. Kate didn't know how to pick up the conversation. Despite the pub din, she heard the clack of computer keys. Patrick was multi-tasking, probably texting with friends or playing an online game while talking to her.

At least he's not at a bar.

Frustrated, she was about to say goodbye when Patrick broke the silence.

"Mom?"

"What?"

"Thanks."

"For what?"

"For coming home when you did."

"Of course. I came home for you. That was never in doubt." She thought about their last conversation in San Bruno. "I'm still thinking about our future, too."

"I gotta get to school."

"Okay, son." Kate fought back a tear. "Be good. I love you."

"Yeah, sure." He disconnected.

Fighting another tear, Kate logged off, shut down her laptop, crammed it back into its case, and rejoined the group. Nick was pontificating about some obscure movie that only he would have seen. Kate flagged a waiter and ordered a double Glenmorangie, neat. When it arrived, she took a large sip, painted on a smile, and pretended to listen to Nick. Her thoughts were in California.

"Did you talk to your son?" Doc's voice in her ear brought Kate back to the pub. Nick had ceased holding court, and the group engaged in one-on-one conversations.

She looked into her glass. "I did."

"How did it go?"

Kate's eyes flashed. "He's fourteen years old and thousands of miles away from his divorced mother. How do you think it went, Doc?"

Taken aback, Doc raised his hands in a conciliatory gesture. "Sorry, Kate. Didn't mean to hit a sore spot." He shrugged. "Teenagers can be difficult."

Kate turned away from Doc toward Nick. "Nick, who's going to win the next Tour de France?"

Warming to the spotlight, Nick launched into a soliloquy on another favorite personal topic.

Kate did not speak to Doc for the rest of the evening.

* * *

Returning to Changi two hours later, the group disembarked the liberty bus for the short walk to *Shenandoah*. Nick set a brisk pace, but Kate felt no desire to rush back to the brow. She felt mellow, and the pier seemed to sway.

Maybe didn't need that last double scotch.

Doc dropped back and matched pace alongside of her.

"About your son—"

284

"Please, Doc. I don't want to talk about it."

He ignored her reluctance. "Don't beat yourself up over a normal rite of passage."

She slowed her pace, looked at him. "Sometimes he acts like his father."

Doc stopped walking. "You've never mentioned Patrick's father. Is he still in the picture? Is he involved in his son's life?"

Kate's voice rose, almost threatening. "No, Doc. He's not. My choice."

Doc pulled back. "Sorry," he said. "I seem to be pushing your buttons tonight."

"Patrick is better off now." She resumed her stride toward the ship.

Doc hurried along beside her. "I understand. If you ever want to talk about it, you know where I live."

"Don't hold your breath, Doc." She picked up her pace, leaving Doc in trail.

Chapter Sixty-Nine

April 20, 2012, Singapore Strait: USS *Shenandoah*

"Underway. Shift colors."

With lines cast off to RSN personnel on the pier, *Shenandoah* moved away from Singapore. Sailors hauled down the flag on the aft jackstaff as another national ensign was run up the mast. After the order from higher authority to disengage from the Korean situation, the flagship returned to its original peacetime schedule. *Shenandoah* headed toward the South China Sea for transit to the Seventh Fleet staff's next scheduled engagement in Thailand.

In the fleet surgeon's stateroom/office, Colonel Preston Davis sat with his arms and legs crossed, his eyes gazing into the overhead. Doc closed the door, eased into his chair, and faced the colonel. The combat-seasoned Marine seized the offensive.

"Ever spend time with the marines, Doc?" The US Navy staff corps served Marines and Navy personnel. The Marine Corps paid the cost of using naval officers and enlisted sailors in certain specialties rather than establishing and maintaining its own medical, legal, or religious ministry capabilities. Most marines cherished their Navy medics.

Doc considered Preston for a second before he replied. "Al Taqaddum. Early days of OIF."

Preston whistled through his teeth. "You must have seen some hard shit there."

Doc sighed. "Many casualties, every day. Intense."

"How did you deal with that? It had to affect you."

Doc shook his head. "We're here to talk about you, Colonel."

"Sure," Preston said. "Just establishing therapeutic rapport, Doc. You and I both know actual combat." He gestured toward the door. "Most of these squids haven't been near it."

"Tell me about your relationship with alcohol, Colonel."

Preston scoffed. "Straight to the point, eh? No chit-chat allowed?"

Doc did not respond.

"Fine, Doc. I have no relationship with booze. It's a substance. I can take it or leave it."

"When did you take your first drink?"

Preston forced a smile. "Legal or otherwise?"

"First time alcohol passed your lips."

"Long time ago, Doc. I was a kid, maybe twelve, fourteen."

"Where did you get it?"

"Snitched it from my stepdad's whiskey stash. Had to take a little at a time. I'd get the belt if the old man caught me."

"How often?"

"He whipped me several times a week. Sometimes for no reason except to remind me he could."

Doc had meant how often his patient had snuck liquor, but he stayed with the colonel's train of thought. "Really?"

"Yeah. He resented my little sister and me because we weren't his. He favored the two kids he and mom had together. Treated Heather and me like white trash."

Doc nodded, but remained silent. Preston swayed in his seat, becoming agitated. "My father was a war hero. After he died in combat, my mom married a jerk who couldn't fight his way out of a bubble. My dad could have destroyed that wimp with one hand."

"You retaliated for abuse by stealing your stepfather's liquor?"

"No, Doc. I took it to ease the pain." Preston's face tightened, flushed. "When I got strong enough, I took the asshole down so hard I thought I might kill him. I wanted to kill him." Preston squeezed his hands together in a choking motion. "I had him on the ground with my hands on his throat. The pussy hissed for mercy until mom made me stop." Preston grinned. "He never bothered Heather or me again."

They sat in silence for a full minute while Preston composed himself.

"Did you get drunk as a teenager?"

"C'mon, Doc. Who didn't?"

"How often?"

"I couldn't tell you. That was a while ago." Preston's eyes darted about the room. His hands opened and closed in a rhythm.

"More than once?" Doc asked. Preston shrugged but said nothing. Doc pressed. "Did you ever get in trouble for drinking as a teenager?"

Preston massaged his chin. "Time or two, maybe. Again, who didn't in those days?"

"Any one episode stands out in your memory?"

"Senior prom. We got a hotel room—most kids did in those

days—six of us, three guys and three girls. We got smashed. The other two guys and one girl passed out. So I did the other two girls at once." He grinned. "One of them squealed like a cat. Someone called the manager."

Preston's voice trailed off. He gazed into the middle space.

"How did that turn out for you?"

Preston leaned toward Doc. "That was the night I took down the old man. He came at me with his belt, and I coldcocked him. Drunk out of my mind, and I still almost killed the bastard."

He sighed. "It went down hard for me. Mom made me apologize to the girls and their parents." Preston stared at the deck, working his fists. "I never saw those girls again."

Doc let the silence drift over them for a minute before resuming the conversation. He figured only half of what he'd just heard was true.

"Let's talk about the present," Doc said. "I'm going to ask you some questions, and I want you to give me the first answers that come to mind."

Preston nodded. The tension left his face and his fists unclenched. He leaned forward on the couch, legs spread, feet on the floor, hands crossing his thighs—a combat-ready Marine.

Doc looked him in the eye. "Have you ever felt you should cut back on your drinking?"

Preston's brow furrowed. "Who hasn't? Maybe when I was younger and didn't know my limits. I'm smarter now. I can handle it."

"That's a 'yes'?"

Preston crossed his arms. "Yes. I sometimes felt like I needed to cut back, if that's what you want to hear."

Doc turned stern. "I'm not interested in what you think I

want to hear. I'm interested in your honest answers to my questions."

"I gave you my honest answer." Preston crossed his legs.

"Next question. Has anyone ever suggested that you cut back or quit drinking?"

Preston leaned back and smirked. "Over-controlling ex-wives included?"

"Anyone."

"It's come up sometimes."

"How did you feel about that?"

"None of their damned business." Preston looked askance at Doc and then spoke in a measured voice. "I can control it. I don't need other people telling me how to manage myself."

Doc tilted his head. "Did you control it the night of the dining out?"

Preston jerked forward, fists clenched. "I let off steam. We had a potential crisis on our hands with the Koreans sinking each other's ships. And this new N3 with her delusions of grandeur, like Princess Frigging Leia wanting to attack the Death Star."

Doc did not respond.

Preston sighed, leaned back, and spoke in a more subdued voice. "We had a lot of tension. I cut loose at the dining out. Maybe I overdid it, but who hasn't once in a while? You've been shit-faced a time or two yourself on liberty, right, Doc?"

Doc kept his expression bland. "Did you feel guilty the next day?"

Preston became agitated. "Damn it, Doc. I'm being honest with you and you attack me. Of course, I felt guilty. It got out of control and caused an unfortunate event for the command." He crossed his arms and legs. "I'll handle it."

"Just a few more questions, then we'll take a break. Not specific to the dining out, have you ever felt guilty about your drinking?"

"I already answered that. Yes. Sometimes. I handle it."

Doc sat stone-faced. "Do you ever take a drink in the morning? To steady your nerves, ease a hangover, that sort of thing?"

Preston bolted off the couch. He charged at Doc, but then he veered to the door. "This is bullshit. We're done here. I have work to do."

Preston stormed out of the room.

Doc did not stop him. "That went well," he said to the empty doorway.

Chapter Seventy

April 20, 2012, Singapore Strait: USS *Shenandoah*

When he returned to his room, Preston went straight to the hiding spot in the bathroom to retrieve his precious bottle. His hands trembled as he unscrewed the cap and raised the mouth to his lips.

He stopped. A wave of primal shame washed over him. He looked at himself in the mirror—not the face of a future brigadier general. Haggard, frightened, and desperate. The face of a derelict, a junkie. He despised that face.

If Kate could see me now.

Preston squeezed his eyes shut. Motionless for a few minutes, he stared at the bottle. On impulse, he turned and emptied it into the toilet. When he reached for the flush handle, his hand stopped, clenched into a fist, and sprang back to strike his forehead. Beads of sweat appeared across his brow.

What the hell am I doing?

He plunged the empty bottle into the toilet bowl to refill it. He exhaled in relief as air bubbled out of the bottle, replaced by his cherished liquid—more blond than brown, diluted by toilet water. Preston chugged a full swig. Brackish liquid burned his taste buds. He gagged and spat it out.

Preston had forgotten that flush water, unlike the potable water the ship made for sinks and showers, contained pure salt water taken from the sea. He looked at the bottle held tightly in his right hand. Both hands trembled. His entire body sweated. The remnants of pale amber liquid in the bottle beckoned him. He sniffed the opening and blotted from his mind the overpowering saline smell in favor of the faint whiskey aroma. However diluted, pain relief was in that bottle.

Take your medicine, Pres.

Preston squeezed his eyes shut, rolled his head back, and poured the entire remaining contents of the bottle straight into his gullet. When done, he clenched his mouth shut, forcing himself not to gag on the brine, but to swallow the entire volume. His reward was a mere semblance of the familiar burn in his stomach, and a taunting hint of warmth spreading in his body.

Seconds later, a powerful torrent of nausea took him to his knees and doubled him over the toilet bowl. He vomited multiple times, losing not only the precious liquid but his entire stomach contents. When he thought he was done, he sat on the bathroom floor and wiped the sweat from his brow. Then he retched again, several times.

Finally spent, Preston leaned against the bulkhead. Wiping his mouth and brow, he remembered that when he or his sister complained of stomach aches, their mother gave them salt water to make them throw up. He closed his eyes against the aftershocks of nausea.

"You just cast your last dice, Colonel," he said aloud.

293

"Crapped out."

Still on the deck, wedged between the toilet and sink in the small head, he reached the flush handle and held it down, allowing torrents of salt water to flush the vomit from the bowl. Struggling to his feet, he ran several liters of hot water and a generous amount of liquid soap through the faux Listerine bottle and tossed it into the trash. Then he rinsed out his mouth and brushed his teeth. Finally, he used wet toilet tissue to mop up the mess on the deck. The head still reeked of vomit, but no one else would be around to smell it.

Back in the bedroom, Preston shut off all the lights and opened his rack. He cast off his stained BDU blouse, bent to unlace his boots, and pulled them off. Then he dropped his trousers to the floor. In his skivvies, he climbed onto the rack and rolled into a fetal position, shaking and moaning. Some kind of hell lay before him over the next hours or days, but he embraced it with all his might.

I've known worse in my life.

After a while, he fell asleep. His last thought was a vision of Kate Mahoney in her flight suit.

Chapter Seventy-One

April 20, 2012, South China Sea: USS *Shenandoah*

Leo LeBlanc stared at the computer screen and rubbed his eyes. He had just plowed through over a hundred "high side" classified e-mails. Most droned on with excess verbiage about routine occurrences or mundane issues affecting the Seventh Fleet. As chief of staff, he must maintain current knowledge of the entire gamut, no matter how trivial. His position required constant anticipation and planning to respond to any question or challenge from the admiral. Intellectual and naturally curious, Darnell Lewis had an insatiable thirst for information, as well as a keen knack for career survival by anticipating the demands of his superiors. Leo considered the day good if he could respond, off the top of his head without notes, to just over half of N00's queries.

He switched to his "low side" unclassified computer. Although the Seventh Fleet's principal operational work flowed through the firewalled and encrypted "high side," the staff officers also maintained vigilance to the unclassified network.

295

Leo opened an email inbox stuffed with a hundred-plus unread messages. He would not read all of them. He scanned down the list, considered the sender and subject, and deleted any items that he deemed unimportant.

One item caught his eye:

Leskowitz CDR CO–Our Conversation

Leo opened the email.

CAPT LeBlanc:

Nice talking to you the other day, sir. WRT the individual we discussed, I've learned that a former subordinate recently checked into your N5. You should look up Lieutenant Commander Toby Windish.

VR/Less

Leo smiled, not only at the information, but the way Les crafted the text with no mention of Kate by name or inference. Leskowitz understood the importance of disciplined email.

Leo had met Lieutenant Commander Windish at a "hail and farewell" reception shortly after the aviator checked embarked *Shenandoah* in Guam during the first port visit of the current underway period. Leo hadn't seen much of the young man since, other than in the flag mess during meal hours. Windish seemed to spend most of his time in the Future Plans (N5) Directorate one deck below the flag spaces.

Leo thought the lieutenant commander unusually shy for a young naval aviator, especially an F/A-18 pilot. He showed none of his community's uber-alpha-male swagger. Embarrassment over a career gone sour? A nonflying staff assignment to a fleet headquarters after an aviation squadron department head tour stuck the officer in terminal grade with no chance for promotion to the next higher rank. In the cutthroat pyramid promotion system, failure to promote would mean an undesired premature exit from the Navy. Assignment to a nonflying, career-ending billet often followed a failure to meet an important milestone, usually an unfavorable officer fitness report.

Did Mahoney destroy this officer's career? Why?

For whatever reason, the naval aviation community had farmed Windish out to Seventh Fleet, expecting him to fade away. His case would not be hopeless. He could restore his aviation career from within the N5 shop, but he must crawl out of that deep career hole first.

If Mahoney had been responsible for his derailment, Windish might want to collaborate with an influential senior officer who could help him salvage his career.

Time to do some mentoring.

* * *

Ten minutes later, a tentative knock on Leo's door interrupted his email scan.

"Come," he called.

The door opened. A wary officer stood in the doorway. About six feet tall and muscular, he wore a green flight suit, with a name tag embroidered with gold pilot's wings and a call sign, *Windy.*

"You wanted to see me, sir?"

Leo beckoned him into the room. The young officer entered and stood at attention in front of Leo's desk.

"At ease, Commander," Leo said.

"Aye, sir." Windish assumed a stiff parade rest position. He gazed forward, focusing on the bulkhead over Leo's head.

"Relax, son," Leo said. "You are not in trouble. I just want to chat. Please, stand at ease."

"Aye, sir." The aviator relaxed his body, although his eyes continued to focus on the bulkhead.

Leo planted a warm smile on his face. "You recently joined the staff, right?"

"Aye, sir."

Leo made a show of perusing the officer's record in front of him. "F/A-18 pilot, previous assignment with VFA-213? Department head tour?"

"Aye, sir. You are correct about my prior assignment, sir."

Leo thought he must sound like a cross-examining lawyer. He tried to soften his voice. "Do you find your current job satisfying after flying combat jets?"

"It is different, sir. Captain Piekarski is a patient teacher. I'm learning a lot about planning, sir."

Leo leaned back in his chair, trying to appear non-threatening. "Commander, this conversation is casual and off the record. You don't need to punctuate every phrase with 'sir.'"

"Yes, sir."

Leo gave up trying to put the nervous officer at ease. "Is this an unusual assignment after an aviation department head tour? Don't pilots move on to other flying billets, as opposed to a nonflying position on a fleet staff?"

For the first time, the lieutenant commander shifted his gaze to Leo. He spoke in a measured voice. "Fortunate to be here, sir."

"Does assignment as an action officer in the N5 enhance your career?"

Windish cocked his head, shuffled his feet. "I figure any job will help my career if I do my best at it. Sir."

Leo sighed. Subtlety was getting him nowhere. "How was your last tour with VFA-213? Any issues?"

"None to speak of, sir."

Leo leaned forward. He dropped all pretenses and got straight to his issue. "Your CO was Captain Mahoney, right? She would have been Commander Mahoney at the time."

A curious expression crossed the young man's face. "Yes, sir."

"What was she like?"

"Sir?"

"As a leader, what was she like?"

Windish pondered before answering. "She was hard, sir. Expected a lot from her officers. Didn't take nonsense from anyone."

"You had problems with her?"

A puzzled wrinkle furrowed his brow. "No, sir. I didn't say that. She was hard, but she was fair. She demanded no more from us than from herself. We became better aviators and officers from her leadership. I haven't known a better pilot or war fighter. I'd follow her into battle any time."

Drat!

Leo sighed. "She was hard on you."

"Not especially on me. Not on any one officer, sir."

Leo looked at the aviator, puzzled. Why would he protect the woman who had derailed his career? What did she have on the young man to exact such loyalty?

Need a different approach. Gloves all the way off.

"Did Commander Mahoney give you a fair fitness report?"

Windish did not hesitate. "Yes, sir. It was very fair."

"Really?" Leo almost exploded. "Isn't it true that you're in this job because Mahoney—Commander Mahoney—gave you a noncompetitive FITREP? That she took you out of the running for advancement in the tactical jet community?"

Windish did not reply. Sensing a crack in the man's shield, Leo pushed his assault. "Do you not feel the least bit betrayed? From your record, you deserved a better evaluation. If she has something on you, you can tell me. We can make it right. She's not allowed to torpedo your career without basis. You have recourse if she blackballed you."

The young officer remained quiet for what seemed like minutes, then he spoke in his measured voice. "No, sir. It was not like that, not like that at all." He looked straight at Leo. "Sir, you said this was off the record. Nothing I say will affect my current position?"

"You have my word," Leo said. "Whatever you say stays in this room between us."

Windish glanced up at the ceiling, and then looked back at Leo. "Truth is, sir, I'm afraid to fly."

Leo stiffened. "Really?"

"Yes, sir. I was one of the better pilots in the training squadron, but flying around the ship for real, I always flew scared. It got worse every time I made an approach to the deck. Halfway through my department head tour, I decided to get out of the Navy when my assignment was done. I couldn't handle the fear."

Windish shuffled his feet. A line of sweat appeared on his brow. "Then I had a near-mishap landing at night in foul weather. Almost hit the ramp. The deck was pitching badly, and I froze on the controls. I figured I'd bought it and prayed I didn't kill anyone else. I was so scared, I shit my pants. Don't know how I made it down.

"I didn't take time to clean myself up. Went straight to Commander Mahoney and asked her to send me home. I sure as hell never wanted to fly again. I figured I was no use to the Navy.

"Commander Mahoney talked me down. She said I was an

outstanding officer, and that didn't change with fear of flying. She encouraged me to stay Navy, to try other options. 'Not everyone needs to fly,' she said, 'even if you're a good stick.' She took me off the flight schedule and offered to help me make a career move, to get me into a community where both the Navy and I would benefit. She said I didn't have to go on being afraid."

The young man relaxed his posture, wiped his brow. "I love the strategic aspects of warfare, the big picture stuff. Commander Mahoney suggested I might want to be a planner instead of a fighter. She got me the orders to N5 here so I could try it out."

Leo's shoulders slumped. "I see."

"I want to do planning, sir. I put in a request for a lateral transfer of communities. Captain Mahoney offered to write me a letter of support. So did the N5." Windish took a deep breath. "I was going to ask you and the admiral for letters too, sir."

"I see," Leo said again. He stared at his desk and then looked up at the former aviator. "Very well, Commander. Thanks for your honesty. I wish you the best on that initiative."

"Thank you, sir." Windish shuffled in place, uncertain what to do next. "Will there be anything else, sir?"

"That will be all, Commander. Thanks for stopping by. We can both forget this conversation happened. I will endorse your transfer request when it gets to my desk, and I will recommend to the admiral that he write you a strong letter of support."

Windish beamed. "Aye, aye, sir. Thank you, sir." He came to attention, then left the room.

When the door closed, Leo slumped back in his chair.
Mahoney the savior. Crap.

- Mike Krentz -

Chapter Seventy-Two

April 20, 2012, South China Sea: USS *Shenandoah*

Later that afternoon, Leo's discussion with the fleet surgeon became heated as they sat facing each other from the comfortable chairs in the chief of staff's office.

"Preston Davis is alcohol dependent," Doc Cushing said.

Leo sat at his desk, arms crossed, face taut. "Can't buy that, Doc. Given his record, he's far from impaired."

"He's built an elaborate wall of self-defense over years. Like many high-performing alcoholics, he can feed his addiction and still do his job. Self-preservation is a powerful force in an addict."

"Proves my point, Doc. Maybe he drinks too much at times, but he does his job. Stellar performer."

Doc Cushing shook his head. "One day, his defenses will fail, and he'll crash hard, with catastrophic personal and professional consequences. That almost happened in Singapore. We can prevent further damage—if we intervene now."

Leo scoffed. "You got all that from a ten-minute interview,

Doc?"

Doc tapped his fingertips together, forming a steeple. "The medical science of substance abuse is straightforward. I've gained a lot of unfortunate experience over my Navy career. The diagnosis is easy. Colonel Davis' case comes right out of the textbook. He hit the bull's-eyes on every diagnostic indicator. I know pathology when I see it. A huge lung tumor on an x-ray would not be more obvious."

He paused, expectant. Leo did not react.

"I'm equally certain," Doc continued, "that without intervention he will deteriorate, as sure as death must follow untreated lung cancer."

Leo raised his hand in a "stop" gesture. "Spare me the dramatics, Doc. I get it. What intervention did you have in mind?"

"Given the depth and lifelong duration of his illness, he needs intense inpatient treatment."

Leo's jaw dropped.

The fleet surgeon looked Leo in the eye. "He needs it now, COS."

Leo blasted back. "That's not going to happen, Doc. Did you not notice that we're underway again?"

"Send him off the ship for inpatient treatment, sir. We can do that from Thailand. I can have it all arranged by the time we get there."

Leo laughed. "You're killing me, Doc. We command the forward deployed naval force here. We engage in real-world ops, not the least of which is this Korean squabble. Colonel Davis is our subject-matter expert on all things Korean. We don't just pluck him off the ship in Thailand and send him to touchy-feely land. We have operational responsibilities."

Doc's eyes hardened. "We have a responsibility to this

Marine, and to the naval forces he serves."

"Give me another solution, Doc. Can't you treat him on the ship?"

"I don't have the tools here. He needs intense inpatient treatment to break down the walls of denial. He must choose to never drink again. The Navy has one of the best programs in the world for treating alcoholism, but it's ashore, not afloat."

Leo leaned back in his chair, his hands folded behind his head. He gazed up at the overhead for an instant and then rocked his chair forward so that he glared into Doc's face. "You'll have to wait until we get back to Japan. I can't afford to let him go now. Treat him as best you can here." He opened his hands, as if in conciliation. "I'll keep him in hack for port visits the rest of the deployment: no drinking and no liberty. Once we get back to Yoko, he's all yours."

Doc folded his arms. "That won't work, sir. He needs to start treatment right away, while the Changi episode is still fresh. Plus, I suspect he has alcohol on the ship, so putting him in hack won't keep him from drinking."

Leo rose out of his chair and pointed his finger at the doctor's chest. "That's a serious accusation. How do you know? You smell alcohol on him? I never have."

Doc didn't back away. "Professional intuition. I've been around the problem long enough to sense it."

Leo threw up his hands. "I will not hang a man's professional reputation out to dry on your intuition, Doctor." He resumed his seat. "Let me be crystal clear. I wasn't asking. I am telling you what will happen. Preston Davis stays on this ship until we return to Japan. You do whatever else you want, but he does not depart before we get back home. You got that, Doc?"

Doc bit his lip. "Aye, aye, sir." In a voice stiff with mock formality, he asked, "Will that be all, sir?"

Leo held his hand to his forehead. "I need Motrin."

"I'll have some sent up to you from *Shenandoah* medical." Doc came to attention. "Thank you, sir."

"Yeah, right," said Leo, as the fleet surgeon departed his office.

Leo waited until the door closed and then punched numbers into his phone pad.

"Pres, come see me. Now."

Chapter Seventy-Three

April 20, 2012, South China Sea: USS *Shenandoah*

The setting sun over the horizon cast orange sparkles on the deep blue water, like dying embers of a recent raging furnace. As a steady breeze cooled the air, sailors and officers emerged from below decks to engage in physical fitness. The breeze, the gentle waves, and the stunning beauty of diminishing sunlight against broken cloud layers made the main deck far more appealing for exercise than the run-down treadmills and other machines in the gray-walled windowless confines of the stuffy ship's gym five decks below.

Dressed out in prescribed Navy workout gear—dark blue ill-fitting shorts with a garish marigold top—Kate and Alexis jogged around the deck with a dozen shipmates of different genders, sizes, physiques, and ability. Eight circuits would equal one mile.

"Getting a little crowded up here," Kate said. "PFA approaching."

The semiannual Navy physical fitness assessment (PFA)

would occur soon after the ship returned to home port. Fear of failure and its negative career consequences motivated a bevy of overfilled human fuel tanks to hit the deck hard, hoping that a few weeks of concerted workouts and food deprivation would overcome the effects of six months' inactivity and overindulgence. Fleshy sailors of both genders pounded the deck in dire earnest.

Like most of their shipmates, Kate and Alexis maintained year-round physical fitness. They ran the deck as a normal routine and a pleasant escape from the stress of their jobs. As they completed the twentieth lap, Alexis pulled up by the ship's superstructure.

"That's enough for me."

Kate almost sighed in relief. She had difficulty keeping up with her younger, fitter colleague. She gladly slowed to match Alexis' cooldown pace. A brisk walking lap around the deck returned them to the superstructure, where they retrieved pre-staged water bottles.

Sipping and walking toward the bow, they came upon an open deck area where Preston Davis, clad in olive green shorts and tee-shirt, led a group of like-clad marines through a vigorous set of jumping jacks. Preston's back was to the two Navy women, so he did not notice them.

When his charges completed their jumping jacks, Preston commanded them in a powerful voice. "On your butts, marines!" Everyone dropped to the deck, including Preston, whose voice resonated with authority. "Four count sit-ups. We'll do thirty. Ready. Begin. Ah, one, two, three, four. Ah, one, two, three, four. Ah, one . . ."

Kate watched Preston count the cadence and perform the sit-ups with a proficiency that showed he could outmatch marines half his age in any fitness challenge, anytime. How could he be the same besotted glob of protoplasm she had encountered at the Changi gate? With a surreptitious closer look, she noted with some satisfaction that the colonel did not appear as robust or energetic as usual. His ruddy complexion had turned sallow.

Alexis noted Kate's interest. "The guy's an enigma."

Kate took a swig from her water bottle and started walking. "Yeah. He can be a consummate jerk."

Alexis looked at her askance. They walked in silence to the ship's bow, where Kate stopped and faced Alexis. "Cone of silence?"

"Sure," Alexis said. They moved under the CWIS gun mount where they could talk in privacy.

"Colonel Davis came on to me at the dining out, on the balcony after dinner." Kate looked at Alexis to gauge her reaction, but the lawyer's face remained inscrutable.

"Not a crime. You're both single. Same rank. Neither reports to the other in the chain of command."

"I don't need a legal opinion, your JAG-ness. I know the fraternization rules."

Alexis wrinkled her brow. "What, then?"

"When it happened, I didn't know what to do. I just left."

"Best option under the circumstances."

"Plenty of men have hit on me. I don't walk away. I take them down. Almost crushed a guy's balls once after he rubbed himself on me."

Alexis gave her a sly smile. "Not a hunky Marine, I'll bet."

"Excuse me?"

"Maybe you found the colonel tempting."

"He was drunk."

"After the dining out, who wasn't?"

"Earlier we had clashed in front of the admiral. Before the dining out, the colonel seldom spoke to me. Then he tried to embarrass us both in the toasts, and afterward he comes on to me? What game is that?"

Alexis regarded Kate with a sisterly smile. "Wouldn't be the first time adversaries became bedfellows."

"No way!" The sudden anger in her voice surprised Kate.

Alexis stepped away from her. The two stared out to sea in silence.

"Sorry," Kate said. "I'm not angry at you."

"I know. But you are angry, and confused."

"Can't figure that man out. He carries that alpha male mystique, and the self-confidence thing." Kate paused, struck by her own words. "Geez, I sound like an infatuated coed."

"Are you?"

"Am I what?"

"Infatuated."

Kate tossed her head toward the superstructure where they had seen Preston and his marines. "That man has monstrous issues." She wiped her brow. "I've trod the Marine road once in my life. Why would I ever go there again?"

"You're a warrior. You like danger, and conquest."

"I didn't take this job for romance. Besides, after Singapore, the colonel has other mountains to climb."

Alexis raised a hand. "I can't talk about that."

"Of course not." The pair walked away from the bow.

Kate fell silent, perplexed by the conversation.

Why did I bring that up?

As they neared the superstructure, Preston and his marines

310

ran toward them, doing their own laps around the deck. As the group passed the two women, Preston diverted his gaze off the ship to the sea and the clouds.

Kate didn't notice his eye avoidance. She was looking down at the deck.

Chapter Seventy-Four

April 20, 2012, South China Sea: USS *Shenandoah*

That evening, Kate sat on Doc's couch without speaking.

Should have eaten more than salad at dinner.

Hunger gnawed at her insides. She hoped it was just hunger. Kate stared into the middle distance, the ajar door tempting her to bolt. She had come to Doc of her own accord, so she could leave anytime. Something more powerful than hunger held her to the couch. She needed to talk about Patrick and her thoughts of leaving the Navy, but her mind wandered.

Preston hovered on the edge of her consciousness.

Doc's voice broke into the vacuum. "A former mentor of mine often said, 'If you leave the Navy after thirty years, or only a day, I will shake your hand and thank you for your service.' No shame if you retire at twenty, especially to be with your son at a critical time in his life."

Kate fidgeted and tugged on the sleeve of her flight suit. "I know that, Doc."

The doorway beckoned.

"I sense something else troubling you," Doc said.

Kate pinched her lips together, and then let out a sigh. "I don't feel like such a wonderful mother."

Doc chewed on the frame of his glasses. "What would Patrick say?"

"Right now, he hates me. Thinks I'm the worst mother in the world."

"Has he said so?"

"Not in words." She blinked. "He barely talks to me."

"That makes him different from other teenagers, how?"

Kate snorted through flared nostrils. "I don't give a rip about another teenager. Patrick's the one I have, and I'm losing him. I'm out here doing this." She waved her arms. "And he's back there taking up with some internet God-knows-what, and bonding with some guy who 'likes kids and video games,' which I don't."

"You don't . . ." Doc paused in mid-sentence, causing Kate to cock her head. ". . . like kids?"

"I meant video games."

"But you said—"

Kate glared at him. Her chest heaved, and her fists tied in knots. "I have to go now." She rose and left the room, pulling the door closed behind her as she scurried into the passageway.

* * *

Back in her own room, Kate pulled a sports drink out of the refrigerator and chugged it. She paced the deck between her rack and desk. Her stomach ached, and she felt lightheaded. Her palms sweat, and her hands trembled. She hyperventilated.

Should I go down to Medical?

She turned off the overhead lights and laid down on her rack instead.

Fragile woman can't handle the stress of real-world operations. That's what COS will say if I go to Medical. No way. It's just a panic attack. Settle the hell down.

Panic attacks plagued her as a younger woman, so long ago that she'd almost forgotten about them. Now she closed her eyes, willing herself back into control.

I like children. I wanted Patrick. I want to be his mother.

"Patrick . . ." Hyperventilating again. She slowed her breathing and closed her eyes to ponder what to do about her son. Foggy images danced behind her eyelids. Patrick, Dodger, Leo, Darnell Lewis, Luke, Preston—all traipsed in and out of her consciousness.

I wanted Patrick.

Kate got out of the rack, stripped, and took a hot shower. Afterwards, she dressed in shorts and tee shirt and returned to her rack, feeling mellow and relaxed. She opened a novel. Her thoughts wandered off the pages, back to her conversation with Doc and how it threw her into a panic attack.

I wanted Patrick.

She put down the book, lay back, closed her eyes and allowed her mind to drift into a fugue where she half-remembered, half dreamed the scenario that had shaped the rest of her life.

Chapter Seventy-Five

1997, Meridian, MS: US Naval Air Station

As he did most nights, Luke had gone out after work with his Marine buddies. Alone in their small townhouse in officers' housing at the Meridian Naval Air Station, Kate went to bed early. She wanted to be asleep when Luke got home.

Sometime later, as Kate lay awake staring at the ceiling, the stench of stale alcohol assailed her nostrils. As if by reflex, she turned onto her side, away from the bedroom door. Luke's lumbering entrance followed. Clumsy footsteps approached the bed.

Stay still. Be asleep.

A flicker of hope teased her when the footsteps moved away from the bed. The bathroom door opened but did not shut. Luke urinated in the dark. The staccato tinkle splashed toilet water, then it spattered on the tile floor.

In the morning, Kate would have to wipe dried urine off the seat and floor before she could use the toilet; not for the first time. She considered bolting out of bed and leaving the house while Luke relieved himself.

Where can I go? What will I do?

His footsteps left the bathroom. Kate sensed his ruttish gaze as he undressed and dropped his clothes on the floor. She closed her eyes and concentrated on holding dead still.

Please be drunk enough to pass out.

Then he was on top of her, hips grinding, hardness poking her at random. His coarse whisper in her ear. "Hey, baby."

The reek of stagnant alcohol nearly made her retch. She buried her face in the pillow, teeth clamped on the solitary diamond in her wedding ring.

"C'mon, baby. I know you're awake. You want this."

Every molecule in her body wanted to fight him. The bite scar on her left shoulder reminded her she would not prevail.

"You want this, Kate."

She made her body limp and let it happen.

* * *

Kate awakened in a cold sweat. Her body trembled, and she hyperventilated.

Where am I?

Her frantic eyes searched in the surrounding darkness.

Father Felix's voice came over the 1MC to recite the evening prayer. Kate was alone in the safety of her *Shenandoah* stateroom.

How many times had she suffered the memory of that night, the humiliating assault that had conceived Patrick?

Chapter Seventy-Six

April 19, San Bruno, CA

"Homework before gaming, Patrick."

Patrick called down the stairs. "Sure thing, Aunt Colleen." He opened the online game. Fuchou had not yet signed on, so Patrick browsed Facebook while he waited for his friend. He did not want to play without his ally.

His iPhone rang. When he picked it up, the caller ID read *Homer House.*

"Hi, Patrick." Mr. Homer's voice. "Sorry to call you at home, but we're in a bit of jam here. One of our other youths on court-ordered service got himself arrested again. He's out for good. Jail time." His voice sounded kind. "Could you possibly come in a couple of weekdays after school, for the next week or two? You'd get your mandatory hours done sooner."

Patrick grimaced. "I don't know. My aunt drives me up from San Bruno on Saturdays, but she works as a nurse during the week."

"We need your help, Patrick. Maybe we can work something

out. If you come up on the BART, one of us could meet you at the station. You won't have to ride the MUNI by yourself. We could drop you back at the BART station when you're ready to go home. We might take you all the way home some evenings."

Patrick's breath quickened. *How cool that would be.* "I have to ask my aunt, but I'd like to do it."

"I can talk to her. If I may say, you impressed us last week. You're a natural at working with these kids. You should stay on after you've finished your court hours."

"I could do that?"

"We always need volunteers, and we'd love to have you. It would be good for you. Nothing more rewarding than helping a kid whose parents don't care about him."

"I'll ask my aunt and let you know," Patrick said. He knew he could manipulate Aunt Colleen into agreeing. Ever since his joyride venture, she'd seemed eager to avoid arguments with him. Plus, he suspected a new love interest in her life. She would probably welcome the opportunity for more alone time.

"I'm pretty sure I can do it," he said.

"See you then," Mr. Homer said.

Patrick switched off his iPhone and returned to the online game.

Fuchou had just signed on.

Patrick's fingers flew over the keyboard.

Fanpan: Guess what I might get to do.

318

Chapter Seventy-Seven

April 20, 2012, South China Sea: USS *Shenandoah*

"Tattoo, tattoo. Lights out in five minutes. Stand by for the evening prayer."

The 1MC announcement disrupted Eric's concentration. Father Felix's amplified voice over the 1MC prayed about fair seas, caring for shipmates, and a successful transit to the next port visit.

Eric concentrated his weary vision on two magnified gray-and-white satellite images displaying the submarine bases along the west coast of North Korea. He had already reviewed a pile of other images of the China coast and other North Korea locations. Now he focused on Pipa Got, a major KPN submarine base on the west coast of North Korea. He compared side-by-side images from different days.

He saw it.

"There you are, you son of a bitch! Got you!"

Father Felix's voice over the 1MC punctuated. "Amen."

Eric punched numbers on his phone.

"Kate? You still up? Can you come down? I got something you want to see. The MIC. Guarantee you will like this."

Chapter Seventy-Eight

April 20, 2012, South China Sea: USS *Shenandoah*

Early the next morning, *Shenandoah* continued north toward its next port visit in Thailand. Kate, Eric, Alexis, and Rusty sat behind Leo in a semicircle, focused on an audio/video transceiver on the chief of staff's desk. The secure video teleconference (VTC) device provided digital encryption of their conversation with Admiral Lewis, who sat in a secure Royal Malaysian Navy conference room in Kuala Lumpur. They could discuss classified information without fear of the prying cyber spies who continuously attacked networks around the Seventh Fleet AOR. The most sophisticated hackers manned computer banks around the clock throughout the People's Republic of China and the Democratic People's Republic of Korea.

As soon as Lewis' face appeared on the screen, Leo got straight to the point. "Admiral, we have a breakthrough in the Korea situation. Captain Mikleson will present the sequence of events leading to the sinking of the two Korean ships."

Eric leaned toward the camera. "Sir, we've analyzed multiple sources to reconstruct what happened that morning. The North Korean ship crossed the Northern Limit Line aggressively. The ROK ship attempted to hail the North Korean ship several times, with no reply."

The Admiral interrupted, impatient as always. "We know that. Who fired first? That's the issue."

Kate intervened. "Admiral, the *Bucheon* did not sink that KPN ship. The salvage team found both her Exocets still in their launchers."

Admiral Lewis' head filled the screen as he leaned forward toward his camera. "Go on."

Eric continued. "The *Bucheon* fired a cannon warning shot, not a missile. The *Sariwon* also fired its cannon, a retaliatory shot. Both ships aimed forward of each other's bows without intent to hit each other. The KPN ship could not have detected an incoming round quickly enough to return fire with any accuracy. Both ships fired, but neither volley hit anything but water."

The admiral's magnified face scrunched up on the monitor. "Quit drawing this out, folks. Who sunk whose ship when, and how do you know?"

Kate nodded at Eric, who looked directly at the video camera and spoke. "Sir, a North Korean *Yono* submarine got underway undetected from Pipa Got a day before the incident. It returned amid all the excitement two days later." He backed away from the camera, chagrined. "We missed her getting underway, sir."

"Not the first time we've missed a sub getting underway, Eric, especially a *Yono*."

"Admiral, the North Korean *Yono* torpedoed its own sister ship, and then launched another torpedo at the *Bucheon*."

322

"Why in the hell would they do that?"

"To make the world believe the ROKs picked a fight," Kate said. "They staged the entire show. The *Sariwon* crew never knew they were on a suicide mission."

"Son of a bitch," said the admiral. "You have data to prove that theory?"

"We do, sir," Eric said. "Including detailed timelines and ELINT tracks, plus a transcript the ROKs provided of their captain telling ROK Fleet that he intended to fire a warning shot."

Kate continued. "Sir, there's more. The salvage team recovered what appear to be remnants of a Chinese-made torpedo near the *Bucheon* sinking."

Lewis scowled. "What do you make of that, Eric?"

"Not sure, sir. We know the PRC sells arms to the DPRK. But the torpedo that sunk the *Cheonan* in 2010 was North Korean, not Chinese."

Leo interjected. "Maybe the North Koreans ran out of stock and had to procure from the PRC."

"Unlikely," Eric said. "They have a huge stockpile. But their inventory is older and marginally effective. The DPRK could have purchased newer stock from the PRC." He wrinkled his brow. "That would be unusual behavior."

Leo said, "How do we know that a Chinese sub wasn't part of the action, too? Maybe the PRC torpedoed one of those ships."

"We can't place any PRC submarine in the area at the time of this event," Eric said. "We've been over the images multiple times. Of course, we can never be one hundred percent certain."

The frown on Leo's brow deepened. "That's not reassuring."

"Admiral," Eric said, "I don't believe we know the complete story. The KPN ship was somebody's sacrificial lamb, and *Bucheon*

323

was someone's target. We assess that the DPRK is the perpetrator. The new kid up north needs to consolidate his power. What better way than to cast the ROK, and us, as aggressors? We believe that, like his father before him, he is capable of any atrocity."

"Whoever is responsible isn't done," Kate said. "We must be ready to respond when the next shot is fired, regardless of who fires it."

Admiral Lewis nodded. "I agree. Resurrect the show of force, but consider it a response force. Do that straight away."

"Sir, we've already worked up a CONOPS," she said. "We've included the JAG's legal analysis, and a suggested public affairs plan from the PAO." Kate felt Leo's eyes boring into her. She hadn't had time to review the plan with him.

Admiral Lewis smiled for the first time. "Very well. I'll call USFK and PacFleet myself." He chuckled. "I will get a VTC with PACOM, just for the pleasure of seeing the four-star's jaw drop. Get the details in place and set up another session this afternoon."

Admiral Lewis looked intently into the camera and scrutinized what he could see of the room. "Chief of Staff, where's the N7?"

Awkward silence filled the room. Surely the admiral knew about the incident at the Changi gate. He would have consented to the low profile, or outright hack, to which Leo had consigned Colonel Davis. Did the boss just hand his N7 a "Get Out of Jail" card?

Leo broke the silence. "Sir, he's engaged in a special project."

"Take him off that and put him on this," Lewis said. "We need his expertise. He must provide full support to the Three and the Two from now until this crisis resolves. Clear?"

Leo grinned. "Aye, aye, sir."

Kate felt her heart in the back of her throat. She dared not wonder why.

Admiral Lewis signed off. The team filed out of the chief of staff's office.

"Mahoney," COS said. "Stay behind and close the door."

When the others had left, Kate wedged the door in its frame but did not quite close it. COS glared at her, red-faced. "Never blindside me with him again, missy."

"Sir, I—"

Crimson-faced, he raised his hand. "You don't talk. You listen and listen well. Do not undermine me with the admiral—ever. You pull that shit again, I will eat you alive."

Kate stared at him, her eyes narrowed.

"Now get your ass out of here," he said.

"Aye, sir." She turned and hurried out.

Chapter Seventy-Nine

April 20, 2012, South China Sea: USS *Shenandoah*

Later that afternoon, the Seventh Fleet staff leadership, this time including Preston Davis, occupied the front row of the Flag Conference Room, conducting another VTC session with Admiral Lewis. Half of the split screen in front of them showed the admiral sitting at a conference table borrowed from the Malaysian Defense Force. The other half cycled through a series of PowerPoint slides the team had produced and pushed electronically, detailing the response plan to further developments in the West Sea. At his end, Lewis could see both the assembled senior staff and the PowerPoint brief.

Eric summarized his data and conclusions regarding the dual sinking in the West Sea.

When he finished speaking, Lewis clapped his hands together. "That should convince even the weak-willed four-stars up our chain of command. I spoke to PacFleet and PACOM. They withheld final approval until they analyze the evidence for themselves." He raised his arms, palms upward like an imam in prayer. Then he looked straight into the video camera.

"What's the plan, Kate?"

Kate glanced at Leo. She had sent him the PowerPoint a half-hour before the teleconference. Had he looked at it? Leo offered a slight nod. Kate led the admiral through her part of the presentation.

"We have some assets now in or near the West Sea that we can move north into attack positions. *Denver* is still supporting the salvage operation. That gives us a flight deck for helo ops. *Stethem* will proceed toward Chinhae. We've asked the ROK Navy for a passing exercise between *Stethem* and *Sejong The Great* in the West Sea as a pretense. To the rest of the world, it will look like a routine encounter between allies, not a rendezvous for tactical ops.

"For undersea warfare, we sent *Michigan* to a port visit in Busan. We can get her into battle on demand. For submarine hunting, we have P-3s on ready alert in Okinawa and I've told *Victorious* to expect imminent orders to the West Sea."

Leo harrumphed.

Kate ignored him and continued her brief. "Admiral, we have the *George Washington* strike group on a twenty-four-hour prepare-to-deploy order, and we've issued a warning order to the *Essex* strike group in Sasebo. They can be underway in less than a week. For additional P-3s, CTF-72 has six ready aircraft and expects two more by week's end."

She turned to Preston Davis, sitting next to her. "Colonel Davis will brief the Marine Corps status."

Preston looked straight into the camera. "A US Marine Corps weapons company recently augmented the ROK garrison on Y-P Do, and another company has joined with ROK marines on P-Y Do. Those are the most vulnerable Northwest Islands. The ROKs have scheduled a live-fire exercise two days from now, which could provoke a North Korean response before we are ready to respond. Defending the islands against an all-out assault presents a hard challenge. Efforts are underway to deter the ROKs from proceeding with the live-fire exercise. I have spoken to the III MEF G3 and also to the USFK J3, both of whom believe the ROK operation will stand down."

Kate resumed the briefing. "We have a solid maritime plan, with concurrence from planners at ROK Fleet and CTF-78, and also USFK. All agree that we can execute the scheme of maneuver that you see on the slide. I spoke to PacFleet N3, who was equivocal as always."

She looked straight at the camera. "We just need your decision, sir."

Admiral Lewis nodded and then addressed Preston. "Any other thoughts, Colonel?"

"Our primary concern remains the PRC," Preston said. "If we compel them to withhold support for North Korea, at least overtly, the new DPRK regime won't risk escalating. This plan sends the proper message to both our potential adversaries. If we could also leak our intelligence information about the *Yono* attack *sub rosa* to the PRC, we might convince them to repudiate the Kim regime."

Admiral Lewis leaned in toward his camera, his face inscrutable. "Chief of Staff?"

"I concur with the N7," Leo said. "I also wonder when the next shoe will drop from the North."

The admiral scanned the faces on his video screen. "Any thoughts on that, people?"

Eric spoke first. "Sir, we don't yet know the DPRK's real purpose in this scenario, what they hope to achieve. They can't be leaning into an all-out war with the South. They would lose."

"I agree," Preston said. "Even if they inflict damage on the ROK in an all-out war, they cannot sustain it, and they cannot win. They need a victory on the political and diplomatic battlefields. With new leadership, and people starving after a long winter, KJU has to paint the ROKs and US as the bad guys. They contrived the West Sea scrap to make the ROKs look like aggressors, as well as to challenge the Northern Limit Line. Look for another provocation, but not an invasion—at least not on the mainland. Northwest Islands might be a different story. In any event, expect them to implicate the ROK/US alliance as the provocateurs."

"Appeasement," said Kate. "They will push until they get appeasement from the world community: handouts, food, money, maybe resuming the six-party talks. They've learned to expect that over the years, just like a spoiled child. They act out till they get what they want." She smiled. "I know how to handle a spoiled child. You don't give them what they want. You give them what they need."

The room went silent for a moment. The admiral spoke. "I agree, Kate. I've had a couple of spoiled kids myself." He chuckled. "Still do." He turned serious. "We must get ahead of these jokers, so if they act out, we're ready to respond swiftly and decisively. I approve your CONOPS, and I'll work to gain support from higher authorities. Preston, I concur with your point about defense of the Northwest Islands. We must get that live fire exercise turned off.

"Folks, you're in the major leagues here. I need you all at the tops of your games, and I need you pulling together as a team. I need vision and imagination. Most of all, I need each of you to perform. For once, don't be afraid to take risks to do what's right. I have your backs, everyone's back. Now get to it."

"Aye, sir," all said in unison.

"That's all," he said. His image disappeared from the screen. The room cleared quickly.

Phase Four: Stabilize

Chapter Eighty

April 21, 2012, South China Sea: USS *Shenandoah*

On the way back to her office, Kate stopped at Doc Cushing's doorway. She leaned in and stared the man down.

"I lost a night of sleep because of you."

Doc turned away from his computer to face her. "What?"

She pointed her finger at him. "You said that I don't want children. You're wrong. I love Patrick."

"Would you like to come in?" Doc gestured toward the couch.

Kate stayed in the doorway and folded her arms. "No. I just wanted you to know that I'm angry with you."

Doc put his glasses on his desk and shook his head. "I never said that, Kate. I repeated what you said."

Kate tossed her head. "I'm not about to play games with you." She turned to leave.

"You didn't say it, either."

She stopped and turned back to him.

"You didn't say you don't *want* kids. You said you don't *like* kids."

Kate's mouth dropped. "Oh."

Doc smiled. "We can talk."

Without another word, she entered the room and sat on the couch.

Ten minutes later, Kate fidgeted in her seat. She had told Doc about her issues with Patrick. "What would you do, Doc?"

"I may not be the one to ask. My kids don't talk to me, and they're both beyond their teens. I could blame my ex-wife, but that would be a lie. I didn't make much effort when they were growing up. Too busy climbing the career ladder. They developed their own lives and learned not to expect anything from their father. These days, they have no use for me at all."

"That may be happening with Patrick and me," Kate said. "I should be home with him. Why should Patrick care that I'm out at sea trying to avert a war? Not his war."

"From what you describe, he's a decent kid. Like most military children, he may have issues of separation, in this case compounded by the absence of a father figure. He may want reassurance that you will be there when he needs you. If he loses you, he becomes an orphan. That's scary, even to a teenager who won't admit the fear."

"I can't give him total reassurance, not with this crisis here. Communication is difficult. I can't keep up with the time zone challenge."

"He may sense that, but he will still test you. Communicate as best you can. Reassure him. If you get nothing back, continue transmitting. He hears you, even if he won't acknowledge it. Making the trip for his court hearing had to mean a lot to him. Let him know you care, even over time and distance."

Psychobabble.

Kate's mind wandered as Doc droned on with advice. How could she close the gap between Patrick and her?

Bring him to live with me in Japan, at least until I sort out my own choices.

Noticing her distraction, Doc had stopped talking. He waited for her to speak.

Kate had left the door open when she entered the room. Random officers and sailors strolled by in the passageway. One junior officer slowed his pace as he glanced into the room.

"Could you close the door, Doc?

"Not a good idea. How about I leave it ajar?"

She scowled. "I don't like talking while people walk by the open door. Someone could pop in at the wrong moment."

He looked at her but didn't move.

"For God's sake, Doc. I'm here for a clinical consultation. Would you hesitate to close the door if I were a man?"

Doc stood and closed the door. His eyes met hers as he reseated himself. "So . . ."

"I appreciate your advice about Patrick, but this Korea situation could turn ugly any time. No matter what, I need to be here."

Doc scowled. "Do I understand you right? The admiral has the entire Seventh Fleet staff on board to support him if something serious goes down in Korea, including a deputy N3. Despite that, the only person in the universe who can help Patrick can't make herself available to her only child?"

He frowned. "Or is it that she *won't*?" He crossed his arms and legs. "What's this about, Kate? Why did you come here? You want me to give you permission *not* to be his mother?"

"I didn't come here to be scolded." She crossed her own arms and legs.

Doc shot back. "Someone has to be the adult here."

Both stared at each other, saying nothing. Doc leaned back in his chair as if he had nothing else to do all day.

Kate wanted to flee from the room but found herself bolted to the seat.

"Of course, I want to be his mother, Doc. It's—complicated." Her chin trembled. "I need to get something off my chest, but I'm frozen. If I open up a curtain, I fear what waits on the other side."

"Sooner or later, we all have to open curtains." He spread his arms. "Safer here than other places. Whatever you say in here stays in here, without judgment or reprisal. You can speak the truth as much as you can handle; or you can leave now. Either way, we remain friends and colleagues. You can talk to Father Felix instead of me, if you'd prefer. He and I are both bound by the same rules of confidentiality." His eyes pierced hers. "You need to talk to someone—soon." He sat back again, impassive.

Kate's eyes darted around the room, but she did not leave. "I don't know where to start."

"Start at the beginning, or the middle, or wherever you will."

Doc remained comfortable with the silence. Kate fidgeted. Her heart raced, and her respirations quickened—a panic attack beginning. The urge to bare her soul raged inside her. The boiling emotional pressure threatened to explode from within, yet she could not force open the escape valve.

"Aren't you supposed to draw it out of me?" Her hands twisted in her lap. A lump rose in her throat.

"When you're ready, Kate." He sat back, silent again.

The pressure continued to steam inside her. "I can't."

Kate rose from the couch. Then, as if from a distance, she heard herself blurt it out. "Luke Walker, Patrick's father, abused me, emotionally and physically. He raped me."

She slumped back into the couch as the dam of denial burst within her and a torrent of emotion rushed out. Watching herself from that safe distance somewhere in the overhead, she beheld a woman vulnerable, emotionally naked. Tears welled in her eyes. Through the wet blur, she measured Doc's reaction. He looked back at her without feeling, nodding his head, understanding without speaking. As her tears flowed, he handed her a tissue.

"I'm sorry for your pain, Kate."

For what seemed forever, she cried. She knew it had been only a minute or two before the crying stopped.

Doc spoke. "Can you tell me about it?"

The Kate Mahoney whom she watched from her detached emotional distance sat meekly on the couch, her soul open like the body of a patient on the operating table. Thus exposed, she poured out her entire history with Luke, from the first erotic days of courtship, the not-so-accidental pregnancy, the brief marital bliss, the miscarriage, and the abuse that followed. Once the storm started, she did not stop talking until she had it all out in the room, including the physical and sexual degradation, the verbal abuse and artful demeaning of her as a person and woman, and the final torment that conceived Patrick—as if he came from the devil's own seed. After thirty minutes, she finished.

Kate felt drained, barren.

They sat in silence. The detached Kate rejoined with the fragile victim weeping on the couch. She dried her eyes and searched for some reaction in Doc's face, but saw not a trace of judgment or pity. Perhaps compassion. Or was it pity, after all?

Doc broke the long silence in a gentle voice. "You've carried that burden around for quite a while. Credit your strength of character that it didn't bring you down or drive you to self-destructive behavior."

She continued to dab with the tissue at her puffy red eyes. "Maybe not immediate self-destruction, like drugs or alcohol. But what have I done to Patrick? Do you know how many times I wished he'd never been born? What horrid mother thinks that?"

Doc leaned forward. "Most mothers think that at one time or another."

"Did I reject him because of how he came to be?"

"You accept Patrick when you accept yourself. Otherwise, you are no use to him, or to anyone."

Kate shook her head. "How?"

"You just made a start, Kate. Abuse causes deep emotional wounds. Healing takes time. Admitting the pain out loud is an excellent first step. Recovery happens when you accept that the abuse is not your fault."

"I know I'm not to blame."

"You may know that in your mind. Yet you repressed the truth for a long time. Owning deep within your core that you are not to blame, that's another matter. That's where the work comes."

Kate nodded, because she didn't know what else to do or say. "I have to get back to work."

She stood.

"Sure." Doc opened the door for her. "We can do more work on this, if you're willing."

Kate tossed her head. "Yeah."

"You know where to find me."

"Aye, Doc." Kate rushed out of the room. As fear flooded her soul, the comfortable walls of denial closed around a still-suppressed terror.

Chapter Eighty-One

April 21, 2012, South China Sea: USS *Shenandoah*

In the chief of staff's office, Leo and Preston watched CNN on the large TV. A banner scrolled along the bottom of the screen:

> *TENSIONS MOUNT IN KOREA! GEORGE WASHINGTON BATTLE GROUP MAY DEPLOY TO YELLOW SEA.*

Above the banner, talking heads swapped face time with taped images of a ranting Kim Jong Un denouncing the United States as an aggressor, threatening "merciless retaliation" if the US Navy sailed its carrier battle group into the West Sea.

"So much for clandestine," said Leo.

"Hard to hide an aircraft carrier getting underway," said Preston. "It's all rhetoric. Kim knows he can't win a fight with us."

"He has dirty weapons."

"Which he won't use."

"And support from the PRC."

Preston shuffled in his chair. "That's the odd part. Why

hasn't the PRC gone public?" He gestured toward the TV screen. "Either the dragon is asleep, or we're sailing into a trap."

"Time was," said Leo, "we'd never worry about that. We ruled the seven seas, the most powerful Navy in the world. We sailed wherever we wanted, whenever we wanted."

"Still can, but we have to be smart about it. Lately, we haven't been so smart. Takes more than firepower these days. You have to win the legal and public affairs battles before you pull the trigger. We've not played this one well. The DPRK and the PRC will spin this show of force to sling mud on our faces."

Leo raised a hand. "Got that, Pres. I'm not the one needs convincing."

Preston shifted his position to face Leo. "Speaking of the N3, what is your next move?"

"I don't follow."

Preston chuckled. "I've never known you to take a whipping, least of all from a woman, without a counterattack. You must have something up your sleeve."

Leo smiled. "I got some ideas, but I'm still gathering intel. Not sure where it's going."

Preston stroked his chin. "There was a Marine Corps F/A-18 squadron in her air wing."

Leo raised his eyebrows. "I had forgotten that. Anyone you know?"

"I could ask around. I'll let you know."

Leo was about to reply when a knock on the door interrupted. Without waiting for an answer, grim-faced Kate Mahoney entered the room. She cast a startled glance at Preston, then addressed Leo, "COS, we just got word that the ROKs are conducting a live fire exercise from Y-P Do."

Leo rose out of his chair. "I thought we turned that off. Did we get any warning?"

Kate shook her head.

"Have you told the admiral?"

"I wanted you to know first."

Leo picked up the phone and punched numbers. "Elijah, set up a secure VTC with the boss, ASAP."

Chapter Eighty-Two

April 21, 2012, South China Sea: USS *Shenandoah*

Fifteen minutes later, Eric and Rusty joined Kate, COS, and Preston on a secure VTC with Admiral Lewis.

The admiral's scowl filled the screen. "What now, people?"

Kate spoke. "Admiral, the ROKs conducted their live fire exercise this morning without advance notification to the DPRK. Or us."

"Or us? I thought we had that turned off."

Kate looked into the camera. "Sir, we thought so too. We don't know who decided, or why they did not inform us."

Lewis did not respond. Eric continued the brief. "They fired to the south as usual, well clear of the disputed maritime zone that the DPRK claim as theirs."

Kate added, "We expect the North Koreans to retaliate."

Lewis scowled. "Preston, what do you think the North Koreans will do?"

Preston looked at Kate before he answered. "I agree with

Kate. KJU will use this as an excuse for another provocation." He glanced back at Kate. "I worry what effect that will have on the PRC, especially if we put our carrier battle group in their backyard. The Chinese won't want to appear weak to the rest of the world. Expect them to denounce our presence in the West Sea."

Kate looked back at Preston. "Colonel, what are the chances of any PRC response beyond a PR campaign? Would they risk a military engagement?" She cocked her head to one side. "What if we tell them what we know about the *Bucheon* incident?"

Preston addressed the admiral. "Captain Mahoney makes a cogent point. The PRC won't risk military action in the West Sea, especially given the DPRK's recent misconduct, known publicly or leaked privately to the PRC. The Chinese may launch heavy rhetoric, but words don't sink ships or shoot down aircraft. We can weather a storm of words."

Kate lifted an eyebrow. "We can weather a verbal storm, but the key question, sir, how much heat will higher authority take from the PRC if we offer our full support for the ROKs and exert our right to freedom of the seas?"

Admiral Lewis smirked. "Higher authority won't take more than a degree or two of heat, based on past performance." He stroked his chin. "We are on the front line. Anticipate a North Korean response to the live-fire exercise, and prepare to go on the offensive, diplomatic or otherwise, with both the DPRK and PRC. As the tactical commander, I require freedom of navigation to operate in the West Sea. We will exert that right. We can hold the PRC in check. What they *don't* say or do will speak the loudest." He paused for a response.

No one disagreed.

"Lady and gents, here's what we do," the admiral said. "First,

343

I will call my ROKN friend, Admiral Lee, to find out what the hell they were thinking with that exercise. Then I'm going to check his pulse for risk-taking. After that, I will speak directly to PACOM. I'll ask him to include me in his next talk with SecDef, so I can share exactly what we know about the ship-sinking incident, and how we know it. I will get this in front of POTUS by the end of the Washington day—if I have to call the White House myself. The PRC has to be told what their psycho protégé in North Korea has been doing behind their backs." He shook his head. "Assuming they don't already know. Kate, get those ships and aircraft moving into the West Sea. If we run ourselves afoul of our own higher headquarters, so be it. I'll assume that risk. Regardless of what the PRC says or does, I want young Kim to feel the heat rising in the vicinity of his ass."

Kate did not allow herself to smile. "Aye, aye, sir."

I love this man.

Admiral Lewis crossed his arms. "We're done here. Carry on, everyone."

Chapter Eighty-Three

April 21, 2012, Pipa Got Naval Base, Democratic People's Republic of Korea

Under cover of darkness, a Korean People's Navy *Yono*-class submarine churned away from the submarine pier at Pipa Got Naval Base. This same *Yono* had rocked the world in early 2010 when it sank *ROKS Cheonan*, the first event in a flurry of North Korean provocations that year.

As soon as it reached open water, the *Yono* submerged. Running silent and deep, it turned to the south where it would linger just west of the Northwest Island chain, south of the Northern Limit Line in ROK territorial waters.

Miles above the earth, a US satellite snapped a series of high-resolution photographs of the submarine base

.

South China Sea: USS Shenandoah

Kate and Preston leaned over maps and PowerPoint printouts in her office—well after evening prayer and Taps.

"You mentioned earlier that the two key players in this drama behave like bratty children," Preston said. Then he whined like a five-year-old. "He started it. He hit me first. Did not. Did too. Did not. Did too. Waaah."

Kate laughed. "You have experience with children?"

Preston shook his head. "Years ago. Didn't turn out well. I claim no expertise in parenthood."

She thought she discerned a flash of pain in his eyes, gone as soon as it appeared.

"As a mom," he said, "how do you intervene when two children fight?"

"Give them time out. Separate them. Send each to a neutral corner and don't let them talk to each other until they cool down."

He leaned in and pointed at the map. "Let's give these brats a time out."

Although she kept her gaze on the table in front of them, Kate felt his face close to hers.

He did not seem to notice. "We give them a little talking to here." He drew a small circle on the map. "Then show them the whacking-stick here. After that, the first kid to act out gets a spanking he'll never forget."

At the word, "spanking," Kate recoiled and stepped away from Preston.

"What's wrong, Kate? You look frightened."

"I—I don't know. I suddenly felt cold." She looked at her watch. "It's late. Maybe it was a caffeine rush."

She willed her nerves to steady. "I like that plan, Colonel. We should prepare to brief it."

"Roger." Preston looked at his watch. "It is late. We've been at this for a long time, and we've got that early morning VTC with PACOM. I suggest we call it a night."

Kate nodded.

He smiled at her like a doting father. "You should switch to decaf or juice in the evenings."

"Right." She headed out. "See you at the VTC."

"Roger." Preston held the door for her, and she accepted the courtesy.

What the hell was that?

Qingdao Naval Base, People's Republic of China

Several thousand miles away from *Shenandoah*, on schedule and hidden by the clutter of activity at the headquarters of the People's Liberation Army Navy (PLAN) North Sea Fleet, a solitary *Song* type 039 diesel-electric submarine slipped away from Pier 5. Operated with professional precision, the boat submerged, undetected by the US reconnaissance satellite orbiting overhead. The disciplined crew prepared to arm the *Song*'s six torpedo tubes with either Yu-4 or Yu-6 torpedoes, or YJ-8 anti-ship missiles, whichever their higher authority ordered when the boat reached its intended position.

In 2006, this same *Song* had approached undetected within five miles from the US Navy's forward deployed aircraft carrier, USS *Kitty Hawk*, then popped up to the surface—within firing range for its missiles and torpedoes—to embarrass the arrogant American Navy.

The crew went about their current mission with full confidence that they could sneak up any time on any targeted vessel—on or below the water's surface.

Clearing the coastline, the *Song* turned northwest and accelerated toward the Yellow Sea.

Chapter Eighty-Four

April 20, 2012, San Francisco, CA

At the Powell Street BART station, Patrick waved good-by to Mr. Homer, then bounded down the escalator to catch the southbound train to San Bruno. He would be in the house before Aunt Colleen got home from work. He planned to eat a quick dinner, then fake doing his homework. He was eager to get online to tell Fuchou what a terrific time he'd had at Homer House.

He and Mr. Homer had talked to an eight-year-old whose father had died two years earlier in Afghanistan. Patrick understood how the child must feel, and he thought he'd helped the boy. Mr. Homer role-played the boy's father. He got the kid to tell him about his life, about school and friends—and his mom—as if he were talking to his real father.

Patrick liked Mr. Homer. A lot.

In their down time between counseling, Patrick and Mr. Homer talked about video and online games. Mr. Homer was not only compassionate as a surrogate father, he was also an expert mentor at online gaming. He told Patrick about some advanced techniques he could use in his WOW game.

Mr. Homer had insisted on riding the MUNI bus with Patrick to the BART station to be sure he got to his train to get home on time.

"We have to get you home on time, or your aunt may not let you keep doing this."

"I definitely want to keep doing it."

Chapter Eighty-Five

April 21, 2012, South China Sea: USS *Shenandoah*

Kate's alarm woke her up four hours after she'd gone to bed. She opened her eyes. During her short slumber, she'd decided.

Patrick must live with me.

The morning video teleconference with PACOM lasted two hours but changed nothing in the plan for Korea. After laborious handwringing over "message" and "optics," no useful guidance came forth. Kate's newest hero, Vice Admiral Darnell Lewis, emerged free to handle the situation without interference—or shared responsibility—from higher headquarters. If the operation failed, they would hang him out to dry. If it succeeded, higher headquarters would allow him some of the credit while they took most of it for themselves.

He and I are in the same boat.

Returning to her room, Kate broke her self-imposed rule to use the ship's commercial international telephone capability to call Patrick's iPhone. With the time zone difference, he should be home from school. After dialing, she heard the ring tone, but no answer. Her call switched over to his voice mail.

"Patrick, it's Mom. This is important. I'll try again in five minutes. Please answer."

Exactly five minutes later, she redialed. This time, he picked up.

"Not a good connection," she said. "Can you move upstairs or go outside?"

He didn't answer right away. Did he walk outside? When spoke again, the connection was no better.

"Where are you, Patrick? I can barely hear you."

Another long silence. Kate worried the call had disconnected. "I'm on the BART."

"Why are you on the BART on a Friday? It's late in the day there."

Long pause. "I'm going to Homer House for my volunteer hours. Mr. Homer needs me this week."

Kate blew into the phone. "Needs you?"

"It's okay, Mom. Aunt Colleen knows."

Kate felt her heart quicken as a wave of electricity passed through her.

If I hadn't already decided, this does it.

"I'll talk to Colleen about it later." She paused for a second. "I need to talk to you about something else."

"I'm almost to The City, Mom. Can it wait?"

"Cannot. I'm calling from sea and it's important. I don't know when I can call you back. Just listen." She took a deep breath. "When this school year ends, and my ship is back in Yokosuka, I want you to move to Japan and live with me. I'll start making the arrangements."

352

Long silence before Patrick spoke. Even with the marginal connection, he sounded upset. "You said 'visit' the last time. You never said I had to live there."

"I know. I've thought a lot about us. I want to be a better mother. That means you stay with me, not Aunt Colleen."

"You'll take me on the ship with you?" Tangible anger in his voice.

"The ship will be in dry dock for three months, so I'll be home during that time. We can figure out how we'll manage after that. We will make it together, not apart."

"I don't want to move to Japan. I have friends here."

"You'll make new friends. You'll still have your online friends."

Maybe not a good thing.

"But Homer House—"

"—is temporary. You will complete your hours before you leave for Japan."

"Mr. Homer says I can stay on after my hours are done."

"Out of the question. I've compromised enough just letting you go there. Now this midweek thing? No. You're coming to Japan, Patrick. We need to be together."

"I won't do it. You can't make me." He disconnected.

His voice frightened Kate.

He sounded like Luke.

Chapter Eighty-Six

April 22, 2012, South China Sea: USS *Shenandoah*

"She's a witch."

Leo held the phone away, glanced at the ceiling, then replaced the receiver to his ear. He was both enticed and repulsed by the vitriol spewing from one Lieutenant Colonel Cameron Mitchell, USMC. The light colonel and Kate had commanded sister F/A-18 squadrons in Carrier Air Wing Eight during the same deployment—just before Kate was assigned to Seventh Fleet.

"Watch your back, Captain. She'll butt-fuck you in a heartbeat to climb another rung on the ladder. Kate Mahoney made everyone's life in the CAG pure hell."

"Do you have any specifics, Colonel? Anything tangible?"

"She got her rocks off by burning our CO asses in front of the Air Wing Commander. Took pleasure in showing us up. No one trusted her."

Leo sighed. "Details?"

"The pilots in her squadron hated her. She rode them hard.

Took all the credit for herself. Didn't give shit for her subordinates. No one could satisfy her. You shoulda heard how they talked about her behind her back. Called her 'KKK' for 'Killer Kunt Kate.'"

The light colonel chortled, a lascivious laugh.

Leo had heard enough. "Clean up the trash talk, Colonel. I don't need foul language or nasty innuendo. I need solid facts. Can you or can you not describe specific instances where Kate Mahoney abused her authority or committed misconduct? Otherwise, it sounds like woman-hating sour grapes. A hard-driving, competitive performer who demands the best from subordinates doesn't make her a female Captain Queeg."

Egad. I just defended Kate Mahoney.

After a long silence, Mitchell spoke. "Sorry, sir. Didn't mean to offend." Another long pause. "Mahoney has a rep among Marine aviators."

Leo stroked his brow. *Another dead end.*

"Completely off the record?" Mitchell asked.

"As I said at the start, Colonel." Leo's patience thinned to gossamer.

Colonel Mitchell hesitated. Leo could almost hear the gears grinding in the man's head before he spoke. "I know something that I'm not supposed to know."

"You have ten seconds before I hang up."

The line went silent for about eight seconds before Mitchell spoke. "She was married to a Marine aviator. Scuttlebutt has it she almost killed him one night. Navy brass covered it up, and she walked. Scot-free." He blew into the phone. "The Marine didn't come out so well."

Leo recalled his earlier conversation with Admiral Sue Hancock. "Was that in Meridian?"

"Yeah," Mitchell said. "I was an instructor there."

"You know the Marine's name?"

"He was a major. Luke Walker."

"Where is Major Walker now?"

"No one knows. He disappeared."

Leo stroked his chin. "Thank you, Colonel. I'll take it from here."

"This conversation never happened," Mitchell said. The line went dead.

Leo punched in the FlagSec's number. "Elijah, find me a number for the Navy legal services office at Meridian Naval Air Station. No, I'll place the call myself. I just need the number."

Chapter Eighty-Seven

April 21, 2012, South China Sea: USS *Shenandoah*

No time for DTs.

Preston's entire body shook. He'd managed to function through most of the day after the escalating crisis in Korea summoned him from exile. The night remained a crucible. He'd slept in fits, often awakened in a sweat—not from nightmares, but from the craving deep in his gut and psyche.

Another morning dawned. Whatever the turmoil, however he sucked it up and performed through the day, he could count on another agonizing night of withdrawal.

Preston took a quick shower, then dressed in clean BDUs. His image in the mirror appeared gaunt and haggard. His hands shook, a fine tremor more felt than seen.

Need food.

The phone rang as he was about to depart for the flag mess. Elijah Kramb's voice sounded weary, suggesting he'd not been to bed at all. "Sorry to disturb you, Colonel. COS needs you in his office for a VTC with the admiral."

Preston brushed his teeth, combed his hair, straightened his uniform, and hustled down the passageway. In the chief of staff's office, he found Kate, Eric, and Leo gathered around the monitor. Eric held up a series of photos to the camera.

"We got this imagery an hour ago," Eric said. "This close-up shows Koampo, about fifty miles from P-Y Do. All new buildings. We assess them to be temporary barracks, suggesting a sudden influx of troops."

"Troops?" said Admiral Lewis.

"Aye, sir." Eric held up another photo. "Along this road, we see a convoy of trucks—troop transports." He pulled a different photo from the stack. "Here's the showstopper. There, and there." He pointed with his finger. "Piers. These images alongside are hovercraft."

"Hovercraft?" said the admiral. "To transport troops for an amphibious assault?"

"LCPAs, sir," Eric said. "Each can transport thirty-five to fifty soldiers. We've counted seventy LCPAs moved into Koampo from the north." Eric looked up from the photos, his gaze intense. "We assess that the North Koreans are preparing to invade P-Y Do, and possibly the other three ROK islands." He swallowed hard. "At the Top-Secret level, we have reliable HUMINT that KPA special forces have infiltrated both P-Y Do and Y-P Do."

"The first step to all-out war with the South," said Leo.

Eric cast a swift glance in Leo's direction before turning back to the camera. "We've seen no troop movements, armor buildups, or unusual activity on the Peninsula itself, no unusual KPA troop movements near the DMZ, and no ship movements on either coast. The pending attack appears to be limited to the Northwest Islands, perhaps only P-Y Do."

Admiral Lewis said, "You think this is a new provocation and not a harbinger of war?"

"We believe so, sir. Perhaps to test our resolve, to see how far we will go to help the ROKs defend the Northwest Islands."

Lewis scoffed. "Then we will show them our resolve. If they intend to start a war, we'll show them their folly." He scanned his computer screen. "Captain Mahoney, what's our force status?"

"We got GW underway under the pretense of unit level training. She's just off the southern point of Kyushu, Japan, and can get into the West Sea in a day. Close enough for flight ops in less than twenty-four hours."

"Get her within striking distance as soon as possible," the admiral said. "What about *Essex*?"

"Home port in Sasebo. We've ordered her and the rest of the strike group to deploy. They're recalling people off leave and liberty as we speak," Kate said.

"What about the MEU?"

Preston replied. "The marines will fly aboard *Essex* after she gets underway. They have to conduct integration training around Okinawa before they can move out as a full-up Navy and Marine Corps unit."

Lewis's voice turned stern. "No time for that. These are professionals who must be ready to fight tonight. Get them aboard now. They can integrate en route to Pen. I want them to prepare for forcible entry, just in case we have to take those islands back from the North Koreans." His face softened a bit. "What else, Kate?"

"*Stethem* is en route to join with *ROKS Sejong The Great* tomorrow under our exercise pretext. *Denver* is still doing salvage ops. No marines on board, but she has helos. We have *Michigan* moving up to the NLL, and *Victorious* will get there in thirty-six hours. The P-3s can depart from Kadena any time for twenty-four-hour antisubmarine surveillance."

Lewis looked pleased. "Very well, Captain."

Eric looked at Kate; she returned an encouraging nod. He looked into the camera. "We have another issue, sir. Sequential imagery of Pipa Got indicates that a *Yono* got underway last night." He gulped. "We don't know where it went."

Lewis ran a hand over his scalp. "Here we go again." He looked in Kate's direction. "Find that boat. Take whatever anti-sub assets you need and find that boat. If we don't know its location by the time this operation unfolds, that binds our hands. We need to concentrate on defending those islands, not protecting our bare asses from a midget."

Kate nodded assent. "Aye, sir."

"Anything else, folks?" said the admiral.

Kate stepped up. "Sir, we need you here on the flagship where you can exert command and control from the sea—as this ship was intended. I'd like to order *Shenandoah* to maneuver within helo range and bring you on board soonest."

She did not look at the COS. She could feel Leo fume.

Preston stepped up. "I agree with the N3, sir. We need you here."

The admiral said, "Make it happen, Kate."

"Aye, aye, sir."

* * *

As the players walked out of the admiral's office, Leo pulled Preston aside.

"What the hell's with you supporting Mahoney?"

Preston shrugged. He glanced at Kate walking away down

the passageway in earnest conversation with Eric. He turned back to Leo.

"There are no enemies on this ship, Leo. Plus, she's right."

Chapter Eighty-Eight

April 22, 2012, Gulf of Thailand: USS *Shenandoah*

"Seventh Fleet, arriving."

Dusk had just turned to night when the olive green HH-60 bearing the Seventh Fleet commander touched down on the *Shenandoah* flight deck. Vice Admiral Lewis moved quickly through the arrival formalities, greeted his chief of staff, and proceeded directly to his office. His senior leaders gathered there to give updates of the day's activities during his kluged hasty transit from Malaysia to Thailand to *Shenandoah* as the flagship idled just within helo range from the coast.

The update brief consumed only thirty minutes, at the end of which everyone concurred that hostilities would begin in the West Sea within the next two days. Satisfied that he had all the information he could expect, Lewis dismissed his staff and picked up his secure phone, ready to begin the marathon of contentious calls he must make to higher authority.

Permission or forgiveness? Doesn't matter. We go all in.

A soft knock on the open door diverted Lewis's attention. He looked up to see the fleet surgeon, Doc Cushing, standing at the threshold.

"Hey, Doc."

"Good evening, Admiral." The physician hovered in the doorway. "May I talk to you in private? I'll be brief. It concerns one of our senior officers."

Lewis put down the phone. "Sure, Doc. Come in, and shut the door."

* * *

Returning to her room after the meeting with the admiral, Kate logged on to Facebook to message Patrick.

He should be up now.

The green dot next to his name showed he was on-line. She opened the message box and typed.

Scarlett: Hi, Patrick.

She waited for a response. Nothing. She typed again.

Scarlett: Need to chat with you.

The message box refreshed, and a new text appeared.

Your message will be delivered to PatWalk's phone.

She looked at the status bar. The green dot had changed to a mobile phone icon. Kate fumed.

The little shit logged off on me!

* * *

In his office, Leo concluded his telephone conversation with the commanding officer of the Navy Legal Services Office at Naval Air Station, Meridian, MS.

"Thank you, Captain. You've been very helpful. If you come across anything else, please let me know. Have a good day."

He disconnected from that call and punched in his FlagSec's

number.

"Elijah, tell the JAG I need to see her in my office. Right away."

* * *

Thirty minutes later, Alexis Sideris emerged from the chief of staff's office, her face grim, skin pale, fists clenched. She walked down the passageway toward Kate Mahoney's stateroom, then stopped and turned around.

I can't tell her now, not with everything else that's happening.

Chapter Eighty-Nine

April 23, 2012: Hwanghae Province, DPRK

A final chill of winter clung to Koampo base, nestled in an inland waterway on North Korea's southwest coastline. The KPA troops awoke to unseasonable cold infiltrating their meager bed coverings. The wooden makeshift barracks had no insulation, so the veteran marines dove into the warmest clothing they possessed: cold weather combat gear. Many shivered as they mustered outside in the frigid darkness. They left nonessential supplies and litter behind in the barracks. They would not return to that place.

Snow flurries sparkled in the floodlights as the assembled invasion force boarded hovercraft, one platoon at a time. Scheduled to launch when day broke, they would reach Baengnyeong Do just as dawn light illuminated their target. By then, KPA's long range artillery would have so weakened the island's defenses that the invasion force would encounter only ineffective return fire from the remnants of the sparse ROK military defending the island. Few of the North Koreans expected the attack on Baengnyeong Do to be more difficult than a morning stroll in light snow. By day's end, the first stepping-stone to South Korea would be in the hands of its rightful owner. The Dear Leader would show his pleasure by rewarding the victorious marauders with lavish public acclaim and recognition. Certain promotions awaited those who led the campaign.

The adrenaline rush of anticipation drove the wintry chill from the invaders' bones. A day of glory lay ahead. For such had they trained. Such was their destiny.

Baengnyeong Island, ROK

Captain Jeremiah Woodson, USMC, pulled his parka close as he stepped out of his quarters into the crisp morning air. White flakes floated before his eyes. He reassured himself that he felt a climatological chill, not one driven by anxiety or fear. When ROK and US intelligence sources had transmitted the news about the troop build-up and hovercraft in Koampo, Jeremiah knew that his Marine Corps weapons company would soon fight alongside their ROK counterparts to defend the island they knew as P-Y Do.

As he sipped coffee and lit a cigarette, Woodson reckoned that the attack would happen that day. What better time to strike than under cover of low thick clouds and light snowfall on a chilly morning? Even as the warm coffee reached his stomach and the nicotine hooked into his lungs, he shivered.

That chill was anxiety.

ROK and US forces had not fought alongside each other since the armistice that paused the Korean War, long before most of the men fighting today were born. His Marines would rise to the task, but they would depend on their ROK counterparts to take point.

Jeremiah would prefer to lead an assault and secure territory—just as the United States Marines had done since the Corps was first established in 1775. Waiting in garrison to defend an obscure hunk of desolated rock did not posture his few good men for certain victory. But a Marine always follows orders. Woodson's orders put him and his men into a supporting role. He gazed at the gray overcast above, then the terrain at his feet. Snow stuck to the cold ground.

Major Huang, the ROK marine leader, joined him on the porch. The two men shared a smoke.

Huang took a deep drag. "Today they will come."

Woodson nodded.

The ROK marine muttered something unintelligible in Korean.

West Sea

On the bridge of USS *Stethem (DDG 63)* loitering in the Yellow Sea a hundred miles south of the Hwanghae coast, Commander Marco Venema issued an unexpected order.

"New heading one two zero. Best speed."

The quartermaster acknowledged as she'd been taught. "Heading to one two zero, aye. Advancing to best speed."

The captain turned to the navigator. "Gator, set up an intercept with *Sejong*. Rendezvous within a thousand yards of her."

"Aye, sir," said the navigator.

Gulf of Thailand: USS *Shenandoah*

Kate had just finished breakfast when one of her junior officers entered the mess and came straight to her. "Ma'am, the N2 needs you right away in the MIC."

"On my way." She chugged the rest of her morning coffee and bounced out of her seat.

In less than a minute, Kate scrambled down the ladder to the third deck amidships location of the Maritime Intelligence Center. She flashed her Top Secret ID badge to the petty officers manning the door—a superfluous motion since they all knew her on sight—and went in to find Eric.

As her eyes accommodated to the dim light in the MIC, she spotted him amid a row of computer monitors manned by earnest young officers and sailors. Kate sensed the heightened tension in the room even before she saw the concern on Eric's face. He motioned her to join him behind one station.

Eric spoke to the petty officer at the keyboard. "Cycle through the photos again, please." He turned to Kate. "These satellite photos are a minute apart, starting about a half-hour ago."

"The KPA base on Koampo," Kate said. She recognized the hovercraft along the pier.

Eric pointed to an area on the screen that to Kate appeared to be rows of dark lines against a slightly lighter gray background. "These are troops in formation."

Kathe shook her head. "If you say so."

"Next photo," said Eric. "The lines are irregular. The troops are boarding the hovercraft."

"Boarding?"

"Today's the day," Eric said. "Next photo. Some of the hovercraft have moved away from the pier. Others seem to take on troops."

"Could it be a drill?"

"Perhaps, but we must assume it's the first phase of an

invasion."

"Concur." Kate grimaced. "Nearest phone?"

Eric pointed to a desk behind them. She picked up the phone and punched in numbers to the flag cabin. After a slight pause, she said, "Admiral, Captain Mahoney. I'm in the MIC with the N2. We have satellite photos of the KPA manning the LCPAs. We believe an invasion of the Northwest Islands is imminent." A short pause, then she said, "Aye, sir." She hung up the phone and turned to Eric. "Admiral's office in five minutes. Please call the COS and the N7. I'm going by the MOC to activate the battle plan."

Eric nodded as he picked up the phone and punched in numbers.

Baengnyeong Island, ROK

Captain Woodson had just started on a ham and kimchee omelet when his operations officer burst into the galley, waving a paper message in his hand. Jeremiah knew the contents before the younger officer spoke.

"Captain, the KPA are on the move," the first lieutenant said.

"I know." Woodson took a generous mouthful of his omelet. A nearby explosion almost caused him to gag on the kimchee.

He looked at his first lieutenant. "Commence fire."

The young man sprinted from the galley.

Korean Strait

The aircraft carrier USS *George Washington (CVN 73)* entered the Korean Strait, making the best speed toward the West Sea. Early morning mist helped to conceal her whereabouts—not at all close to her last reported position off the southern coast of Japan. During the night, she had stolen swiftly north to reduce the flight time between her deck and the Korean Peninsula.

The floating airport turned into the wind. On the flight deck, the air boss had already set flight quarters. As air crew hastened to their aircraft, the decibel level rose with each successive engine roaring alive. The familiar aroma of JP-5 jet-fuel exhaust filled the air just as the morning mist cleared.

The HH-60 plane guard helicopter lifted off the deck to take up its position flying ovals along the starboard side of the ship, a maneuver referred to as "Starboard Delta." As soon as the helicopter took position, an E-2 Hawkeye radar plane shot off the forward catapult. Its two thundering propellers drove the aircraft into a steady climb to altitude. The Hawkeye flew north to its station over the West Sea. The radar dome, spinning like a giant Frisbee atop the fuselage, would provide real time situational awareness to the three flight officers manning screens and computers in the plane's aft cabin. They would relay this information to all allied ships and aircraft in the area.

Next, a pair of EA-6B Prowlers catapulted in succession off the deck. Both carried radar-jamming and electronic warfare capability to thwart the North Korean ground-based anti-aircraft arsenal. A third EA-6B launched behind the first two. Carrying 300-gallon external fuel tanks, it climbed to a position overhead the carrier; the "Texaco" station set up for aerial refueling of the F/A-18 Hornets before they pushed on to their objectives.

Throaty afterburner roars announced the launch of Hornets in successive tandems. The ignited fuels from twin tailpipes sparked a fiery trail as each jet soared into the sky. After their Texaco stops, the Hornets flew north in formations to positions between the carrier and the Northwest Islands. Some carried AAMRAM air-to-air missiles to fly combat air patrol in protection of the carrier and her escorts—and also for ROKS *Sejong The Great* and the other ROKN ships in the West Sea.

Besides the AAMRAM, the final four Super Hornets carried laser-guided bombs. They would speed to the Korean coastline near the Northwest Islands. Once the Prowlers defeated the North Korean air defense radar, the Hornet drivers hoped to introduce the DPRK to the full power of the United States naval air force.

Kadena Air Force Base - Okinawa, Japan

Loaded and armed, with Lieutenant Commander Cricket Squire as pilot in command, the P-3 *Orion began* its takeoff run. When it reached take-off speed, Cricket nudged the control wheel toward her chest. The nose edged upward, and the wheels left the ground. The four engines accelerated the bird on its climb to altitude. Cricket flew a gradual turn toward the plane's destination in the Yellow Sea. Once on station there, the submarine hunter would join USS *Michigan* and USNS *Victorious* to find, pursue, and kill the North Korean *Yono*—and any other hostile submarines that might show up in the Korean theater of operations.

Once in level flight, Cricket reviewed the mission orders with her crew in the back of the aircraft.

A puzzled crewmember looked at her. "Ma'am, did they change the AROE without telling us? If not, we are about to violate international law."

"We're here to carry out orders," she said. "If that means fucking over a KPN sub, fine by me. Let the JAGs worry about AROEs."

West Sea

"Advance to best speed, heading three zero zero."

ROKS *Sejong The Great* steamed into the West Sea, 150 miles southwest of Y-P Do. The crew manned their general quarters' stations while the fires team executed the pre-launch check on the weapons system. Commander Huang sat in the bridge captain's chair and peered through the early morning mist. His cool demeanor infected the entire crew as they went about their business, preparing a military action that the ROK Navy had often practiced but never executed. Today would be a glorious day for Huang, his crew, and his family. A devout Christian, he silently praised God for selecting him to be the instrument of revenge for North Korean atrocities committed upon his forebears many years ago.

Huang's attention turned to a pair of rapidly advancing blips on his air-defense radar. He looked past the bridge wing just in time to spot the pair of US Navy Hornets streaking past his ship in a choreographed fly-by. The sun was peeking over the horizon to clear the mist. The American jets waggled their wings in greeting as they passed by. Huang returned a friendly wave, but the speeding aircraft were well into their climb to a combat air patrol (CAP) station over his ship.

Chapter Ninety

April 23, 2012: Koampo Base, Hwanghae Province, DPRK

The KPA commander looked at his watch. Long range artillery batteries along the coast had pounded Baengnyeong Do and the other Northwest Islands for almost two hours. He planned to wait a bit longer for the withering fire to achieve full effect. Then he would launch the hovercraft invasion. By nightfall, the KPA would control all the Northwest Islands.

A piercing whistle eclipsed his gloating chuckle, followed by an enormous explosion on the beach below him; then another, closer to where he stood. He dove for cover.

"The fuckers are shooting at us!" He picked up his field phone and gave the order, "Launch the assault! Launch the assault!"

When the first hovercraft invaders moved out, the remaining craft were still loading troops at the pier. Precision artillery rounds from the south put them out of commission. The KPA invasion force was reduced to half-strength before it began its assault.

"Get those craft loaded and away from the pier!"

A massive explosion splintered the pier, throwing hovercraft shards and human bodies skyward in a geyser of water.

"That was no artillery!"

A roar of jet engines sounded overhead, just before the headquarters building and artillery batteries went up in serial explosions.

The KPA commander ran for deeper cover.

Baengnyeong Island, ROK

When the first KPA artillery round hit, Captain Woodson and his ROK partner ordered the combined USMC and ROK long-range artillery batteries on Y-P Do and P-Y Do to fire on their respective targets, primarily Koampo Base. They heard the scream of the attacking ROK Air Force jets overhead, joining with those of the US Navy. Then they heard sounds of explosions from the north.

A smile lit up Woodson's face. He slapped his ROK partner on the back. "Oo-rah! Not even half-time and we're way ahead!"

The ROK marine officer smiled back and offered a polite nod.

West Sea

Soon after *Stethem* acquired *Sejong The Great* on its SPY radar, the two captains reviewed strategy by secure radio. *Stethem's* radar swept the coastline and found no threats. The EA-6Bs and companion ROK air assets had done their job. *Sejong* readied its Vertical Launch System (VLS). Captain Huang addressed the *Stethem* skipper. "We teach young Kim a lesson he will not soon forget. ROKs will never again cower like mice in the face of insane provocation." His voice swelled through the receiver. "Today we declare independence, sir."

A half hour later, news of the North Korean attack on P-Y Do reached *Stethem*. Commander Venema knew Sejong would also have the news. He looked toward the cruising South Korean ship to see the blazing contrails from the Hyunmoo-3 cruise missiles launched from *Sejong's* VLS.

Koampo Base, Hwanghae Province, DPRK

The remaining buildings and piers at Koampo Base rocked and disintegrated amid massive explosions as two 500-kilogram warheads from Hyunmoo missiles hit their targets. A few of the hovercraft loaded with troops had already begun their advance on P-Y Do, but most were still on the inland waterway. They were destroyed, or—absent orders from the now demolished command post—turned around to begin a search and rescue operation for their own troops.

Those who led the advance on P-Y Do heard the explosions behind them. Knowing that something had gone terribly wrong, they pushed on with a dispirited attack, soon overcome by the collective firepower of the US and ROK marine defenders. None of the erstwhile marauders made it onto the beach, nor did they return to the north.

West Sea

News of the successful cruise missile attack on Koampo Base and the thwarting of the KPA invasion of P-Y Do soon reached the captain of *Sejong The Great*. He smiled and pumped his fist in the air.

Sejong's work was not yet done. Another score remained to

be settled.

Huang ordered his ship to a new course and readied the VLS, where several missiles remained. As soon as they were programmed for the next target, he gave the order to fire.

The missiles thrust from the silos in rapid succession. With targeting data supplied from nearby *Stethem*, they screamed along the terrain at Mach 1 to the DPRK submarine base at Pipa Got. In successive waves of detonation, the headquarters building and several tunnels that housed DPRK submarines went up in massive explosions.

A short time later, the battle damage reports from US satellite images reached *Sejong*. The entire crew cheered and wept at the same time. The submarine base that launched evil attacks was destroyed and out of service. ROKS *Cheonan* and ROKS *Bucheon* were avenged.

Thirty miles away, the covert North Korean *Yono* snuck closer to *Sejong* and *Stethem*. USS *Michigan (SSN 762)*, the *Los Angeles*-class attack submarine, which had picked up the *Yono* as it crossed the NLL, moved ahead in silent pursuit. The *Michigan* skipper gave the order to arm the Mark-48 torpedoes to take out the KPN mini-sub before it could close to *Stethem* or *Sejong*. Either or both ships could be the *Yono's* targets.

Suddenly, *Michigan* lost contact with the *Yono*. The skipper scratched his head. USNS *Victorious,* the ocean surveillance ship operated by Military Sealift Command, had not yet arrived on station. The submarine captains hoped that the P-3 would detect the *Yono* and warn *Stethem* and *Sejong* to counter the imminent attack.

As suddenly as he had lost contact, he had it again. No, this was a new contact, not the *Yono*. This contact was larger and faster and appeared to speed in a direct line toward *Stethem*. He turned his boat in pursuit. With no other US submarine in these waters, the new contact had to be a hostile, an immediate threat to both *Stethem* and *Sejong*.

"Torpedoes in the water." The call came from the petty officer manning the sonar. "Moving away."

"All stop," commanded the skipper. His fists jammed into his sides.

Too late.

Chapter Ninety-One

April 23, 2012, Gulf of Thailand: USS *Shenandoah*

Sitting at her central position in the Maritime Operation Center, Kate felt like a TV show director. Symbols for actual air and sea units moved in real time on the giant video screens in front of her.

Patrick would consider this the ultimate video game.

For the past four hours, she had watched the plan unfold exactly as she and Preston had envisioned.

Until now.

The North Korean *Yono* dropped off the screen. Alarmed, Kate asked aloud to the room, "Where's the *Yono*?"

A petty officer spoke up. "All units report lost contact with the *Yono,* ma'am."

"What about *Michigan*?" Kate's voice rose in pitch. "Do we still have *Michigan*?"

"Unknown, ma'am. Missed her comms window."

Damn. Just when we thought we'd won.

"*Sejong*?"

"Still there, ma'am," said the petty officer. "Where she's supposed to be."

"*Stethem*?"

Another voice spoke from elsewhere in the room. "*Stethem* reports an underwater disturbance several miles aft of her position. Maybe torpedoes."

"Hitting what?" Kate looked around for anyone who would have an answer. Blank expressions came back to her.

"Until we know otherwise, assume we've lost *Michigan*," Kate said. "All other units' top priority is to find that *Yono* before it strikes again."

The petty officer spoke up, his voice more excited. "Ma'am, the P-3 reports a new contact. POSSUB HIGH. But it's not the *Yono*, nor *Michigan*."

Kate turned wide-eyed toward the petty officer. "Someone else is out there?"

"Ma'am, *Victorious* reports new sub contact with line of bearing away from the one-twenty-four. Appears to be heading toward the PRC."

"*Victorious* reports it? She's still south of the action. Is the *Yono* running away south?" Kate felt the situation unraveling in front of her. "Get the N2 up here right away." As soon as she spoke, the phone next to her elbow rang. *Eric.*

"You're absolutely telepathic," she said.

"Excuse me?" Preston's voice.

Kate exhaled. "Sorry, Colonel. I was expecting the N2."

"Sorry to disappoint," said Preston. "I wanted to report an interesting call I received from the Pentagon."

"Can you come to the MOC, sir? We could use your help."

"On my way." Did she detect eagerness in his voice?

379

* * *

A few minutes later, Kate, Eric, and Preston huddled at her desk in the MOC.

Eric spoke in a strained voice. "A *Song* submarine got under way from Qingdao yesterday morning. She's unaccounted for since she left port."

Preston said, "My Pentagon contacts cite a reliable source that POTUS spoke to Premier Hu this morning, gave him all the information we gathered on the *Bucheon* incident, plus the pending attack on the Northwest Islands. He told Hu that if the PRC won't control the DPRK, the US for sure will. He must have been persuasive, because the PRC issued an ultimatum to the DPRK. Cease further provocations or else lose PRC support. KJU told the Chinese to pack sand."

Kate looked at Preston. "I know another way to control a bratty kid."

Preston nodded. "Stand aside and let big brother have a whack at him?"

"Precisely."

The flag aide entered the MOC and approached the threesome. "The admiral wants you three and the COS in his office right away."

As the trio headed toward the door, a petty officer shouted, "We have contact with *Michigan!* She reports fully operational."

* * *

They stood with Leo in front of Admiral Lewis, who beamed at them.

"I just took a call from PACOM. We've learned through diplomatic channels and the national command authorities that the PRC will publicly repudiate the latest North Korean shenanigans, including the trumped-up charges of South Korean aggression."

The four leaders rejoiced, but the admiral held up a hand. "The PRC will also demarche the ROKs for taking 'excessive' military action today, and the US for supporting it." He chuckled. "Of course, they won't do anything beyond the verbal and written diatribes. That's diplomacy, folks.

"The Chinese guarantee that the DPRK will not retaliate for the attacks on Koampo and Pipa Got. The repudiation alone should force KJU and his military cabal back into their cages to lick their wounds." He turned to Kate. "Captain Mahoney, you can phase down the operation now."

Kate heaved a long sigh and nodded.

The admiral smiled. "Get with *Shenandoah* leadership to execute the next port visit."

Kate beamed. "Aye, sir."

"One other thing. The PRC reports that the KPN has lost a *Yono*-class submarine. A PRC frigate found debris in the West Sea in the general vicinity of the one-twenty-four line, positively identified as a North Korean *Yono*. No survivors." The admiral winked. "Appears the submarine suffered some unfortunate internal accident."

Chapter Ninety-Two

April 23, 2012, Gulf of Thailand: USS *Shenandoah*

Phasing down the operation took little personal effort on Kate's part. She delegated most of the tasks to her staff, keeping enough battle forces in the West Sea to deter any change of heart by the North Korean regime or its gorilla neighbor. Once she'd given direction, she hurried off to her stateroom. She wanted to try Patrick again.

She found Alexis Sideris waiting at her door. The JAG looked at her with haunted eyes. "I need to tell you something."

Kate leaned close to her friend. "Are you okay? Did someone die?"

Alexis tilted her head toward Kate's door, replied in a whisper. "Cone of silence. Please."

Kate unlocked the door and led Alexis into her room. She motioned her to sit, but the JAG remained standing.

Kate crossed her arms, brow furrowed. "Out with it."

Alexis shuffled from side to side. A wet film covered her eyes. "COS called me to his office last night." She wrung her hands.

"Asked me pointed questions about your case."

A shiver ran up Kate's spine. "My case?"

"He knows about Meridian, Kate. That I was your lawyer. He demanded—"

Kate cut her off. "What does he know?"

"He wanted me to tell him what I knew, but of course I said—"

Kate moved closer, just inches away from her friend. Her voice rose. "What does he know, Alex?"

Alexis shook her head, arms held out. "That's just it. I don't know what he knows. He . . . tried to pry information out of me, but I claimed attorney-client privilege. He got angry. Told me that if he found out I helped you—'get off' were the words he used—he would ruin me."

"He said 'get off'?"

"Yes. He believes you were guilty, that someone covered it up."

Kate's head felt about to explode. Her nostrils flared. Her fists clenched. She elbowed Alexis aside and stormed out of her room, heading up the passageway to the chief of staff's office.

Alexis ran behind her. "Wait, Kate. Think about this."

Kate slammed through Leo's door without knocking.

Leo looked up from his desk and scowled. "Knocking would be—"

Kate circled behind his desk, stood over him, and leaned into his face. "You've been asking questions about me." She stared him in the eye. "Let me save you the trouble. I can tell you whatever you need to know."

Alexis entered the room. Leo looked at her. "What did you—?"

Kate kept her gaze on Leo. "Get out, Alexis. You do not want to witness this." She held a fist in Leo's face.

He pushed his chair away from Kate's fury, then stood to give himself a height advantage.

With both hands, Kate shoved him back into his chair.

"You stay, JAG," Leo said. "I will not let Captain Mahoney assault me without a witness."

Kate glared at him. "Fine. She stays. As a lawyer, not a friend." She stepped away from the agitated chief of staff. "I won't hit you, Leo. Wouldn't be a fair fight."

Leo stayed seated. Kate stepped back to allow the adrenalin to seep from her body. She sat on the edge of his desk, facing him. "You want to know what happened at Meridian? Why?"

"I'm the chief of staff. It's my responsibility to know if one of my senior staff, not to mention the deputy chief of staff, committed an unrequited felony."

"Bullshit." Kate tossed her head. "From the day I stepped aboard, you've tried to discredit me. I've put up with your sexism and insults because I came here to do a job—which you've made more difficult by your behavior toward me." She narrowed her gaze. "I could have filed harassment charges against you—the JAG here suggested that—but I didn't want to distract the staff or Admiral Lewis with petty crap. Nor will I stoop to your level of slime."

Leo did not speak.

Kate moved closer, leaned into his face. "You think you've got something on me? Think you're going to drive me out of *your* Navy? Think you have a gun to my chest, and you can't wait to pull that trigger, can you?"

Leo did not speak.

"If you have a need to know what happened in Meridian, I

384

will tell you—*all* of what happened in Meridian—because I have nothing to hide." She shook her head. "You don't have a need or a right to know. Makes me wonder who you've talked to; what deals you've made to get your unauthorized half-truths. If we dig into that, I bet we find that you've abused your authority and status as a senior naval officer and chief of staff." She shot him a sarcastic smile. "Am I getting warm, Leo?"

He didn't speak. Didn't move.

"Thought so." Kate resumed her seat on the edge of Leo's desk. "Here's the deal, COS. You will swear, right here and now, in front of the JAG, that you will cease any further harassment of me. You will treat me at all times like a respected professional colleague. You will never again threaten me or undermine my ability to do my job. You will conduct no unauthorized investigations into my past."

She glanced at Alexis. "Are you getting all this down, JAG?

Alexis shot back a terrified look.

"Take notes, Alex." Kate turned back to Leo. "I say again. You will conduct no unauthorized investigations into my past, either in person or through a surrogate. You will make no more incriminating insinuations about my ethics or morality. Understood?"

Leo did not speak. Kate moved closer to him. She smelled his fear.

Spineless coward.

"Should you refuse, should you not agree to my demands in spoken word in front of this witness within the next thirty seconds, the three of us will march across the passageway and lay this all out in complete detail to Vice Admiral Lewis. When we are done, when the whole truth is out in the open, one of us will no longer have a job on this staff, or in the United States Navy. It won't be me, Leo. I swear it."

Leo did not speak.

"Am I crystal clear?"

Leo nodded.

"You have about ten seconds to speak, or we march to the admiral."

Leo looked at Alexis and then at Kate. He sighed. "Okay, Kate. You win."

Kate scowled at him. "That's 'Captain Mahoney' to you." She moved toward the door. "You must explicitly state what you intend to do and not do. I'll give you ten more seconds."

Leo's eyes flamed with hatred. "Okay, *Captain Mahoney*, I will not harass you. I will treat you with respect. I will conduct no further investigations into your past."

"Ma'am," Kate said.

Leo glowered. "Ma'am."

"Thank you, Leo."

Kate walked out of the room, Alexis trailing behind. In the passageway, she turned to the JAG. "How was that for a show of force?"

Kate turned toward her stateroom. Alexis followed. Kate wheeled on her, raised her hand. "Don't."

In her stateroom, Kate locked the door, stripped off her clothes, and headed to her shower. She turned on the water full blast and stepped in. She screamed—a mournful, primal wail. Sliding her back down the metal shower wall, Kate sat on the wood slats over the drain, allowing the water to flow over her. She hugged her knees to her chest in the confined space, laid her head in the crook of an elbow, and allowed the tears to gush in gut-wrenching waves.

Chapter Ninety-Three

April 23, 2012, Gulf of Thailand: USS *Shenandoah*

Kate stayed in the shower so long that her skin looked like an octogenarian's. She dried off, put on fresh underwear and a royal blue tee shirt, and climbed back into her flight suit and boots. Then she sat at the computer, opened Facebook, and messaged Patrick. He was not online, nor had he replied to her previous message. She typed a new message.

Scarlett: Patrick, please let's chat.

Your message will be sent to PatWalk's phone.

Frustrated and famished, she went to the flag mess for dinner—the first time she'd not eaten at her desk in three days. None of the fat-laden choices on the buffet line appealed to her, so she settled for salad supplemented with canned tuna. At the table, the mindless chit-chat and boisterous male bonding of the junior officers annoyed her. She saw no one there whom she wanted to join in casual conversation.

Thought Preston might be here.

She rushed through her salad, washed it down with a cup of chicken soup, munched a chocolate chip cookie, stuck another one in her pocket, and headed toward her stateroom. Tired to the bone, she thought she might grab a quick nap—if she could force her mind to throttle back.

Instead, she found herself at the fleet surgeon's door.

She heard herself say, "Got a minute, Doc?"

Doc looked up and smiled. "Sure, Kate. Come in."

As if stepping off a hurtling train onto a serene platform, she entered the room and shut the door behind her. Doc made no move to reopen it. Kate lay on the couch, her head at the end closest to Doc, facing away from him.

She stared up at the overhead beams. "Okay," she said. "Let's play doctor. You be the shrink, and I'll be the screwed-up naval aviator."

Doc did not respond. She sensed him looking at her, but she continued to stare at the overhead. Then she heard him maneuver his chair behind her to sit out of her field of view.

"Okay," he said. She blinked at the harsh fluorescent light over her head.

"Could you douse the overhead, Doc?"

He flipped off the light. The room was now dimly lit by Doc's desk lamp and computer monitor. Kate closed her eyes. Memory fragments floated around in her mind with emerging clarity.

"A little while ago, I thought I would kill the COS."

"Uh, huh."

She told him what had happened, leaving out the specifics about what COS was investigating. By the end, she hyperventilated. Early sign of a panic attack.

Doc spoke. "Kate, this is your safe place. No one can harm

you here."

The gentleness in his voice soothed her more than his words did.

Kate drifted into deeper relaxation and confidence. She closed her eyes, appreciating Doc's presence, and his silence even more. Blurred images danced on the edge of her consciousness. She hyperventilated again. A terrible fright swept over her. In a blink, it was gone.

Kate opened her eyes. Still in Doc's room. Safe.

Doc spoke. "I wonder why your anger scares you so much."

"I hate to lose control." A single sob escaped her throat.

"You're okay, Kate. You can let it out. Let it all out."

Like a dam broken, she sobbed for what seemed like an eternity. Maybe just a minute or two?

Doc sat behind her, not moving or speaking.

Eventually, the paroxysms abated.

He handed her a tissue but said nothing.

Kate closed her eyes again. No longer in Doc's room. Another place, a cold and scary place, a dark place. From somewhere in the room, she heard words gush. Her voice, but as if she heard herself speak from a distance.

"Bless me, Father. I'm not a naughty girl, Father. I'm not a naughty girl."

Doc's voice—was it Doc's voice?—filtered through a mask. "You are good."

Her voice. "Forgive me, Father. I'm not a bad girl. I'm a good girl. Really, I am."

"Yes, you are." The filtered parental voice.

"I wanted to kill him," her voice said. "I wanted him dead."

Kate squeezed her eyelids and screwed her face tight.

"Forgive me, Father. I wanted to kill him! I didn't want to do it, Father. He made me. I'm a good girl. Please forgive me, Father. Please . . ."

Her voice trailed off to a whisper. Her body felt drained. The sobbing stopped. She lay still for several minutes, her mind void. As if her body and mind had blown into pieces, then come together in a different way.

She opened her eyes to the reality of Doc's room and his silent presence.

"Who abused you as a child, Kate?"

She sat up with a start. "What did you say?"

"You heard me."

A steel curtain closed around her. She was desperate to fly from the room, but could not move her muscles. Trapped, she struggled against the curtain, suffocating, panicked. With one immense effort, she tore away the barrier. She yanked it down and faced the ugly truth hidden there. Her mouth struggled to utter the words that her mind already knew. Her face turned hard as granite.

"My father. He raped me when I was thirteen years old. He said I deserved it because I was a naughty girl." She hyperventilated but willed it to stop.

"Can you tell me about it?" Doc's gentle voice calmed her.

She took a deep breath.

"Something happened when I was six years old. I don't remember much. My mother's yelling woke me up. Daddy was sitting on my bed. Mom screamed she would kill him if he didn't stop.

"That was the only time I ever heard her yell at him. He took her out of the room. I heard him hit her. She cried out in pain. 'My fault,' I thought. He hurt her because of me—because she yelled at

391

him about me. I did not know what I had done.

"I wanted him to love me. He left me alone after that. Until the day I turned thirteen. He came to my room that night, and . . ."

Kate opened her eyes and sat up. "I can't do this. Too much pain. I hate him. I'm glad he's dead." She rolled into a fetal position, facing away from Doc. He did not touch her, but she felt his kindness and compassion. Maybe she was safe now, maybe for the first time.

Please let it be over.

She woke with a start, still lying on her side away from the doctor. She turned to face him.

He had not moved. "Good nap?"

"How long was I out?"

"Maybe ten minutes. How do you feel?"

She sat up and poked herself, as if to verify reality over a dream. "Okay. I feel okay."

Doc spoke in a kind, subdued voice. "We may have found the root cause for your deeply repressed anger that explodes into rage when men push the wrong buttons."

Kate's mouth dropped. She blew out a long breath. "Guess so." She stood and used Doc's sink to wash her face and dab her swollen eyes with a cold washcloth. She returned to the couch, not sure what to do.

"Many people who get into abusive adult relationships suffered abuse as a child," Doc said. "That abused child grows up with a subconscious label that says, 'I'm no good,' or even worse, 'I'm evil.' That label drives relationship choices. We seek someone as bad as we think we are, to punish us, to validate our own negative feelings. Sometimes, not always, we find a hidden reservoir of courage. We fight back. Even that heroic act carries a heavy burden of guilt.

"We break that cycle only when we believe that what happened early in life was never our fault. Maltreatment defines the abuser, not the victim. Once we respect ourselves as innocents, our life can change."

Kate fixed her gaze on the fleet surgeon. "'We,' Doc? You too?"

He glanced away. "We're done for now. You can come back to talk, or nap on the couch, anytime you want. When we return to home port, I can hook you up with a mental health professional. You have an arduous journey ahead of you, but a rewarding one. You are on your way to recovery. Be proud of yourself."

"Not sure I believe that, Doc. But thanks."

"Thank yourself, Kate. You did all the work."

A few minutes later, she emerged from Doc's room and returned to her stateroom. Although it was early in the evening, she lay down on her rack and fell asleep. No dreams came that night. She slept until reveille and awoke with a start.

Patrick!

Chapter Ninety-Four

April 24, 2012, Gulf of Thailand: USS *Shenandoah*

The day before *Shenandoah* was to arrive in Laem Chabang, Thailand, Vice Admiral Lewis's office became the equivalent of a military courtroom for the formal process known as admiral's mast, or non-judicial punishment. With the ship underway from home port, the admiral had full judicial authority to determine innocence or guilt in most cases, and to award just punishment.

The conference table and couches had been moved aside to make room for a podium with space in front of it. Attired in his service dress white uniform with a combination cover for one of the rare occasions that prescribed headwear indoors, Darnell Lewis stood at ease but stiff behind the podium. Even the most casual observer would recognize his displeasure at conducting his first admiral's mast since taking command of the Seventh Fleet almost a year earlier.

The evidence and testimony he had just heard did not improve his mood.

Facing Vice Admiral Lewis in front of the podium, Ensigns Zipp and Robinson, also clad in service dress whites and combination covers, stood at rigid attention. Master-at-arms petty officers flanked each ensign. Behind the two accused women, COS LeBlanc, Kate, Alexis Sideris, Chaplain Armando, Doc Cushing, and other officers called as character witnesses stood at parade rest. All wore the same formal white uniforms and covers.

Lewis blew out a breath and leaned forward, staring down at each of the accused officers. "Did you or did you not accompany Colonel Davis to his hotel room on the night in question?"

Ensign Robinson answered, "Sir, he said nothing about a hotel room. We just went drinking and dancing."

Admiral Lewis turned to Ensign Zipp, who stared at her feet. "Look up, Ensign Zipp." He pointed to the space between his eyes. "Look right here." The young woman did as ordered, her own eyes moist.

"Did you accompany Colonel Davis to a hotel room?"

"No, sir. We went to Clarke Quay and hit a couple of nightclubs. We had drinks and danced. When we realized we'd busted curfew, we caught a taxi to take us back to the ship."

Kate maintained her parade-rest posture but turned livid as she heard the testimony.

No hotel room! What did he mean when he . . .?

"Captain Mahoney."

Kate blinked, pulling her mind back to the immediate matter at hand. The admiral regarded her with pleading eyes. "I have read your written statement. Do you have anything to add?"

Kate cleared her throat, hoping to control the nervous falsetto. She looked between each of the ensigns. "Admiral, once in my career, a wise leader gave me a second chance after I'd done something that could discredit myself and the Navy. That second chance rescued my career." She paused for effect. "I recommend you give these young officers similar opportunities."

In preparing her statement, she had intended to say no more. Without thinking, she continued. Her voice seethed without a hint of falsetto. "While the ensigns must own accountability for their behavior that night, the poor example and inadequate leadership of the senior officer with them mitigates their culpability. They held Colonel Davis in the highest respect and admiration. The colonel unduly influenced these young officers. The onus for this unfortunate international embarrassment rests on his shoulders."

Kate wondered if she would have said all that had Preston been in the room. No matter. She'd said it and felt good about it.

Admiral Lewis stared at her for a few seconds before a trace of a smile perked up the corners of his mouth. "I will consider your recommendation, Captain Mahoney." The room remained silent while he rifled through the documents and notes in front of him. Then he stiffened and faced the two accused ensigns, prepared to render judgment.

Kate and the others snapped to attention. The admiral's baritone voice overwhelmed the small room. He stared down at the two ensigns, both of whom looked at the deck.

The admiral's eyes narrowed. "Heads up, ladies." Again, he pointed to his forehead. "Here."

The ensigns did as commanded.

"Service as an officer in the United States Navy, especially as a member of a fleet commander's staff, demands standards of conduct beyond the Navy's basic core values of honor, courage and commitment. Serving this great nation, as an officer in this most prestigious Navy, is both a privilege and a responsibility. The latter seems to have escaped you two ladies.

"Further, service to the Seventh Fleet command makes you ambassadors of our nation in areas of the world where not everyone loves or respects us, where we must win and maintain the peace, one interaction at a time. Your irresponsible actions not only tarnished your professional integrity and reputations, but you put the US Navy and the United States of America into an unfavorable posture with one of our most significant regional allies. Fortunately for all of us, we limited the damage.

"My experience and my personal code of honor cry out for justice. My instinct tells me to boot the two of you as far as possible out of my Navy." He glanced at Kate. "For some unfathomable reason, Captain Mahoney believes she can make decent officers out of you." He raised his eyebrows. "Against my gut instincts, I will give her—and both of you—that chance.

"I award each of you a non-punitive letter of caution, declaring that you have put your Navy careers in extreme jeopardy, and spelling out explicit instructions on how you may recover—if you so choose. You will attend alcohol abuse prevention training as recommended by the fleet surgeon, and you will meet weekly with Captain Mahoney for individual mentoring."

The admiral pursed his lips, glanced again at Kate. "I'll expect an interim report of your progress in six weeks and a final report in three months. If I see or hear anything less than stellar, I will throw you both out of the Navy with my own hands. I will pin such a tarnished paper trail onto each of you that you'll be lucky to get the most menial and low-paying civilian jobs." He leaned over the podium and glared at the young women. "Understood?"

Each ensign held her head high and whispered. "Aye, aye, sir."

"I can't hear you."

The ensigns spoke in firm but tremulous voices. "Aye, aye, sir."

"That's better. You both will take watch on the ship during the duration of any future port visits. The next time your feet hit dry land will be back at home port."

The two women looked at each other.

Admiral Lewis stared at them. "Would you prefer time in the Singapore Navy brig instead?"

"No, sir," said Ensign Zipp.

"Thank you, sir," said Ensign Robinson.

Admiral Lewis shook his head. He turned to Kate. "Frankly, Captain, I think you're wasting your time and energy."

Kate shot a reassuring glance at the ensigns, then addressed the admiral. "Sir, I believe they can become fine officers, once properly mentored, and not led astray by errant senior officers."

Lewis dropped the stiff formality. "I hope you're right, Kate. I'll be the most delighted sailor on this ship if you prove me wrong."

He came to attention, cast a weary look around the room, then back to the two ensigns. "Dismissed."

The ensigns saluted, pivoted on their heels in a crisp about-face, and left the room. Neither looked at Kate as they passed her.

Chapter Ninety-Five

April 24, 2012, Gulf of Thailand: USS *Shenandoah*

After a half-hour break, Admiral Lewis stood again at the podium, still attired in a white uniform and covered. In front of him, Colonel Preston Davis stood at ramrod attention in his Marine Corps dress uniform with a white combination cover. A solitary master-at-arms petty officer stood to the side and somewhat behind the colonel. The cadre of other personnel in the room had diminished from the prior session. Only COS, Kate, Alexis, Doc, and the chaplain remained.

Beads of perspiration emerged on the admiral's forehead beneath the brim of his cover. "Colonel, after the dining out, did you invite Ensigns Zipp and Robinson to your hotel room in Singapore?"

"No, sir."

"Were you drunk, Colonel?"

"Yes, sir."

"Were the two ensigns drunk?"

"I believe so, sir."

"Perhaps you invited them to your room, but don't remember

it?"

"No, sir." Preston cleared his throat. "I didn't book a hotel room in Singapore. I slept on the ship that night—in the medical ward."

Kate felt herself go crimson with fury. She clenched her fists, trying to channel the rage away from her face, desperate to make her angry reaction less obvious.

The admiral scanned his notes, then looked back to Preston. "Do you remember coming back to the ship that night, Colonel?"

Preston glanced away from the admiral, recovered, and looked back. "No, sir. I was very drunk. I don't remember anything between hailing a cab at Clarke Quay and waking up in *Shenandoah* medical sometime later."

He fidgeted a bit, but kept his feet planted on the deck, hands stiff at his sides, thumbs along the creases of his pants. His right hand held a one-page printed document. "Sir, if I may make a statement?"

Admiral Lewis nodded. "You have that right, Colonel."

Preston lifted the hand with the document but did not look at it as he spoke. "I make no excuses and seek no mercy for my behavior. From the time the dining out began, I allowed alcohol to take control over my mind and body. That resulted in behavior unbecoming an officer, especially a senior officer of the United States Marine Corps. I not only tarnished the Navy and Marine Corps team in front of our allies, but I also offended fellow officers whom I deeply respect."

He made a brief glance in Kate's direction. She did not move.

"Further, I jeopardized the professional standing of two young officers who deserved better leadership. I make no excuses for what I did, and for what I failed to do. I take full responsibility not only for myself, but for those junior officers. For my deplorable conduct and regrettable failure as an officer and gentleman, I stand prepared to receive your judgment and to pay whatever price I must."

A wave of nausea almost overcame Kate. She wanted to bolt from the room.

Admiral Lewis shuffled through his notes and then looked up at Preston.

"In my naval career, I've never been more disappointed than I am at this moment, Colonel. I feel physically ill, in my stomach and in my heart. I want to believe. I need to believe that you speak sincerely and truthfully. I want to accept your remorse and your apology."

He pursed his lips. "I will take your statement at face value, but I must interject a modicum of skepticism. I heard the fleet surgeon's assessment that you have an addiction to alcohol. I buy that." The admiral leaned forward, frowned. "Addiction or none, I must hold you accountable for what you did in Singapore and for the effects of your actions. You cannot blame alcohol or any external factor. Period.

"Even if your repentance is genuine, you have wrought irreparable damage to your career. You cannot apologize away the destruction you have brought upon yourself."

Admiral Lewis blew out a long breath. "I must consider ending your distinguished career, right here, right now." His voice broke. He turned away. When he looked back at Preston, he struck the podium with his fist. "What a waste, Preston. What a lamentable waste."

Preston looked down. "Yes, sir. I truly regret putting you in this position."

The admiral wiped a dollop of sweat from his brow. "If I end your career, I fear not for the United States Marine Corps, or the US Navy. We can and will replace you, no matter your talents and accomplishments. No person is indispensable.

"I fear for you. I fear for Preston Davis, the man. While it may seem right and just to drum you out of the Corps in shame, I cannot and will not condemn another human being to a life of continued self-destruction. My Navy does not expect me to take your life, physically or spiritually."

The admiral huffed. "I choose to look deep beneath the foul surface tarnish to find the inner man, the Marine, the professional officer whom I have known and respected for half my career. Maybe, just maybe, we can restore that man back to health.

He glared at Preston. "You must help me. You must help yourself."

Preston raised his gaze to meet the admiral's dark eyes. "I understand, sir."

"I will give you that chance, Colonel. I doubt that I, or anyone, can salvage your career from this disgrace; but I will try to save your life, if you are willing." He pointed his finger at Preston's face. "You must take the first step. You must admit your addiction. You must accept that you cannot control it. You must comply with the fleet surgeon's recommendation. You must commit, I emphasize, commit yourself to treatment." He stared into Preston's eyes. "Am I clear?"

"Yes, sir."

"Am I clear you are the one deciding here, not me?"

"Yes, sir. I want the treatment, sir."

"I hope you are sincere, Colonel. I'll accept your statement.

We'll find out soon enough if you're serious."

"Aye, sir," Preston said. "I understand, fully."

"As of this moment, you are under Doctor Cushing's care. You will do exactly as he says, no compromise, no debate. At the next port, you will leave the ship with an escort and proceed directly to inpatient treatment. You are relieved of all other military duties, and you are no longer cleared for access to classified material or briefings. Clear?"

Preston's head jerked back as his mouth fell open. "Sir, I—"

The admiral raised his hand. "This is not a discussion, Colonel. Are you clear? Or not clear?"

"Clear, sir."

"Very well," said the admiral. "Dismissed."

Preston saluted, made a perfect about face, and strode out of the room with his head held high, eyes straight ahead. Kate did not dare to look at him. She needed all her strength to fight off the tears.

When Preston had left the room, Admiral Lewis removed his cover and relaxed. The others followed his lead.

"That was unpleasant," he said. "Good luck with this, Doc. I didn't find him very convincing. Keep me posted on progress." He looked around the room. "You all can go, except for COS. Thank you for your time."

As the others filed out, Kate heard Lewis say, "Sit down, Leo. We need to talk."

Chapter Ninety-Six

April 24, 2012, Gulf of Thailand: USS *Shenandoah*

"Seventh Fleet, departing."

Leo and Preston sat on the soft chairs in Leo's office watching the video image of the helicopter departing from the flight deck with Admiral Lewis on board. As the ship approached port in Thailand, the admiral would fly the short distance to Bangkok for his formal visits to Thai government officials. By evening, he would be driven to his hotel in nearby Pattaya to await *Shenandoah*'s arrival in port the next day. Two nights hence, he would host a gala reception on the flagship's main deck for local Thai dignitaries and military brass. With the business of war averted, the Seventh Fleet staff made a seamless transition to its other primary mission in the region: fostering friendship and maritime security partnerships among US allies.

As Director for Theater Security, Preston would have played a lead role in coordinating the in-port engagements. Now a fresh set of challenges lay in front of him. As the helicopter lifted off the deck, Leo turned to Preston. "I convinced the boss not to fill your position, Pres. We'll make do with an acting N7, expecting you to return soon. The Navy owes you that chance. Admiral Lewis is skeptical. I've never seen him so upset. But he respects your record, and at the core he's a compassionate man. He's giving you one hell of a chance."

Preston's eyes avoided the chief of staff. "I appreciate that, Leo. I'll do what I have to do. I'm a Marine. I survive."

"We need you here, Pres. The fleet needs you. Hell, the nation needs you. Put this behind you, for good. Take care of your issues and get back here, ready to go to work."

"Oo-rah," said Preston with a downcast smirk. He paused, then changed the subject.

"How will you handle Mahoney now?"

"Handle? I won't. I can't touch her. I can only hope to direct her considerable energy and ambition to serve the common good."

"Common good? Strange words coming from you."

"The boss chewed my ass big time after the mast hearings. He gave me specific rudder orders. My job and career are on the line. I'm supposed to be more 'collegial' in my dealings with the ACOSes, especially Mahoney." He smirked. "She'll screw up, eventually. Ambitious women always do."

Preston thought for a moment. "I hope she doesn't crash and burn."

"What?"

"The Navy needs officers like Kate Mahoney, unafraid to challenge assumptions and take chances. As an institution, we've become too stodgy, too risk-averse. Nowadays, many officers won't take a stand against higher authority, afraid to kill their promotion chances. Kate cares more about being right than being proper, less about moving up the career ladder. Even you must admit that's a fresh new attitude." He smiled. "Worked out for the best in the last operation."

Leo sniggered. "She got help from you."

"Because she was right. I took too long to see it."

Leo stared at his friend. "Pres, I want you to get your head straight on this alcohol thing, but don't you dare go soft on me. The Navy needs good men like you."

Preston stood up. "The Navy needs officers who put mission and people first over personal gain. Gender is irrelevant."

Leo scoffed. He stood and reached out his hand in a warm gesture. "Fair winds, shipmate."

Preston nodded as he shook the chief of staff's hand. "Thanks, Leo." Then he turned and left the room.

Scheduled to disembark the ship as soon as it made port, Preston knew he should pack up. His feet took him to the flag mess instead. Maybe Kate would be there. She had not spoken to him since the admiral's mast. He opened the door and looked in. No Kate.

What would I say to her?

Heading toward his stateroom, he took a detour past Kate's office. She was not there. He detoured again to walk by her stateroom. His steps hesitated in front of the closed door, sensing her presence on the other side.

Don't be a fool.

Preston walked on to his own stateroom.

Chapter Ninety-Seven

April 24, 2012, Gulf of Thailand: USS *Shenandoah*

In her stateroom, Kate fought the urge to smash her fist through her computer screen to destroy the mocking Facebook message box.

Your message will be sent to PatWalk's phone.

She typed again.

Scarlett: Patrick, you cannot avoid me forever. We need to work through this. My ship just pulled into Thailand. I'm staying at a hotel for the next few nights. I will call you from there tonight. You need to answer the phone when I call. If you don't, I'll have Colleen take it away from you.

She waited for a response, even though she knew Patrick had not logged on. Then the text box refreshed.

Your message will be sent to PatWalk's phone.

Kate buried her head in her hands. She looked up as footsteps approached and stopped outside her door. After a few seconds, the footsteps moved away.

She sighed. Kate felt trapped, incarcerated inside her steel-walled room with no windows, a small cell within a floating metal fortress, populated by people with agendas.

What is Kate's agenda? Where do I go from here? What the hell do I want?

The outcome of her Korea operation promised success in her current job—as long as Darnell Lewis remained the commander. She allowed herself a smile as she recalled how she had bluffed Leo LeBlanc into abandoning his efforts to derail her. Would he ever realize how close he'd come?

I could still lose Patrick—if I haven't already.

What a pathetic coincidence that Patrick's parent crisis happened around the same age as hers.

Am I any better as a parent than Tom Mahoney?

"Get a grip, woman," she said aloud. "Nowhere close to that degree of terrible."

She shook off her melancholy mood and turned back to her unclassified computer to enter a Google search: *Job opportunities for pilots.*

The screen came alive with a credible list of sites seeking pilots with jet experience—not only with airlines, but with companies throughout the world. For an hour, Kate browsed those sites, bookmarking the ones with the most appeal.

I will find a better life for me and Preston.

She scowled and shook her head.

I mean Patrick and me, of course.

Chapter Ninety-Eight

April 25, 2012, Laem Chabang, Thailand

Liberty call had begun. Lines of sailors and officers in dappled resort wear streamed off their respective brows to board liberty buses for the ride into Pattaya Beach. Many looked forward to a raucous weekend taking part in the annual Thai New Year's water festival, the *Songkran*. Wet days and nights—in more than one sense—lay ahead of them.

Preston emerged onto the quarterdeck, dressed in muted civilian clothes, hefting a full sea bag. A *Shenandoah* junior medical officer, also attired in civilian clothes but carrying a smaller suitcase, joined him. Preston's assigned escort no doubt had orders to never let the colonel out of his site, even for head calls, until delivered to the Navy alcohol rehabilitation center in San Diego.

Addressing the officer of the deck, Preston held up his ID card. "I have permission to go ashore."

The OOD saluted. "Aye, aye, Colonel. Best wishes, sir."

Preston nodded to the young Navy officer. He stepped onto

the brow, turned to face aft, and saluted toward the national ensign. He turned back and descended the brow to an official van waiting on the pier, threw his sea bag into the back of the van, and took the front seat next to the driver. His medical escort climbed into the back.

As the vehicle moved, Preston looked back at the ship and noticed Kate hefting a suitcase down the brow. She wore khaki slacks and a yellow blouse, her hair in a casual ponytail. Alexis Sideris and Eric Mikleson accompanied her, casually attired but bearing smaller pieces of baggage.

"Stop the van," Preston told the driver. As Kate and her friends descended the brow, he got out and stood by the van. They had to pass him as they walked down the pier.

When she passed him, Kate looked away. Preston called after her. She stopped and turned around, but did not walk back toward him.

Preston gestured to his van. "Can I offer you all a lift?"

"No thanks," said Kate. "We have our own ride into Pattaya. Wouldn't want to risk you missing your flight."

"Suit yourself," Preston said.

Kate and her friends walked away. After a few paces, she stopped, asked them to wait, and returned to where Preston stood.

"Colonel, I hope things work out for you." Her voice had a sharp, formal edge. "The staff needs your expertise." She hesitated, glanced away, then looked at him. "I never thanked you for your support in the last phase of the operation." She shrugged. "So, uh, thanks. I wish you well."

A hint of a smile crossed Preston's face. "Thanks, Kate. That means a lot. You take care of yourself now." He reached out to shake her hand, but she turned to rejoin her friends.

He called after her. "Kate."

She stopped and looked at him.

"I hope everything works out with your son."

She glared at him. "Thanks." She turned away and did not look back.

* * *

"Our own ride?" said Alexis when Kate caught up with them.

"That liberty bus over there. The ride may not be as comfortable as a van, but the company is better."

Alexis and Eric looked at each other.

As they walked toward the liberty bus, the van passed them. Preston saluted Kate through the window. She stopped walking and stared after the vehicle until it disappeared from view.

Chapter Ninety-Nine

April 25, 2012, San Bruno, CA

"I won't move to Japan."

Patrick had answered his iPhone; not because his mom had threatened, but because he had to make her understand. On his computer, he continued to melee with Fuchou and the rest of their Horde team. "My life is here."

"I understand how you feel," she said.

Then stop bugging me about it.

She continued to talk. No surprise. "As your mother, I decide what's best—for both of us. We need to spend more time together."

"Then quit the Navy, like you said before."

"I can't just leave. I have to stay another year until I can retire. After that, we can live wherever we want."

"I'll stay here until then." On the screen, his best crane kick took out three enemies at once.

"We've already drifted too far apart," she said. "We need to reconnect."

"That won't work. You'll go off on that ship. I'll be in Japan by myself. What kind of connection is that?"

"You'll have friends."

"I have friends here. I don't need new ones." He hesitated, then said it. "Plus, I have a job here."

His mother blew into the phone. She spoke in a trembling voice. "You do not have a job. You have payback for a crime that you would not have committed if I'd been closer to you. Your Homer House arrangement stops as soon as you've finished your required hours." She huffed. "It may have to stop sooner. There are other ways to get those hours."

Shocked, Patrick shouted into the phone. "No way. I like it there. I'm good for those kids."

The phone went silent. When she talked again, her voice had calmed. "I'm proud of you for that, son. But right now, family has to come first."

Family? What family?

"I'm not moving to Japan, Mom."

"Yes, you are. You don't get to choose."

Patrick squinted against the tears in his eyes. Then he had a thought—a welcome thought. He steadied his voice, attempted to sound resigned. "Okay, Mom. You win. Whatever you say."

She paused. He heard her heavy breathing. "I promise I'll make it work for us—for both of us."

"Sure, Mom."

"I love you," she said.

"You too," he said.

They both disconnected. Patrick punched in the speed-dial for Homer House.

413

- Mike Krentz -

Chapter One Hundred

April 25, 2012, Pattaya Beach, Thailand

Lush foliage surrounded the Marriott's free-form pool within a sequestered courtyard that shut out the chaos and street noise as the locals launched into celebrating the weekend water festival. Wearing a modest two-piece bathing suit and matching cover, Kate found a secluded lounge chair lit by warm sunshine. She spotted a few other refugees from the *Shenandoah* and Seventh Fleet Staff around the pool, but all seemed engrossed in their own private worlds, happy to get away from enforced camaraderie on the ship. They would not bother Kate. She ordered a Mai Tai from the roving waiter, slipped off her cover, and stretched out on the lounge chair. The sensuous warmth of the sun bathed her bare skin as she relaxed her mind.

She opened a romance novel, eager to escape into a provocative universe removed from her real world. Immersed in the novel, she rode the pages like waves, each one taking her farther away from *Shenandoah* and the recent events there.

Memory of her conversation with Patrick blocked her escape.

415

Kate gave up reading and closed her eyes. Her mind swirled. Maybe Patrick had not been entirely sincere, but at least he agreed.

A start. Movement.

The intoxicating sun, the rum, and the cumulative fatigue of the last two weeks soon caused her to doze off. The book fell onto the pool deck.

* * *

Kate awoke from an erotic dream, startled by someone standing next to her. She opened her eyes to a tall, well-built male figure silhouetted against the sun behind him. He wore swim shorts and a tee shirt. Even with his face obscured in shade, Kate recognized Preston Davis.

"Sorry, Kate. I didn't mean to startle you."

Was this man in her dream? Was she still asleep? Shaking herself to full consciousness, she felt a warm delight. Then she remembered to be angry.

"What? You're supposed to be . . ."

She sat up on the edge of the lounge—hastening to don her bathing suit cover—and looked up at him. He stepped back into the sunlight, his face relaxed, smiling.

"Flight canceled. Had to rebook for tomorrow. We got rooms here."

"Another mythical hotel room, Colonel?" She hoped that her voice projected the irritated edge that she intended.

"This one is real."

Kate searched the surrounding space. "Where's your escort?"

Preston chuckled. "The young doc? I bought him a drink at the bar and negotiated 'honor time.' I'm allowed to hang out unescorted around the hotel, but I can't leave the premises."

Kate shook her head. "Ever the manipulator."

He seemed taken aback by that.

She squinted at him. "You couldn't get a hotel at the Bangkok airport?"

Preston shrugged. "Just as easy to have the van bring us back here to be around friends and shipmates. You know, for the baby doc. I hate he has to miss a great port visit on my account."

Kate waved him away. "Go find friends then."

He stood his ground, rubbed his hand through his hair. "Look Kate, I'm very sorry about what I said to you that night in Singapore. I was way out of line. Not the man I want to be around you—then, or now."

Kate refused to accept his apology. She pointed to his hand gripping a glass of amber-colored liquid, poured over ice, and raised her eyebrows.

"Ginger ale." He held the glass out to her. "Want some?"

She held up her hand. "No, thanks." An awkward silence descended. "What time is it?"

"About 1700."

"I slept too long." Her chest and upper thighs felt hot, moist from the heat. From the dream?

Preston shuffled, uneasy. "Would you be interested in dinner? I can't leave the hotel, but the restaurant here looks pretty good."

She winced. "Bad idea."

"It's just dinner, Kate. No drinks. Well, you can have a drink. I won't."

She found it difficult to stay angry. "Maybe I have plans."

Preston tilted his head. "I'm not going anywhere. I'll either eat with you or by myself."

She thought about it. Conversation might be better than

isolated anxiety. "I plan to dine at the restaurant at 1830. You can join me there if you want."

He smiled. "1830, aye."

Kate rose to leave.

Preston raised the romance novel that had fallen to the deck when she fell asleep.

"I think you dropped this. I picked it up so it wouldn't get wet."

She blushed as she reached out her hand. "Thanks."

He turned the book in his hand. "I enjoy her novels. Haven't read this one yet." He smiled as he handed her the book. "See you at 1830. I'm going to get in a quick swim first."

She watched as he took off his tee shirt and dove into the water.

What the hell are you doing now, Mahoney?

She hurried back to her room, bounding across the patio like a giddy coed.

Chapter One Hundred One

April 25, 2012, Pattaya Beach, Thailand

"Would you like some wine?"

Kate frowned across the table at Preston. "Do you think that's a good idea?"

He smiled, patronizing. "I won't have any, but you can. It won't bother me."

"I don't understand how you turn off the craving—or whatever it is." Kate winced, embarrassed at her directness.

Preston smiled, looked her in the eye. "Hi. I'm Preston, and I'm an alcoholic." He shrugged. "It's easy to say it. I know what I am. I accept what I must do. This is not my first sobriety rodeo. I figured you'd have guessed that by now."

"I didn't mean to pry." She looked at her plate.

Preston flagged down a waiter. "Please bring the lady a glass of—?" He turned to Kate.

"I don't need wine." Her voice sounded sharper than she'd

419

intended.

"You've earned a relaxing evening. I will regret it if my personal problems stifle you."

"Fine." She glanced over the wine list, then looked at the waiter. "I'll have a glass of the Mollydooker Shiraz."

"I'll have soda with a splash of grenadine," Preston said.

They perused their menus in silence until the waiter brought the drinks. Preston raised his glass to Kate. "Here's to the architect of an innovative, successful military strategy. You should be proud of what you did in the last weeks. Cheers."

Reluctant, she raised her glass and touched his, glancing down as she did. "Thank you, sir. It wasn't all me. Your support with the admiral sold the deal."

"Your plan sold itself, on its own merits, Kate. And please don't call me 'sir'."

She looked at him and smiled. "Aye, aye, sir."

After the waiter took their food orders, Preston again raised his glass to her. "Let's try this again. Here's to you, Kate."

Even more uncomfortable, she raised her glass and touched his again. She looked away.

He gave her a sly smile. "If you don't make eye contact when you toast someone, you are doomed to seven years of unsatisfying sex."

Annoyed, Kate picked up her half-empty glass of wine, cleared her throat, and raised her glass. "Better than no sex at all. Cheers." As they touched glasses, she looked him in the eye and held her gaze until he glanced away. Then she downed the rest of her drink, savoring the warmth that washed through her.

"That's excellent wine. I'll have another glass, with your permission, sir."

She looked straight at him until he averted his eyes.

"You win, Captain." Preston raised his hands in a gesture of surrender. "Again." Then he beckoned the waiter.

Chapter One Hundred Two

April 25, 2012, Pattaya Beach, Thailand

"I'll walk you to your room." Preston made it a declarative statement, as if he'd just described the weather.

"I can make it okay." Kate felt giddy after the wine and the after-dinner cordials. During the evening, she had lost her discomfort at drinking in front of him.

"I insist," he said. "I am still an officer and a gentleman. A Marine never lets a lady walk home alone."

Kate didn't reply. She'd heard that line from Luke Walker years ago.

She and Preston strolled across the pool area in silence. Kate felt her pulse pick up. The night was warm and the air clear. The sequestered confines of the hotel courtyard sheltered them from the raucous street celebrations a block away. *Shenandoah* and all its stresses, Leo LeBlanc—even Patrick—seemed a world away.

Kate's room edged the courtyard, near to the swimming pool.

When they reached it, she fumbled with her key card.

Am I that nervous? Or just drunk?

"Need help?" Preston's voice, still declarative, neither joked nor jibed. Kate refused help, got the door open, and stood in the doorway. She held out her hand.

"Thank you for sharing dinner with me, Colonel. I wish you—Oh, my God." She pulled him into the room and closed the door.

Preston's eyes widened. "What the—"

Kate held a hand to her mouth. "Doc Cushing. Walking across the courtyard as if he was looking for someone. I—sorry, I panicked. I didn't want him to see us together."

Preston chuckled. "You didn't before now? He was at the pool this afternoon. No doubt saw us talking there. He was in the lounge while we were at dinner."

Kate flushed. "What must he think?"

Preston furrowed his brow. "Why care? Men and women who know each other and work together as professional colleagues talk. Sometimes they have dinner together." He looked at her askance. "Why should you be afraid of what he might think?"

Kate's shoulders drooped. "We have a relationship."

Preston laughed. "You and the doc? Isn't he a bit old for you?"

She made a sour face. "Yuk. Not *that* kind of relationship. I meant a therapeutic relationship. He's helped me through some tough emotional times lately."

"Not a reason to hide." He squinted. "Or is it me you wanted to hide?" He stepped back. "What's going on, Kate?"

Kate felt a warmth rise within her, much more than she would expect from the alcohol in her body. She bit her lip, then

423

looked into Preston's eyes. He looked tentative, yet sensitive and warm.

"Well," she said. "I seem to have an issue about falling for marines. It never ends well."

"Doesn't mean the next one won't."

A longing arose in Kate that she'd not known for many years. She drew closer to him, looking up at him and parting her lips. "Pres, I—"

He backed away. "The doc is probably gone now." His voice turned flat, distant. He opened the door a crack and peeked out. "Coast looks clear." He turned to her. "Thanks, Kate."

I don't want you to go.

"I—you could—"

He grasped her shoulders, leaned forward, and planted a chaste kiss on her forehead, like a kind uncle. "Good night, Kate."

He opened the door and started out. She went after him. "Colonel."

Preston turned. Kate thought she saw longing in his eyes.

"Good luck," she said. "I hope you come back." She put her hand to her cheek. "To Seventh Fleet, I mean."

"Thanks, Captain. I intend to do that." Then he was gone.

Kate closed the door. If Doc was still skulking about, she didn't want him to see the tears on her face.

* * *

Alone in her room, Kate undressed, donned a large tee shirt, and went to bed. She felt charged up, not at all sleepy. She read her romance novel but became frustrated by the erotic descriptions of lovemaking.

Kate tossed the book aside, turned out the light, and tried to sleep.

Two minutes later, she turned the light back on and reopened her book. She read through the love scene, but could not stop thinking about Preston and how he walked out just as she'd wanted him to stay. She touched her forehead where he had placed his avuncular peck. At once, she fumed.

He treated me like a child.

Kate turned off the light and tossed in the bed, awash in frustration. She flipped the light back on, got out of bed, and opened the minibar. She found two small bottles of Courvoisier, which she emptied into a drinking glass from the bathroom. Picking up the romance novel, she sat in the chair sipping the cognac and reading. After a couple of pages, she had trouble focusing and gave up. Then she sat on the edge of the bed and put her hand on the bedside phone.

What would I say to him?

Angry with herself, Kate turned off the light and got back into bed. She flopped around like a wounded fish. Never had she felt such sexual frustration. Finally, she kicked away the covers, turned on her side, and pulled the pillow between her legs.

* * *

Kate opened her eyes to the sound of the alarm clock. The dim light coming through the curtain suggested early dawn. She sat up and looked at the clock: 4:30.

The ring was not the alarm clock, but her Blackberry on the desk across the room.

Wrapping herself in the top sheet, Kate walked over to the desk and answered.

"Ma'am, this is the Seventh Fleet watch officer. Sorry to disturb you this early, but we just received a call from your sister in California. She asks that you call her right away. It's an emergency."

425

Chapter One Hundred Three

April 25, 2012, Pattaya Beach, Thailand

As the first light of dawn peeked into his room, Preston Davis lay on his back and stared at the ceiling. He had slept in fits and starts through the night, remembering how Kate had looked at him with those inviting green eyes. He had wanted her far more than the warm flush in his head had indicated.

Yet he had pushed her away. Why? How? He could not deny his feelings for her, unlike any he could remember. Kate felt something too, at that moment, inside her room. She had sent a clear signal. Preston could have swept her into his arms.

It was neither the time nor the place. How ironic was that?

As much as Preston desired Kate, at that moment her fragility matched his own. Whatever was happening between them could easily break and disappear forever. Preston could not risk having that responsibility on his conscience on top of everything else.

Sometimes you must love someone enough to pretend you

427

don't.

Preston had a harder challenge ahead. He harbored no illusions—even to himself—that he could salvage his career in the Marine Corps. No chance in hell. The words of Darnell Lewis echoed in his mind. Preston Davis, the man, was worth saving. Preston would save that man, even at the loss of what would have been a very pleasant night with Kate Mahoney.

He glanced at the minibar. At another time in his life, those little bottles would ease the disappointment of a missed opportunity. Preston had kept the bar closed. A small step. Why? For Kate? Darnell? No. For himself. For his own life.

As the light continued to grow in the room, he looked at the bedside clock. 5:05. Soon, he needed to get dressed and meet his ride to Bangkok for the long trip to permanent sobriety.

Ten minutes later, his bedside phone rang. He had not left a wake-up call.

A smile crossed his face when he recognized Kate's voice—until he realized she was talking through tears.

"Colonel, this is Kate Mahoney. Sorry to call so early, but I didn't know where else to turn." She gulped and then continued. "I wonder if—could I ride with you to the airport?"

He waited for her to explain, but all he heard was her distressed breathing. "Of course," he said. "What's wrong, Kate?"

"My son is missing. I have to go find him."

"I'll be right there."

Chapter One Hundred Four

April 26, 2012, San Francisco International Airport

Almost twenty-four hours after her frantic early morning call, Kate, Preston, and his escort deplaned into the San Francisco international terminal. With Preston's help, Kate had booked the first available flight connecting out of Bangkok through Tokyo to San Francisco. Preston and his escort were already booked on the same itinerary with a follow-on connection from San Francisco to San Diego for Preston's admission to the Navy's inpatient alcohol treatment center.

They had ridden in the van from Pattaya to Bangkok in nervous silence. When they checked in, Preston manipulated the seat assignments so that he and Kate sat next to each other on all the flights. In between meals and naps, Kate told Preston about her entire history with Patrick—including her marriage to Luke. In a subdued voice, she told him about her assault on Luke and its aftermath, including Leo LeBlanc's recent attempt to dig up the details. She also told him of her concerns about Patrick's online life, his escapade with Colleen's car, and his infatuation with a man called Homer.

"I told Colleen to call Homer House and ask if Patrick was there. They said they hadn't seen him. I don't believe it. If he wanted to leave home, that's where he would go."

"What about the police?"

"They won't get involved until he's been missing for forty-eight hours. They told Colleen that most runaway kids Patrick's age return home within that time."

"That's absurd," Preston said. "Check out this Homer House for yourself."

"Exactly what I intend to do."

He looked at her with eyes that showed genuine concern. "Be careful."

"I can take care of myself."

"I have no doubt, Kate." He smiled. "But be careful."

The flight attendant announced the final approach to San Francisco, ending their conversation.

* * *

Once they cleared customs, they came to a juncture that divided connecting passengers from those ending their travel in San Francisco. Preston stopped, gave his escort a commanding look that said to back off, and turned towards Kate. The young doctor excused himself to go to the bathroom.

Preston took her hand. "I wish you the best, Kate. It will all work out for you."

"Thank you, Pres." She heaved a sigh. "I wish you the same. I look forward to your return to Seventh Fleet."

"Thanks. That means more to me than you know."

As he walked away, she called after him.

"Preston, wait."

She dropped her bags and walked up to him. "Thank you for not crossing the line with me in my room the other night."

Preston smiled, a warm glow in his eyes. "Maybe we can cross that line someday. When all our ghosts are behind us. And . . ." He gave her a knowing smile. "When both of us are sober."

Kate's mouth dropped.

Preston frowned. "I'm sorry. I didn't mean that the way it sounded."

She looked at him with the same firm gaze she had used at dinner, when she met his challenge to look him in the eye as they toasted.

"If had been sober, I would not have let you leave my room."

He looked puzzled.

"Because," she said, "I would have known that I and not the buzz wanted you."

He opened his arms, and she fell into his embrace. Their lips brushed together, tentative; then their mouths locked into a deep, passionate kiss. It lasted a few seconds, and an eternity.

When they pulled apart, Kate saw the escort approaching. She wiped her eyes and whispered, "Take care, Pres. Please come back."

She walked away and did not look behind her.

* * *

Preston watched her until she was out of sight. He turned to his escort. "I got to hit the head myself, Doc. If you could do the luggage drop, I'll catch up with you at the gate."

431

Chapter One Hundred Five

April 26, 2012, San Francisco, CA

Colleen turned her car onto Haight Street. "There's no place to park."

Kate had insisted that Colleen drive her from the airport straight to Homer House. By the time they navigated through the traffic, they had reached the end of rush hour. Neighborhood residents had taken all the on-street parking.

"Just drop me off," Kate said. "Drive around the block. If Patrick's not there, I'll come right out."

Kate found the front door to Homer House open. She entered a small, vacant reception area. Behind the counter, a light at the end of an otherwise dark hallway

"Hello?" No response. She walked around the counter and called again. "Hello? Mister Homer?"

A gravelly male voice answered. "In the back."

Her spine tingling, Kate walked with caution down the

hallway to a small office, the source of the solitary light. She stopped to peek around the open door. The room reeked of stale tobacco. Behind an ancient desk, the back of a thin man with long, sandy brown hair. He faced a computer terminal, typing. Two suitcases, one large, one smaller, stood beside the desk.

"Mister Homer?"

The man spun his chair around to face her. A wicked smile crossed his face. "Hello, Kate."

She gasped. Her hands came up to her face, and a band tightened around her chest. For a second, she could not breathe. The man looked so much thinner than Kate remembered. No muscle mass. His face had grizzled with age, most of it obscured by the graying beard and long hair.

The cold, steely blue eyes that bored into her soul could belong only to one man.

Luke Walker leaned forward in his chair and extended his arms over the desk in a gesture of welcome. "I've been expecting you."

Kate's fragile world collapsed around her. Her instincts told her to run, but her knees trembled, and she could not move her feet. She took a deep breath.

No running away. Finish this.

Her heart pounded in her chest. While she struggled with the sudden change in reality, Luke stared at her. He rose from his chair. Kate inched backward toward the open doorway.

"What's wrong, babe?" She knew that mocking voice so well. "Not scared, I hope. I thought you would be happy to see me, after so many years."

Terrified, Kate thought about Patrick and found her voice—quivering and shrill. "What? What are you doing here?"

Luke made a circling gesture with his arm. "I run this center for abandoned children. Something about which I have much experience."

His evil grin brought Kate down to earth. She glanced at the suitcases. "Going on a trip?"

He sat down. "Maybe."

Kate fathomed what was happening. "Is Patrick here?"

Luke leaned back, put his hands behind his head. "Not at the moment. He lives here now—by choice. After your sister called looking for him yesterday, I figured you'd show up in whatever time it takes to get here from Sayonaraland. I sent him on some errands. Won't be back soon."

"Does he know you—?"

Luke shook his head. "You and I talk first. Alone."

Kate felt as if a hammer pounded the top of her head. "How did you—"

Luke shot her a wicked grin. "I've worked this a long time, Kate. My turn to be his parent."

"No way."

"You don't get to choose. He's fourteen. He can choose for himself."

"You manipulated him."

"What a cruel accusation." Luke scoffed. "Don't tell me about manipulation. Not after what you pulled."

"I don't know what you mean."

In a sudden rage, Luke pounded his fist on the desk. "The hell you don't!"

His angry eruption forced Kate back on her heels. She glanced behind to assure herself the doorway would provide a ready exit.

Luke didn't notice. He went into a rant. "First you trap me into giving you a kid, and then you get your high and mighty Navy brass to bully me into giving him up." His face turned crimson. "I lost my career. I lost my dignity. Change my identity, just to get a job to support myself."

"I never trapped you. You raped me."

"Not how I remember it."

"Figures. You were drunk out of your gourd that night."

"You didn't say no." He sneered. "How did you get pregnant, Kate? Forget your pills again? You knew what you were doing."

Kate felt like she'd been gut-punched. "I never—"

Luke raised a hand. "Shut it." He shook his head. "You got what you wanted, then walked away. You took my son and never looked back. Didn't give a crap about me. Never. You used me. When I was no more use to you, you kicked me into the garbage like a piece of trash."

Kate moved back a step.

The man has lost his grip on reality.

Luke glared at her through narrowed eyes. "You've had this coming for a long time, Kate Mahoney. Now, I have my son. For once, you are going into the trash where you belong."

The man is unstable. Do not play his game.

"Where is Patrick? I've come to take him home."

"This is his home. He'll be back soon. Ask him if he wants to go anywhere with you, least of all halfway around the world to Japan."

Kate bit her lip. How much of his life had Patrick revealed to this "Mr. Homer"? Gloom engulfed her like a thick black cloud. Desperate to flee this man and this place, she could not do that—if Patrick might come through that door.

435

Seize the advantage.

Her eyes flitted around the room, looking for something that she could use as a defensive weapon.

Luke noticed. "No kitchen knives here, Kate. The only knife we have . . ." He opened a drawer in his desk. "Is this one." He pulled out a naval aviator's survival knife and set it on top of the desk. "Don't get any stupid ideas about going physical."

He drew the knife out of its sheath, ran his finger along the edge, picked up a piece of paper, and sliced it in half with one swift slash.

"Sharpened it this morning."

Chapter One Hundred Six

April 26, 2012, San Francisco, CA

Patrick lugged two bags of groceries through the front door. Earnest voices came from Mister Homer's office. Thinking it was a parent or counselor with Mr. Homer, Patrick did not want to interrupt. He climbed the stairs to the second-floor apartment and put away the groceries. Then he sat at the kitchen table to log onto his laptop. Maybe he could connect to Fuchou and set up the next gaming session. He left the apartment door open so he would hear Mr. Homer's guest depart.

The downstairs voices grew louder, angry. Mr. Homer was arguing with a woman. That would be strange. Curious, Patrick walked halfway down the stairs.

His mother's voice!

He descended the stairs, crept down the hall to Mr. Homer's office, and peeked through the open door. His mother stood facing Mr. Homer's desk.

Crap. She found me.

Patrick stole backwards up the hallway. He did not want his mother to see him. Homer would get rid of her. Patrick could hide upstairs until the coast was clear. As he reached the stairs, his mother's high-pitched voice caught his attention.

"Luke, you don't have to do this."

Luke?

In a flash, Patrick recognized what he had suspected—and hoped—since he first met Mr. Homer. He ran down the hallway and rushed into the room.

His mother stood in front of the desk. Homer—Luke?—stood behind it, cradling a knife in his hand. He stopped talking when he saw Patrick. The knife clattered onto the desk.

"Here's Patrick now."

His mother turned, grabbed Patrick's arm, spun him around, and shoved him toward the doorway. "We have to get out of here now."

Patrick dug his heels into the carpet and yanked his arm away. He stood between his mother and the door. She tried to push him through it. He shoved back.

She stumbled backwards.

Homer had yanked her by the hair from behind. His other hand held the knife.

"No one goes anywhere until I say so."

Homer pointed the knife at Patrick's mother with one hand and pushed her into a chair with the other. "Sit down, Kate. This won't take long. Then we can all go our own ways."

He looked at Patrick and spoke in a kind but firm voice. "Please sit in the other chair while I explain."

With a mix of terror and anger in her eyes, his mother

motioned Patrick to the chair next to her. He sat.

"Patrick," she said in an icy voice, "This is your father, Luke Walker. That's his real name. Mr. Homer is a fake."

Patrick studied the man leaning on the edge of his desk. "You've been around me before now. Before—"

Luke Walker smiled. "I've known you a long time, son. I could not reveal myself until now. Until you were old enough to choose for yourself."

His mother stared daggers at his father. "You stalked him?"

In a casual motion, Patrick's father brandished the knife. "Please shut up while I speak to my son. You've had your years with him. My turn now."

His mother turned to him. "You don't have to do this, Patrick. We can leave."

At once Patrick seethed. "I have a right, Mom. You can't keep me from knowing my father."

She looked up at the ceiling. Then she glared at Luke Walker. "Have your say. When you're done, Patrick and I are leaving."

"We'll see about that," Luke said.

Down the hallway, the front door to Homer House opened. All heads turned toward the sound.

Colleen's voice. "Kate, are you here? I found a parking spot. I got worried when you didn't come out. Hello?"

Luke turned on Kate. "Get rid of her." He pointed at Patrick. "Nothing about this."

Mom got out of her chair, went to the door, and poked her head out. "I'm back here, Sis, talking to Mr. Homer. Patrick's not here, but we might have a lead. I'll be out soon. You can wait in the car."

Aunt Colleen's voice sounded strange. "I'll just wait here." Patrick's mother turned back into the room and shut the door behind her.

Luke Walker stroked the knife's blade. "We will all use our quiet voices now." He looked back and forth between Patrick and his mother. Then he looked straight at Patrick. "I don't know what Kate has told you, son. I can only imagine. But—"

Patrick interrupted. "She never told me anything."

Luke looked at Kate and raised his eyebrows. "Really?" He looked back at Patrick. "I would have thought otherwise. Truth is, we had some hard times when you were a baby. I did some shameful things. Your mom took you away. Maybe she needed to do that."

He leaned forward, shifting his eyes between Patrick and his mother. "She never gave me a chance to come back, to get it right, or to know you. She ruined me. Ruined you and me both."

Mom stood and took Patrick's arm. "We will not listen to this."

Luke leaned over the desk and pointed the knife at her chest. "Sit down. I get my say."

Terror rose in Patrick's chest. His mother sat. Luke Walker, his father, looked at him.

"I made myself better, and then I found you. You had just turned five."

A flash of recognition struck Patrick. "My birthday party."

His father nodded. "After that, I watched from a distance as you grew up. I saw what she did to you."

He scowled, ugly-faced. "She was no mother. How many times did she go away and leave you with your aunt, like she's done now? You think she'd even think about you now if Auntie hadn't sounded the alarm?"

Patrick stared at the floor.

"She took you away from your father, yet she refused to be your mother. You deserve better. You deserve a full-time parent. That's me. In your mom's life, you'll always be second. For me, you will always be number one."

His mother spoke. "Stop it. You speak poison."

His dad flared. "Shut up. You got no right." He moved around beside the desk. "You got no power in here. This is my turf."

Mom tensed and her fists clenched, but she didn't speak. She reached out to hold his hand.

Patrick needed her to do that.

Luke scoffed. "Really, Kate. *Now* you hold his hand? A little late."

He turned his eyes on Patrick. "You are old enough now. You can make your own choice about where you live, with which parent. We can go to court. The judge will rule for whatever you want. You can choose to stay with me."

Mom snorted. "No court is going to place a child with you. Not with your record. Not after what you did." She motioned at the knife in his hand. "Certainly not after this act."

Luke glared at her. "I told you to shut up. Since you mentioned my 'record,' your son should know that they railroaded me out to save your precious female naval aviator ass."

Patrick looked at his mom. "What?"

"Go ahead, Kate. Tell our son how you tried to kill me. How your Navy brass covered it up, and you walked. Tell Patrick who you really are."

"I've told him all about that night, Luke. He knows how you got drunk and tried to hurt him."

Luke scoffed. "So you say. You never had to prove anything.

You walked, and I paid. Now it's payback time."

Mom stood. "No more of this. Come on, Patrick." With a strength that surprised him, she yanked him out of the chair and pulled him to the door. She grasped the doorknob. "Colleen!"

In a flash, Luke body-blocked her into the door frame. He raised the knife.

Patrick lunged at his father.

Chapter One Hundred Seven

April 26, 2012, San Francisco, CA

Kate struggled to free herself from the weight of Luke's body, shoving her against the doorjamb. His left hand circled her throat. His other hand raised the knife, aimed at her chest.

Patrick lunged and knocked Luke off balance. The knife skittered under the desk. All three of them fell to the floor in a heap against the closed door.

Footsteps approached from the hallway. Colleen's voice. "What's going on in there?"

Colleen tried to push open the door, but the three heaped bodies blocked it. Luke and Patrick rolled off Kate.

Patrick helped his mother to her feet.

Luke Walker had backed away into the corner of the room, both arms raised. "Patrick, I was fooling with that knife. I would never hurt your mother, or you."

Kate got to her feet, put herself between Patrick and Luke.

She spoke without taking her eyes off Luke. "Patrick, please get that knife from under the desk."

"Really, Kate? You're going to come at me with a knife? Again?"

She glared at him. "You started this."

He shook his head. "Just having some fun with you and the boy. No harm meant."

Patrick crawled under the desk and retrieved the knife.

Kate reached out her hand. "Give it to me."

He stepped away. "No."

Luke chuckled. "That's my boy. I'll take it."

"Not giving it to you, either." Patrick snarled. "You are both disgusting."

"Patrick," Kate said. "Get out of here. Go to Aunt Colleen."

Where the hell is she? Why didn't she open the door when we moved away from it?

Multiple sets of footsteps sounded from the hallway. Had Colleen called the police?

The door burst open. Kate turned.

Preston Davis stood in the doorway, Colleen behind him. Preston surveyed the scene in front of him, locked eyes with Luke. "Are you all right, Kate?"

Kate glared at Luke. "We're fine, Colonel. Just a show of force here." She took Patrick by the arm and steered him toward the door. "We were just leaving."

Preston stood aside to let them into the hallway. As Patrick, Preston, and Colleen headed toward the front door, Kate turned, stood in the doorway, and pointed at Luke.

"You and I are not done."

Phase Five: Enable

Chapter One Hundred Eight

April 26, 2012, San Francisco International Airport

"I won't be long," Kate said to Colleen and Patrick as she and Preston alighted from Colleen's car at San Francisco International Airport. She turned to Preston. "I'll walk with you as far as security."

"You should have called the police," Preston said as they entered the airport. "You still should."

Kate shook her head. "I can't. That would dig up the past. All of it. None of us, least of all Patrick, need that." She slowed her pace. "I did what I had to do in Meridian to save Patrick. Worse, I wanted to kill Luke. Like I wanted to kill my father."

Preston looked at her with empathy, not judgment. "Luke is a sick man. No telling what he'll do next. If you won't have him arrested, at least take precautions—for you and for Patrick."

"Patrick will come back to Japan with me. Beyond that, we'll see." She gulped. "I was wrong to make Patrick grow up not

447

knowing his father. No matter how twisted Luke may have been, I had no right to erase him from Patrick's life. I need to fix that."

They reached the ticket counter. Kate held back while Preston exchanged his boarding pass for a later flight. She thought about Luke, how he had persevered to stay on the fringe of Patrick's life. Maybe he deserved better than he got.

He was right about one thing. I wanted to get pregnant. I wanted Patrick. I used Luke to get him.

She felt her throat where Luke had almost choked her. She visualized the glint of the knife point.

Maybe I deserved that.

She forced the thought from her head.

Delusion of an abused child, not of a free woman.

She should share that with Doc. No, she would never return to the fleet surgeon's room.

I'll find a real shrink and get my head right once and for all. Patrick deserves that. I deserve it.

She looked at Preston as he stood at the ticket counter. How different he seemed now—not at all the besotted waste of a man she'd loathed in Singapore. Today he had risked what little military future he had left and come for her. She remembered their passionate kiss a few hours ago. Kate wanted to feel that again, with that man who had proved himself a loyal friend.

Preston walked toward her, talking into his Blackberry. When he reached her side, he put it away. "The baby doc escort is waiting for me on the other side of security."

"I hope you don't face more trouble on account of—this." (She had started to say, "on account of me.")

"Doubt it. I've got this doc pretty well buffaloed, poor guy. I told him I received an emergency call from an old friend who needed immediate help with a dire problem. Couldn't leave that friend in the lurch."

"How noble of you." She smiled.

He stopped and turned to her. "Noble has nothing to do with friendship. When you care about someone, you do what you must."

Kate's throat felt dry. "Thank you." She shrugged. "Don't know what else to say. I'm not accustomed to anyone caring about me."

"You said enough."

"You saved my life."

"You saved mine first."

She squinted at him. "How?"

Preston smirked. "No way did Leo LeBlanc start me down this rehab road on his own initiative. I reckon you bullied him into doing it, even when I repulsed you. I owe you my life, Kate."

Preston looked away, but not before Kate saw the moisture in his eyes. When he looked back, the moisture was gone. "Time to go."

They embraced. She wanted to kiss him, but he made no move. She looked up at him. "This can't be the end."

"It's not. I'll see you back on the flagship." Then he kissed her, soft and quick—neither chaste nor passionate, but on the lips with feeling. He turned and walked through security. On the other side, he looked back and waved to her.

Kate watched him until he went out of sight. A tear formed in the corner of her eye. She wanted to trust him, but a familiar ache deep inside said it would never happen, not for Katherine Mahoney.

She turned away and walked back toward the front of the airport, back to Patrick.

Believe, Kate.

- Mike Krentz -

Chapter One Hundred Nine

April 26, 2012, San Francisco, CA

Alone in his apartment, Luke Walker limped to the refrigerator and grabbed two cans of beer. He opened one and took a deep quaff. The other he pressed against the welt on his side where Kate had kicked him. He limped back to his desk, lit a cigarette, fired up his computer, and logged onto the internet. Luke sucked down the rest of the beer and then opened the second can.

Typing with fury, he started his online game and opened a message box.

Fuchou: Fanpan, let's play.

THE END

- Mike Krentz -

FREE BOOKS and OTHER PRIZES

Sign up to receive Mike's regular newsletter that offers insights into military and emergency medicine, news about Mike's books, and a monthly contest for gift cards, novellas, and signed paperback books. No spam.

Join Mike's newsletter mailing list here:

https://mikejkrentz.com/newsletter

ALSO BY MIKE KRENTZ

Dr. Zack Winston Medical Conspiracy Thrillers

DEAD ALREADY

A drug-laced conspiracy. A former Navy surgeon with a harrowing history. Will a covert frame job end his career… and his life?

WARM AND DEAD

He flourishes in the heart of a hectic ER, but the threatened loss of family becomes his greatest fear. Can an intrepid doctor protect his own from a twisted mind?

TOXIC DEATH (Coming in 2024)

NEAR DEATH (Coming in 2025)

Mahoney & Squire Women's Military

ACKNOWLEDGEMENTS

This novel has trod a long and winding road with several stops over more than a decade to reach its present form.

Ten years ago, faced with the inevitability of retirement from the Navy, I made the glib decision to become a writer for my next career. This edition of my initial sortie into novel writing has weathered many false starts and random meanderings through the daunting world of a craft and business of which I knew very little, and still don't know much. With humble yet ardent gratitude, I acknowledge those who inspired and helped me along the way:

My wife, Kathryn not only signed onto the great Navy adventure with me but also sacrificed to support and endure my Piscean forays into rotating hobbies and avocations. You are more than the "ideal Navy wife." You are the perfect life companion.

My son, Matthew moved thirteen times in twenty years and attended seven different schools by high school graduation. You have risen to the challenge of being a military child. Whatever course your life takes, I am always proud of you.

My older children, Jewls, Lisa, Debi, and Michael. You've endured more than a fair share of your imperfect dad's life wanderings, yet remained loving and loyal through it all. You will always have my constant and unconditional love and gratitude.

My stepchildren, Kate and James suffered family disruption and turmoil plus the vicissitudes of a blended military family. Your adaptability and indomitable spirits are models for all of us.

Jayne Ann Krentz, cherished cousin-in-law, for your encouragement, support, gentle nudges, and solid counsel. Your confidence helped me to believe in myself as a writer. A special salute to Frank, who is more like a brother than a cousin to me.

My colleagues at The Muse Writers studio whose cogent commentaries and enthusiastic support elevated the quality of my writing: Kelly Sokol, the late John Cameron, Kim Engebrigtsen, Susan Paxton, Kelley McGee, John Aguiar, Hope Dahmen, Lea Ann Douglas, Jim Hodges, and Tamako Takamatsu. You all are fabulous writers whose works deserve publication. A huge thanks to Michael Khandelwal, founder and guiding light of The Muse for establishing a world-class writers' community in our hometown, and to Shawn Gervin who keeps the ship sailing north.

Lauran Strait and staff at Hampton Roads Writers. Their annual writers' conference rivals those hosted on a national level.

Cissy Hartley, Susan Simpson, Degan Outridge, and the staff at Writerspace/Killer Books for guiding me through the book promotion process.

A special salute to the men and especially the women of The World's Finest Staff — the officers, Sailors, Marines, and civilians who serve the Seventh Fleet commander in winning the peace over a vast world region ever teetering on the verge of conflict. Your consummate professionalism and selfless commitment to commander and mission represent the finest tradition of naval service. Few Americans will ever know or understand your sacrifices for our nation and its ideals. However unsung, you are all my heroes, and I am ever honored to have served with you aboard the flagship.

Most of thanks to my readers. I appreciate your investment

458

in my novels, in time and money. I hope you enjoyed reading this story as much as I did writing it.

If you are so inclined, I would appreciate a review on Amazon, Barnes and Noble, Goodreads, BookBub, and/or other retail platforms.

- Mike Krentz -

AUTHOR'S NOTE

Behind the scenes of any international military confrontation, a
dedicated team of warfighters labors around the clock to guide and
support the operational and tactical missions. These men and women
come from all walks of life and professions—career warriors,
logisticians, engineers, information systems experts, doctors,
lawyers, chaplains, public affairs specialists. Brand new sailors, mid-
career hopefuls, and seasoned veterans. They represent a cross-
section of the nation they serve. Their stories seldom appear in
national media. They don't carry weapons. They don't sail the ships,
fly the airplanes, drop the bombs, or storm the beaches. Look for
them behind desks and computers aboard the most sophisticated
floating command-and-control platform in the world: the fleet
flagship. Armed with complex, redundant technologies, these
warriors bring to bear their collective training, knowledge, and
experience to inform the fleet commander's critical decisions—high
stakes judgments that must either avert war or guarantee decisive
victory if the shooting starts.

The unsung men and women on a fleet commander's staff
work long hours in an austere and stressful environment, separated
from families, loved ones, and comforts of home. Like all who travel
the road of human condition, each one has a unique story—of joy
and pain, love and disappointed love, hopes and fears, triumph and

460

tragedy. Amid the realities of war and the threat of war, their human sojourns become even more inspirational. The fictional characters in this novel portray those stories.

Over the course of a twenty-year career as a Navy physician, I had the privilege and honor to serve alongside the Sailors and Marines who dedicate their lives to keep the peace around the world and to protect American interests abroad. The actual men and women of the flagship far overshadow my imaginary characters in upholding Navy core values of honor, courage, and commitment. While some may struggle with personal flaws and challenges, they rise above them as they accomplish sometimes horrific missions.

The people and situations in this novel are make believe. The actual military women and men who do the nation's work every day are true American heroes who never pale in the face of a real or potential enemy. God bless them all, keep them safe from harm, and return them intact in body and spirit to their loved ones at home.

Bravo Zulu and Semper Fidelis.

—   MJK

ABOUT THE AUTHOR

Mike Krentz writes medical suspense, psychological thrillers, and military fiction based on his experiences as an emergency physician and US Navy medical officer.

Born and raised in Arizona, Mike earned a classical degree in English from the University of San Francisco, a Doctor of Medicine degree from the Medical College of Wisconsin, and a Master of Public Health Degree from Johns Hopkins University.

Following a stellar civilian career in emergency medicine, Mike rededicated his professional life to serve America's Navy and Marine Corps heroes and their families, in both land-based clinical settings and afloat warships. His last active-duty assignment was as Seventh Fleet Surgeon on board the flagship, USS *Blue Ridge.*

After retiring from the US Navy, Mike continued his service as a consultant to the Navy and Marine Corps Public Health Center, Health Analysis Department. Upon completion of that mission, he returned to his earliest life passion as a full-time writer.

Mike serves as Vice-Chairman the Board of Directors of The Muse Writers Center, where he also teaches fiction writing and leads an advanced fiction studio.

Mike, his wife Kathryn, and miniature schnauzer Yoshi live in Norfolk, VA.

PREVIEW:

HER PACIFIC

SHOWDOWN

By Mike Krentz

Mahoney & Squire Series

Book 2

Chapter One

April 8, 2012, West (Yellow) Sea

The US Navy P-3 *Orion* maritime patrol plane arrived over the chaotic scene unfolding in the Yellow Sea, known as the West Sea by the Republic of Korea and its United States ally.

Lieutenant Commander Jessica "Cricket" Squire, United States Navy, put the four-engine turboprop aircraft into a descent to five hundred feet above the surface over the wreckage of ROKS *Bucheon,* a Republic of Korea *Pohang*-class corvette.

Not far to the north, a similar scene involved a *Sariwon*-class corvette from the Democratic People's Republic of Korea.

By emergency direction from the US Seventh Fleet, the P-3 had broken off from a routine submarine-hunting mission to provide on-scene surveillance and a live feed from the scene of the latest skirmish between the two nations on the divided Korean peninsula.

Cricket flew the P-3 in sequential figure-eight tracks over both doomed warships. The aircrew in the back of the plane transmitted photos and videos to their base in Okinawa, Japan, from where the images would be relayed to USS *Shenandoah*, flagship of the Seventh Fleet, underway in the South China Sea.

From her left-seat vantage point, Cricket noted almost identical disasters evolving on both sides of the imaginary Northern Limit Line that divided the West Sea into North and South Korean territorial waters. Amidst the wreckage, she spotted desperate human beings either clinging to flotsam, flailing about in the open sea, or sinking below the surface.

Cricket and her crew could do nothing to help. The P-3 had no rescue capability. The closest US Navy ship, USS *Stethem,* would arrive too late to save the perishing humans below their aircraft.

"What the hell happened down there?" Cricket said.

A voice came over the radio. "Hunter one-zero-three, Seventh Fleet has all they need. RTB."

Cricket advanced the throttles, put the aircraft into a climb, and turned toward home base on Kadena Air Force Base, Okinawa, Japan.

April 8, 2012, Okinawa, Japan: Kadena Air Force Base

The post-flight brief complete, Cricket left her squadron's hangar, still shaken by the human carnage she'd seen in the West Sea. She considered foregoing her usual gym workout in favor of heading to the Officers' Club to drown her sorrows in generous libations.

A petty officer interrupted. "Boss wants to see you, ma'am."

Minutes later, Cricket stood at parade rest before Commander Brett Hawke, her squadron commander. Neither would characterize the other as among their favorite people.

"At ease," Hawke said.

Cricket relaxed her posture but declined the proffered chair next to the CO's desk.

The man shrugged. "This is your lucky day, Lieutenant Commander Squire. You get to go home tomorrow."

Cricket blinked. Why would they send her back to Honolulu

465

in mid-tour? Was she being fired?

"Sir?"

The commander gave her a sly grin. "It will be a quick turn. You'll bring the P-8 back here."

The P-8 *Poseidon* was the Navy's newest aerial surveillance platform, with highly classified electronic intelligence (ELINT) capabilities. Cricket had been among the first pilots to qualify in the complex jet.

"This mission is hush-hush," the commander said, "so you'll bring it back under cover of darkness. Then we hide it until or if it's needed. We for sure don't want other, uh, players in the region to know we have it."

"I don't understand, sir. Why now?"

"I don't have the complete picture. Seventh Fleet wants it in theater. Ours is not to reason why . . ."

"Got it, sir."

"Then you'd best go pack. You and your crew are on an early transport flight to Honolulu."

Back in her room at the Bachelor Officers Quarters, Cricket placed a call to Honolulu.

"I'm coming home, love. Quick turnaround, but we can get that license signed."

Chapter Two

April 27, 2012, San Bruno, CA

The longest day in Captain Kate Mahoney's life had begun with a jarring phone call to her Thailand hotel room sixteen time zones away from San Francisco Bay.

"Patrick's missing." Her sister Colleen's grim message had shattered Kate's pre-dawn erotic dreams and flung her emerging consciousness against the harsh wall of reality.

Teenage son in trouble. Absentee single mom naval officer thousands of miles away. Again.

Thirty-six hours later, the time approached four AM. Kate was the only one awake in Colleen's split-level home in San Bruno, CA. She poured a full glass of Shiraz, took a generous quaff, and welcomed the near-immediate numbness washing over her body. She carried the bottle and glass into the living room, kicked off her shoes, plopped into the recliner chair, flipped on the TV, and muted the sound.

Kate doused the lamp and sat alone and pensive in the flickering glow of the screen. In synchrony with the shifting light, random images of the day's trauma flitted across her memory:

Luke's aviator survival knife aimed at her chest had not frightened her. She'd recognized his desperate but empty threat. A

467

show of force for Patrick? Outrage that she'd found him and interrupted his contrived reunion with their son?

Patrick's body-block on Luke had taken Kate by surprise. The boy hated his mother, and he admired Luke. No, he'd admired the man he knew as Mr. Homer, a kind mentor dedicated to serving abandoned children. Kate's unannounced arrival at Homer House had blown that cover.

A teenager discovers his long-lost father minutes before the man attacks the boy's mother. Of course, Patrick reacted.

Her son's snarling words reverberated in Kate's brain like electronic feedback. "You two are disgusting."

Preston Davis had burst into the room like an avenging warrior, too late to do anything but gawk. He had risked what little remained of his plummeting Marine Corps' career to follow her from the airport.

The same Colonel Preston Davis she might love. If she knew how.

Patrick had not spoken to Kate since she, Colleen, and Preston had whisked him out of Mr. Homer's/Luke's Haight Ashbury habitat.

Three men in Kate's life. Preston had gone on to alcohol rehab, Patrick slumbered upstairs, and Luke?

What will he pull next?

When they were both young officers in flight school, they'd gotten pregnant and married, in that order. She should have killed Luke when she had the chance. A mother defending her infant son from an abusing drunken father would have prevailed in court. She thought she'd accomplished the same end when her Navy superiors forced Luke Walker to disappear from their lives.

Now he's back. And Patrick knows him.

468

She sipped the wine. Somewhere in the fog, Kate's mind found clarity.

What Luke or I deserve doesn't matter. We've cast our dice. Patrick's life matters now. She drained the rest of the glass. *Tomorrow, I'll make a plan.*

Still unable to sleep, Kate switched on the lamp and turned off the TV. She refilled the wine glass and picked up the day's newspaper. A column below the fold caught her eye.

China Unlikely To Budge On Thorny South China Sea Dispute
Reuters
By Morris Grimes

BEIJING - Pressured at home and increasingly sensing a concerted regional effort to diminish its territorial claims, the People's Republic of China (PRC) will be in no mood to make concessions on vast areas of the disputed South China Sea at two key East Asia summits later this week.

China claims the most extensive historic sovereignty rights in the oil- and gas-rich region, including uninhabited atolls near the equatorial northern coast of Borneo and west of the Philippines archipelago, collectively known as the Spratly Islands.

Vietnam, the Philippines, Taiwan, Malaysia, and Brunei are the other claimants in the area. Along with the United States and Japan, they are pressuring Beijing to seek some way forward on the knotty issue of sovereignty, which has flared up again this year with often tense maritime standoffs.

469

"China is prominent and pretty powerful now, so why back down?" said Kelsey Hargraves of the Asia Program at Chatham House, a London foreign policy institute.

"It would be odd for it to do so when you consider the extents of its strategic needs, its energy needs, and the potential that these disputed territories have to fulfill those," Hargraves added.

Kate threw the paper on the floor. "Not my problem today." Her voice sounded less convincing than she wanted. Kate had two weeks of leave with Patrick before she had to rejoin USS *Shenandoah,* the US Seventh Fleet flagship, when it returned home to Japan. She had personal decisions to make, every bit as weighty—and in the end more serious—than anything she might do in her official role as Seventh Fleet Director of Operations.

Captain Kate Mahoney, United States Navy, could almost but not quite admit that she missed being in the middle of that maritime action.

* * *

Sometime later, Kate nodded awake, still in the living room. The lamp remained lit; the newspaper littered the floor. Her bottle of Shiraz, two-thirds empty, stood beside the drained glass.

Her head ached, and her mouth felt parched. Groggy, she looked at her watch.

Four AM. Jet lagged.

Not yet forty-eight hours since she and Preston Davis had boarded their flight in Bangkok. She closed her eyes and tried to sleep, to no avail.

How can a person be exhausted to the marrow but not sleep?

Kate padded barefoot into the kitchen, found Colleen's

coffee maker, and started a pot. As she ascended the stairs to the bathroom on the upper level, she noticed a glow of light from beneath Patrick's door.

At four in the morning? Is he up early or late? Maybe he fell asleep with the light on like I did.

She started to knock on his door, then thought better of it. Patrick had avoided her since they got home from The City. If he was asleep, he would rage if re-awakened.

Back downstairs, Kate poured a cup of coffee and returned to the front room recliner. There she sat in silence, pondering. As the caffeine coursed through her body, her mind clarified. By the time the first morning light seeped through the window blinds, she knew what she had to do.

* * *

"Did you not go to bed, Kate?" Colleen appeared in the doorway, already dressed for her shift as a nurse in a local hospital emergency department. Kate wondered how her older sister could appear so prim and properly coiffed first thing in the morning. Maybe liberating herself from a toxic marriage had brought peace and meaning into Colleen's life.

At least she didn't have children to suffer through a family break-up.

"I dozed in the chair," Kate said. "Mind on a rampage."

Colleen went into the kitchen and emerged with a travel mug of coffee. "What are you going to do?"

"I have to go back there. I hope to talk to Mr. Homer rather than Luke Walker."

Her sister cast her a wary eye. "Only a fool would go back into that lion's den."

"No matter what he's done, he's Patrick's father. He deserves

471

a chance to make it real. More important, Patrick deserves to know him and maybe have a healthy relationship with him." She shrugged. "I have to try, Sis."

"Hasn't Luke Walker caused you enough grief for one lifetime?" Colleen gathered up her purse and car keys. She looked at Kate and shook her head. "Don't let me see you in the ER later today." She turned and left the house.

Kate heard Patrick's door open. Had he overheard her conversation with Colleen? She called up to him, but he went straight to the bathroom, the slamming-door sound followed by the shower running. Kate went up the stairs and knocked on the bathroom door.

"Yeah?" His voice sounded angry.

"Do you want some toast or cereal before you go to school?"

"No."

She fixed the toast anyway.

When he came down the stairs, dressed and ready for school, Patrick ate it with gusto. "Thanks, Mom." Then he was out the door.

Kate finished her coffee, then showered and dressed. When she came back down the stairs, she had a battle plan laid out in her mind. She rehearsed it as she walked the several blocks to the Millbrae BART station for the train into San Francisco. She would spend some time wandering around the city. Kate intended to reach Homer House after it closed—when Luke Walker, aka Mr. Homer, would be alone.

Chapter Three

April 27, 2012, San Francisco, CA

Dusk had settled over San Francisco's Haight-Ashbury neighborhood where Luke Walker ran Homer House, a day care and counseling center for abandoned children or those from broken homes.

Luke sensed the intruder's presence before he heard the footsteps on the stairs. They stopped at his opened office door. Turning from his computer, Luke gazed across his desk into the somber eyes of the woman who, years ago, almost killed him.

Standing in the doorway, Kate Mahoney brandished her Blackberry like a weapon at Luke's face. "I've set up an emergency message to 911. One move toward me, and I'll bring the police—like I should have done yesterday."

Luke leaned back in mock alarm. "A Blackberry, Kate? You threaten me with a Blackberry?" He tilted his head as if to look behind her. "I'm the one who should call 911. You've either got a knife in your underwear, or your jarhead bodyguard is out in the hall." He affected a lascivious grin. "Or should I say, 'Marine lover'?"

Kate's eyes darted left and then back.

Guessed right, Luke thought.

473

"He's Colonel Davis to you." Kate fixed her gaze on his eyes. "I came alone, unarmed."

Luke spread his hands like an amiable host. "Do come in and sit down, Kate. I promise to be good."

She kept the Blackberry pointed toward Luke's face. "I'll stand right here. I know you have that survival knife in your drawer."

Luke shrugged. "From yesterday? That was just horseplay, a little show of force. I wouldn't have stabbed you, as much as you deserve it. How did I know you had a personal protection force waiting outside to ambush me?"

Kate lowered the Blackberry to her side. Her voice took on a higher pitch, as it usually did whenever she felt nervous or threatened. "I came to talk about Patrick."

"And here I thought you'd come to make up to me, after all the years."

Her eyes flashed. "I don't give a shit if you live or die, except you are Patrick's father."

Luke's eyes flared. "You got a lot of nerve. Thirteen years after you stole our son—and you tried to kill me—now you care that I'm his father?" He made a show of reaching for his phone. "I'm calling 911. They need to cart you off to the loony bin."

Kate's eyes turned hard as flint. "I should have killed you that night. Patrick and I would be better off now."

Luke scoffed. "Cut the histrionics, Kate. You got away with attempted murder while I got railroaded out of the Marine Corps and out of aviation. I lost my dream, and you took my only child away from me. Hell, you'd be in Leavenworth right now if Naval Air hadn't rolled in to save your precious female jet-jockey ass."

"That's enough." Her voice trembled.

474

Luke pressed his attack. "You're right. You should have killed me, but you didn't. You were no better at killing than you were at flying. All you did was cripple me and then pretend I didn't exist. You told Patrick that his dad died in combat, right? Well, I found him despite you. We were building our own relationship until you and your boyfriend stormed in."

"Stop it. I will leave right now. You will never see Patrick again." Her voice shrilled.

Luke stood and pointed his finger at her. "You got no right to talk to me about Patrick. You will not steal my son again. You want to leave, leave. You have nothing to say that I want to hear."

He folded his arms. "You cannot deny my right to see my son."

To Luke's surprise, Kate put the Blackberry in her pocket. Her shoulders slumped, and she swayed on her feet. "That's why I came to talk to you." Her voice had turned quiet, almost plaintive.

Could victory be this easy?

Luke sat back down but said nothing, poised to seize the advantage but waiting to see what Kate would do next.

"I took Patrick away because I feared for his life—and mine. You abused us. You were a drunk, a terrorizing husband, and a tyrannical father. We had to get away from you. It took all my strength to do it."

Luke responded, but she raised a hand.

"Hear me out. To keep my sanity, I had to erase you from my life, and I had to keep Patrick from knowing the truth about you." Kate looked down and swallowed hard. She looked back at him with moist eyes. "Maybe I had no right to erase you from his life. But that's in the past. Now I—*we* need to figure out how to make it right." She sighed. "For Patrick's sake."

Luke cocked his head. The simpering woman before him was a far cry from the warrior Kate Mahoney he'd known in the past or had seen yesterday. What had changed in twenty-four hours?

Kate seemed to read his thoughts. "How I reached this point in my life does not concern you. I had no clue that you stalked us all those years. Why? Revenge? You could have shown yourself any time, but you hid in shadows. Why?"

Luke opened his mouth to speak. He meant to say that reuniting with his son had become the driving force in his life, but that he had waited until Patrick was old enough to choose him over her.

Kate waved him off before he could utter a word. "I don't want to know. I don't want anything to do with you. Patrick's old enough to decide for himself if he wants a relationship with you. I owe him that choice. You are free to contact him. But be direct and honest, not some bogus identity like this 'Mr. Homer' crap."

Luke tried to pierce her with his eyes. "He came to Homer House to live with me because I gave him hope and the chance to feel good about himself. Helping abandoned kids was therapy for him."

"You tricked him. Would he have come here if he knew you were his father, '*Mr. Homer*'?" She paused. When she spoke again, her voice turned bitter. "Here's the deal. I offer you an open relationship with him, but he lives with me."

Luke forced his own sarcastic laugh. "I must be ill-informed. I thought he lived in San Bruno with your sister."

"He stayed with Colleen while I deployed. I'm taking him to Japan with me when I'm done with my leave here."

A flame ignited in Luke's gut, but he stifled the urge to jump over the desk and attack her. "How are you going to do that? Stow him in your stateroom on that gray relic they call a flagship?" He shook his head. "You really are nuts."

"Where and how he lives with me is my business. I'll tell you where and when he can see you."

She's got no clue. Making this up as she goes along.

Luke spoke in an even voice. "So, the great deal you offer me here is that you take Patrick to Japan—to live God-knows-where while you're underway—but I get to have an 'open' relationship with him, on your terms? That sounds so fair, Captain Mahoney. No wonder the Seventh Fleet put you in charge of operations. You got no logic at all."

"I have another year at Seventh Fleet, then I can retire from the Navy. Patrick and I will return to the US. I'll get a job that supports being a proper mother."

Luke cocked his head. "The Kate Mahoney that I knew— loved once—had so much ambition that she scored the only tactical jet assignment open to our aviator class. Then she blew the crap out of the Iraqis—after beating her husband half dead. She climbed onto the fast track to command, a high-profile fleet staff job, and a shoo-in to flag rank." He shook his head. "You let no one stand in the way of your career, least of all our son. Now you want me to believe that you will cash in a guaranteed admiral's star for a civilian job?" He leaned forward, menacing. "I want a toke of whatever you're smoking, Kate."

"I'm forty-two years old, and I've never been an exemplary mother. Because of that, I almost lost Patrick. I mean to start over now, and I want to give you the chance to be a worthy father. No matter what happened between us, we are Patrick's parents. He deserves the best we can give him. I'll work with you on that. You just have to promise to be honest about who you are."

By God, she's serious.

He scrutinized her over tented hands as he considered his options.

"Okay," he said. "I'm in. How could I not be?"

Relief relaxed Kate's face. "I choose to believe you. We have to make this work for Patrick's sake." She turned to leave. "I'll be in touch with details."

"Not so fast. I have one condition."

She turned back; her eyes narrowed. "What?"

"You don't take Patrick to Japan. He stays in the Bay Area, where I have access to him without either of us trucking across the friggin' Pacific Ocean. He can stay with Colleen if you can't stomach him living with me."

Kate stiffened. "No way."

Luke folded his arms. "No deal then."

"You can't—"

"I can, and I will." He gave her a dismissive wave. "I'm done talking."

Kate's face turned crimson. "I hate you." She stormed out of the room.

Luke went to the door and called after her. "See you in court."

- HER SHOW OF FORCE -

HER SHOW OF FORCE
(Mahoney and Squire, Book 1)
By Mike Krentz

Published by Purple Papaya

Copyright © 2023 Mike Krentz
All rights reserved.

ISBN: 978-1621812029

Cover Design: GetCovers.com

Connect with Mike Krentz online https://mikejkrentz.com/

Revised, Second Edition
First edition published as RIVEN DAWN, by Mike J. Krentz
Copyright © 2012 Michael Krentz

Printed in the United States of America.

Made in United States
Troutdale, OR
10/16/2023